PRAISE FOR
The Lady's Guide to Petticoats and Piracy

"[Lee] develops a world rich in historical detail, crafts a plot wild with unexpected turns, and explores complex topics like colonization and identity. An empowering and energetic adventure that celebrates friendship between women."
—*KIRKUS REVIEWS* (STARRED REVIEW)

"An incredible, must-have follow-up full of old characters and new, blood and guts, and a delightful barrage of sarcasm."
—*SLJ* (STARRED REVIEW)

"This action-driven adventure is a joy."
—ALA *BOOKLIST* (STARRED REVIEW)

"A beautifully brilliant story about feminism, female friendship, privilege, sexism in the seventeenth century, and doing all you can to fulfill your passion and dreams."   **—BUZZFEED**

"A feminist feast that challenges societal norms and forgoes all romance, which is unconventional, albeit refreshing, in young adult literature."   **—BOOKPAGE**

"[A] strong feminist credo."   **—*THE HORN BOOK***

"*The Lady's Guide to Petticoats and Piracy* is fun while still being thoughtful, feminist, and an ode to female friendship."
—BUSTLE

The Lady's Guide to Petticoats and Piracy

Mackenzi Lee

KATHERINE TEGEN BOOKS
An Imprint of HarperCollins Publishers

For Janell, who would have loved this

Katherine Tegen Books is an imprint of HarperCollins Publishers.

The Lady's Guide to Petticoats and Piracy
Copyright © 2018 by Mackenzie Van Engelenhoven

Library of Congress Control Number: 2018933261
ISBN 978-0-06-279533-5

Typography by Carla Weise
Map by David Curtis
20 21 22 23 24   PC/LSCH   10 9 8 7 6 5 4 3 2 1
❖
First paperback edition, 2020

The Lady's Guide to Petticoats and Piracy

Don't tell me women
are not the stuff of heroes.
—Qiu Jin

A highly dowered girl was faced by a great venture, a great quest. The life before her was an uncharted sea. She had to find herself, to find her way, to find her work.
—Margaret Todd, MD, *The Life of Sophia Jex-Blake*

To Do:
- Purchase *Anatomy of Surgery*
- Pick up candied almonds for Callum
- Send Percy homeopathy paper
- Inquire with surgeon's board about apprenticeship
- Scream in frustration over the plight of women in medicine

Edinburgh

Why is it always gra[y] here?!

Monty + Percy

London

Kunstkammer = Cabinet of Curiosities

Zurich

Gibraltar

Mediterrane[an] Sea

We're off the edge of the map

Algiers

Medical capital
of the country
UNLESS YOU'RE
A BLOODY WOMAN!!!

N
W   E
S

Stuttgart

Edinburgh

17—

1

I have just taken an overly large bite of iced bun when Callum slices his finger off.

We are in the middle of our usual nightly routine, after the bakery is shut and the lamps along the Cowgate are lit, their syrupy glow creating halos against the twilight. I wash the day's dishes and Callum dries. Since I am always finished first, I get to dip into whatever baked goods are left over from the day while I wait for him to count the till. Still on the counter are the three iced buns I have been eyeing all day, the sort Callum piles with sticky, translucent frosting to make up for all the years his father, who had the shop before him, skimped on it. Their domes are beginning to collapse from a long day unpurchased, the cherries that top them slipping down the sides. Fortunately, I have never been a girl overbothered with aesthetics. I would have happily

3

tucked in to buns far uglier than these.

Callum is always a bit of a hand wringer who doesn't enjoy eye contact, but he's jumpier than usual tonight. He stepped on a butter mold this morning, cracking it in half, and burned two trays of brioche. He fumbles every dish I pass him and stares up at the ceiling as I prod the conversation along, his already ruddy cheeks going even redder.

I do not particularly mind being the foremost conversationalist out of the pair of us. Even on his chattiest days, I usually am. Or he lets me be. As he finishes drying the cutlery, I am telling him about the time that has elapsed since the last letter I sent to the Royal Infirmary about my admission to their teaching hospital and the private physician who last week responded to my request to sit in on one of his dissections with a three-word missive—*no, thank you.*

"Maybe I need a different approach," I say, pinching the top off an iced bun and bringing it up to my lips, though I know full well it's too large for a single bite.

Callum looks up from the knife he's wiping and cries, "Wait, don't eat that!" with such vehemence that I startle, and he startles, and the knife pops through the towel and straight through the tip of his finger. There's a small *plop* as the severed tip lands in the dishwater.

The blood starts at once, dripping from his hand and into the soapy water, where it blossoms through the suds like poppies bursting from their buds. All the color leaves his face as he stares down at his hand, then says, "Oh dear."

It is, I must confess, the most excited I have ever been in Callum's presence. I can't remember the last time I was so excited. Here I am with an actual medical emergency and no male physicians to push me out of the way to handle it. With a chunk of his finger missing, Callum is the most interesting he has ever been to me.

I leaf through the mental compendium of medical knowledge I have compiled over years of study, and I land, as I almost always do, on Dr. Alexander Platt's *Treaties on Human Blood and Its Movement through the Body*. In it, he writes that hands are complex instruments: each contains twenty-seven bones, four tendons, three main nerves, two arteries, two major muscle groups, and a complex network of veins that I am still trying to memorize, all wrapped up in tissue and skin and capped with fingernails. There are sensory components and motor functions—affecting everything from the ability to take a pinch of salt to bending at the elbow—that begin in the hand and run all the way into the arm, any of which can be mucked up by a misplaced knife.

Callum is staring wide-eyed at his finger, still as a rabbit dazed by the snap of a snare and making no attempt to staunch the blood. I snatch the towel from his hand and swaddle the tip of his finger in it, for the priority when dealing with a wound spouting excessive blood is to remind that blood that it will do far more good inside the body than out. It soaks through the cloth almost immediately, leaving my palms red and sticky.

My hands are steady, I notice with a blush of pride, even after the good jolt my heart was given when the actual severing occurred. I have read the books. I have studied anatomical drawings. I once cut open my own foot in a horribly misguided attempt to understand what the blue veins I can see through my skin look like up close. And though comparing books about medicine to the actual practice is like comparing a garden puddle to the ocean, I am as prepared for this as I could possibly be.

This is not how I envisioned attending to my first true medical patient in Edinburgh—in the backroom of the tiny bakeshop I've been toiling in to keep myself afloat between failed petition after failed petition to the university and a whole slew of private surgeons, begging for permission to study. But after the year I've had, I'll take whatever opportunities to put my knowledge into practice that are presented. Gift horses and mouths and all that.

"Here, sit down." I guide Callum to the stool behind the counter, where I take coins from his customers, for I can make change faster than Mr. Brown, the second clerk. "Hand over your head," I say, for if nothing else, gravity will work in favor of keeping his blood inside his body. He obeys. I then fish the wayward fingertip from the washbasin, coming up with several chunks of slimy dough before I finally find it.

I return to Callum, who still has both hands over his head so that it looks as though he's surrendering. He's pale as flour, or perhaps that is actually flour dusting his cheeks. He's not a clean sort. "Is it bad?" he croaks.

"Well, it's not good, but it certainly could have been worse. Here, let me have a look." He starts to unwrap the towel, and I qualify, "No, lower your arms. I can't look at it all the way up there."

The bleeding has not stopped, but it has slowed enough that I can remove the towel long enough for a look. The finger is less severed than I expected. While he sliced off a good piece of his fingerprint and a wicked crescent of the nail, the bone is untouched. If one must lose a part of one's finger, this is the best that can be hoped for.

I pull the skin on either side of the wound up over it. I have a sewing kit in my bag, as I have three times lost the button from my cloak this winter and grew tired of walking around with the ghastly wind of the Nor Loch flapping its tails. All it takes is three stitches—in a style I learned not from *A General System of Surgery* but rather from a hideous pillow cover my mother pestered me into embroidering a daft-looking dog upon—to hold the flap in place. A few drops of blood still ooze up between the stitches, and I frown down at them. Had they truly been upon a pillowcase, I would have ripped them out and tried again.

But considering how little practice I've had with sealing an amputation—particularly one so small and delicate—and how much it slowed the bleeding, I allow myself a moment of pride before I move on to the second priority of Dr. Platt's treaty on wounds of the flesh: holding infection at bay.

"Stay here," I say, as though he has any inclination to move. "I'll be right back."

In the kitchen, I bring water to a quick boil over the stove, still warm and easily stoked, then add wine and vinegar before soaking a towel in the mixture and returning to where Callum is still sitting wide-eyed behind the counter.

"You're not going to . . . do you have to . . . cut it off?" he asks.

"No, you already did that," I reply. "We're not amputating anything, just cleaning it up."

"Oh." He looks at the wine bottle in my fist and swallows hard. "I thought you were trying to douse me."

"I thought you might want it."

I offer him the bottle, but he doesn't take it. "I was saving that."

"What for? Here, give me your hand." I blot the

stitching—which is much cleaner than I had previously thought; I am far too hard on myself—with the soaked towel. Callum coughs with his cheeks puffed out when the vinegar tang strikes the air. Then it's a strip of cheesecloth around the finger, bound and tucked.

Stitched, bandaged, and sorted. I haven't even broken a sweat.

A year of men telling me I am incapable of this work only gives my pride a more savage edge, and I feel, for the first time in so many long, cold, discouraging months, that I am as clever and capable and fit for the medical profession as any of the men who have denied me a place in it.

I wipe my hands off on my skirt and straighten, surveying the bakery. In addition to every other task that needs doing before we close up for the night, the dishes will need to be rewashed. There's a long dribble of blood along the floor that will have to be scrubbed before it dries, another on my sleeve, and a splatter across Callum's apron that should be soaked out before tomorrow. There is also a fingertip to be disposed of.

Beside me, Callum takes a long, deep breath and lets it hiss out between pursed lips as he examines his hand. "Well, this rather spoils the night."

"We were just washing up."

"Well, I had something . . . else." He pushes his chin against his chest. "For you."

"Can it wait?" I ask. I'm already calculating how long this will leave Callum useless over the ovens, whether Mr. Brown will be able to lend a hand, how much this will cut into my time off this week, which I had planned to use to begin a draft of a treaty in favor of educational equality.

"No, it's not . . . I mean, I suppose . . . it could, but . . ." He's picking at the edges of the bandage but stops before I can reprimand him. He's still pale, but a bit of the ruddiness is starting to return to the apples of his cheeks. "It's not something that will last."

"Is it something for eating?" I ask.

"Something of a . . . just . . . stay there." He wobbles to his feet in spite of my protestations and disappears into the kitchen. I hadn't noticed anything special when I was mixing the wine and vinegar, but I also hadn't been particularly looking for it. I check my fingers for blood, then swipe a clean one over the iced bun I had previously targeted. "Don't strain yourself," I call to him.

"I'm not," he replies, immediately followed by a crash like something tin knocked over. "I'm fine. Don't come back here!"

He appears behind the counter again, more red-faced than before and one sleeve sopping with what must have been the milk he so raucously spilled. He's also clutching a fine china plate before him in presentation, and upon it sits a single, perfect cream puff.

My stomach drops, the sight of that pastry sending a tremble through me that a waterfall of blood had not.

"What are you eating?" he asks at the same moment I say "What is that?"

He sets the plate on the counter, then holds out his uninjured hand in presentation. "It's a cream puff."

"I can see that."

"It is, more specifically, because I know you love specificity—"

"I do, yes."

"—exactly the cream puff I gave you the day we met." His smile falters, and he qualifies, "Well, not *exactly* that one. As that was months ago. And since you ate that one, and several more—"

"Why did you make me this?" I look down at the two choux halves with whorls of thick cream sculpted between them—he's never this careful with his craftsmanship, his loaves and cakes the kind of rustic you'd expect to be made by a big-handed baker of good Scotch stock. But this is so deliberate and decorative and—zounds, I can't believe I know exactly what type of pastry this is and how important it is to let the flour mixture cool before whisking in the egg. All this baking nonsense is taking up important space in my head that should be filled with notations on treating popliteal aneurisms and the different types of hernias outlined in *Treaties on Ruptures*, which I took great pains to memorize.

"Maybe we should sit down," he says. "I'm a little . . . faint."

"Likely because you lost blood."

"Or . . . yes. That must be it."

"This really can't wait?" I ask as I lead him over to one of the tables crowded in the front of the shop. He carries the cream puff, and it wobbles on the plate as his hand shakes. "You should go home and rest. At least close the shop tomorrow. Or Mr. Brown can supervise the apprentices and we can keep everything simple. They can't muck up a bread roll too badly." He makes to pull the chair out for me, but I wave him away. "If you are insistent upon moving forward with whatever this is, at least sit down before you fall over."

We take opposite sides, pressed up against the cold, damp window. Down the road, the clock from Saint Giles' is striking the hour. The buildings along the Cowgate are gray with the twilight, and the sky is gray, and everyone passing the bakery is wrapped in gray wool, and I swear I haven't seen color since I came to this godforsaken place.

Callum sets the cream puff on the table between us, then stares at me, fiddling with his sleeve. "Oh, the wine." He casts a glance over at the counter, seems to decide it's not worth going back for, then looks again to me, his hands resting on the tabletop. His knuckles are cracked from the dry winter air, fingernails short and chewed raw around the edges.

"Do you remember the first day we met?" he blurts.

I look down at the cream puff, dread beginning to spread in my stomach like a drop of ink in water. "I remember quite a lot of days."

"But that one in particular?"

"Yes, of course." It was a humiliating day—it still stings to think of it. Having written three letters to the university on the subject of my admission and received not a word in reply for over two months, I went to the office myself to investigate whether they had arrived. As soon as I gave my name to the secretary, he informed me that my correspondence had indeed been received, but no, it had not been passed on to the board of governors. My petition had been denied without ever being heard, because I was a woman, and women were not permitted to enroll in the hospital teaching courses. I was then escorted from the building by a soldier on patrol, which just seemed excessive, though it would be a lie to say I did not consider sprinting past the secretary and bursting through the door into the governors' hall without permission. I wear practical shoes and can run very fast.

But, having been unceremoniously deposited on the street, I had consoled myself at the bakeshop across the road, drowning my sorrows in a cream puff made for me by a round-faced baker with the figure of a man to whom cakes are too available. When I had tried to pay him for it, he'd given me my coins back. And as I was finishing it, at this very table beside this very window (oh, Callum was truly digging in the talons of sentimentality by sitting us here), he made a tentative approach with a mug of warm cider and, after a good chat, an offer of employment.

He had looked then like he was trying to lure a snappish dog in from the cold to lie beside his fire. Like he knew what was best for me, if only my stubborn heart could be enticed there. He looks the same way now, earnestly presenting me that same sort of cream puff, his chin tipped down so that he's looking up at me through the hedgerow of his eyebrows. "Felicity," he says, my name wobbling in his throat. "We've known each other for a while now."

"We have," I say, and the dread thickens.

"And I've become quite fond of you. As you know."

"I do."

And I did. After months of counting coins with my side pressed against his in the cramped space behind the counter and our hands overlapping when he passed me trays of warm rolls, it had become apparent that Callum was fond of me in a way I couldn't make myself be fond of him. And though I had known of the existence of this fondness for a time, it had not been a matter of any urgency that required addressing.

But now he's giving me a cream puff and recollecting.

Telling me how fond he is of me.

I jump when he takes my hand across the table—an impulsive, lunging gesture. He pulls away just as fast, and I feel terrible for startling, so I hold my hand out in invitation and let him try again. His palms are sweating and my grip so unenthusiastic I imagine it must be akin to cuddling a filleted fish.

"Felicity," he says, and then again, "I'm very fond of you."

"Yes," I say.

"Very fond."

"Yes." I try to focus on what he's saying and not of how to get my hand out of his without hurting his feelings and also if there's any possible scenario in which I can walk away from this with that cream puff but without having to do any more than hold his hand.

"Felicity," he says again, and when I look up, he's leaning across the table toward me with his eyes closed and his lips jutting out.

And here it is. The inevitable kiss.

When Callum and I first met, I had been lonely enough to not only accept his employment, but also the companionship that came with it, which gave him the idea that men often get in their heads when a woman pays some kind of attention to them: that it was a sign I want him to smash his mouth—and possibly other body parts—against mine. Which I do not.

But I close my eyes and let him kiss me.

There is more of a lunge into the initial approach than I would prefer, and our teeth knock in a way that makes me wonder if there's a business in selling Dr. John Hunter's newly advertised live tooth transplants to women who have been kissed by overly enthusiastic men. It's nowhere near as unenjoyable as my only previous experience with the act, though just as wet and just as dispassionate a gesture, the oral equivalent of a handshake.

Best to get it over with, I think, so I stay still and let him press his lips to mine, feeling as though I'm being stamped like a ledger. Which is apparently the wrong thing to do, because he stops very abruptly and falls back into his chair, wiping his mouth on his sleeve. "I'm sorry, I shouldn't have done that."

"No, it's all right," I say quickly. And it was. It hadn't been hostile or forced upon me. Had I turned away, I know he wouldn't have chased me. Because Callum is a good man. He walks on the outside of the pavement so he takes the splash of the carriage wheels through the snow instead of me. He listens to every story I tell, even when I know I've been taking up more than my share of the conversation. He stopped adding almonds to the sweet breads when I told him almonds make my throat itch.

"Felicity," Callum says, "I'd like to marry you."

Then he drops off his chair and lands with a hard *thunk* against the floor that makes me concerned for his kneecaps. "Sorry, I got the order wrong."

I almost drop too—though not in chivalry. I'm feeling far fainter in the face of matrimony than I did at the sight of half a finger in the dishwater. "What?"

"Did you . . ." He swallows so hard I see his throat travel the entire course of his neck. "Did you not know I was going to ask you?"

In truth, I had expected nothing more than a kiss but suddenly feel foolish for thinking that was all he wanted from me. I fumble around for an explanation for my willful ignorance and only come up with "We hardly know each other!"

"We've known each other almost a year," he replies.

"A year is nothing!" I protest. "I've had dresses I wore for a year and then woke up one morning and thought, 'Why am I wearing this insane dress that makes me look like a terrier mated with a lobster?'"

"You never look like a lobster," he says.

"I do when I wear red," I say. "And when I blush. And my hair is too red. And I wouldn't have time to plan a wedding right now because I'm busy. And tired. And I have so much to read. And I'm going to London!"

"You are?" he asks.

You are? I ask myself at the same time I hear myself saying, "Yes. I'm leaving tomorrow."

"Tomorrow?"

"Yes, tomorrow." Another revelation to myself—I have no plans to go to London. It sprang from me, a spontaneous and fictitious excuse crafted entirely from panic. But he's still on his knee, so I push on with it. "I have to see my brother there; he has . . ." I pause too long for my next word to be anything but a lie, then say, "Syphilis." It's the first thing that comes to mind when I think of Monty.

"Oh. Oh dear." Callum, to his credit, seems to be making a true effort to understand my nonsensical ramblings.

"Well, no, not syphilis," I say. "But he's having terrible spells of . . . boredom . . . and asked me to come and . . . read to him. And I'm going to be petitioning the hospital for admission again in the spring when they bring in new attending physicians, and that will take all my attention."

"Well, if we married, you wouldn't have to worry about that."

"Worry about what?" I ask. "Planning a wedding?"

"No." He picks himself up off his bended knee and sinks back into his chair with far more slump to his shoulders than before. "About schooling."

"I want to worry about that," I reply, the back of my neck prickling. "I'm going to get a license and become a physician."

"But that will . . ." He stops, teeth pressing so hard into his bottom lip it mottles white.

I fold my arms. "That will what?"

"You're not serious about that, are you?"

"If I wasn't serious, I wouldn't have been able to sew you up just now."

"I know—"

"You'd still be bleeding out over your washbasin."

"I know that, and that was . . . You did a wonderful job." He reaches out, like he might pat my hand, but I pull it off the table, for I am not a dog and therefore need no patting. "But we all have silly things that we . . . we want . . . dreams, you know . . . and then one day you . . ." He scoops at the air with a hand, like he's trying to conjure appropriate phraseology between us rather than be forced to say what he means. "For example, when I was a boy, I wanted to train tigers for the Tower menagerie in London."

"So train tigers," I reply flatly.

He laughs, a small, nervous trill. "Well, I don't want to anymore, because I have the shop, and I have a house here. What I meant is, we all have silly things we lose interest in because we want something real, like a house and a shop and a spouse and children. Not—not today," he stammers, for I must look petrified, "but someday."

A different sort of dread begins to distill inside me now, strong and bitter as whiskey. *Silly little things.*

That's all he thought my grand ambitions ever were. All this time, all these chats over scones, all his intense listening to me explain how, if the head were to be sawed off a corpse, one could trace paths of the twelve nerves connecting to the brain all the way through the body. One of the few who had not told me to give up, even when I had nearly told myself to, when I had written to surgeon after surgeon in the city, begging for teaching and received only rejections. I hadn't even been granted a single a meeting once they discovered I was a woman. All the while we had been together he'd been wondering when it was that I'd give up on this passing fancy, like it was a fashion trend that would disappear from shop windows by the end of the summer.

"I'm not training tigers," I say. "It's medicine. I want to be a doctor."

"I know."

"They're not even comparable! There are doctors all over this city. No one would say it was silly or impossible if I was a man. You couldn't train tigers because you're just a baker from Scotland, but I have *actual skills*." His face falls before I register what I've said, and I try to back step. "Not that you . . . sorry, I didn't mean that."

"I know," he says. "But someday, you'll want something real. And I'd like to be that something for you."

He looks very intently at me, and I think he wants me to say something to assure him I take his meaning, and yes, he's right, I'm just a flighty thing with a passing interest in medicine that can be siphoned off once a ring is placed upon my finger. But all I can think to say is a snappish *And maybe someday the stars will fall from the sky.* So I offer nothing in return but a frosty stare, the sort of look my brother once told me could put out a cigar.

Callum tucks his chin into his chest, then blows out a long, hard breath that ruffles his fringey hair. "And if you don't want that too, then I don't want to do this anymore."

"Do what?"

"I don't want you working here whenever you need money and showing up at any hour you please and eating all the buns and taking advantage of me because you know I've an affection for you. I either want to marry you, or I don't want to see you anymore."

I can't argue with any of that, though the fact that my heart sinks far further at the thought of losing this job than of losing Callum speaks volumes about the ill-advised nature of a union between us. I'm sure I could find something else to sustain me in this bleak, punishing city, but it would likely be even more menial and tedious than counting coins in a bakery and would most certainly not include free desserts. I'd ruin my eyes making buttons in a smoggy factory or wear myself ragged as a domestic, be blind and bent and consumptive by twenty-five, and medical school would be soundly put to bed before I'd had a proper shot.

We stare at each other—I'm not sure if he wants me to apologize, or agree, or admit that yes, that's what I've been doing, and yes, I've known I was using him badly, and yes, I will agree to his proposal in penance and it will all have been worth it. But I stay quiet.

"We should finish cleaning up," he says at last, standing up and wiping his hands off on his apron with a wince. "You can eat the cream puff. Even if you can't say yes right now."

I wish I could believe that yes was inevitable, the same way he seems to. It would be so much easier to want to say yes, to want a house on the Cowgate and a whole brood of round Doyle children with stubby Montague legs and a solid life with this kind, solid man. A small part of me—the part that traces my finger in the sifted sugar dusted around the edges of the choux and almost calls him back—knows that there are far worse things for a woman to be than a kind man's wife. It would be so much easier than being a single-minded woman with a chalk drawing on the floor of her boardinghouse bedroom mapping out every vein and nerve and artery and organ she reads about, adding notations about the size and properties of each. It would be so much easier if I did not want to know everything so badly. If I did not want so badly to be reliant upon no soul but myself.

When Monty, Percy, and I returned to England after what can be generously called a Tour, the idea of a life in Edinburgh as an independent woman was thrilling. The university had a newly minted medical school; the Royal Infirmary allowed student observation; an anatomy theater was being built in College Garden. It was the city where Alexander Platt had arrived after his dishonorable navy discharge with no references and no prospects and had made a name for himself simply by refusing to stop talking about the radical notions that had gotten him booted from the service. Edinburgh had given Alexander Platt a leg up from nothing because it had seen in him a brilliant mind, no matter that it came from a working-class lad with no experience and a stripped title. I was certain that it would do the same for me.

Instead I was here, in a bakeshop with a proposal pastry.

Callum is kind, I tell myself as I stare at the cream puff. *Callum is sweet. Callum loves bread and wakes early and cleans up after himself. He doesn't mind that I don't wear cosmetics and make very little attempt to dress my hair. He listens to me, and he doesn't make me feel unsafe.*

I could do much worse than a kind man.

The scent of sugar and wood smoke starts to return to the room as Callum smothers the ovens, drowning out the faint hint of blood that still lingers, sharp and metallic as a new sewing needle. I do not want to spend the rest of my life smelling sugar. I don't want pastry beneath my fingernails and a man content with the hand life has dealt him and my heart a hungry, wild creature savaging me from the inside out.

Fleeing to London had truly been a fiction, but suddenly it begins to unspool in my head. London isn't a medical hub like Edinburgh, but there are hospitals and plenty of physicians who offer private classes. There's a guild. None of the hospitals or private offices or even barbaric barber surgeons on the Grassmarket have allowed me to get a toe in their door. But the hospitals in London don't know my name. I'm smarter now, after a year of rejection—I've learned not to walk in with pistols drawn, but rather to keep them hidden in my petticoats with a hand surreptitiously upon the heel. This time, I will approach stealthily. Find a way to make them let me in before I ever have to show my hand.

And what is the point of having a fallen gentleman in the city for a brother if I don't take advantage of his gentlemanly hospitality?

London

2

Moorfields is a stinking, rotting neighborhood that greets me like a fist to the teeth. The noise is fantastic—sermons of preachers damning the poor from street corners argue with screams from the brothels. Cattle bellow as they're herded through the road to market. Tinkers call for pots to mend. Vendors sell oysters, nuts, apples, fish, turnips—new wares every few steps, all of them oily and all of them shouted about. I'm ankle-deep in mud all the way from the stagecoach stop, the thick, greasy sort that traps carts and steals shoes. Dead cats and rotten fruit bob up from the quagmire, and the thick haze of smoke and gin makes the air feel gauzy. It's miraculous that I do not have my pockets picked on the walk and will be equally miraculous if I ever manage to scrape all the mud and offal off the soles of my boots.

My brother, always one for histrionics, has made his

fall into poverty as dramatic as possible.

Even as I mount the stairs of his building, I'm not certain what emotion is most strongly associated with the impending reunion with Monty. We parted on good terms—or if not good, at least good-adjacent—but only after a lifetime of sniping at each other like feral foxes. And fencing for soft underbellies is a hard habit to break. We've both said enough unkind things to each other that would justify a reluctance on his part to greet me with warmth.

So it is unexpected that my first reaction upon seeing his face when he opens the door is perhaps closest cousin to fondness. This miserable year apart has made me terribly soft.

What he offers back is shock. "Felicity."

"Surprise!" I say weakly. Then I throw my hands in the air like it's some sort of celebration and try not to regret coming here at all. "Sorry, I can go."

"No, don't . . . Dear Lord, Felicity!" He grabs my arm as I turn, pulling me back to him and then into an embrace, which I don't know what to do with. I consider trying to pry myself free, but it will likely be over faster if I don't resist, so I stand, stiff-armed and chewing the inside of my cheek.

"What are you doing here?" He pushes me back to arm's length for a better look. "And you're so tall! When did you get so tall?"

I have never aspired to impressive stature, based primarily on Monty's example—we are both of a solid, hard-to-knock-over stock that sacrifices height for shoulder width—but I've had to let the hem of my skirt out since summer, and in my heeled shoes and him in stocking feet, I could put my nose to his forehead. Pettiness must die a very slow death indeed because, in spite of that momentary pinch of fondness, I'm delighted to be officially taller.

His hug prevented me from getting a good look at him until he stepped backward to assess my height, and I examine him in return. He's gotten thinner—that's the first thing I notice. Thin in a way that can no longer be described as *willowy*, but rather the sort that comes from not having enough to eat. He's paler as well, though that's less alarming—the last time we saw each other we'd just finished a stretch in the Cyclades islands so we were both of us brown as nuts. The short, bleak days that populate London in the winter have made it impossible not to notice the scars on his face, far more livid than I expected. They run raised and red, like a splatter of paint across his forehead and in patches down to his neck, made more visible because he's cut his hair short, though it somehow still has that effortless tousle to it, like someone's sculpted it to look rumpled just so.

"Here, come inside." Monty ushers me into the flat, floorboards protesting more loudly than I feel they should while still maintaining structural stability. I haul myself and my knapsack over the threshold.

The flat is crowded as a party. There's a washbasin balanced atop a set of trunks stacked on each other that seem to be functioning as both storage and a dining table, bumping knees with a sooty stove that looks like it's pushing down the floor. I consider taking off my boots but decide I'd rather not risk trodding these boards sock-footed for fear of a splinter impaling me.

Monty steps into the middle of what can be generously termed the front room, though there's only a thin partition to designate its edges. "I know it's shit," he says before I have to come up with a compliment that is actually a lie. "But it's our shit. So long as we pay the rent. Which we have. Mostly. Only one close call so far. And we have a stove, which is grand. And there are significantly fewer cockroaches than there were in the summer. More mice now, but fewer cockroaches." He does a little victorious gesture with his hands clasped above his head. "Here, Percy's in bed. Come say your hallos. I think he's still awake."

"Why's Percy abed?" I follow Monty around the partition as Percy raises his head from where he's burrowed into their mattress. He hasn't become as dramatically waifish as Monty, though his dark skin hides any pallor. That, and Percy has been a stretched-out creature since youth, every suit a bit too short in the sleeves and his limbs thin with lean muscles jutting out like tangerines wrapped in burlap.

It occurs to me suddenly why the pair of them may be lounging in the middle of the day, and I freeze, blushing before I have confirmation of my suspicions. "Oh no. Am I interrupting something marital and romantic?"

"Felicity, please, it's six in the evening," Monty says with great indignance, then adds, "We've been fornicating all day."

I resist using up my first eye roll of the visit this early. "Really, Percy, why are you in bed?"

"Because it has not been a very good week." Monty sinks down at Percy's side and nestles into his shoulder, his deaf side away from me.

Percy gives me a weak smile, his head listing against Monty's. "Just a fit yesterday," he says, and Monty wrinkles his nose at the word.

"Oh." It comes out more relieved than I meant it to—I'm far more comfortable discussing epilepsy than fornication. Percy is an epileptic, temporarily incapacitated at periodic intervals by convulsions that physicians since Hippocrates have been attempting—and largely failing—to both understand and treat. After several years of his guardian aunt and uncle bringing a parade of so-called experts in to cup and bleed and dose him in attempt to lessen the severity, they finally decided upon permanent imprisonment in the sort of barbaric asylum that people with untreatable ills are confined to. It would have happened, too, had he not absconded with my brother—so dedicated were they to keeping his illness a secret for fear of the social embarrassment that neither Monty nor I knew of it until we were abroad.

I am tempted to ask after the paper I sent the previous month on homeopathy and the treatment of convulsive fits through quinine. But Percy looks drowsy and ill, and Monty will stop listening once I begin to talk of anything medical, so all I say instead is "Epilepsy is a son of a bitch."

"Oh my, but Scotland has made you vulgar," Monty says with delight. "What brings you down from those highlands to us? Not that this isn't a delightful surprise. But it is a surprise. Did you write? Because you reached us before the letter."

"No, this was . . . unplanned." I look down at my shoes as a chunk of some unknown substance crumbles from the sole. I have never been good at asking things of others, and it sticks in my throat. "I was hoping you'd put me up for a bit."

"Are you all right?" Percy asks, which should have been my brother's first question, though I'm not shocked it wasn't.

"Oh, I'm fine." I try to make it sound sincere, for I am well in all the ways he's concerned for. I'm feeling rather trapped between the foot of the bed and the partition—when I try to scoot back, I nearly knock the screen over entirely. "I can find somewhere else to stay. A boardinghouse or something."

But Monty waves that away. "Don't be absurd. We can make room."

Where? I almost say, but they're both watching me with such a thick undercoat of concern it makes me look down again at my shoes. Eye contact in return somehow feels both too vulnerable and too invasive, so I mumble, "Sorry."

"What are you sorry for?" Monty asks.

I was sorry that my great plan hadn't worked out. Sorry I was here relying on my brother's Christian charity—what little he had to spare—because my plan for my future had lost its footing at every mile marker. Because I was born a girl but too stubborn to accept the lot that came with my sex.

"Felicity." Monty sits up and leans forward with his arms around his knees, looking very intently at me. "Apologize for nothing. It has been made clear in many a letter you are always welcome with us. I was anticipating if you ever took us up on that offer, there would be some notice, so you'll have to put up with our current states of invalidity and concern for said invalidity. But had you written, I swear to God our answer would have been 'board the first coach south.'"

Thank God—something I can be indignant about.

It's far more comfortable than sentimentality. "*Many a letter*? Really?" When Monty gives me a quizzical look, I fill in, "You have not once written to me."

"I write!"

"No, Percy writes me long lovely letters in his very legible penmanship and then you scrawl something offensive at the bottom about Scottish men and their kilts." Monty grins, unsurprisingly, but Percy snorts as well. When I glare at him, he pulls the quilt up over his nose. "Don't encourage him."

Monty leans over and gives a gentle nip at Percy's jaw, then presses a kiss to the same spot. "Oh, he loves it when I'm filthy."

I look away, right at a pair of trousers tellingly discarded upon the floor, and resign myself to the fact that their affection is unavoidable. Particularly if I'm to be staying with them. "Are you two still nauseatingly obsessed with each other? I thought by now you'd have mellowed."

"We remain completely unbearable. Come here, my most dearest darling love of loves." Monty pulls Percy's face toward him and kisses him on the mouth this time, sloppy and showy, and somehow he manages to look at me the whole time as if to convey just how smug he is about making me uncomfortable. That initial fondness I felt toward him has already begun to rot like an overripe melon.

I can resist the eye roll no longer, though I fear for my vision as soon as I look to the ceiling—it seems to be peeling off in chalky lumps. If there is a piece of this flat that isn't playing skip rope with the line between habitable and condemned, I have yet to see it. "I will leave."

When they pull apart, Percy at least has the good sense to look sheepish about the show. Monty just looks obnoxiously pleased with himself. Somehow his dimples are even jauntier than I remember them.

"He's showing off," Percy assures me. "We never touch each other."

"Well, please don't start for my benefit," I reply.

"Come here, darling, and we'll give you a cuddle as well." Monty pats the bed between them. "A proper Monty-Percy sandwich."

I give him a sweet smile in return. "Oh, *darling*, I'd rather set myself on fire."

It has taken me, admittedly, a time to reconcile the idea that Percy and Monty seem to have found honest affection for each other in what I was taught was the sin of all sins. Perhaps the distance helped, or at least gave me space to ponder it and make my peace with it and move from cringing tolerance to something nearer to understanding that their love is probably truer than most of the pairings I saw growing up. Anyone who put up with my brother certainly would not be doing it unless they really, sincerely loved him. And Percy's the sort of decent lad who actually might. When stripped of the illegalities and the Biblical condemnation, their attraction is no stranger to me than anyone's attraction to anyone.

Percy nudges the side of Monty's head with his nose. "You should get to work."

"Must I?" he replies. "Felicity just arrived."

I perk up in a way that I'm certain makes me look more squirrel-like than is flattering, but I can't resist a taunt. It's owed him after that clogged drain of a kiss. "I'm sorry, Percy, I'm not sure I heard right, because it sounded as though you said *work*, which would imply that my brother has tricked someone into employing him."

"Thank you, I have been consistently employed since we arrived in London," Monty says. Percy coughs, and he adds, "Somewhat consistently."

I follow Monty around the partition, perching myself at its edge so I can keep them both in my conversation as Monty starts pawing his way through the trunks. "May I guess what sort of employment you're rushing off to? You're a horse jockey. No, wait—a nightclub performer. A bare-knuckled boxer. A brothel bully."

From the bed, Percy laughs. "He'd be smaller than most of the tarts."

"Ha, ha, ha. I won't have you two ganging up upon me while you're here." Monty surfaces from a trunk with a jumper that looks like it was vomited up by an aging housecat and wrestles it over his head. "I'll have you know," he says as he fights to get his hands through the sleeves, "that I have a respectable position in Covent Garden."

"Respectable?" I cross my arms. "That sounds fake."

"It's not! It's very respectable, isn't it, Percy?" he calls, but Percy has suddenly become occupied with a thread coming undone from the quilt.

"So tell me what it is you're doing respectably in *Covent Garden*," I say with an eyebrow arched over the neighborhood.

As a newly monogamous man, he pretends to not understand my emphasis on the notorious cruising grounds he once frequented. "I play cards for a casino."

"You play *for* the casino?"

"I stay sober but pretend to be drunk to play against the men who actually are tipsy and win their money and give it to the house. They pay me a portion."

I let out a bark of laughter before I can stop myself. "Yes. *Respectable* is the first word that comes to my mind when I hear that."

"Better than making plum cakes with *your* little plum cake," he returns with a sly grin.

And suddenly none of it is fun or funny any longer—it's the savage sniping of our youth, both of us jabbing gently until someone presses a little too hard and it draws blood. Monty might not sense the change in the weather, but Percy does, for he says sternly to Monty, "Be nice. She's only been here twenty minutes."

"Has it only been twenty minutes?" I mumble, and Percy swats his hand at me.

"You have to be nice too. That road runs both ways."

"Yes, mother," I say, and Monty laughs, this time less at me than with me, and we trade a look that is, shall we say, not hostile. Which is good enough.

It takes Monty an excessively long time to dress. There's the jumper, mostly obscured by a jacket and an overly large coat, then heavy boots and fraying gloves, all topped by an adorably misshapen cap that I like to imagine Percy knit for him. It also takes him half a dozen false starts before he actually manages to reach the street—first he has to come back for his scarf, then to change into thicker socks, but most times the thing he comes back for is one more kiss with Percy.

When Monty finally leaves in earnest—the whole building seems to tip a bit more westward when the door slams behind him—Percy smiles at me and pats the spot on the bed beside him. "You can sit down, if you like. I promise I won't try to cuddle you."

I perch myself on the edge of the bed. I'm assuming he's going to dive face-first into an interrogation on the subject of why exactly I have made my bedraggled appearance on their doorstep begging for shelter. But instead he says, "Thank you for the paper you sent."

I was so prepared to make protestations that my surprise visit to London is not a sign of an impending crisis that I turn a bit too hard into this subject. "Wasn't it fascinating? I mean, it's annoying that he calls it Saint Valentine's Malady the whole bleeding paper, but it's brilliant how many physicians are advocating alternatives to bloodlettings and surgeries. Particularly for a disease like epilepsy where we still don't have much of a real idea where it originates. And his footnote about the unlikeliness of epilepsy having any relation to illicit sexual desires was gratifying—that isn't often acknowledged. But the whole idea of a consistent preventative dose of pharmaceuticals rather than treating in a moment of crisis—preventative rather than prescriptive—for a chronic illness that doesn't manifest every . . ." I trail off. I can tell Percy is struggling to follow so many words spouted so quickly and with so much vigor. "Sorry, I'm rambling."

"Don't be sorry. I wish I had something intelligent to offer in return. Maybe when I'm a bit more . . ." He waves a hand vaguely to indicate his current invalidity.

"Have you tried anything suggested? He makes a good case for quinine."

"Not yet. We don't have the money right now. But the Royal Academy of Music here in London will be looking for violinists in the fall, and one of the lads in my quartet is a student of Bononcini and said he'd introduce me— I'm hoping something will come of that." He leans back against the headboard as he studies me, legs curling into his chest so that his toes are no longer hanging off the end of the bed. "Are you all right?"

"Me? Yes, of course."

"Because we are very happy to see you, but your arrival seems rather . . . unplanned. Which would cause a concerned party to wonder if you had left Edinburgh in some kind of distress."

"It would give cause, wouldn't it?" I hope my casual tone might stall him, but he goes on staring at me, and I sigh, my posture sinking into a very unladylike slouch. "Mr. Doyle—the baker, you know, the one I work for." Percy nods, and I continue with great reluctance. "He has expressed an interest in someday making a proposal of marriage to me."

I expected some fantastic start, the same sort of surprise that struck me when Callum made the actual ask, but Percy's face hardly changes. "How very clinical."

"You don't seem surprised."

"Should I be? Were you?"

"Yes! How did you know?"

"Because of everything you wrote about him! Unmarried gentlemen don't pay young ladies that sort of attention unless they have long-term plans. Though I suppose you Montagues are first-rate at not noticing when someone is smitten with you." He might mean for it to make me laugh, but instead I take a strong interest in picking at the pills of wool on my skirt where my ruck-sack rubbed. "You don't sound very excited."

"Well, considering that after he asked me, I immediately booked a carriage here and wrote to Saint Bartholomew's about an appointment with the hospital governors' board, I can't say that I am."

"I thought you liked Callum."

These woolly little bastards are really clinging. I catch the ragged edge of my thumbnail in the grain of the material and pull up a loop of thread. "I do. He's kind, and he makes me laugh—sometimes, if the joke is clever—and he works very hard. But I like a lot of people. I like you—doesn't mean I want to marry you."

"Thank God, because I'm spoken for."

I'm resisting the urge to fall face-forward into the bed—I would have been more likely to indulge had I not been concerned that the mattress would offer no give and I'd be left with a broken nose. "Callum is sweet. And he's helped me. But he thinks he's saving me from all my ambition when really I can't see any future scenario where I come to be as interested in Callum as I am in medicine. Or interested in anyone that much. Or interested in doing anything other than studying medicine." I release a long breath, fluttering the fine hairs escaping my plait. "But I could do much worse than a kind baker who owns a shop and worships me."

"In my experience, it's less gratifying for both parties

if that worship is single-sided." Percy rubs a hand over his face. I can tell he's getting drowsy, and I think he might beg to retire, but instead he says, "Not to abandon this subject entirely, but can we return to something for a moment? What was that about the Saint Bart's Hospital board?"

"Oh." The subject inspires in me an entirely different sort of anxiety than talking about Callum. "I requested an appointment with the hospital governors."

"To be admitted as . . . a patient?"

"No. To make a petition to study medicine there. Though they don't know that's what I want to talk to them about. I may have implied the meeting would be to discuss a financial donation I wanted to make to the hospital." I scrape my teeth over my bottom lip. It sounds far worse when I say it aloud. Particularly to Saint Percy. "Should I not have done that?"

He shrugs. "You could have picked a less dramatically different reason. They're all going to wrench their necks from the shift in topic."

"It was the only way I could be sure they'd see me. Nowhere in Edinburgh will have me as a student—not any of the hospitals or the private physicians or teachers. I'd have to leave eventually if I want schooling and a license." I let my head fall forward so that it's resting against the headboard of the bed. "I didn't realize it would be so hard."

"To study medicine?"

Yes, I think, but also to be a woman alone in the world. My character was forged by independence and self-sufficiency in the face of loneliness, so I assumed the tools for survival were already in my kit, it was just a matter of learning to use them. But not only do I not have the tools, I have no plans and no supplies and seem to be working in a different medium entirely. And, because I'm a woman, I'm forced to do it all with my hands tied behind my back.

Percy shifts his weight and flinches, a shudder running up his arm and twisting his shoulder. I sit up. "Are you all right?"

"I'm sore. I'm always so sore after a fit."

"Did you fall?"

"No, I was asleep when it happened. In bed. Maybe I wasn't asleep." He presses the heel of his hand into his forehead. "I don't remember. Sorry, I was feeling awake but I'm getting fuzzy again, and I can't remember the last thing we talked about."

"You should sleep."

"Do you mind?"

"Of course not." I stand up, smoothing out my skirt where it's gotten rucked up over my knees. "I am more than capable of entertaining myself. Do you need anything?"

"I'm all right." He burrows down into the blankets,

the bed frame letting out an ominous creak. The weight of the day settles through me: exposed to the freezing winds as I rode the imperial of the coach down from Scotland, reeking of the horses relieving themselves and the man next to me asking again and again for my name, where I live, why won't I smile? I'm weary, and cold, and Percy is a soft place to land.

"Could I . . . ?"

He opens his eyes. I suddenly feel very small and meek, a child begging to crawl into bed with her mother when she's woken at night by frightful dreams. But I don't even have to ask. He tosses back the quilt and slides over to make room for me.

I kick my boots across the floor and strip off my coat, but leave my jumper on, then lie down beside him, pulling the quilt over us both. I roll over onto my back and let the silence settle over us like a fine layer of dust before I say, my face to the ceiling and not entirely certain Percy's still awake, "I've missed you. Both of you."

I can hear the soft smile in his voice when he replies, "I won't tell Monty."

3

The appointment at Saint Bart's is confirmed for a week after I arrive in London—somehow the address in Moorfields didn't tip them off to the fact that I haven't any spare coinage to be tossing at their establishment. I have a half-hour slot, just before they recess for lunch, so they'll all be hungry and irritable and disinclined to rule in my favor.

I sleep as well as a girl can hope to the night before a meeting that could change the course of her life. Which is to say, I do not sleep at all, but rather lie awake for hours, mentally reviewing the process of lancing boils, like they might quiz me on that one very specific thing I just happened to study, and trying not to let my thoughts spin into hypotheticals of where I would live if they did admit me, or how I'd pay the fifty pounds tuition, or what I would do if my tutors did not subscribe to an anatomist philosophy. When I do fall asleep, it's into dreams of missing my meeting time, or my feet turning to stones as I race toward the assigned room, or the board asking me why I should be allowed to study medicine and I cannot come up with a single coherent reason.

Why are you here, Miss Montague? they ask, and I can't reply because my throat is clamped shut and my head is empty. *Why should you be admitted here when you're just a girl, when you're just a child, when this is all just a silly passing fancy?*

The third time I wake from this particular dream, I get up. Monty isn't home yet, and Percy is dead asleep beside me with his head all the way under the blanket, so I risk lighting a candle from the smoldering ashes of the stove. I retrieve my book of Platt's treaties from my knapsack and rip out the final blank page. Then, with a pencil from Percy's music stand, I sit cross-legged on the floor at the foot of the bed and begin to make a list.

Reasons I Should Be Allowed to Study Medicine at Saint Bartholomew's Hospital

First, *women comprise half the population of this city and the country and have unique afflictions of their sex that male physicians are incapable of understanding or treating effectively.*

Second, *the perspective of a woman on the subject of medicine is an untapped resource in a field dedicated to progress.*

Third, *women have been practicing medicine for hundreds of years and have only been excluded in this country in recent history.*

Fourth, *I can read and write Latin, French, and some German, in addition to English. I am schooled in mathematics and have read widely on subjects related to medicine. My favorite writer is Dr. Alexander Platt, and if you were to present me now with pen and paper, I could draw you a map of the bronchial tree from memory. Also I recently mended a gentleman's amputated finger with no prior schooling on the subject, and he is expected to recover entirely.*

Fifth, *I want nothing else in the world so much as to know things about the workings of the human body and to improve upon our knowledge and study of them.*

I frown at the last one. It's a bit overly sentimental and will do nothing to make a case for the stout heart of a woman. It is also not entirely true—I do not want to know things. I want to *understand* things. I want to answer every question ever posed me. I want to leave no room for anyone to doubt me. Every time I blink or breathe or twitch or stretch, every time I feel pain or awake or alive, I want to know why. I want to understand everything I can about myself in a world that often makes no sense, even if the only things to be known for certain are on a chemical level. I want there to be right answers, and I want to know them, and myself because I know them.

I don't know who I am without this. That's the truest thing I could say. Half my heart is this hunger. My being is constructed by an aching to know the answers to every mystery of the frail ligaments that connected us to life and death. That wanting feels a part of me. It has seeped into my skin like mercury injected into a vein to trace its shape through the body. One drop colored my whole being. It is the only way I can see myself.

This, I remind myself, is a fresh start. A new city. Another place to try again and prove that I deserve a spot in this world.

I write that at the top—not for the board, but a reminder to myself. *You deserve to be here.*

There's a crash and a curse on the other side of the partition. I startle so fantastically that I accidentally poke the tip of the pencil all the way through the paper, skewering the final *e* in *here*. "Monty," I hiss, peering out from behind the partition with my candle raised. I make out the shape of my brother, bent double massaging his kneecap, which, judging by the clatter, he slammed into the stove.

"This flat's a bloody death trap," he says, words fizzing through his clenched teeth. "What are you doing? It's four in the morning."

"I'm . . ." I look down at the paper mashed between my hands. "Thinking."

"Can you think in bed with the light out so that I can sleep?"

"Yes, sorry." I crease the paper and shove it into the pocket of my skirt hung upon the partition.

Monty watches me, one hand still rubbing his knee. "What were you writing?"

"Nothing of consequence." The list suddenly feels silly and small, the sermon of an idealistic missionary who has yet to accept that no one cares about her gospel. "Just some notes for my appointment."

"Are you nervous?"

"Of course not," I reply. "Just wanted to be prepared." I blow out the candle and return to bed before he can ask further. I can hear him rooting around the flat for several minutes longer, dressing for bed. He pauses on the other side of the screen, and I hear the crunch of unfolded paper. There's a silence, then another rustle as it's returned to its place.

I don't get up, and he doesn't say anything to me as he gropes his way to bed through the darkness and curls up on Percy's other side. He's snoring in minutes, but I lie awake for hours longer, counting the beats of my heart and repeating to myself over and over *You deserve to be here.*

When I wake again, the morning light flitting in through the cracks in the wall is the warm gold of a soft-boiled egg. At my side, Percy is curled up with his knees pulled to his chest and Monty's head—still swathed in that ridiculous slab of a hat—resting on his chest. It's the same way we sometimes slept on our Tour, the nights we all three shoved ourselves into lumpy beds in dodgy inns or laid out beneath the white poplars in farmer's fields blushing with lavender.

I try to make my rising quiet, though the floorboards render that impossible. The whole flat seems to be conspiring against me, for I immediately run into the screen, and it nearly collapses. It's a testament to how exhausted they both must be, for Monty continues to drool into Percy's nightshirt, and Percy doesn't stir.

There's no room for true privacy in the tiny flat, and though I've shared tighter quarters with these two lads, I'm not about to strip to my skin in the middle of the room and pretend as though my modesty is as easy to put out of sight as it was when we were stowed away together in the bowels of a xebec. I manage to change into fresh underthings on the other side of the screen without disrobing entirely, though I bang my elbow hard at least three times on three separate things and almost tip over like a falling tree when I catch my toe in a hole in my petticoat. When I tie my pockets around my waist, I check to make certain the list is still there. It is, though in the right, rather than the left where I placed it. Monty remains a terrible thief.

The stove is still warm from the night before, but nowhere near enough for it to do anything useful like boil water for coffee or thaw me under my jumper. I throw on a pair of logs and blow until they catch, then wrap myself in my brother's coat before crouching with my back to the belly of the stove, waiting for the heat to become too much to sit so close and listening for chimes down the road, though I know from the light it's still early. But it's more comfortable to worry about being late to the meeting than to worry about the meeting itself.

There's a creak behind me, first from the bed ropes, then the floorboards, and Percy comes around the screen, wrapped in a battered dressing gown that looks as though it was made in the previous century for a man half his height. His hair is puffed up on one side and flat on the other, and his face is heavy, like he's still waking himself. "Good morning," he says. I press a finger to my lips with a meaningful look at where Monty is still asleep, now spread over the entirety of the bed like he was dropped there from a great height.

Percy waves me away. "He's lying on his good ear. He'd sleep through the end of the world."

"Oh. Well then. Good morning. Better today?"

"Much." He sits down cross-legged in front of the stove, his shoulders curled toward its warmth. "Why are you up so early? I thought your meeting wasn't until eleven."

"Just gathering my thoughts." I resist the urge to reach into my pocket for my list again. "You?"

"My quartet is playing at a luncheon today, and I actually think I might make it through the entire concert without vomiting."

"Oh. Good." I don't mean to sound upset, but it comes out with a bit of a wilting end. It isn't that I expected him or Monty to come along with me—the most they could offer is silent encouragement from the back of the room. And I've always known I would be doing this alone. Everything I've done up to this point has been alone. But disappointment still knocks against my rib cage. "That's all right."

Percy looks up. "Hm?"

I had waited too long to say it, and also he hadn't been apologizing for anything. I shove down that annoying disappointment, chiding it that it has no business being here. "Nothing." I smile at him, then push myself to my feet. "Let me make you coffee before I go."

I give myself an hour to walk to Saint Bart's, though it's only a mile, in addition to a half hour to sit anxiously in the hallway before the scheduled time of the appointment. Percy sees me off at the door with more affirming words but no hug or even a pat upon the shoulder. Thank God for friends who learn to speak to you in your own language rather than making you learn theirs.

I'm already on the street, hood pulled up and hands jammed into my muff and trying to remember to breathe, when I hear the door to their building slam behind me. I turn as Monty stumbles down the stoop, trying to lace one of his boots while still moving forward and doing neither effectively.

"Sorry," he calls as he staggers toward me. "I swear, I was going to be up on time, but I didn't think you'd be leaving so goddamn early."

"What are you doing?" I ask.

He gives up on the boot and jogs to catch me up, laces dragging in the mud. "I'm coming with you. Someone should make certain you don't get arrested." He's still got that little tea cozy of a hat on, and he reaches up to pull it down so it's covering his scars as much as possible without it impeding his vision. He notices me staring at it and asks, "Should I have worn a wig? This seems now like it might be a wig-wearing sort of gathering. I've got one upstairs—I can go fetch it. But it's been growing mold since the fall, and I assumed that wasn't the sort of impression—"

"Thank you," I interrupt.

He pauses. "For not wearing my moldering wig?"

"Yes. Definitely for that. But thank you for coming."

He scrubs his hands together and gives a short puff on them for warmth. "Percy would too, if he could. But he's missed too many shows this week, and epilepsy is, in professional medical terms, a son of a bitch."

I nearly laugh, but then he'll be pleased with himself, and if I have to see those dimples this early, I might punch him.

We fall into step together—or rather, as into step as a pair can on these ragged roads. I dart around a puddle of what I'm fairly certain is piss gathering in the frozen rut of a wagon wheel, then duck around Monty so I'm not on his deaf side.

"You really think I'd let you do this alone, you goose?" he says as we walk. "It's a lot to take on by yourself."

"I've taken on a lot by myself," I reply.

"I'm not saying you're not capable. But it's nice sometimes, to have someone to cheer you on. Metaphorically," he adds quickly. "I promise I won't do any actual cheering. Even though it's tempting because of how much it would embarrass you."

I glance sideways at him, and he looks at me at the same time. The corners of his mouth start to turn up in the sly triumph of having caught me in a moment

54

of sentimentality, but I toss my head back so my hood shields my face before he can say anything. "That hat is idiotic."

"I know," he says. "Percy made it for me."

"I didn't know Percy knew how to knit."

"He doesn't," Monty replies, and the brim of the hat falls in front of his eyes as though in emphasis.

"I'm glad you've got Percy," I say.

"So am I." As we cross into the square, the caving tenement houses open into gray sky. The light is a slick sheen over the muddy streets like the scales of a herring. "And don't be cross with me for saying this, but I wish you had someone too. I worry about you."

"You do not."

"I do." He dodges a stream of brown water dumped from a high window, and our shoulders bump. "Ask Perce. I wake up in the middle of the night in panic about my lonely sister up in Scotland."

"I'm not lonely."

"I didn't think I was either."

I shrug so my cloak falls closed in front of me. "Do you want me to marry Mr. Doyle because you think I need a man to protect me? Or complete me? I'll pass on that, thank you very much."

"No," he says. "I just wish you had someone cheering for you all the time, because you deserve it."

We stop on a street corner, waiting for a flock of

sedan chairs to cross the road ahead of us, their footmen calling greetings and japes to each other as they pass. "Love has made you terribly soft, you know," I say to him without looking.

"I do," he replies. "Isn't it grand?"

4

At eleven o'clock, Monty and I are shown into Saint Bartholomew's Great Hall by a spotty adolescent clerk with too much powder cracking along his hairline. It's a high-ceilinged, gold-leafed room with two levels of windows framed by dark wooden plaques, the names of donors painted in long, neat rows. Men. All of them men. A portrait of Saint Bartholomew hangs over a marble mantelpiece, his blue robe one of the only spots of color in the dark room.

It would be more impressive if we had not walked through the filthy hospital ward, where haggard nurses shook lice out of gray linens, buckets of waste were carried about by patients forced to work to earn their keep, and a man I assumed was a surgeon screamed at a woman about using the name of the Lord in vain, to get here. The hallways reeked of sickness, intertwined with the sharp, metallic tang from the meat market it adjoins. All this grandeur seems like appalling waste.

But I'm here. My heart hiccups. I am about to speak to a board of hospital governors. I've never made it this far before.

There are a few rows of chairs lined up before a tall wooden bench, behind which sit the governors. Them I do find impressive, though aside from their wigs and fine clothes, it's likely to do with the fact that they are men in a large group, which always ignites a sort of primal fear in me. Flanked as they are by busts of the governors before them and loomed over by all those names along the walls, I feel generations of men who have kept women from their schools staring me down. Men like this never die—they're chiseled in marble and erected in these halls.

Monty settles himself in one of the chairs and puts his feet up on the one in front of him. The clerk nearly faints. I consider chiding him, but I would rather my first impression with these men not be that of a stern governess correcting her overgrown man-child on his manners. While I, in tartan and wool and work boots, am in no place to be casting judgment upon anyone's fashion, his trousers have more holes than I noticed on the walk here, one distressingly near a sensitive area. He could have gone to a bit more effort not to look waifish.

I lay my winter things over the chair beside him, fish

my notations out from my pocket, and resist the urge to wear out all my anxiety on its corners as I take my place before the board, none of whom look at me. Rather, they're speaking to one another, or going through the forms in front of them. One of them is discussing what he's going to eat for his luncheon today. Another laughs at a joke from his fellow about their horse-racing bets.

I feel small enough without being made to wait for them to decide they're ready to address me, so I speak first. "Good morning, gentlemen."

Perhaps not the best strategy, but it gets their attention. That, and Monty hisses a hush from the back like we're in school. I almost turn to glare at him—so much for the promise of not embarrassing me—but the men are starting to look my way. They're all old, all of them fair skinned and robust. At the center of the table, the gentleman with the largest wig folds his hands and surveys me. "Miss Montague. Good morning."

I take a breath and it sticks in my throat like cold porridge. "Good morning, gentlemen." And then I realize I have already said that and nearly turn on my heel and dash from the room in panic.

You are Felicity Montague, I remind myself as I take another porridgy breath. *You have sailed with pirates and robbed tombs and held a human heart in your hands and sewn your brother's face back together after he got it shot off over said human heart. You have read* De Humani

59

Corporis Fabrica *three times, twice in Latin, and you can name all the bones in the body, and you deserve to be here.*

You deserve to be here. I glance down at where it's written upon the top of my list. *You deserve to be here. You deserve to exist. You deserve to take up space in this world of men.* My heart begins to even itself out. I take a breath, and it doesn't stick. I push up my spectacles and look at the board.

And then of course I say "Good morning" one more time.

One of the governors snorts—the same mutton-faced man who was boasting about the chops he was about to eat as soon as they're finished here—and it sets off a flare inside me. I square my shoulders, raise my chin, and say with as much confidence as I can muster, "I have come today to petition the board on the matter of granting me permission to study medicine at Saint Bartholomew's Hospital."

I glance down at my notes again, ready to launch into my first argument with only a small reminder of what that argument is, but the wigged chairman who seems to speak for the group interrupts. "I'm sorry. I must have the wrong appointment." When I look up, he's flipping through his papers. "I was told that this was to discuss a donation. Higgins!"

"No, sir, that's right," I say, nearly knocking Higgins the clerk out cold as I throw up an arm to halt his scurry forward from the back of the room. The chairman looks at me, and I amend, "I mean, it's not right."

"Are you Miss Felicity Montague?"

"Yes, sir."

"And you scheduled this appointment to discuss a financial donation you wished to be made from a late relative's estate?"

"Yes, sir, but that was a pretense in order for the board to see me."

"So there's no money?" the chops man whispers to his neighbor.

The chairman folds his hands and leans forward over them, his eyes narrowing. "You felt the need to seek refuge in a pretense?"

"Only because I have made appeals to several different boards at several different hospitals and not been granted permission to make my plea."

"And what plea would that be?"

I resist the urge to glance down at my paper, just for somewhere to look that isn't into those hawk-black eyes of a man who has never been denied anything in his life. "I would ask the board's permission to be granted a chance to study medicine at the hospital, with the intention of obtaining a post and license to practice."

I had expected laughter from the board. Instead, they're looking back and forth at one another, as though questioning whether the others are also seeing this terrier of a girl who dares to ask them for the moon, or if she's simply a figment of their pre-luncheon hunger pangs.

"I can show her out, sir," Higgins says, and I jump—somehow he's snuck up to my shoulder without my noticing and is already reaching to take me by the arm.

"Not yet," the chairman replies. My fist closes involuntarily around my notes, crushing them. That *yet* raises my hackles, as though my being thrown from this room is merely a matter of time. "Miss Montague," he says, his tone the auditory equivalent of looking down his nose. Which he is also doing, as he's seated higher than me. "Why do you think you have previously been denied a chance to petition a hospital board on this matter?"

It's a snare of a question, one that I know I have to walk into or he'll lead me in circles until I trip it, and I'd rather not be led anywhere. My chin rises—if I raise my head any higher, they'll be staring up my nose—and I say, "Because I am a woman."

"Precisely." He looks down the bench and says, "So, that's our recess, gentlemen. We'll reconvene here at two."

The men begin to stand up, reaching for their cloaks and gathering their cases and papers and all talking at full volume. I feel Higgins behind me, closing in to make good on that *yet*. He actually gets his bony little fingers around my arm this time, but I shake him off before he can get a good grip. I take a few steps forward and say as loudly as I can without shouting, "You haven't heard my case."

The chairman tosses his cloak over his shoulders and gives me a smile that he likely thinks is kind, but is, in fact, the smirk of a man about to explain something to a woman that she already knows. "There's nothing more to hear. Your case is contained within that single statement. You are a woman, Miss Montague, and women are not permitted to study at the hospital. It's our policy."

I take another step toward the bench. "That policy is antiquated and foolish, sir."

"*Antiquated* is quite a large word, madam," he says.

So is patronizing, I think, but bite my tongue.

Most of the board is listening again now. I have a sense that, more than anything, they're hoping to have a good story to share at the pub, but I'll take any attention I'm offered.

"Have you previously studied medicine at a hospital or academic institution?" the chairman asks.

"No, sir."

"Have you had any kind of formal schooling?"

He's baiting the water again, and the best I can do is sidestep. "I was educated at home. And I've read quite a lot of books."

"That isn't healthy for you," one of the other men

interrupts. "Reading in excess causes the female brain to shrink."

"Oh, for God's sake," I burst out, my temper snatching the reins. "You can't actually believe that."

The man leans backward, as though I've frightened him, but another leans in to add, "If you've read so many books, why do you need a hospital education?"

"Because a hospital education is required in order to obtain licensure and establish a practice," I say. "And because reading Alexander Platt's treaties on human bones is not adequate preparation for setting a broken leg when the wound is bloody and the bone has splintered under the skin and already starting to fester with gangrene."

I had hoped Dr. Platt's name would conjure something closer to adoration among the men, but instead, a low murmur ripples through them. A man on the end with a pointed chin and tufts of coarse blond hair sticking out from under his wig raises his eyebrows.

"Then let a man set that bone and let the woman see the injured has a good meal and a bed," the chops man murmurs, loud enough for everyone to hear. There's a smattering of laughter from these men with clean fingernails who hardly know the color of blood.

The chairman flicks his gaze in their direction but does nothing to silence them. "Miss Montague," he says, his eyes returning to mine, "I have no doubt that you are very bright for a young lady. But even if we were to consider admitting a female to our student ranks, the cost of necessary arrangements for her—"

"What arrangements, sir?" I demand.

"Well, to begin, she would be unable to attend anatomy dissections."

"Why? Do you think my nerves so weak and fragile that I could not handle the sight? The women on the streets of London witness more death and dying in a single day than you likely have in your lifetime."

"I have yet to meet a woman with a stomach for the sort of dissections we undertake," he says, "not to mention the nakedness of the male form, which would be inappropriate for you to see outside the bonds of marriage."

He glances over my shoulder at Monty, who raises his hand and says, "Brother," as though that's the most important matter to set straight here.

I resist throwing something over my head and hoping it catches him in the nose, and instead remain focused on the chairman. "I can assure you, sir, I would not become hysterical."

"You seem hysterical now."

"I'm not," I say, annoyed that my voice pitches on the second word. "I'm speaking passionately."

"Not to mention the concessions that would have to be made so the male students would not be distracted by the presence of a woman," one of the other men adds, and the rest of the board nods in support of what an excellent, nonsense point he has made.

It takes every ounce of strength in me not to roll my eyes. "Well then, you might consider covering up table legs lest the mere reminder of the existence of the female form send your students into an erotic frenzy."

"Madam—" the chairman begins, and I can feel Higgins right over my shoulder again, but I press on, using my argument as a plow this time.

"Women make up more than half the population of this city, this country, and the world. Their intelligence and ideas are an untapped resource, particularly in a field that claims such a commitment to progress. There is no proof women are unequipped to study medicine—quite the contrary, women have been practicing medicine for hundreds of years and have only been excluded in recent history as surgery became regulated by institutions run by men. Institutions that are now so bogged down in bureaucracy that they have ceased to serve even their most basic functions for those in need." I hadn't planned to say that, but the stink of the hospital wards is still in the back of my throat. The chairman's eyebrows have risen so high they're about to disappear under his wig, but I press on. "You make money off the poor and the sick. You charge them to take up space in your hospital wards. You make them work to earn their keep so less salaried staff is required. You charge absurd amounts for treatments you know don't work so that you can fund research you refuse to share with those who need it."

It is perhaps not the wisest thing to insult the institution in which I'm standing, but I've so much rage bottled up inside me about so many things, and it's all pouring from me in a spurt, like shaken champagne violently uncorked.

"In addition," I say, "there are elements of feminine health that male physicians are not equipped to address and have made no attempt to understand or improve treatments for. Would you deny your mothers and sisters and daughters the most effective medical care?"

"There are no treatments women are denied because of their sex," the chairman interrupts. "We treat female patients here, the same as we treat men."

"That's not what I'm talking about. I'm talking about a lack of any research to provide relief from the debilitating pain that regularly restricts the most basic tasks of daily life for women."

"I don't know what you're referencing, madam," the chairman says, his voice raised over mine.

"I'm talking about menstruation, sir!" I shout in return.

It's like I set the hall on fire, manifested a venomous

snake from thin air, also set that snake on fire, and then threw it at the board. The men all erupt into protestations and a fair number of horrified gasps. I swear one of them actually swoons at the mention of womanly bleeding. Higgins snatches his hand back from my shoulder.

The chairman has gone bright red. He slams a book against the desk, trying to cram a lid over the Pandora's box I have flung open. "Miss Montague, we'll hear no more protestations from you. Based on your insubstantial and, frankly, hysterical case made before us today, I could not in good conscience allow you to enroll as a student here. You can see yourself out, or I'll have Higgins escort you."

I want to stay—I want to keep fighting them. I want to be allowed to finish the points upon my list. I want to tell them how I stole medical treaties from the bookshop in Chester because the seller wouldn't let me buy them, how I cut the pages out so carefully and reconstructed them into the binding of Eliza Haywood's amatory fiction to hide what I was actually reading after my mother found a copy of *Anatomical Exercise on the Motion of the Heart and Blood in Animals* in my bedroom and thrown it in the fire without a word to me. How sometimes the only reason I feel like I belong to myself and not the world is because I understand the way blood moves through my body.

I also want to cry, or shout that I hope all their

genitals sprout wings and fly away, or perhaps travel back in time to the start of the meeting and go about this whole thing differently. I want to shut up the small, nasty voice in my head whispering that maybe they're right and maybe I am unsuited for this and maybe I am hysterical, because even though I don't think I am, it's hard to be raised in a world where you're taught to always believe what men say without doubting yourself at every step.

Before Higgins can at last get a good grip on my arm, I push past him, not waiting for Monty or looking backward at the governors or the Great Hall. I've never wanted to be away from somewhere so badly in all my life.

Outside, the winter air is a welcome slap across my burning face. I plow through the hospital courtyard, past the line at the dispensary and the nurses emptying sludgy buckets into the gutter, until I'm through the gates and out on the street. The cold has pried the tears from my eyes, though it's easier to blame them on the winter than humiliation. I stop on the pavement so suddenly that I force a sedan to redirect its course. A dog on the lead of a vagrant growls at me.

I pull my sleeves up over my hands and press them against my face, my nails digging hard into my forehead. A gust of wind carries a sprinkling of snow off the hospital wall and deposits it on the back of my neck. It feels greasy and clogged with soot, but I let it melt in a slow trickle down my spine, imagining each vertebra as it passes, counting bones with every breath.

Running footsteps slap the stones behind me. I drop my hands from my face as Monty comes barreling out of the gates, stopping short when he realizes I haven't made it any farther than that. My cloak and muff, abandoned back in the Great Hall, are slung over his arm. He extends them to me, and when I don't move to take them, he makes an awkward toss of the cloak around my shoulders. He starts to wedge the muff in between my elbows, rethinks it when he realizes how close this puts him to accidentally grabbing my breast, and instead lets his hands fall, the muff hanging limp at his side.

We look at each other. The city boils around us. I want to strike flint and set it aflame. Burn everything from the sky down and start the world over.

"Well," Monty says at last, then again, "Well. That didn't quite go as planned."

"It went exactly as I planned," I say, my voice a snap like a rib cracking.

"Really? That was your ideal scenario?"

"I said what I wanted to." I snatch my muff from him and shove my hands into it. "Every point I made is irrefutable. Their exclusionary policies rest entirely on the fragility of their own masculinity, but it doesn't matter because they're men and I'm a woman so it's not even going to be a fight and it was never going to be a fight. It was always going to be them walking all over me, and I was stupid to think it could ever be anything more than that, and don't you dare try to hug me."

His arms, which had been rising, freeze midair, and he lets them hover there, like he's carrying something large and round and invisible. "I wasn't going to."

I swipe the back of my hand over my eyes, knocking my spectacles askew. I want so badly to be away from here, but I've got nowhere to run to. Not back to their flat, too small for me to have a good, private cry. Even the fact that it's *their* flat reminds me how much more together my brother's life is than mine. Not back to Edinburgh, into the arms of a man who smells like bread and aniseed and says he likes me for my spirit but wants it broken just enough that he can take me out in public. Not back to my parents' house, where I grew up unacknowledged by anyone unless it was to voice some disapproval for the way I dressed and spoke and brought books with me to parties. For all my efforts, I haven't even a bed of my own to throw myself upon and sob.

"Miss Montague," someone says behind me, and I turn too quickly, for a tear rips itself loose from my eye and sets a course down my cheek.

One of the governors is standing behind me—the man with the ill-fitting wig who gave me an eyebrow wiggle at the mention of Dr. Platt. His cloak is thrown over his arm and he's breathing fast, a bit of a wheeze to his lungs that sounds like a lingering winter cold.

I can feel that tear sitting against the corner of my mouth, and I'm not certain if wiping it away will make its presence more or less noticeable, so I leave it there. "Good day, sir."

He scrubs his hands together, an uncertain gesture that seems to be both an attempt to generate warmth and also just something to do. "That was quite a scene," he says, and my heart sinks.

"You don't have to put it like that, mate," Monty interrupts. He's reaching out for me again, like he intends to put a protective and brotherly arm around my shoulders. I glare at him, and he turns it into brushing some invisible dust off my arm.

"My apologies." The governor extends a hand to me. "Dr. William Cheselden."

"Oh." In spite of how sour I'm feeling toward all men in medicine, I go a bit light-headed at hearing the name. "I've read your paper on lithotomy."

"Have you?" He looks surprised, as though my entire presentation in the Great Hall was a fabrication. "What did you think of it?"

"I think your method is undeniably better for removing bladder stones," I reply, then add, "but I wonder why you wouldn't devote more energy to the study of how to reduce their occurrence altogether rather than removing them once they've already caused pain."

He stares at me, his mouth slightly open and his head canting to the side. I'm ready to turn and walk away, nursing the satisfaction that I was able to tell off at least one of the Saint Bart's governors. But then he smiles. "You subscribe to Alexander Platt's school of preventative medicine?"

"Emphatically," I reply. "Though I've had very little chance to apply anything practically."

"Of course." He slaps his gloves against his palm, then says, "I wanted to offer my apologies for the ungentlemanly way you were treated just now. Some men seem to think that if a lady behaves in a way that they consider unbecoming of her sex, they are justified in speaking in a way that is unbecoming of theirs. So first, my apologies."

I nod, not sure what more I can say other than "Thank you."

"Second, I wish to offer you a few suggestions."

"Suggestions?" I repeat.

"If your heart is set upon studying medicine, you might seek an apprenticeship with an herbalist or a midwife."

"I'm not interested in either of those subjects."

"But they are"—he drags out his thought with a hum through pursed lips, then finishes—"adjacent to medicine."

"So is body snatching, and yet you aren't suggesting I become a grave robber."

The tip of his nose is going red from the cold. "Perhaps employment as a nurse at the hospital, then. They're always looking for young women here, and at Bethlem. I'd be happy to put in a word."

I fold my arms. "You mean spooning soup into mouths of invalids and sweeping up the wards after the surgeons walk through it?" I had not woken today thinking I would get in an argument with a famous physician, but if I wanted to cook for men, I'd have stayed in Edinburgh and married Callum. "I don't want to be a midwife. Or a nurse."

"You're so determined to become a lady doctor then," he says.

"No, sir," I reply, "I'm determined to become a doctor. The matter of my sex I would prefer to be incidental rather than an amendment."

He sighs, though it comes out round with a chuckle. "It's a shame you weren't here a few weeks ago, Miss Montague. I would have handed you off to Alexander Platt. You two would get on famously."

Even knowing that it is anatomically impossible in relation to my continued state of living, I swear my heart actually stops. "Alexander Platt . . . as in the author of *Treaties on the Anatomy of Human Bones*?" As in Alexander Platt, my idol, the working-class surgeon among all these wigged fops who man the hospitals. Alexander Platt, who was discharged from his post as a navy surgeon for his tireless campaign for anatomical dissections to better understand what killed men on the sea. Alexander Platt, who cut his teeth and dirtied his hands walking hospital wards in the French Antilles before he ever was allowed to set foot in an Edinburgh hospital. Alexander Platt, whose work on arsenate poisoning earned him a spot as a visiting lecturer in Padua when he was just twenty-two. Alexander Platt, who had proved one did not need money or a title to be a physician—just a good brain and a determination to use it.

Cheselden beams. "The same. He was here last month."

"Giving lectures?" I ask.

"No, it's a rather unfortunate situation. He had his license suspended several years ago and . . . well, it's all a very sticky business." He laughs, too high, his eyes darting away from mine before he finishes, "But he was here seeking hands for an expedition he's undertaking."

"He left on an expedition?" I ask, and it comes out pinched by disappointment.

"Not yet—he's gone to the Continent, to be married. He sets off for the Barbary States on the first of the month to complete some research. You should write to him and say I recommended you—he's less likely be put off by your sex than the men here in London. He's taken on work with women before."

Of course he has! I want to shout. *He's Dr. Alexander Platt, and I have excellent taste in idols!* "Do you know where I might write him?"

"He's staying with his intended and her family in Stuttgart—the uncle's surname is Hoffman, and the bride is . . . give me a moment, it will come to me . . . Josephine? No, that's not it. Joan?" He runs a hand over his chin. "Something beginning with a *J* and an *O*."

My joy turns bloated and sick. When the name of one's only childhood friend is brought up unexpectedly, years' worth of memories you vowed to rid yourself of entirely bob to the surface. Particularly when that friendship ended as poorly as ours did.

"Johanna?" I squeak, hoping he'll say otherwise.

But he snaps his fingers. "Yes, exactly that. Johanna Hoffman. Very clever of you."

Of course. Of course another felled tree blocks my path. Of course the woman marrying Dr. Platt is the last person who'd want to welcome me into her home.

Oblivious to my strife, Cheselden goes on, "You might write to Dr. Platt via Miss Hoffman. I know he's intending to set out as soon as the wedding is finished, so you may be too late, but you've no loss dropping a line."

"When's the wedding?" I ask.

"Three weeks from Sunday. Perhaps a bit optimistic for a letter to arrive by then."

It is almost impossible that, in such a short time, my letter could find its way to Dr. Platt *and* he would find time amid marriage and planning an expedition to read it *and* he would be so taken with my written plea alone that he would offer me a position and I would then have enough time to travel to wherever he was leaving from and make his acquaintance. An even slimmer chance that any letter bearing my name would not immediately be ripped to shreds by Johanna Hoffman, a girl with whom I have a checkered history as expansive as the list of names upon the walls of the Great Hall.

But . . . if it wasn't a letter that showed up on his doorstep, but rather me in the passionate, intelligent flesh, then I might have more of a chance.

Dr. Cheselden fishes in his coat pocket for a calling card and hands it to me. "Do tell Alex I advised you to write him."

"I will, sir. Thank you."

"And Miss Montague—the very best of luck to you." He touches two fingers to his forehead, then turns down the street, his coat collar turned up against the wind.

I wait until he's out of sight before I spin to face Monty and grab his arm, though he's so bundled I mostly get a handful of sweater. "Look at that! I told you it all went according to my plan."

Monty is looking far less enthusiastic than I'd anticipated—I had even been willing to let him hug me had he offered, but instead he's rubbing the back of his neck with a frown. "That was . . . something."

"Try not to sound too excited."

"He was bloody patronizing to you."

"Much less than anyone else was. And he gave me a card!" I wave the creamy stock engraved with Cheselden's name and office address at him. "And told me to write to Dr. Platt—*the* Dr. Alexander Platt. You know, I was telling you about him yesterday at breakfast."

"The one who lost his license to practice surgery?" he says.

"Because he's a radical," I reply. "He doesn't think like the other doctors. I'm certain that's why." Monty scuffs his toe against the pavement, eyes downcast. I press the card between my hands like I'm praying over it. "I'm going to go to Stuttgart. I have to meet him."

"What was that?" Monty's head snaps up. "What happened to writing?"

"A letter will not get his attention in the way I need to," I reply. "I'm going to show up and introduce myself, and he'll be taken with me and offer me the position."

"You think you're just going to show up on his doorstep and he's going to hire you?"

"No, I'm going to go to the wedding and dazzle him with my exceptional promise and work ethic, and then he will hire me. And," I add, though I know this trail is more treacherous, "I know Johanna Hoffman—you remember her, don't you?"

"Of course I do," he replies, "but I didn't think you two parted on good terms."

"So we had a small falling-out," I say with a flippant wave to undercut the grandness of this understatement. "Doesn't mean it won't seem perfectly innocent for me to show up at her wedding. We're friends! I'm celebrating with her!"

"And how will you pay your way there?" he asks. "Travel is expensive. London is expensive—is Dr. Platt going to pay you for this work? Because as much as Percy and I adore you, sharing our bed is not a long-term living arrangement I am thrilled about. If he had a job for you that was studying medicine or working toward some kind of degree or license, that would be one thing, but it sounds like you'd be taken advantage of."

"Well, maybe I'm going to let him take advantage of me. Not like . . ." I blow out a sharp breath, and it comes out wispy and white against the cold air. "You know what I mean."

"Come on, Feli." Monty reaches out for my hand, but I pull away. "You're too smart for that."

"Then what am I supposed to do?" I cry, and it comes out ferocious. "I can't give up on medicine, and I can't go back to Edinburgh, and I can't marry Callum— I just can't!" The only reason I'm not crying is that I'm so aggravated by the fact that I'm almost crying again. I haven't cried in ages—even those first gray, lonely weeks in Edinburgh I had been stiff-lipped and stout-hearted— but in the space of a single hour, I've been on the verge of it three times. "I'm not going to spend the rest of my life hiding the things I love behind the covers of books that are considered appropriate for my sex. I want this too much to not try every last damn thing possible to make it happen. Fine, now you may hug me."

He does. It is not my favorite. But if he can't understand the hurt, I can at least let him apply a familiar balm. I stand in his arms, my cheek pressed against the scratchy wool of his coat, and let myself be held.

"Everyone wants things," Monty says. "Everyone's got a hunger like that. It passes. Or it gets easier to live with. It stops eating you up inside."

I scrunch my nose and sniff. Maybe everyone has hunger like this—impossible, insatiable, but all-consuming in spite of it all. Maybe the desert dreams of spilling rivers, valleys of a view. Maybe that hunger will one day pass.

But if it does, I will be left shelled and halved and hollowed out, and who can live like that?

5

By the next evening, Monty and I have descended from civilized point-and-counterpoint to full-on bickering on the subject of my going to Stuttgart.

It is our only topic of conversation as the three of us walk to the pub in Shadwell called the Minced Nancy, which from the name alone brands itself a place where mollies like my brother and his beau can be together openly. We're supping with Scipio and his sailors, whom Monty and Percy have been conspiring for a reunion with since their crew docked several weeks previous. The pavement is narrow, and we walk with me squashed between Monty and Percy, all of us tripping over one another in an attempt to huddle against the cold and also avoid being mowed down by carts. The air reeks of burning pitch from the riverside, so strong I'll be swallowing the smell all night. Soot falls in great clumps, as London sets everything that burns aflame to keep warm. Lacking coinage to spare for a lamplighter, our only illumination comes from the spitting spray off the knife grinders' wheels and the blacksmiths stamping out their embers for the day as we pass their shops. By the time we find the address, I'm so tired of being cold and wet and hearing my brother's infuriatingly sensible arguments about why I should not go to Stuttgart on a whim that I'm ready to turn around and return to the flat as soon as we arrive.

I expect the club will be crowded, loud, and reeking of booze, but it feels more like a coffeehouse, dark and warm, with oyster shells littering the floor so that the boards sparkle and crack under our boots. A thin veneer of smoke hangs in the air, but it's a sweet tobacco, and welcome relief from the sludgy evening outside. The noise is mostly conversation at a level volume, combined with the soft clatter of cutlery on plates. There's a man with a theorbo sitting on the bar, his feet up as he tunes the strings.

"You chose this place?" I ask Monty as I look around. "Your taste has gotten far more civil since I last saw you. No one's got their top off."

"Please don't compliment me on my morals; it makes me feel very obsolete." He's put on his best coat for the occasion—a coat he apparently could not spare for accompanying me to the hospital—and his face is washed. It's an approximation of looking presentable, though he still looks less like a gentleman and more like the raw ore mined to create one. "It's just that I can't hear a bloody thing if it's noisier than this."

"There's Scipio." Percy waves, and I follow his gaze to the familiar crowd in one corner. Monty fumbles for Percy's hand, and I follow them across the room.

Privateering suits the crew of the *Eleftheria*. They are all better dressed and less gaunt than the last time I saw them. Most of them still sport sailor's beards, but their cheeks don't valley beneath them anymore. The ranks have shifted—I know Scipio, Ebrahim, and King George, now a whole foot taller (but just as enamored with Percy, as proved by his sprint across the room and tackle-hug). But with them are two other dark-skinned men I don't recognize, one with a curled mustache and golden earring, the other with three fingers missing on his left hand. There's a third, much smaller and smooth-faced person, in a shapeless tunic and a headscarf, so hunched over a mug that I can't immediately tell if they're a man or a woman.

Scipio claps Monty and Percy warmly on their backs and gives Monty's newly shorn hair an affectionate ruffle before he takes my hand in both of his and kisses it. "Felicity Montague, what are you doing here? Did you come all the way from Scotland just to see us?" Before I have a chance to answer, he asks, "And have you grown taller, or am I shorter than when we last met?"

"She's not; it's those damned boots of hers." Monty slings himself into the booth beside Ebrahim. "They've got the thickest soles I've ever seen."

"He's sore I'm taller than him," I say.

Scipio laughs through his nose. "He lost several inches in cutting that hair."

"Don't." Monty claps a hand to his heart in reverence. "I'm still in mourning."

"You've got a new crew." Percy reaches down to shake hands with the two men I don't recognize, then slides into the booth beside Monty, unfolding his long legs under the table while I take the chair across from them.

"We needed more hands sooner than expected," Scipio says. "This is Zaire and Tumelo, picked up from the tobacco trade in Portugal. And that"—he points down to the slouching youth at the end of the table— "is Sim, from Algiers, who adopted a legitimate life to join us."

Sim looks up from her beer. Her face is heart-shaped and small, made even more pointed by the frame of her headscarf. Her features seem almost too large for such a small canvas. The two men stand to shake hands around, but she doesn't move.

"How have you found sailing as merchants under the British crown?" Percy asks as we all settle into the booth.

Scipio laughs. "I am of a far calmer temperament than I was when we sailed without patronage. We're still questioned more than most British crews when we're on European soil, but at least we have letters now."

"Where have you been traveling?" I ask.

"Still in the Mediterranean, mostly," he replies. "Portugal and Algiers and Tunis and Alexandria. It's all dead cargo—your uncle's kept us away from the Royal African Company," he says to Percy. "We saw him in Liverpool last month and he seemed very well."

Percy smiles. Percy's aunt and uncle, though ready to see him committed to an asylum, were far from tyrants. His uncle had been gracious in using his position to aid the crew of the *Eleftheria* as thanks for the role they'd played in our safety while abroad. In contrast, Monty and I had each written one letter to our father, letting him know only that we were not deceased but also not coming home, and received nothing in return. While my father had been hostile to Monty and indifferent to me, he was the sort of man who would have cut off his own hand if it meant avoiding scandal. And two children mysteriously disappearing on the same trip to the Continent would have all the bees buzzing back in Cheshire.

"Oh, tell Felicity the story about the goats in Tunis," Monty demands, though I'm spared by the distraction of Georgie returning with the beer.

"Have you been corresponding?" I ask Scipio. I know

Percy organized this reunion but not that there has been much more communication between them.

"On occasion," Scipio replies.

"Here, Miss Montague, you and Sim may have something in common," Ebrahim interrupts, and calls down the table. "Sim, what do you think of London?"

She raises her head. Her face doesn't change, but I can feel the rehearsed nature of this bit, like she has been called upon to do it more than once and is growing tired. "I hate it."

"Why do you hate it?" he goads.

"Too many white men," she replies. Ebrahim laughs. Sim doesn't. Across the table, she meets my eyes, and some invisible string seems to tighten between us. Her head cants to the side as she inspects me. It makes me feel like a specimen pinned open on a corkboard for students to study.

I'm given an excuse to look away when Scipio says to me, "How have you taken to the north? Percy said you'd been in Scotland."

"She's already tired of Scotland," Monty answers. To compensate for his deafness, he's taken to either staring with off-putting intensity at whoever he's speaking to or turning away so his good ear is toward them. I know it's necessary for his hearing, but the latter makes it look as though he isn't paying attention, magnifying the already dismissive air he's prone to giving off. I shouldn't be annoyed by it, but I'm an easily stoked fire tonight. Monty pokes me in the ribs with his elbow. "Maybe Scipio will take you to the Continent."

When I don't smile, Scipio looks between us. "Are you traveling again?"

"No. Monty is being cruel," I say.

"I'm not being cruel!" he protests. "It was an honest suggestion! You've got no other means to travel."

I glare at him. "And you know Stuttgart is entirely landlocked, don't you?"

"I do now," he says into his beer.

Across from me, Sim's head snaps up. She has both fists resting on the table, knuckles notched into each other and her thumbs pressed into a steeple.

"What business is taking you to Stuttgart?" Ebrahim asks.

I let out a heavier sigh than I mean to, and my spectacles fog. "My friend Johanna Hoffman is getting married."

It seems the simplest explanation, but leave it to Monty to show off the dirty underside of everything. "She wants to go to Stuttgart because her friend is marrying a famous doctor Felicity's obsessed with and wants to work for."

"I am not obsessed with Alexander Platt," I snap.

"She's been turned down by every surgeon and hospital in Edinburgh, and she doesn't have any money or way to travel, but she's still ready to go gallivanting off because Dr. Cheese Den told her that this Platt fellow is theoretically possibly maybe hiring a secretary." Monty looks to Scipio. "Tell her it's a terrible idea."

I want to kick Monty under the table, but there are so many legs tangled up I'm afraid I'd misjudge and dig an unwarranted toe into an innocent stander by. "It is not a terrible idea," I snap before Scipio can answer him. "And it's Cheselden. Not cheese den."

"Do you have any opposition to oysters and eggs for supper?" Scipio calls down the table, interrupting Monty and me before we can properly show our claws. "Georgie, come help me carry plates."

As soon as they've gone and Ebrahim has turned down to converse with the other two men, I give my brother a hard stare. I would have tossed that mug of warm beer in his face if I hadn't suspected I'd soon need it, as I am no great lover of oysters.

In return, he adopts a wide-eyed innocence. "What's that look for?"

I lean in, my tone clipped as a fingernail. "First, you don't have to be a smug prick about the fact that I don't have money or means to travel or that I was barred from the hospital, because in spite of what you and Callum and everyone else seem to want, I am not going to give up and settle down. Second, you are not in control of my actions simply because you are the closest man to me.

What I do is not up to you, nor to anyone, particularly someone so ignorant of the difficulties of my current position. And third, Monty, that's *my* leg."

The ascent his foot has been making up my thigh halts. Percy peers under the table, where his legs are stretched out parallel to mine, then pats his own knee. "Is this what you're after?"

Monty flops backward into the booth, raising a puff of dust from the upholstery. "You can't be serious about traveling, Fel. It's insane."

"No more than giving up your inheritance to live a skilless sod in London," I snap. "You're a professional card player, remember; you're not curing cholera."

"Stop it, both of you," Percy interrupts, a hand going up over the table between us like he's refereeing a boxing match. "This is meant to be a nice evening, and you're ruining it." There's a pause, then he says to Monty with a frown, "My legs aren't actually thinner than Felicity's, are they?"

"Oh, stop it, Perce, you know you have magnificent calves," Monty says, then adds, "And Felicity has very hairy socks."

"Magnificent calves," I scoff. "Could you have picked a less erogenous body part?"

It was an unwise door to open, for Percy pipes up, "Monty has nice shoulders."

Monty pillows his cheek upon his fist in a swoon.

"Do you really think so, darling?"

"You think he's got deep dimples in his cheeks," Percy says to me, "you should see his shoulders."

Here I thought nothing could inflate my brother's head more. I swear his chest actually puffs up. I'm no great lover of this mealy beer, but I take a drink just for the drama of it before I reply, "I pray nightly I never again have occasion to see my brother's bare shoulders."

"Come on now." Monty knocks his foot into mine—then peers beneath the table to make sure he's aimed correctly this time. "If you're going to be a doctor, you mustn't be shy about human anatomy."

"It's not human anatomy that makes me queasy, it's *your* anatomy."

"My anatomy is excellent," he replies.

"Yes, it is," Percy adds, pressing his lips to Monty's jawline, just below his earlobe.

"Dear God, stop." I resist the urge to cover my eyes. "You're still in public, you know."

Monty drags himself away from Percy and gives me a saccharine smile. "Felicity, my darling, you know we love you dearly and are so very delighted that you're staying with us for the time being, but it does place some limitations upon the sort of, shall we say, *activities* that we are accustomed to engaging in both frequently and privately—"

"Stop talking now," I interrupt, "and go find a back room somewhere and suck each other's faces off."

Monty grins, his hands suspiciously out of sight beneath the table. "That's not what I intend to be sucking."

"You are the filthiest creature on God's green earth," I tell him.

Percy wraps an arm around Monty's shoulder and pulls him into his chest. Their vast height difference is only slightly less comical when they are seated. "Isn't it adorable?"

That roguish grin goes wider. "I told you I'm adorable."

They slink off together, though *slink* is far too sheepish a word for it, as there's absolutely nothing sheepish about it. They strut, hand in hand and tripping over each other in delight. Obnoxiously proud to be in love.

Scipio and Georgie return with food—neither of them asking where the gents disappeared to, thank god. I don't eat much, or talk—Scipio asks a few gentle questions about how I'm doing, but my answers must be brisk and simple enough that he knows I'm not in the mood. By the end of the meal, I'm sitting alone at the edge of the group, picking at the cracked white paint on the tabletop and wishing Monty weren't so right. It's mad to go to Stuttgart alone. More than mad—it's impossible. I have almost no money. Certainly not enough to get to the Continent. And what would I do once I arrived? What does one say to a friend who broke your heart? *Hallo, remember me? We were young together and used to collect bugs in jars and broke chicken bones from supper so we could practice setting them, but then you called me a pig in a party dress in front of all your new friends and I said you were shallow and uninteresting. Congratulations on your union; may I talk to your husband about a job?* I sink down in my seat without meaning to, one hand sliding into my pocket and fiddling with the edges of my list.

Someone sits down at the table across from me, and I look up, expecting Monty and Percy returned from their backroom romp.

It's Sim. In spite of the trousers and loose shirt, she's far more feminine-looking in close proximity. The bones of her face are fine and elegant in the lamplight. She doesn't say anything, and I'm not sure what it is she wants from me. We stare at each other for a moment, both of us waiting for the other to speak.

"Am I interrupting your sulking?" she says at last.

"I'm not sulking," I reply, though I very clearly was.

"So your posture is always that terrible?" Her English has the same accent as Ebrahim's; he was raised speaking Darija in Marrakesh before being kidnapped and sold into slavery in the American colonies. Before I can reply, she presses on, "You want to go to Stuttgart."

I throw my hands up, a gesture that nearly overturns my mug. "Good, so everyone overheard that."

"No one overheard it," she says. "We just *heard* it. Your brother speaks very loudly."

"He's deaf," I say, then add, "and obnoxious."

Her face doesn't change. "I want to take you."

"Take me where?"

"To the Continent."

"The Continent?"

"To Stuttgart." She pauses, then says, "Do you want to repeat that as well?" Her tone snaps with impatience that I can't keep up, as though she's proposing something as casual as paying a call together. Though I might have been flummoxed even if her choice of conversation had been more conventional, for her eyes are very dark and very intense and they've got me fumbling for an answer. "You want to go there," she says slowly, tapping a finger on the table between us. "I want to take you."

"You want to . . . why?"

"You know Johanna Hoffman, and you're invited to her wedding."

None of that answers my question. I'm also most definitely not invited to the wedding, but a correction would overturn a complicated grave, so I ask, "I'm sorry, who are you?"

"Oh, do we need to make some preliminaries?" She

holds a hand over the table, which I don't take. "I'm Sim. I work for Scipio."

I almost roll my eyes. "Well, now that the niceties are out of the way."

"I can do more," she says. "The weather's cold. Ebrahim thinks it's funny to hear me say there are too many white men in London. You should wash your hair more."

"Excuse me?"

"Your braid fell in your beer when you were slouching." She folds her hands upon the table with a nod, satisfied with the perfunctory chat. "I'm Sim; you're Felicity; I want to take you to Germany."

If she's joking, I can't tell. Her face is impossible to read, those enormous eyes offering no hints. I'm more accustomed to Monty, who can't make a jape without congratulating himself.

"Why do you want to take me to Germany?" I ask again.

Her boot knocks my shin under the table, and I'm annoyed that it's me who moves to give her room. "Because I need to go to the Hoffman house, and that will be easier if I have you to help me."

"Why do you need to get to the Hoffmans'?"

"It doesn't matter."

"No, actually, that matters quite a lot to me." I sit up straighter and match her folded hands upon the table. "If you're going there to, say, as what I hope is an extreme example, murder someone, or set the house on fire, I'd rather not be complicit in that. Your introduction from the captain included mention of sailing legitimately, which implies that you once didn't."

A flash of irritation breaks over her face, just for a moment, but enough for me to think that this stoic façade may be just that. She's working very hard to appear much cooler and tougher than she actually is, like she hopes that will balance out the fact that she's ripped open and vulnerable in asking me for this. "I'm not murdering anyone."

"And yet you're silent about arson."

"I'll pay your way. All your expenses to Stuttgart. The *Eleftheria*'s payout was good—I can prove it if you want. All I ask is that you let me pretend to be your maid so that the Hoffmans will put us up in the house. You can do what you like while we're there—go to the wedding or accost that man you're obsessed with—"

"I'm not obsessed—"

"And I promise, no one will be in danger or hurt." She sucks in her cheeks, making a hard, unflattering face. The lamp on the table turns her skin the bright amber of monarch wings. "You can trust me. I'm one of Scipio's crew."

"You're a sailor," I say. "What does a sailor want

with an English family abroad?" I'm trying to remember if Johanna's family has any connection to trade or sailing, but by the time her father died and she left England to live with her uncle, we were seeing as little as possible of each other.

Sim works her mouth into a hard line, then, with great care, says, "To reclaim something that was taken from my family."

"So you're a thief?"

"That's not what I said."

"*Reclaim* is just *theft* in fancy dress."

"It's not theft," she says. "There is an item that belonged to my family, and I believe it's now in possession of the Hoffmans. All I want is a location."

"The Hoffmans are an upstanding family," I say. "Johanna's father was an aristocrat, and her uncle's a businessman. What sort of dealings would they have with . . ."

I trail off, but Sim finishes for me. "With someone like me?"

"With common sailors," I say. "What's this mysterious item of unknown location? Is it treasure?"

She stares down at the table, digging her thumb into a chip of white paint until it snaps free. "More like a birthright."

"That's a very abstract concept to be stealing."

"All right. You're not interested; I'm finished." She

stands up to go, but almost before I realize I've spoken, the word "Wait!" tumbles from me.

She pauses, her chin to her shoulder so that her headscarf obscures most of her face.

This is a bad idea, and I know it. Humans have instincts specifically for situations like this. Everything in me is saying there is danger lurking in this forest, eyes bright and hungry through the dark.

I want to walk in anyway.

Because it's Alexander Platt. It's medical schooling. It's a chance to plant my feet firmly in a direction away from Callum and wifedom and general gentility. What does it matter to me what clandestine mission is drawing her to the same house as me? She's just a bank with credit to travel. I'm doing nothing wrong so long as she doesn't.

"If we go," I say, "you are there only for a location. You have to promise me there won't be a theft or damage or harm done to any person or item. I won't let you into their house just to make a robbery of it. That's my condition."

"I said I wouldn't steal anything."

"Promise me."

"Why are you so certain I'm villainous?"

"Because the alternative is that you're simply doing a good turn for a stranger, and your initial approach would lead me to believe otherwise."

I have suppressed enough eye rolls in my lifetime to know she's working very hard to do so. "I promise."

"We'd have to leave soon," I tell her. "The wedding is in three weeks." Even as I say it, it hardly feels like enough time, particularly if we're traveling on limited funds. There's a chance we'll arrive only to find Dr. Platt and Johanna have already traded their vows and are now cozied up in some honeymoon suite leagues away. Arriving uninvited to a wedding is one thing—bursting in on a honeymoon quite another.

"I'm ready to leave whenever you are," she replies.

"Will you be missed?" She shakes her head. "And you won't tell my brother?"

"Does that mean you're in?" She holds out a hand again, and this time I take it. I expect a firm shake, but instead she pulls me up, so that we're nose to nose. She's a few inches taller than I am, thin but powerful. Perhaps those hungry eyes are hers. Perhaps I don't care.

"Yes," I say, and it feels like a step off a cliff. My pulse flutters with the freefall. "I'm in."

6

I wait until the next morning to tell Monty I'm leaving.

I hoped to catch both him and Percy at the same time so that Percy could provide a buffer between my brother and me, but he departed early for a concert, and Monty woke late from a night at his casino, so he has his breakfast while I take luncheon, though they're both comprised of the same stale bread and coffee. He receives the news with indifference—most likely because all I say is that I'm leaving, with no additional details about where or with whom that departure will be made.

From his perch upon the stove, rippling the surface of his steaming coffee with his breath, Monty asks, "So what are you going to say to Mr. Doyle? Should I be checking the post for a wedding invitation?"

I drop a cube of bread into my coffee to soften it.

"Actually, I'm not going to Edinburgh. I'm going to Johanna's wedding."

"What?" He looks up. "How?"

"That's not important."

"I think that's rather critical information."

I fish the bread out of my cup with my spoon. I can feel him staring at me, but I refuse to look. "The woman we had supper with—from Scipio's crew. She's helping me."

"Why?"

"Because I want to go to Stuttgart."

"That's not what I meant. Why is she helping you?"

He may not be the sharpest scalpel in the surgical kit, but he'll raise the concerns I have forced myself to ignore at the mention of *reclaiming a birthright*, so instead I offer up a question in deflection. "Why are you making that face at me?"

"You're going to meet that doctor, aren't you?"

"I am going because Johanna is my friend, and I'd like to see her married," I say.

Monty snorts. "Is she? I seem to remember you two shouting at each other at Caroline Peele's birthday party, and you making a very impassioned decree that you had no further interest in her company."

I set my mug on the stack of trunks that serves as their table, a little harder than I mean to. A few drops slosh out over my hand. "Why are you being such an ass about this?"

"Because this sounds like a terrible idea, and I'm worried about you."

"Well, that's not reason enough for me not to go," I say. "I worry constantly about you and Percy being pilloried or tossed in the Marshalsea or you setting your flat on fire because you don't know how to boil water, but I don't stop you."

"I'm not trying to stop you from studying medicine, but I'm not going to pretend I think this is the way to do it."

"What other way is there?" I ask. I'm annoyed that my tone is rising while his is staying maddeningly even. I am not usually the first of us to grow agitated. "I may not get another chance like this."

"But you're smart. And you work hard. And you don't give up. It's not a matter of if, it's when."

He's not going to understand. It crystalizes for me in a moment. We may have grown up in the same house, two restless children with contrary hearts, but our parents sought to sand down our edges in different ways. Monty suffered under the hand of a father who paid far too much attention to his son's every movement, while mine was a youth of neglect. Unacknowledged. Unimportant. While Monty might have someday run the estate, the best that could be hoped for me was I'd leave it in the arms of a wealthy man. Had he stayed, Monty would have been that wealthy man to some other girl. That was the best either of us could hope for.

We may have both left home. Defied our parents and our upbringings in favor of our passions. But there are rocks in my road Monty can't understand how to navigate, or even conceive of being there in the first place.

He drains his coffee, wipes his mouth on his sleeve, then says, "Stay a few more weeks with us. Or we can find you a room somewhere and help you with the rent. Write to your Dr. Platt and see what he says. Visit a few more of the hospitals here." He bites his lip, and I know I won't like what he says next. "Just don't go to Stuttgart with that woman, all right? It's a bad idea."

He's not going to understand. Better to pretend that I do. "Fine," I say.

He looks up, and I wonder if my tone was curt enough to raise suspicion—I had tried to sound sincere but had fallen rather short. "Really?" he says. "You agree with me?"

"Of course I do. It's far more sensible to stay in London."

"Yes!" He slaps a hand upon his knee. "Exactly, yes. Remember this day, Felicity: the day you agreed I am the more sensible out of the pair of us."

"I'll mark it in my diary," I say dryly, then stand up to refill my mug. Hopefully the movement will disrupt the conversation enough that he'll truly think me a changed woman and we can move forward to something else.

I shall not get Monty's permission to go to Stuttgart. Luckily, I don't need it.

I continue the charade of planning to stay in London for the next two days before Sim and I are to depart. I let Percy suggest neighborhoods in which I might look for a flat and Monty make ludicrous propositions about how I shall break into the field of medicine, all the while gathering my meager possessions in my knapsack under the pretense of tidying up the flat. It is a traditionally feminine enough activity that neither Monty nor Percy seems suspicious.

Then, in the wee hours of the last day of the week, I get up after a sleepless night, dress silently in the dark, and let myself out of the flat, my knapsack knocking against the backs of my knees.

It will be two weeks of travel to Stuttgart, then the wedding festivities provided we manage to weasel our way into the household. If the position with Dr. Platt comes to fruition, I don't intend to return to Moorfields, particularly not as a dependent houseguest. Neither do I intend to return to Edinburgh. On my way to the harbor, I drop a three-line missive at the post office to Callum, saying that I will be staying in London longer than planned, as my brother's syphilis/boredom is more serious than anticipated, leaving out any mention of the fact that I am going to the Continent with a stranger to make a future for myself that will not include him.

I have challenged fate to chess and am now attempting to keep all my confidence from puddling in my boots. What if I'm the only one betting on myself because everyone but me can see I am not suited to play at all?

You are Felicity Montague, I say to myself, and touch the paper in my pocket listing my arguments, which, if all goes according to this impossible plan, will now be made in some variation before Alexander Platt. Dr. Cheselden's card is nestled in its folds. *You have stowed aboard a ship and traveled forty-eight days with a single outfit. You are not a fool, you're a fighter, and you deserve to be here. You deserve to take up space in this world.*

The harbors are perhaps the vilest part of a vile city. The ground is slick with a foul combination of fish intestines, yellow spittle, gull droppings, vomit, and other fluids I'd rather not give too much thought to. Even at this early hour, the narrow docks are packed, every person certain their business is most important and therefore that snapping at others to get out of their way is justified. The wind off the water picks up a spray from the fetid Thames and spews it in my face as I search the crowd for Sim. I find her lingering near the end of the queue of passengers waiting to board the packet, and when she sees me coming, she steps into the line in earnest. She's swapped her sailing duds for a muslin dress and unembroidered shawl tucked into the stomacher, topped with a heavy wool cloak.

When I join her, she forgoes a greeting and instead says, "You look upset."

"And your scarf has a hole in it," I snap. "Oh, look, we're all making observations." She doesn't reply, and perhaps I imagine her shifting her weight so she's facing away from me, but I press my hands to my face and give my head a good shake to clear it. "I'm sorry. I'm anxious, that's all."

"About leaving?"

"No, more about the fact that . . ." It seems unwise to tell her that no one knows where I am, so instead I say, "My brother's an ass. That's all."

"So are mine."

"Your what?"

"My brothers. They're all asses."

"Brothers plural?" Had I been forced to grow up in a household of multiple Montys, I would have got myself to a nunnery just for some quiet. "How many have you got?"

"Four."

"Four?" I nearly swoon. "Older or younger?"

"All younger." She grimaces. "All very loud."

"Are they sailors too?"

She nods, adjusting her grip on her bag. "Or they will be. The littlest one is only eight, but he'll be at sea soon. All my family are sailors."

"What sort of sailors?" I ask.

But Sim is already turned away from me, instead peering ahead to the front of the queue, where boarding cards are being checked before we're allowed on the deck, and though I know she's heard me, she doesn't answer.

"That's fine," I say. I'm more annoyed at her silence than I likely should be, but in my defense, it has been an exceedingly stressful few weeks and all my emotions seem to be operating at a higher level than usual. "We needn't exchange any personal information—we'll only be together constantly for the next several weeks; I'd rather remain strangers in proximity." I push myself up on my toes, trying to see over the heads of the other passengers. "This is taking too long."

"Maybe you're impatient," Sim says, still aggravatingly calm.

"I am not impatient. I just know how long things should take."

She blows into her hands. "Then maybe you're opinionated."

"Well, my opinion is that you shouldn't pass judgments upon me." I cross my arms, turning away from her and the line to instead look around the harbor. The sails of the moored ships flutter in the wind, smaller boats flitting between them with punters digging their poles into the bottom of the Thames. The ropes of a sledge crane nearby have snapped, and a merchant in a fine suit speckled with salt is shouting at a group of boys about the damage to his goods. Several planks down from us, there's a mess of raw fish spilled and trampled into the boards. A porter slips on the guts and drops the trunk he's carrying, grabbing on to a stranger beside him for balance. A stranger in a ridiculous hat.

It's Monty.

"Oh no."

Sim looks up from her hands. "What?"

I pivot sharply, my back to Monty, though that will hardly be a hiding place for long. "My brother's here."

"Is that a problem?"

"I didn't . . . I didn't tell him I was leaving. I mean, I did, but he wasn't thrilled about that, so I lied and said I wasn't, but in the process gave him just enough details that if I was to disappear in the middle of the night, he'd know where I was going."

"And you disappeared in the middle of the night?"

"Not the middle of the night," I protest. "The very early hours of the morning."

Sim must spot Monty as well, for she ducks down at my side. "He's coming this way."

Of course he's coming this way—we're standing in line for the ferry to Calais, the first place to seek out your sister fleeing to the Continent. "Come on." I pull Sim out of the line, up the dock, and then out of sight behind the cargo dropped by the crane. I turn to her, my knapsack knocking me hard in the small of the back. "What do we do?"

"I don't know; he's your brother," she replies.

"He's also a human man, which I assume you've had dealings with in the past." I press my face into the collar of my cloak, trying to examine the situation as though it were far more scientific than it is.

The problem: avoiding Monty, who is paying careful attention to everyone boarding the ship to Calais. The resources at our disposal: little to nothing. Sim, me, my knapsack, which is mostly mittens and books and underthings. Though I suppose throwing a book at his face and then running aboard would not be a bad distraction. That or just shout something about menstruation and watch the entire dock erupt into chaos—it worked so effectively with the hospital board.

We do not have time to wait for another ship. The sky is clear today, and winter weather is an unpredictable horse to bet upon. Tomorrow might be stormy, the channel so chopped up that no ships can break through it. The wind may be too strong, the air too cold, the water too treacherous with chunks of ice. Our window to get to Stuttgart is so narrow there's a chance we might miss the wedding even with everything running on time. We have to be on that boat, whether Monty is in the way or not.

"We have to distract him," I say. "He hasn't got a

boarding card, so he can't follow us onto the boat, so we only need occupy him long enough to make a run for it. And probably wait for the queue to die down. We'll have the best chance right as they're about to cast off."

"How are you going to distract him without him seeing you?" Sim asks.

"We get someone else," I say, trying to sound more confident and not like I'm making this up on the spot. "We pay someone."

"We can't afford to pay someone."

"How much money do you have, exactly?"

She screws up her lips, then says very carefully, "Enough to get us to Stuttgart."

"Brilliant," I grumble.

"If you want to pay someone to go punch your brother in the face, that can be your share for dinner tonight."

"I don't want someone to punch him," I protest, then add, "I mean, I do. But not right now. But we need some kind of distraction . . ."

Had I more time to think this through, I could certainly come up with a more elegant plan. But time is not on our side. I set out from behind our hiding place, Sim chasing me down with a yelp of surprise at my sudden movement. Away from the water and the ships, the dock is teeming with sailors and deckhands, some of them working, some of them huddled around smoking braziers, warming their hands over the flames. There's a bakery window selling cakes and mulled wine, the kind where you help yourself and drop some coins into the box on your honor. Having more crisis than honor, I take a mug without paying and start toward one of the clusters of men, but Sim stops me. "Tell me what you're doing."

"Asking a man to distract my brother long enough that we can board the boat."

I expect she'll argue—not only is it vague, but most of my plans are talked back to by participating parties. But she just nods, then scans the groups of sailors closest to us.

"You think that will work?" I ask, my voice peaking on the last word. I am unaccustomed to being trusted so absolutely, and Sim is not someone I had expected to offer up that trust easily.

"It will certainly do something. Ask that one." She points to a man huddled alone against the wall of a dock office. I can smell from here that he's in his altitudes, or perhaps coming down off a binge the night before. His skin is withered from the sun; the strips poking out of the too-short sleeves of his coat are covered in blue ink. Several other drawings crawl up from his collar and along the back of his neck. He does not look like the sort of man I want to trust my escape to.

But Sim put her faith in me. The least I can do is the same.

I stride up to the gentleman, careful not to spill

my mug of hot wine. He looks up from his pipe as we approach, regarding us with a squint though the sun has hardly risen. "Good morning, sir," I say. "I would like to offer you this drink."

"All right, then." He's reaching for it before I've finished my sentence, and I have to snatch it away, nearly dumping it all over Sim.

"Wait—first, you must do something for me."

"Don't want to do anything for you," he replies, tucking back into his pipe packing.

"It's very simple," I say. "Do you see that man over there by standing by the dredge? He's short and has his hair cut, scars on his face."

The sailor glances up. "The one with the adorable hat?"

Damn it, Monty—now I wish our distraction *was* punching him in the face. "That one exactly. I need you to go over to him and pour this drink down his front, but make it seem like an accident, and then take a good long time telling him you're sorry and helping him clean up."

"Then I don't get the drink," the man says slowly.

"Well spotted," I reply. "But you don't have to pour all of it."

He stares at us, his head weaving, though I can't tell if that's because he's actually considering the offer or about to tip over. Then he hawks a ball of spit at the boards and sticks his pipe in his mouth. "No, thanks."

I'm ready to move on and try another, dafter sailor,

but Sim steps forward. "Come here," she says, crooking a finger at him. "I want to tell you something."

The man runs his tongue around his mouth, eyes flashing as he leans in. Sim grabs him by the collar and yanks him to her, a long, black knife drawn from her boot and pressed against the soft meat of his throat. It is, if the throat is to be slit, not technically the best place to approach from—she'd have better luck going in from the side, stabbing into the carotid artery, then moving forward and down to the vocal cords to ensure silence and letting out both major blood supplies to the brain simultaneously.

But I'm less concerned about that and far more concerned by the fact that first, Sim has a knife in her boot that she brought along with her for unknown but likely unsavory reasons, and second, she is about to use that knife to *slit a man's throat.*

The sailor gurgles with fear, his eyes bulging in his head. Sim tosses back her sleeve, and I watch the man's eyes travel from her knife to her forearm, and somehow he looks even more afraid. "You see this?" she says to him, and he nods.

"You sail under the bleeding Crown and Cleaver," he says, his voice higher than a moment before.

Sim presses the knife harder, though not enough to draw blood. The man lets out a whimper. "You know what that means, do you?" She looks pointedly at the ink on his neck, and he doesn't nod this time—the knife is pressed in too deep to risk any sudden movements. "You do as she says," Sim says, then shoves him into the wall. She replaces the knife in her boot, then straightens and nods me toward him. I don't know if she's expecting me to acknowledge my gratitude for her help, but my throat has gone dry. The instinct to step back from her, to pull away and run and unknot myself from our alliance rises inside me, primal and animal, the compass of my heart pointing straight to *flee*. That knife and that threat has confirmed the very likely truth that I have avoided looking in the eyes since Sim dropped her proposition upon me at the Minced Nancy: I am likely taking up with a dangerous person, who might hurt me or the people to whom I'm exposing her. If someone in the Haus Hoffman is to have their throat cut in their bed, she might take me as well, just to ensure my silence.

Below us, the sailor asks, "Can I have the drink?"

I take a deep breath and turn to him, trying to look less shaken than I am. "You may hold it, but you may not drink it. And do not move until I signal you." A harbor bell begins to toll the hour, and one of the sailors on board our ship shouts down to the man on the dock checking the manifest. "Signal," I say, yanking our man to his feet and shoving him forward. "Go make yourself a nuisance."

Sim and I watch together as he makes a halting

stagger through the crowd, tracking his progress with our own path along the dock and back toward the ship, ducking behind every crate and cart and barrel that will hide us. The gent moves much slower than I had hoped he would move. The harbor bells are finishing, and the sailors about our packet are pulling in the gangplank, and Monty is starting toward the man at the end of it, like he might ask after the names on the manifest to see if I'm listed there. Our drunken friend veers sharply, raises his glass in the most theatrical of gestures . . .

. . . and pours it over a complete stranger.

Which certainly causes a commotion, though among the wrong people. I curse under my breath, ready to just run for the ship, but Sim grabs my arm. I flinch without meaning to, still thinking of that knife, but she's only directing my eyes. The commotion is close enough to Monty that he has to dodge out of the way to avoid the ruckus, and he glances over at our sailor, right as the sailor realizes his error and looks back at us as if we might be holding some kind of sign with printed directions of what to do now. Monty follows his gaze, and, across the harbor, our eyes lock. My stomach drops.

He starts toward me, and I'm ready to run, but then our sailor, clearly afraid of Sim's wrath should he fail, throws himself at Monty and tackles him. The sailor is a fair bit bigger than my brother, and the force of the hit knocks him more sideways than I imagine was intended, because both Monty and the sailor plummet over the edge of the pier and into the rancid, freezing Thames.

"That works," Sim says, and I feel her hand on my back, pushing me forward. "Go now."

I almost don't. Partly because there is a chance real harm has been done to my brother—exactly the thing I had hoped to avoid with drink-pouring rather than face-punching as a distraction. And more than partly because of Sim's bright icicle of a knife and the fear in the man's eyes when he recognized her.

If you're going to run, this is the time. Do it before you leave London, before you're far enough from home that you'd never get back on your own.

I glance down the dock, to where a few kind souls are fishing my brother and our sailor out of the river. They both look unharmed. No visible blood or limbs pointing the wrong direction. They're sopping wet and shivering, but Monty will be a bloodhound after my scent as soon as his feet are on dry land again.

Last chance, I think, staring forward up the gang-plank. *Last chance to run. To change your mind. To find another fight, or surrender altogether and trade in whatever danger undoubtedly lies ahead for a cozy bakeshop and a kind baker back in Edinburgh.*

But I'm not giving up on a spot with Alexander Platt. If I'm going to place a bet, it's going to be on me and my ability to outfox and outrun Sim, should the need arise.

You are Felicity Montague, I tell myself. *And you are not afraid of anything.*

And when Sim sprints down the dock and up the gangplank of the packet, I follow her.

It's a day on the water to Calais. If the sky stays clear and the channel cooperative, we'll be in France by sunset. We don't take a cabin, and below deck is frigid and wet and smells foul, so we sit upon the benches lined against the rails, where the air is cold but fresh. The hood of my cloak refuses to stay up, and the wind has its way with my hair, twisting and whirling it out of its pins and into thick clumps that I try to untangle with my fingers, even though I know it's pointless.

At my side, Sim watches me struggle with a snarl at the back of my head, her own hands clamped over her headscarf to keep it in place. "Do you want help?" she asks.

"I'm fine," I say, then give a hard pull that pricks all the way to my eyes. The knot remains maddeningly knotted.

"You're going to rip your hair out of your scalp."

"I think I almost have it."

"You don't. Here, stop." She stands up, brushing her hands off on her skirt before climbing over the bench so she's behind me. "Let me."

I don't like this. I don't like turning my back to her, letting her put her hands in my hair, her wrist brushing my neck. I'm thinking of that knife against the sailor's throat and how easily it could be against mine at any moment but especially this moment, with my eyes forward and my skin exposed.

She's gentler than I expected. As soon as I think it, I feel guilty for imagining her to be rough and tug at my scalp. I can feel her hands combing through my ends, working with careful precision like it's surgical thread she's untangling. "I think I'll have to cut it out."

"What?" I spring to my feet and whip around to face her. Her hands are still in my hair, and I feel the sharp pull of leaping without warning, my nerves searing.

"It's just a bit of hair," she says. "You won't even notice."

I reach back and touch the knot to make certain she isn't bluffing. I can feel the impossible snarl. "With your knife?" I blurt before I can stop myself.

"My . . . oh." She reaches down into her boot, slowly and with her eyes on me, like she wants to be certain I don't spook. "It's not a knife. It's a marlinespike." She holds it up for my inspection, and it is, indeed, not a knife in the most traditional sense. It's a long, tapering spike with a chiseled end, made from black iron and rough along its edges. "It's a sailor's tool," she explains. "For sailing ropes."

It hardly matters what it was called—confidence is half of any bluff, and she had wielded it with the sureness and threat of a blade. "You still could have killed that man in the harbor with it," I say.

She looks sideways at me. I lift my chin. I want her to know that I know she's dangerous and I'm here anyway. I want her to think me braver than I am, and just as dangerous as her.

"Could I?" she says.

I'm not sure if she's asking sincerely or if she's testing me. I'm also not sure I should tell her. "Had you pressed it down and hooked it below the clavicle bone, just here"—I tap my own over my cloak—"it would have gone into his lungs. Perhaps his heart, if you had the angle right. A punctured lung might not have killed him straightaway, but he didn't seem like the sort who'd go running for a doctor. So it would have likely been a long, drawn-out death with a lot of wheezing and shortness of breath. And then there would still be the blood, and he could easily lose enough to prove fatal. Why are you looking at me like that?"

"How do you know all of that?" she asks.

"I read a lot of books."

"By that man? The one we're going to see?"

"Among others."

She rolls the marlinespike between her hands, the patches rubbed silver by her fingers glinting. "You want to be a surgeon."

"A physician, actually. It's a different license and

requires more—it doesn't matter." I sit down again and turn my back to her, tossing my hair over my shoulder, though the wind immediately yanks it back across my face. "Go on then."

Behind me, she lets out a small, breathy laugh. "So spirited."

"I'm not spirited," I say, sharper than I mean to.

Her hand, which I had felt hovering near my neck, jerks away at the spark in my voice. "All right, easy. I didn't mean it as an insult."

I cross my arms, letting myself sink into a slouch. "No one calls a girl spirited or opinionated or intimidating or any of those words you can pretend are complimentary and means it to be. They're all just different ways of calling her a bitch."

Her fingers tug at the ends of my hair. "You've heard those words a lot, have you?"

"Girls like me do. It's a shorthand for telling them they're undesirable."

"Girls like you." She laughs outright this time. "And here I thought the spectacles were decorative."

I twist around to face her. "What's that supposed to mean?"

"The only girls who talk like that are the ones who assume there are no other women like them in the world."

"I'm not saying I'm a rare breed," I reply. "I just mean . . . you don't meet many girls like me."

"Maybe not," Sim replies, fingering the marlinespike again. "Or maybe you just don't look for them."

I turn back around with more of a petulant huff than I intend. "Just unknot my hair."

There's a pause, then I feel her fingers against my neck, sweeping my hair over my shoulder so that she's holding the knot on its own. "You're right," she says softly.

"Right about what?"

"I've never met a woman quite like you." There's a sharp pinch and a sound like ripping cloth, and then she touches my shoulder. "Here." I hold out my hand, and she drops the knot into it. "No blood spilt."

"Thank you." I run my fingers through my hair, trying to find the shorter strands. "I should wrap my hair like yours. It would be more practical."

"I'm a Muslim," she says. "That's why I wear it. Not because it's practical."

"Oh." I feel silly for not realizing it. Then wonder if I am permitted to ask any questions on the subject or whether that will only prove how ignorant I am on almost all matters of religion, particularly those outside of Europe. "I've heard Muslims pray quite a lot. Do you need . . . ?" I trail off with a shrug. When she goes on looking at me, I finish, "Somewhere private or incense or something?"

She picks a few stray hairs off the end of her

marlinespike, then holds them on her open palm for the wind to snatch. "Have you met a Muslim before?"

"Ebrahim is as well, isn't he?" I say. "From the *Eleftheria*."

"Most of their crew is," she says. "Or were born into it. Not the Portuguese men, but the lads from the Barbary Coast."

The Barbary Coast pricks a vein inside my mind. I am not so foolish as to think there is only one kind of sailor that comes from the Barbary Coast of Africa, but there is a particular sort of ship that makes berth there, and most of them are in the business of piracy. And most are not the sort of cuddly pirates with career aspirations that we found in Scipio and his men. I remember the fear in the sailor's eyes when Sim showed him her arm, too intense to be raised by a scratch or a scar.

"What's on your arm?" I ask before I can stop myself. I'm not certain if she can follow the complex footwork that led me to this conversational pivot, but I say, "I'm not stupid. You showed that man something, and suddenly he was willing to help us."

She doesn't turn, just darts me another sideways glance—I almost miss it in the fall of her scarf. "It's a mark."

"Like a mole?"

I can hear her teeth grind. "No, not like a mole."

"Is it a crown and a cleaver?"

She lets out a tense sigh, lips pursed so hard her skin pinks. "I didn't think you heard that."

"How did you know it would frighten him?"

"He's got ink on him that means he's sailed where frightening things happen to honest sailors who cross that banner."

"Are you one of the honest sailors?" I ask.

"No," she replies, and sticks the marlinespike hard into her boot.

"Oh." I turn forward. She straightens. We both stare out across the gray water, watching England disappear into the fog, and all I can think is that if she's not one of the honest sailors, it may mean she's one of the frightening things.

Stuttgart

7

Our journey from Calais to Stuttgart is done in crowded diligences that hop from city to city along rutted roads, close quarters our only barrier against the cold. I may wear holes in my cloak for all the scrubbing up and down arms I have done, and I fear for my already deteriorating posture, for with every passing mile I feel more and more concave, my shoulders pulling over my knees, my back in a half moon, with my cloak tented around me.

We sleep mostly on the coaches, only two nights in roadside inns, where Sim and I are forced to separate because of our respective skin colors, and while I am opposed to inequality in all forms, it's the only time we have apart all the while we're on the road, and it's not unwelcome. Sim is a quiet companion. She doesn't seem to need the company of books or chatter to find diligence journeys bearable. She doesn't fill silence with conversation unless I initiate it. She lets me talk to most of the ticket clerks and innkeepers and diligence drivers, both of us knowing that most would be even less forthcoming to an African woman than they are to a fair-skinned one—and I have to field my share of questions about who I'm traveling with and where's my chaperone and why it is I'm going anywhere with just a maid hardly older than me. I can see the hard line of her jaw tense every time I step up instead of her, but neither of us says anything about it.

When we reach Stuttgart—a quaint Germanic town with half-timbered houses crowded around squares, all draped in a gentle cloak of new snow—I get the Hoffmans' address from the records office, while Sim finds a dressmaker who can fix me something that will be appropriate for wedding festivities but in a forgettable-enough color that no one will notice repeat wearings.

We start out on foot for the address several miles outside of town. The countryside is heavily wooded, but the austerity of winter has rendered the trees no more than rickety silhouettes, their tops wrapped in thorny mistletoe. We pass a farmhouse with a thin drizzle of smoke rising from its chimney and a stork nested against its shingles. The thin layer of snow coating the earth has been trampled to mud and turned to ice, so that the ground looks bruised and worn. It all seems a charcoal drawing of a landscape.

"How do you know her?" Sim asks as we walk. Her breath is coming out in short, white puffs against the air. "Miss Hoffman," she qualifies when I don't answer right away. "Because so far you've only spoken of the doctor she's marrying."

"We grew up together," I reply, for it seems the simplest answer.

It does not satisfy Sim. "Were you close?"

Close seems too small a word for my single childhood friend; Johanna an only child with an absent mother and father often abroad and I with parents who I was sure sometimes forgot my name, found a whole world within each other. We tore up the forest between our houses, made up stories about being explorers in faraway corners of the world, foraging for medicinal plants and discovering new species that we would name after ourselves. She was famous naturalist Sybille Glass, and I the equally famous Dr. Elizabeth Brilliant—even as a youth, my imagination was very literal. Then Dr. Bess Hippocrates, when I started reading on my own. Then Dr. Helen von Humboldt. I had a hard time committing to a make-believe persona, but Johanna was always Miss Glass, the fearless adventurer who often had to be saved—usually from the grievous injuries her bravery and fondness for risk brought upon her—by my level-headed doctor, who would then advise her to act with more prudence before they set off on their next wild adventure.

"She'll remember me," I say to Sim.

I'm just not sure Johanna will remember any of those childhood games. They're all obscured now by the long, lean shadow of our sour parting. The three years that stretched between then and now feel impossibly vast as we turn up the drive of the house.

Haus Hoffman is painted the bright pink of grapefruit pulp, with gold-and-white trimming and shingles in the same shades capping it like a crown. It looks made of cake and frosting, an extravagant birthday treat that will leave your teeth aching from the sweetness. The drive is split by a fountain, frozen in repose, the hedges rimming it bare as the trees but still imposing.

It has been so very easy to divorce Johanna from this scheme. I had enough to think about aside from her—Alexander Platt, whatever the crown and cleaver upon Sim's arm means, and why she is so desperate for a spot in this house. But as we climb the drive, knapsacks thumping in time against our backs, I think, for the first time, of the next few weeks in their entirety, without skipping over the part where I must see Johanna again.

I don't know what I'll say. I don't know if I want to apologize, or if I want her to.

We are a bedraggled pair that pulls the bell chord—far rougher around the edges than is likely to create a believable image of a rich English girl come from boarding school to her best friend's wedding, attended by her maid.

"What's your surname again?" Sim asks, both of us staring at the door.

"Montague. Why?"

"I'm going to introduce you."

"No, let me do the talking."

"It makes more sense—"

She breaks off as the door opens. A butler greets us, a tall, aging gent with more hair in his ears than atop his head. He looks wrung out and put out and like he'll fall for nothing.

I have learned that men respond best to nonthreatening women whose presence and space in the world does not somehow imperil their manhood, and so, as much as it pains me, I put on a smile so big it hurts my face and try to think like Monty, which is infuriating.

Be charming, I tell myself. *Do not scowl.*

But when his eyes meet mine, I'm gut-stuck with the sudden fear that we shall be foiled before we're even permitted to cross the threshold. I shall never meet Alexander Platt. I shall never escape Edinburgh and Callum and a future filled with bread and buns and babies. I shall always have to push myself aside to make room for others in my own life.

But then I will also never have to face Johanna Hoffman. The scales tip.

"Good day," I say, right at the same time Sim does. We glare at each other. The butler looks ready to shut the door in our faces due to a lack of communication and decorum, so I say quickly, "My name is Miss Felicity Montague. I'm here for the wedding."

"I was not told to expect any more guests," he says.

I swallow—my mouth has gone very dry, as if all the moisture in the body was slowly sucked from me by the long walk—reaffix my best sweet, innocent-slip-of-a-thing face, which uses muscles that have grown stiff from lack of practice, and, Lord help me, the actual phrase *What would Monty do?* manifests like an unwanted houseguest in my mind. "Did my letter not arrive? Johanna—Miss Hoffman—and I are good friends from childhood. I grew up in Cheshire with her. I've been at school not far from here, and I heard she was to be married and I simply had to come. She's the best friend I've ever had, and I couldn't miss her nuptials."

Perhaps it was not the wisest play to show all my cards immediately upon arrival—I have just offered up the entirety of the story I am reliant upon to get us a place in this house in a single mouthful, and I'm not certain he's swallowing it, so I tack on, for good, pathetic measure, "Did the letter truly not arrive?"

Rather than answering, the butler simply repeats, "Miss Hoffman did not inform me to expect any more guests."

"Oh." My heart hiccups, but this fight is far from over. I select the next weapon from my feminine arsenal—the damsel in distress. "Well, I suppose I could just . . . go back to the town and wait to see if you receive the letter." I heave the weariest sigh I can muster. "Zounds, it was such a trip. And my girl has been limping on a twisted ankle since Stuttgart." I give Sim a nudge, and she obediently begins rubbing her ankle. It's a far less convincing performance than mine, but I turn back to the butler and attempt to bat my eyelashes.

It must come off rather more as trying to rid my eyes of something irritating for he asks, "Do you require a handkerchief, madam?"

I was hoping to elicit pity, but this ghoul of a man seems to have not a single drop of charity to be wrung from him. Simpering seemed the best method—simpering and simple, my two least favorite things for a woman to be, but the two things men like most—to approach a gentleman such as this fuzzy-eared sod, but he's so obviously unmoved, and also I think I shall faint from the effort if I'm forced to remain this repressed. So instead, I change course dramatically, and rather than playing my brother, I play myself.

I stand straight with my hands upon my hips, drop my dimpled smile, and adopt the tone I found most effective in ordering Monty about on our Tour when he was dragging his feet and moaning about his poor toes as though we had some other choice of how to travel and were simply holding out on him. "Sir," I say to the butler, "we have come a great distance, as is obvious if you care to make any observation of our current state. I am exhausted, as is my lady, and here I am telling you my dearest friend in the world"—I am unintentionally escalating the significance of my relationship to Johanna with each retelling, but I press on—"is to be wed and you will not even allow me to cross through your door. I demand first an audience with Miss Hoffman so that she can make judgments for herself to our acquaintance, and, should she decline to allow us to attend her wedding, you can at least have the decency to put us up for the night."

Which cracks him for the first time—the guardian of the grapefruit house rendered stunned and mute by how firmly and confidently I spoke to him. Sim, in contrast, looks rather impressed.

Then the butler says, "I believe Miss Hoffman is dressing for dinner."

"Zounds, really?" I say before I can help it. It's hardly midafternoon.

The butler either chooses not to comment or his ears are so encased in hair he does not hear my aside, for he continues, "I will see if she is available for an audience."

"Thank you." I take two fistfuls of my skirts and push past him into the entryway, thinking it will make me seem as impressive and authoritative as my tone led him to believe I am, only to then have to stop dead and wait for him to lead, as I've no idea where I'm going. He doesn't offer to take my winter things. He doesn't seem to think I'll be staying long.

Sim appears at my side and makes a big show of leaning over to unfasten my cloak while really using it as an excuse to hiss into my ear, "No snapping her head off, crocodile. You're friends, remember?"

"I'm not going to be cross with Johanna unless she's as much of a stooge to me as her butler was," I reply, then add, against my better judgment but compelled to defend myself, "And I'm not a crocodile. If I am to be an animal, I would like to be a fox."

"Well then, foxy." She whips the cloak off from around my shoulders, then smooths the collar of my dress, her hands lingering on my breastbone. "You've only got one chance at this, so make it count."

"I'd make it count even if I had twenty, thank you."

"And you wonder why I worry about you charming your way into a wedding party," she murmurs, and I truly cannot tell if she's about to smile or grimace.

The butler returns before I can reply, leaving Sim aggravatingly with the last word. I'm escorted into a sitting room off the entryway and seated upon a sofa. I try to neither settle too far back upon it nor sit too close to the edge, wishing for perhaps the first time that I actually had sat a lesson at the finishing school my father was determined to send me to just to better create the illusion of ladyship. There are so many invisible layers to decorum that you don't think of until you're staring them down across a fancy parlor. I have never done any sofa sitting in my life that felt as though it mattered as much as this.

There are footsteps in the hallway, and I stand, expecting the butler, but instead in prances a dog the size of the sofa, gangly limbs and swinging jowls and a coiffure of a tail that bobs above him like a feather in a jaunty cap. His coat is shiny with care, blemished only by the bubbles of saliva gathering in the folds of his lips.

The dog bounds over to me and presses his head into my knees with such enthusiasm that I promptly sit down again on the sofa, which only delights him further, for it makes my face more accessible to his mouth. He leaps at me with what I guess from his tail and perked ears is joy at the prospect of a new friend, but he's overly zealous and comes at me with his enormous jaws gaping wide. I shriek without meaning to, though in my defense, what rational being wouldn't when approached by an open mouth in which your whole head could fit?

"Maximus, down! Off, get off her! Max, come here!"

The dog is wrangled off me, our only connection the long strings of drool that run between his mouth and my shoulders.

"Sorry, sorry, he's harmless. He's such a big love; he just wants to be chums with everyone and doesn't seem to realize he's bigger than they are."

I look up, and she looks up at the same time from where she's crouched on the floor with her arms around the neck of her dog, and there is Johanna Hoffman.

It is not so long that we have been apart, but in this moment, our two years of separation feel more enormous than all the years we spent together. The difference between fourteen and sixteen feels like centuries, time the greatest distance that can stretch between two people. There is no chance I would not have recognized her, but somehow she's a different person from my memories. Her hair is the same brown, so dark it's almost black, eyes hooded and deep green, but it's like she's better settled into her own skin. She was a round child with spotty cheeks adolescence wasn't kind to, but either time or expensive milk baths or a very well-laced set of silk stays has made her into a Renaissance muse, shapely and curved in a way my stocky, geometric frame never will be. Even under the wide panniers at her waist, her hips swing. Her face is powdered white with just the faintest hint of rouge, as though she has been caught in a maidenly blush.

Or maybe she's blushing in earnest to see me. I might be as well. For even as I look at her, in a bright, dreamy blue day dress with an embroidered bodice and a tiered skirt and two strings of pearls around her neck, all I can think of is the girl who used to walk barefoot with me in streams, never caring if her hems muddied, who grabbed a snake by the throat and carried him off the road to save him from being bisected by a carriage. Who went with me to the butcher's shop to watch them empty entrails from the pigs and cows and helped me understand how everything inside of a thing wound together. Johanna Hoffman had never minded dirt under her fingernails, until suddenly she had, and that was when she had left me behind in favor of company she had decided was more appropriate for her new self.

A part of me, I realize as she stands, one hand resting upon her massive dog's head (the only sound is him panting like a windstorm), had hoped that I would find her with muddy knees from running through the grounds, shoes worn through at the toes, her hair studded with twigs and her pockets full of the baby birds she'd rescued when they fell from their nests.

But instead, with her hair curled and her breasts pushed up, she's the cream puff that I cut all ties with.

"Felicity," she says, and zounds, I had forgotten how high her voice is—it was a singsong soprano even when we were children, but in that excessive dress, it feels put on, like she's playing up the girlish simper. I scrunch up my forehead without meaning to, then remember I am trying to win her over. I am trying to remind her we were friends.

Dear Lord, were we?

"Johanna," I say in return, and I make myself smile, because she is marrying Dr. Platt, and I want to work for Dr. Platt, and there's no chance I'll ruin that by making a bad impression on the person who likely has the most influence over him. Or rather, I'll try not to ruin things any more than I did two years ago. "It's so good to see you."

She does not return the smile. "What are you doing here?"

"I'm . . . what am I . . . that's actually rather a good story. So since we last saw each other . . . or rather, since you left . . . your father died, which is . . . I'm . . . Sorry, is your dog all right?" I'm trying not to stare at the saliva foaming upon his lips, but it's impossible not to. "He's breathing rather heavily."

Johanna doesn't look away from me, nor does she uncuff the beastie. "He's fine. That's just how he sounds."

"Consumptive?"

"Alpenmastiffs have a lot of excess skin to breathe through." She reaches down and swipes a handful of slobber ribbons from under his mouth, and for a moment, there she is—my best friend who loved animals and feared no mess. But then she looks around for something to wipe her hand upon and, finding nothing, waves it about with her fingers splayed until the butler appears with a handkerchief.

Then we're alone again, staring. Each a ghost to the other.

"May I sit down?" I ask.

She gives me an indifferent shrug, so I resume my perch upon the couch. Max lunges forward, my face once again at the perfect angle for examining it with his tongue, but Johanna catches him by a roll of back fat— so many folds and so much hair I lose sight of her hand for a moment—and pulls him over with her to a chair, where she wraps her arms around his neck and rests her chin upon his head, pinning him in place. "What are you doing here?" she asks again, her eyes fixed on me.

"I'm here for your wedding."

"I thought you might write."

"I tried, but your gentleman said it didn't arrive, so I expect a week after you're wed you'll get my missive about coming to your wedding—"

"I don't mean about the wedding," she interrupts. "I thought someday you might write to me. As a friend."

A vein splits open inside me, guilt and hurt spilling out in equal measure. "I did," I say. "About the wedding."

She looks away, the tip of her tongue jutting out between her teeth. "How did you hear I was getting married?"

"Oh, you know, things travel around. Gossip and . . ." I stop. Johanna licks her lips. Max also licks his, tongue wrapping all the way around his nose. "I've been at school," I say, which is the lie I decided upon, for it most closely aligns with what I am currently supposed to be doing—it's unlikely that Johanna, so far from home, would have heard about my disappearance during my Tour, and even unlikelier that, had she known, she would have run to my father and put an X upon the map for him to mark my location. Most unlikely of all that he would care. But lies are easiest to believe—and to remember—when they bump against the truth. And school is a good excuse for my limited wardrobe.

"School?" She smiles, and it is the first time she's looked like herself. "You finally got to go."

"I mean, it's not quite . . . yes." It's not worth digging into the injustice of the fact that the school I should currently be attending is one for manners and not medicine. "Yes, I got to go to school. And you . . . have a giant dog! And you're getting married! That's . . . a thing that is happening and that's wonderful for you, it's so wonderful. Just . . . wonderful. That we both got . . ."

"Got what we wanted," she finishes for me.

Did we? I want to shout at her. *Because once we wanted to go on an expedition together and collect previously unknown medicinal plants and species and bring them back to London to be cultivated and studied.* I thought I had long ago cut Johanna from me like a cancer, but you cannot simply hack yourself apart in hopes of healing faster.

Best not to have friends at all, I remind myself. *Best to explore the jungles alone.*

I am unraveling, and Johanna is still staring at me like I'm a spider crawled up from the floorboards and inching toward her. What I would like to say is that I remember when she aspired to more than a rich husband and domestic bliss. I remember how she audaciously declared that she would be the first woman to present before the Royal Society. That she would go on expeditions. Bring new species home to England to study.

"I can't wait to meet your fiancé!" I blurt. "Dr. . . ."

I fake a fumble for the name, like he hasn't been a saint to me for years and like he's definitely not the reason I'm here.

"Platt," Johanna finishes for me. "Alexander Platt. You don't have to pretend."

"Pretend what?"

"That you don't know who he is. You love his books."

"You remember that?"

"You wanted me to name that kitten I found under our house Alexander Platt, even though she was a girl."

"Alexander could be a . . . gender-neutral name." I scratch the back of my neck. The collar of my dress feels very tight. I was hoping she had forgotten my obsession with Alexander Platt so that she could have no leverage against me. Knowing how much I want to meet him, how much I admire him, means she knows where to wound me. She knows how savage it would be to turn me out now. "How did you two meet?"

"He and my uncle are in business together." She mashes her thumbs behind the dog's ears, and he closes his eyes in bliss. "Dr. Platt is organizing a scientific expedition, and my uncle is providing the ship for the voyage. He came over for dinner one evening to discuss finances and I was just . . . smitten!" She throws her hands up in the air like she's tossing confetti.

I wonder if it's appropriate to ask how soon they're leaving and what research he's working on. All I want to ask about is Platt.

But then Johanna pulls in her cheeks too hard and bites down upon them so that she looks like a fish. It's a nervous habit from childhood, one she used to do so often in the presence of her father that the insides of her cheeks would bleed. And for a moment, I'm ten years old again, and I know her as well as I know the sound of my

141

own voice. As much as I had told myself over and over that I wasn't here for Johanna, she didn't matter, I am here only for Platt and don't care what she thinks of me anymore, I suddenly find myself blurting, "I should have written."

Her face relaxes, lips falling back into their painted part.

I swallow. "I mean, I shouldn't have had to write, because I should have apologized after your father died. Before you left. I should have apologized, and we should have been writing each other all this time because we were friends. And I'm sorry I didn't do any of that."

"I wish you had." The dog rests his head upon her lap, and she strokes his nose absently, her eyes still on me.

"I'm sorry I'm here," I say. "I can leave, if you want."

From out in the hallway, I swear I hear Sim choke.

"No," Johanna says quickly. "No, don't leave. I want you to stay."

I take perhaps my first deep breath since we left England, so loud it rivals Max's consumptive snuffles. "Really?"

"You sound surprised."

"I am. I mean, if I were you, I wouldn't want anything to do with me."

She stands up, her hand disappearing again into the folds of her dog. Her skirt fans around her, a cascade of brocade silk and too many petticoats, the edges fringed with lace and bows. When she looks at me, I am disarmed. "Well then," she says, and I don't know how I shall survive these next few days without drowning in her. "Lucky you're not me."

8

At dinner, I expect I shall get my first glimpse of Alexander Platt.

The dining room is crowded, and I am relegated to a place of dishonor as far from the head of the table, where Johanna's uncle Herr Hoffman sits, as is possible. I practically need a telescope to see him, and Johanna sitting beside him, with another empty chair beside her. Maddeningly empty, and no doubt reserved for her intended.

It is still empty when the first course is served. It is still empty when the man beside me, who has to keep putting down his knife to pick up his ear trumpet, asks me, "How do you know Miss Hoffman?"

"We were friends as children," I say, jamming a frustrated knife at my mutton.

"Excuse me?"

"We grew up together," I say louder.

He cups a hand to the end of his ear trumpet. "What?"

"Friends."

"What?"

I nearly fling my knife down. "We were accomplices in a massive diamond heist in which we stole jewels off the neck of the queen of Prussia, and now I'm here to claim what is owed me by any means necessary."

"Excuse me?" The woman next to me leans forward in alarm, but the man just smiles. "Oh, how nice."

To top the fact that Alexander Platt is not even here, the dress Sim purchased in town was made with a waistline that can only be described as aspirational. Sim had to fish me out of the silk and tighten my stays three times before I achieved the inconceivably small diameter deemed appropriate for a lady to make an impression at a social occasion. My bulbous shoulders feel likely to burst free at any moment.

It's hard to focus on the meal when I'm thinking about Dr. Platt, and when I can't properly breathe, and also every time Johanna laughs, my heartbeat stammers. How is it, I wonder, that the brain and the heart can be so at odds and yet have such a profound effect upon the functions of the other?

Dr. Platt has still not arrived by the end of dinner. The men go to the formal sitting room, while the ladies make their way upstairs. I, for longer than is natural, stand in the hallway, weighing my options but likely

145

looking as though I'm a shape-shifting fairy-tale creature able to choose which sex I would rather be for the evening. If Dr. Platt is to show up, he will certainly not be up in Johanna's rooms with the ladies. And I am not here to waste time talking about ribbon and music and whatever other insubstantial nonsense gets passed around in rooms full of women.

I start toward the parlor, hoping that if I walk with enough confidence I'll not be stopped, but the hairy-eared butler has me by the collar before I've crossed the threshold. "The ladies are upstairs, Miss Montague."

"Oh." I smile but do not attempt the eyelash bat again. "I've just got one quick thing to say to Herr Hoffman and then I'll follow."

He is unmoved. "I can convey the message to him."

"Oh, thank you, but actually I lost an earring here earlier and I wanted to look for it."

"I'll search for you."

I pretend to see someone in the room over his shoulder and wave. "I'll be right in!" I call to this imaginary person. The butler doesn't move. I consider faking a fainting spell just for an excuse to call for a doctor and hope it's Platt, but that hardly seems an appropriate situation to then funnel into an intellectual discussion. "Please," I say to the butler, and I hate how pleading my voice sounds. I do not like pleading—reliance upon the whims of others makes me far too vulnerable to feel comfortable.

"Excuse me," someone says behind me, and the butler pulls me out of the way so the man can pass into the room.

I glance sideways and recognize him at once from the etching of his likeness on the title page of *Treaties on Human Blood and Its Movement through the Body*.

"Alexander Platt," I blurt.

He stops. Turns back to me. "Can I help you?" It's not a courteous question—it's brusque and annoyed.

He looks exactly like himself, but more rumpled than I expected. He's unshaven, dark stubble in sharp contrast to his blond wig with its ratty queue. His housecoat is not the sort of thing you'd wear to a party before your wedding in which you're trying to make a good impression in the home of your bride. He has an intense gaze, small dark eyes made smaller by a fringe of thick brows, and when he frowns at me, I forget every word I know.

All I manage to stammer is, "You're Alexander Platt."

He flips the lid of the snuffbox in his hand, glancing over his shoulder at the room full of gentlemen waiting for him. "Do we know each other?"

"I'm Johanna Hoffman. I mean, I'm a friend of Johanna's. I'm for the wedding. Here for the wedding." Am I having a stroke? Not only are all the words I wish to say putting themselves in a random order in my brain, but I'm almost certain my voice is far too loud and my movements far too exaggerated. I've gone completely blank, all my planned brilliance with which I was going to win him over washed away at the sight of Alexander Platt in the flesh.

He's looking at me, and all I can think to say is, "Hullo!" And it comes out much higher than my voice usually is. Perhaps this is how people feel when they talk to someone they fancy—all fluttery and silly and everything tuned to the highest key. I've certainly heard Monty's voice pitch when Percy walked into a room.

I remember suddenly I have Dr. Cheselden's card in my pocket, stashed there for exactly this meeting, and I start to paw at my excessively large skirt for it.

"Dr. Platt, you join us at last!" Johanna's uncle calls from the room, and Platt raises a hand. Before I've even had a chance to find my damn pocket, he gives me a nod and says, "Have a good night."

"Wait, no!" I try to chase after him, but the butler catches me again. My arm whips out as he pulls me back, knocking a portrait off the wall. The glass cracks when it strikes the tile. Dr. Platt glances over his shoulder, and I'm not sure if I imagine it or if he actually winces. The butler stares at the broken frame, then at me.

"I'll show myself to Miss Hoffman's rooms," I say, and slink away.

There is a unique sort of agony to entering a party alone.

It is the shuffle in, the survey, trying to spot allies and cracks in the fortress of guests where you might slide into a conversation with such ease that they will think you've been there all the while. It is the keen pinch of hanging in the doorway and knowing that people have seen you come in but no one is pulling you over to their conversation or waving in greeting. Wondering if you can sidle up to the fringes of a conversation and laugh at just the right moment and they'll part.

It is an even more pernicious pain when it comes upon the heels of the social equivalent of vomiting partially digested entrails upon my idol.

Johanna's apartments are swarming with women from dinner, all with waists tinier and hair taller than mine. The aroma of scent bags and a garden of fragrances crowd the air. I haven't any powder on—I never wore it at my parents' house unless a maid managed to catch me off guard and blow a puff in my face—and my skin feels garishly ruddy and freckled in the presence of these girls dusted pale as icing sugar with tiny pox patches spotting their cheeks. Their maids trail them, rearranging trains when they sit upon the silk couches, fetching them flutes of champagne, using a single finger wetted by a tongue to fix a smear of rouge.

There are card tables, where whist and faro are being dealt. Another table is laid with bonbons, silky pink entremets topped with chocolate flakes sculpted like sparrows, gingerbread, and salted toffees wrapped with spun sugar as fragile and translucent as the wings of a dragonfly, along with bottles of champagne and a pot of spiced wine.

Johanna is both literally and figuratively in the center of it all, talking to a small crowd of girls while others wait their turn to kiss her cheeks and offer her their congratulations. She drinks champagne and talks with her hands and speaks in arias. She wiggles her shoulders, points her tiny, perfect feet, sucks in her cheeks to make her face look thinner.

It aggravates me, in the same way it did back in Cheshire, but not because she's putting on a party persona. It's because she's so bloody good at it.

From his spot at the buffet table, Max galumphs over to me, an enormous pink silk bow around his neck. He smashes his forehead into my knees until I consent to massage his ears, then he walks over to the dessert table again and sits with an expectant look, as though greeting me has made him worthy of a treat.

I almost bolt. I want nothing more than to run back to my room and hide in a book the same way I have always done in the face of these gatherings.

But I'm trying to make an impression. I'm trying to

pretend I am an indoor cat. I am trying to get to Dr. Platt, and since my impression was so disastrous, the best way to do that will be through Johanna.

You are Felicity Montague, I remind myself. *You had your brother tackled into the London harbor and found Alexander Platt and are absolutely going to make up for that embarrassing incident earlier.*

Since the knot of women around Johanna is too intimidating to breach just yet, I take a tentative seat on a couch near the door, next to a woman who looks a little older than me. She catches my eye and gives me an obligatory smile over her champagne. I look away, am then mortified that was my reaction to being smiled at, and say too loudly and without introduction, "I like your eyebrows."

I had spun a mental wheel and picked the least flattering feature to compliment a woman on. She looks surprised. As any person would at such a bizarre statement so loudly uttered. "Oh. Thank you." She purses her lips, looks me up and down, then says, "Yours are also nice."

"Yes." I stare at her for a moment longer. Then I nod too vigorously. Then I ask, "How many bones in the human body can you name?" And dear Lord, what is happening to me? Why don't I know how to talk politely to other women? "Excuse me."

I flee to the food, take up a glass of spiced wine, and

think about a pastry as well but decide I'd rather not risk spilling something down my front. There's a knot of women standing by the dressing room staring at me, and when I look back at them, they all duck and giggle, and I hate these girls. I hate them so much. I hate the way they giggle, and look at me when I don't, and then it feels as though I'm being laughed at and they're all in on it and I'm not. It's my whole childhood, being sneered at by watery girls for a joke I didn't understand because I was reading books they could never understand.

For a woman who boasts that she doesn't give a fig what anyone thinks of her, I certainly have a lot of party-related anxiety.

Max seats himself upon my hem and looks up at me with his drooping eyes. The white spots above them make him look grotesquely expressive. "You have very nice eyebrows," I tell him, and give him a flat-handed pat to the head. He licks his lips, then goes on staring at my glass. Of course, the moment I get around other females my own age, I end up socializing with the dog.

"Well, don't you look aggressively miserable," someone says, and I turn. Johanna has extricated herself from her harem and come to stand beside me at the window. Max leans into her, his tail thumping happily between her backside and mine.

"It's a nice party," I say.

"It is," she replies, reaching down to massage Max's

head. "So why do you look like you're having your teeth pulled? What's the matter?"

"I'm just . . ." I consider lying. Saying I'm tired from my trip or ate something at supper that didn't agree with me. But a strange sort of instinct sets in when I meet her eyes. I used to tell Johanna everything. "I'm so bad at this," I say.

"At what?"

"This." I flap a general hand at the room full of women. "Talking to girls and socializing and being normal."

"You're normal."

"I'm not." I feel like a wild animal in a menagerie, ragged and feral and unsocialized among all these women who don't tip over in heels or itch the powder off their face. As Sim proclaimed, a crocodile in a cage full of swans. "I'm prickly and off-putting and odd and not always nice."

Johanna takes a macaron from the buffet table and licks a dab of filling off her finger. "No one's good at these things."

"Everyone here is."

"Everyone is faking it," she says. "Most of these women don't know each other—they likely all feel just as misplaced and awkward as you."

"You don't."

"Well, it's my party."

"But you're good at this," I say. "You always have

been. That's why people liked you back home, and not me. Girls like me are meant to have books instead of friends."

"Why can't you have both?" She takes a bite of her macaron, then tosses the rest to Max, who, in spite of how large an area his mouth covers, misses it entirely and has to chase it down under the table. "I think you need to give people a chance. Including yourself." She reaches out and puts a light hand on my elbow. "Promise me you'll stay tonight and at least try to have a good time."

I run my tongue along my teeth, then let out a sigh through my nose. I feel like I owe this to her. And also am completely maddened by that. I do not enjoy being beholden, so perhaps it's best if I pay off this debt as quickly as possible. "Must I?"

"And you have to talk to at least three people."

"All right, you're one."

"Three people you don't already know. Max does not count," she says, reading my mind.

"If I talk to three people, may I then leave?"

Her head cants to the side, and I can't tell if her smile actually saddens or if it's simply the angle. "Are you really that desperate to be away from me?"

I look away, to our reflections in the glass, made black by the darkness. It feels like looking through a window into a shadow version of ourselves, the girls who could have existed if Johanna and I hadn't fought. Maybe, if things had gone differently, I'd be here as an attendant at her wedding, invited and wanted and not kicking my feet in the corner. Or maybe we'd neither of us be here. Maybe we'd have run away together long ago, gone to find her mother who had left her and her father when she was a child, or found a world of our own, away from all of this.

"Miss Johanna!" someone calls, and we turn as a very blond, very pretty girl with a very narrow waist comes over to us. She wraps an arm around Johanna's stomach from behind and cuddles into her neck. Max leans into them both. The girl looks up at me with enormous blue eyes. "Who's this?"

"This is my friend Felicity Montague," Johanna replies. "We grew up together."

"Oh, in England? You've come from so far!" The girl holds out her hand to me over Johanna's shoulder. "Christina Gottschalk."

With her hand in front of her stomach and out of Christina's sight, Johanna holds up a single finger and mouths to me, *That's one*. I almost laugh.

Christina gives me a smile I'm not sure I believe is genuine, then turns her face back up to Johanna. "I have to give you a scolding."

"Me?" Johanna presses a hand to her breasts. "Why?"

"Your Dr. Platt about scared my poor girl to death last night."

A conversation I was about to be forced to tolerate has just become sincerely interesting to me, as it involves Platt. Perhaps I'll actually be quite good at socializing after all. "What happened?" I ask.

"My maid went last night to fetch me milk, and he gave her a terrible scare!" Christina says. "He was up in the library at god-knows-what hour pacing and jabbering to himself. Said he started to shout at her for creeping about."

Johanna runs a finger around the rim of her glass. She does not look at all thrilled by this conversation topic. "Yes, he's a bit manic when he's dosed."

"That's the peril of marrying a genius, isn't it?" Christina says. "They're either depressingly gloomy or terribly insane. Sometimes both at once."

"Is he often in the library?" I ask.

Johanna's eyes narrow at me—she knows exactly the game I'm playing but won't give it a name in front of her friend. "He works late and sleeps late; it's his way. We don't see him until supper most days."

"And not even supper today," Christina says, which is perhaps meant to make Johanna feel better, but instead has her sucking in her cheeks again.

If Dr. Platt is hanging about the Hoffman library alone each night, that will give me the perfect opportunity to chat with him, without butlers or gentlemen or my inability to have articulate conversations with no warning getting in the way.

But Johanna has me trapped, both in this conversation, which is turning to a discussion of melon water in comparison to cucumber for a smooth complexion, and by my promise to speak to three new people. There has to be a way to create a good reason to slip away and position myself in wait for Dr. Platt without wasting time making good on that promise.

So the next time Max knocks into me, I use it as an excuse to empty my wineglass down my front.

I only intend for it to be a dribble, a small splatter that would give me enough reason to say I just have to run back to my room and change but in truth sneak down to the library and wait for Platt. It is, however, a more effective display than planned. Firstly, I had not drunk as much as I thought, so rather than a few small drops discreetly spilled, I pour almost a full glass of wine straight down the front of my dress. It's such a direct shot that I can feel it soak all the way into my knickers. Johanna and Christina both shriek in surprise. I open my mouth to make an excuse and pretend like I have just spilled a normal amount of drink rather than poured a glass down my front, but before I can get a word out, Max leaps at me, trying to lick it off. His weight sends me flying backward. I throw out a hand to steady myself, miss my mark at the edge of the buffet table, and smash it straight into the creamy center of a plate of entremets.

Max, now with even more opportunity for carnage, leaps forward, paws upon the table, and plunges his nose in after me, splattering me with thick globs of cream.

It effectively grinds the party to a halt. It is also a bit more embarrassing than I had expected it to be, particularly considering that I was the architect of the disaster. Well, the first part, at least.

Johanna apologizes over and over as she wrestles Max off the food, long strings of saliva trailing from his lips to the pastry as he tries desperately to gulp a few more bites before Johanna reaches down his throat and pulls out an entire metal spoon he inhaled in his haste. She's covered up to her elbow in slime. I've got wine down the front of my dress and pastry cream splattered across my side and fur clinging to both. Christina has a small splatter of wine on her skirt and seems intent on pretending she is as victimized as I am.

"I'm so sorry," I say, and Johanna looks up from Max. I can see in her eyes she knows exactly how intentional this was, whether or not I meant for it to ruin the party.

"Just go," she says, her voice so low no one hears but me. "It's what you wanted, isn't it?"

And yes, it's exactly what I wanted. But as I make my head-down, tail-tucked exit, I rather wish it hadn't been.

Sim isn't in our shared room, which is unfortunate, as it leaves me with the task of getting myself out of this dress alone. The rules of fashion dictate that anything a man wears, a lady must wear more of; it must be more uncomfortable for her; and it must require at least two people to get her into and out of it, so that she is rendered incapable of an independent existence. I can't even reach the damn buttons running up the back, let alone unfasten them. I keep turning in circles like a dog chasing its tail, trying each time to stretch my arm just a bit farther while holding on to the deranged hope that perhaps if I catch the buttons by surprise they won't dart away from me. And every second I waste spinning is a second I might be missing Dr. Platt in the library. At last, I give up, decide to wear the wine with confidence even though it's starting to turn from sticky to crunchy, and head below stairs.

The gentlemen's party in the parlor is still loudly in progress, so I make a quiet slip into the library, in case the hairy-eared butler is lurking, ready to send me back to Johanna's rooms. The room is warm and smells like dust, and just the presence of so many books makes it easier to breathe. It's remarkable how being around books, even those you've never read, can have a calming effect, like walking into a crowded party and finding it full of people you know.

"What are you doing here?"

I spin around with a squeak. Sim is standing behind me, lurking in between two of the stacks and either unaware or unperturbed by the scare she just gave me. "Zounds, don't do that."

"Do what? Address you?"

"Sneak up on me like that! Or sneak around, full stop. People will think you're up to something."

"What people? You people?"

"Yes, me people. What are *you* doing here? You're supposed to be a maid, remember? I'm fairly certain this room is off-limits."

"I'm cleaning it." She swabs a sleeve along the nearest shelf without looking at it. "There. All clean."

"Have you found your birthright yet?" I ask.

It's too dark to really tell, but I swear I hear her eyes narrow. "Have you talked to your Dr. Platt yet?"

"Is that it?" I point to the large leather book she's got tucked under her arm, and she immediately pushes it behind her skirt.

"Is what it?"

"That book you're ineffectively hiding. You can't take it with you—no stealing, remember? That's our agreement. Is it what you're looking for?" She doesn't say anything, so I hold out my hands. "May I?"

Reluctantly, she surrenders. It's not a book, I realize as I carry it over to one of the reading stands with a lit lantern upon it, but more a folio. The cover is monogrammed with the initials *SG* and a date almost twenty years previous. Inside are intricate botanical drawings—cross sections of tulip bulbs and mulberry trees, the delicate veins of leaves mapped like tributaries and a whole page dedicated to the many ways of looking at a mushroom. It's all done in the sort of minute detail that makes my hand shake just to think of attempting it.

I look up at Sim, standing on the other side of the lectern, watching me turn the portfolio pages with her teeth working on her thumbnail. "Did you come all the way here to look at a book about nature?" I ask.

She keeps her nail in her mouth, speaking through teeth gritted around it. "Why does it matter?"

"It doesn't," I say. "That's just very much something I would do."

She stops grinding her teeth, then a slow smile spreads over her lips. "And here you thought we'd have nothing in common."

I turn another page and stare down at a sketch of a long snake moving through water, its nostrils bobbing above the surface. I can't imagine what it is about this work that drew her from a continent away just to see it. I thumb the edges, realizing that, more than anything, it's a relief. No matter Sim's protestations otherwise, and that she came to me through Scipio, a small part of me had been chewing its fingernails with certainty that she was here to slit a throat or steal a diamond and I would be complicit for the access I provided.

"What's so special about this book?" I ask.

"It's not a book, it's a portfolio," she replies. "And it's the only copy."

"Well, yes, I assumed that if it existed elsewhere, you would have picked it up from a printer in London."

"Of course you did."

I look up, and through the sallow glow of the lantern, our eyes meet. In this light, her skin looks bronzed, something burnished and worn into battle by ancient warriors. "It would have saved you a lot of trouble."

"Maybe I wanted the trouble."

There's a snap behind us as the latch of the library door clicks open. "Have a good evening," someone calls, then the creak of hinges as it's closed again. We're out of sight, tucked between the shelves, but I can hear footsteps down the next aisle over, heading toward the fireplace. I nearly trip over myself in my haste to grab Sim and shove her out of the room. She tries to take the folio with her, but I slap it shut and shake my head. "No thieving."

"I'm not thieving. I'm looking," she hisses in return. "It's not stealing just because you take something from where it belongs."

"That is the actual definition of stealing," I reply, my voice louder than I mean for it to be, for through the stacks, a man calls, "Is someone there?"

I usher Sim toward the door, but she's already going, her slippers a soft tread on the rug. I straighten myself out as best I can in a dress that's mostly dessert, toss my hair back over my shoulders so I will not be tempted to nervously fuss with it, then go the opposite way, toward the firelight.

Dr. Platt has taken off his wig and jacket and made a flop down in an armchair beside the mantelpiece. He kicks his feet up as he fishes in his jacket, emerging a moment later with the same snuff box he was fiddling with when I attempted to flag him down. He tips some of the powder into a cupped hand, crushes it with his thumb, and snorts it.

I have been lurking for too long to make my entrance anything less than invasive. I consider doubling back as silently as possible and then reentering the library loudly so as not to alarm him.

But then he looks up, and I'm standing there, and he startles, spilling snuff down his shirt, and I startle, and suddenly I remember there's spiced wine all over my dress, and for some reason my brain decides clarifying that point is first priority, and I blurt, "This isn't blood."

"Goddammit." He's brushing the snuff off his front, trying to collect it into his hand and then tip it back into the box. "What the hell do you think you're doing?"

"I'm so sorry!" I take a step forward, as if there's anything I can do to help, but as soon as I'm properly in the firelight, he catches sight of my dress and yelps. "It's just wine!" I cry. "I spilled wine. And fell into a cake."

I'm pushing my skirts behind me, like I might hide the stain from his view, but there's not much to be done about the fact that I have just snuck up on him in a dark room and the first thing I did was assure him I'm not covered in blood. And here I thought nothing could be worse than our meeting after supper.

"Do you need something?" he asks, his voice clipped. He's still trying to collect any of the spilled snuff that can be salvaged.

"Yes, I, um, I shouted at you earlier. In the hallway. After supper."

"And now you've come to yell at me again?" He gives up on the snuff and slumps back down in his chair, running a hand over his cropped hair and looking around for something to do that will dismiss me. I'm tempted to ask him if I could excuse myself, take a good, deep breath, then reenter and try this entire encounter again but this time with my head on straight. And preferably no wine spilled down my dress.

"I'm sorry about the snuff," I say, feeling like a kicked puppy that only wanted a pat on the head. "I can replace it." He sighs, one leg bouncing up and down so that his shadow in the firelight jumps. There's a smear of it still on his lapel, and against the dark material, there are flecks of incandescent blue hidden in it. "It is snuff, isn't it?"

"It's *madak*," he says, the word presented in a tone

of expectation that the other party will not recognize it.

But I do. "That's opium and tobacco."

He gives me the first proper look since I arrived. I wouldn't say he looks impressed, but he's certainly not indifferent. "From Java, yes."

"There are more effective ways to take opium," I say. "Medicinally speaking, dissolved in alcohol and drunk will move through the body much faster and more effectively, as it is the most direct route to the digestive system."

He squints at me, and I immediately feel foolish for explaining laudanum to Alexander Platt. But instead he says, "Who are you, exactly?"

"I'm a great admirer of yours. Academically," I add quickly. "Not . . . I know you're getting married. Not like that. But I've read all your books. Most of them. All the ones I could get. Some of them I read twice so perhaps that makes up for the ones I missed. But I've read most. I'm Felicity Montague." I stick out my hand, like he might shake it. When he makes no move to, I pretend that my intention all along was to brush something off my skirt. A large glob of dried pastry cream crumbles onto the carpet. We both look at it. I consider picking it up, but, having nothing to then do with it, I instead look back at him with a sheepish smile.

To my great relief, he returns it. "An admirer?" He pours himself a glass of whatever amber spirit is in the bottle on the mantel, then says, "My admirers are usually much older and grayer and . . . well, men. They're usually men."

"Yes, sir, that's actually what I came to talk to you about. Not the men. But that I'm a woman. No, this is coming out entirely wrong." I press my hands to my stomach and force myself to take a breath so deep I swear my ridiculous stays pop. "I've been trying to gain admission to a medical school in Edinburgh, but they won't have me on account of my sex. When I made inquiries in London, I was given your name by Dr. William Cheselden." I fish around in my pocket, unwrapping the calling card from my list and handing it to him. "He said you were in London looking for a fellow. Or an assistant. Or something, for an expedition. And he thought you might take me on."

Platt listens without interrupting, which I appreciate, but he also keeps his face entirely unreadable, which I appreciate less, as I'm unsure what effect my speech is having upon him and whether I should press on with it until he says, "I'm not sure where Cheselden got the impression I was looking for a fellow, but I'm not."

"Oh." All the breath leaves my lungs in that single exhalation and yet it still comes out very small. I have to look down at my feet to make certain I'm still standing and not on my knees, for the world feels to have dropped away from me so suddenly, it's like falling. I've never felt so foolish in my whole life, not being thrown from the university in Scotland or standing before the governors in London or when my mother presented me with enrollment in finishing school like she was making all my dreams for education come true. I've come all this way. I've bargained and begged and compromised so much. I didn't realize how much hope I had pinned to this moment, and how little I had truly let myself consider the possibility of defeat, until it's snuffed me out like a candle. My whole world reformed in a second by the dashing of a hope I have not just lived with, but lived inside.

My collapse must be more obvious than I hoped, for Platt turns Cheselden's card over between his fingers, then says, "You really came all the way here to ask me about a position?"

"Yes," I say, my voice just as small and just as kinked up with disappointment as before. I swipe the heel of my hand against my cheek, then add, "And I know Johanna. I'm not here entirely under pretense."

Platt's glass halts at his lips. "You do?"

"We were friends when we were children," I explain. "We grew up together."

"In England? What did you say your name was?"

"Felicity Montague."

He takes a sip of the whiskey, regarding me over the rim, then hooks his foot around a stool and pulls it in front of him. "Come sit down." I take a tentative seat, and he tips his glass at me. "Care for a drink?" When I shake my head, he takes another sip and says, "Why do you want to study medicine, Miss Montague? It's not a passion one sees in many young ladies."

I may not have gotten to use my answers on the Saint Bart's board, but I've got them ready. I reach into my pocket before I can stop myself and pull out that battered list, now folded and unfolded so many times in varying states of dampness that I can hardly read the words overlapping the creases.

"First," I start, but Platt cuts me off.

"What's that? Do you have to read off a paper to remember your own heart?"

I raise my head. "Oh, no, sir, I just had this prepared for—"

"Give it here; let me see." He holds out a hand, and I surrender my list, biting back the temptation to snatch it back in embarrassment of both my penmanship and earnestness. Platt scans the list with a loud sip from his glass. Then he sets both glass and list upon the end table and begins fishing in his coat pocket. "None of this will get you taken seriously by physicians in London."

"Sir?"

"All this nonsense about women contributing to the field? No one will listen to that argument. Don't even mention you're a woman. No one wants to hear about women. Act as though it's no barrier and that you, as you so appropriately say, deserve to be here." He finds a pencil nub in his jacket and crosses out my first point. I feel an actual lurch in my stomach when his pencil makes violent contact with the paper, like he's scrubbing out part of my soul. "And while I appreciate the naming here, so what if you can read and write Latin, French, and German? Any idiot with an Eton education can do more. They don't want to hear that, they want to see it in the way you carry yourself. The way you speak." He makes a note, then his eyes flit down the list, one brow arching. "Did you really mend an amputated finger?"

"Yes, sir. My friend—"

"Lead in with that," he interrupts, scrawling the point at the top of my paper. "Experience is everything. Say it is one of many instances, even if it is not. And tell them you'll work for free, and harder than anyone else, even if it isn't true. None of this nonsense about lady surgeons in history. You can't name a lady surgeon from history because there aren't any that matter to these men. You need to talk about Paracelsus and Antonio Benivieni and Galen—"

"Galen?" I laugh before I can help it, then immediately clap my hands over my mouth, horrified that I have just laughed in the face of Dr. Alexander Platt. But he looks up from my paper with a curious expression, and I press on. "He's a man who wrote about the body without ever making an actual study of one. Half his theories were disproved by Vesalius and no one even took the time to prove the rest wrong because they're so obviously idiotic. Paracelsus burned his books. Who reads Galen anymore?"

"Clearly not you." Platt presses his fingers together, my paper between them. "You favor human dissection, then?"

"Strongly," I reply. "Though particularly when that dissection is used in conjunction with your school of discovering the cause rather than the cure."

"Ha. I didn't know anyone thought of it as a school." He makes another note on my paper. "Had you been granted hospital education, you would have found my theories as disregarded as Galen's."

"Prevention would decrease the business of hospitals and make it more difficult for them to exploit the poor, so I understand why they will not invest in it. With all due respect to the hospital boards in London." I pause, then add, "Actually, no. No respect is due to them, because they're all asses."

He stares at me, and I fear I've spoken too boldly, but then he laughs, a burst like a bullet through glass. "No wonder those toffs in London didn't like you. Where did you find all these opinions?"

"I didn't find them, I formulated them," I say. "From reading your books. And others."

He leans forward, elbows on his knees, and I'm suddenly very aware of the fact that it's just the pair of us, talking alone in a library at night. Which sounds far more like a scene from the amatory novels I used to pretend to read than the medical texts I was actually studying.

Platt wipes the corner of his mouth with his thumb. "You're lucky the hospitals didn't admit you. You'd be better off getting a venereal disease instead of a practical education. They'll both make you unsuitable for jobs and undesirable to men." He looks at me like he's expecting me to laugh at that, but the best I can offer is not frowning. Perhaps I have placed too much hope in Dr. Platt being entirely divorced from the notion of a woman's primary value being how much she's desired.

"The hospital schools in London are populated by the sons of rich men whose fathers pay for them to sleep through their lectures and skip hospital rounds," he goes on. "And then buy their way into the guilds. You would have been wasted there."

"Then what would you suggest I do?" I ask.

He drains his glass, then sets it hard on the desk, like the end of a toast. "You take my suggestions and you improve your arguments and you try your petition with someone who would actually have something to teach you. Go to Padua or Geneva or Amsterdam. They're more forward-thinking than we English."

He returns my list to me, and I look down at his

scribbled notes in the margins, his handwriting only slightly worse than mine. Platt is already settling back into his chair, pulling a foot up under him and reaching again for the bottle. And this may be the only chance I ever get, so I clear my throat—bit of a dramatic gesture— and start.

"Well then, sir, I would like to make a petition to you for a position." He looks up, but I press forward before he can tell me this was not what he meant. "You may not be looking for an assistant, but you will not know how badly you were wanting for one until I begin. You will wonder how you ever got by without me. I will work harder than any other student you may have had, because this opportunity would be too precious to me to waste. I already have some practical knowledge, having completed successful surgical procedures on multiple occasions under situations of duress, in addition to the knowledge I have gained from reading books such as Antonio Benivieni's *De Abditis Morborum Causis*, both of which will provide a strong foundation to be built upon. I am a supporter of human dissection and anatomical studies, which align well with the school you practice, and I believe that my contributions to your work, as well as the knowledge you could provide for me, would leave us both better for our partnership."

I take a deep breath. It shakes a little more than I'd like. Platt hasn't said a word the whole time I was speaking, nor did he try to interrupt me. He kept his head tipped to the side, swirling his empty glass between his thumb and first finger, but when I pause for that breath, he says, "Are you finished?"

I'm not sure if that's an invitation to continue or a request to stop, so I just reply, "For now."

"Well then." He nods once. "Bravo."

"Really?"

"It's not the best argument I've heard, but you're certainly fearless—I mean, my God, you came all the way here just to see me. And you're willing to learn—that's the most important thing." He rubs his palms together like he's trying to warm them, or perhaps scheming. It's hard to say. Then he asks, "Will you be at the Polterabend?"

"The what?"

"It's another one of the insane wedding customs here. Friends all come in fancy dress on the theme of fish and fowl the night before the wedding and smash pottery. *Scherben bringen Glück*—shards bring luck, that's the saying. It's all a waste of time and good china, but the bride must be appeased. Will you be there?"

I don't love the way he speaks of Johanna. I also don't say yes in case his next sentence was going to be an offer to skip the society party with him and instead bury ourselves up to our eyeballs in medical texts. "If I'm invited."

"I'm inviting you." He leans into a luxurious stretch, arms over his head and his back arched before he reaches again for his snuffbox. "We should find each other there and have a chat—I'm going to Heidelberg tomorrow to pick up a prescription, and I won't be back until the party, but I'll think while I'm gone over where a mind like yours might be best put to use."

I don't want to say no, but also I don't want to wait. I don't want to talk to him the night before his wedding—his attention will be split between too many things, and that's not enough time for any position to be secured before he departs. And there's no such thing as a substantial conversation at a party.

"Dr. Cheselden mentioned you're going to the Barbary States," I venture, and he nods. "Are you leaving soon?"

"After the wedding. Miss Hoffman and I are honeymooning in Zurich for a week, and then I'll depart from Nice."

"Zurich. How . . ." I fumble for a word. It is not the ideal location for a romantic, postnuptial retreat. "Cold."

"Not so cold. And not for long. I'll be on the Mediterranean by the first of the month, and Miss Hoffman on her way to my home in London."

"Do you think there might be a place—" I venture, but he cuts me off.

"My crew is already set. The work we're undertaking

is quite sensitive, so the ranks have to be monitored rather judiciously."

"Of course."

He snaps the snuffbox open and shut a few times, staring down into it like he's thinking hard. "But come find me at the Polterabend. We'll talk more, I promise." I don't quite know what that means, other than I now need to make certain I have a dress for the night that is not decorated with tonight's dessert. As though he read my thoughts, Platt looks me up and down and laughs. "I'm a little disappointed it isn't blood your dress is covered in. I would quite like to see a lady surgeon at her post."

And that recognition, in spite of the irksome modifier, that pride and belief in his voice where usually I only find scorn, makes me feel seen, for perhaps the first time in my life.

I can hear the Polterabend carrying up the stairs and through my bedroom door, so grand and sparkling that it spooks me before I've seen the source. I would have had a book tucked into my skirt—and am truly still considering it—or chosen to not attend at all had it not been for Dr. Platt's invitation to talk more at the party. Since our meeting in the library, he's been absent from the house, only returning a few hours earlier and immediately being swept off by Herr Hoffman to make himself ready. And with the ceremony tomorrow, this is a precious final chance to speak with him.

Sim manifested another dress from the modiste in Stuttgart, this one with a far more appropriate waistline for my square torso but made from a shiny black crepe that strongly suggests it was meant for a funeral. That, and its ready-made nature. Death is even more unpredictable than sitting in a cake at a party.

It's not on the appointed theme of fish and fowl, but I could make a good argument for the entomological nature of my outfit, for I feel like a beetle in this skirt, the material made stiff and wide by panniers and thin ribbons dangling off the waist like antennae. "I think you tied it wrong," I said at least five times to Sim while she helped me dress, and each time she replied, "I have not tied it wrong."

I am still contemplating as I stand alone in my room, teetering before the mirror, trying not to be self-conscious about the fact that my hair is up off my neck and that I have several very large spots on my chin and also absolutely maddened by the fact that I care about these things when Dr. Platt is waiting for me downstairs. *Your beauty is not a tax you are required to pay to take up space in this world*, I remind myself, and my hand flits unconsciously to my pocket where my list is still tucked. *You deserve to be here.*

Someone knocks on my bedroom door, a frantic rap that's certainly not Sim's tap of warning before she lets herself in each time. "Felicity?" comes hissed over the knock. "Felicity, are you there?"

"Johanna?"

The door flies open, and she comes scampering into the room without invitation, Max bounding at her heels like they're about to have a romp. She's dressed for the party—white powder, perfect pink cheeks, and a heart-shaped mouche placed with surgical precision on her left cheek. Tiny pearls drip down her neck, spilling over the elegant slope of her shoulders and in between her breasts.

She slams the door behind her, Max perching himself at her feet with his tail thumping the floor hard enough to rattle the windowpanes. "I need your help," she says, breathless, and I realize that the color in her cheeks isn't from rouge.

"My help?" I'm still shocked she didn't throw me out of her home after my scene at the party. "What do you need my help with?"

"I ruined my dress." She turns around, trying to see her own back like a dog chasing its tail, and Max mimics with foamy delight. "Look."

It's a tent's worth of material, and so adorned I can't see anything amiss at first. I peer at her, trying to find the rip or tear or the big spot of drool from the dog.

"On the back," she says, and I fight my way around the skirt as she keeps turning, and there it is—a small, but very noticeable against the blue, spot of blood.

"I didn't realize I had started until I put the dress on," Johanna moans. Max lets out a low yowl in solidarity.

It's impossible to have an interest in medicine without picking up several methods for removing bloodstains along the way. It is also impossible to be a woman without that knowledge, though Johanna is limited by its location. "I think I can get this out," I say.

"Can you really?"

"Stay here." I dash into my dressing room and fish out a fingerful of talc from its silver casing, then mix it with a few drops of water from the washbasin before returning to her. I press the salve carefully into the stain, then fan it with my hand. "It has to dry," I explain when she casts me a quizzical glance over her shoulder. And who can blame her? I'm currently waving at her backside while Max dances delightedly between us like this is some sort of fantastic game, his jowls swinging.

"What if it doesn't work?" Johanna asks, her hands pressed to either side of her neck.

"Then I'll throw a glass of wine at you to cover it up and you can tell everyone the stain was my fault. I had quite a lot of practice the other night."

I thought I did a rather good job of making light of the incident, but Johanna doesn't laugh. She puts her chin to her shoulder, eyes downcast. "You could have just told me you were miserable instead of destroying the dessert table."

I stop flapping. "In my defense, I didn't mean to do that. And also in my defense . . . I have no other defense. I'm sorry I ruined your party."

"Oh, you hardly ruined it. One can still have a marvelous party without desserts. Though they certainly help."

It is exceedingly odd to converse with someone while standing behind them, but facing Johanna, looking her in the eyes, still feels too daunting. Too easy to see the way she has settled into herself like an impression in the sand, while I have just grown stranger. I stare at the clasp of her necklace and the fine hairs that curl along the back of her neck. "I wouldn't know."

"Why? Because you've never been to a party?"

"No, I have."

"I know."

"I meant—"

"Caring about things like parties is beneath a woman like you?"

"I didn't say that."

"Well, not just now, no." She turns. Makes me look at her. "But you did. Once."

She's speaking gently—not a thorn could grow from that spritely voice. But something about it makes me want to snap back at her. "And you said I was an ugly shrew and would die alone."

She takes a step backward. "I didn't."

"It may not have been exactly those words," I say. "But you made it very clear you thought me less of a woman because I don't care about balls and card parties and boys and ridiculous blue dresses."

She folds her arms. "Well, you seemed to think I was less of a person because I did."

"Well, you're certainly a less interesting person now than you were."

I want to take it back as soon as I say it. Or better yet, want to go back and try this conversation again and not say it at all. Or maybe go back even further and never fight with her. Because I used to know Johanna like she was another version of myself—I had forgotten just how intimate our friendship was until I saw her again. The hollow spaces in my shadow, the second set of footsteps beside mine. I could have listed her favorite foods, animals, plants, books in preferential order like I had memorized them out of an encyclopedia. We made up a song about the four humors before I stopped taking Galen seriously as a medical writer. We got poison oak from hiking along the River Dee looking for sea monsters and didn't tell anyone for fear of being kept apart. But standing beside her now, it doesn't feel the same. It likely never will. Returning to a place you once knew as well as your own shadow isn't the same as never leaving at all.

"I'm sorry," I start, "I shouldn't have said—"

"It's not a blue dress; it's indigo," she interrupts. "I chose this shade because it comes from *Persicaria tinctoria*, which is a flower like buckwheat that my mother collected while she was in Japan and brought back to Amsterdam for cultivation."

We stare at each other, the silence between us thick and fragile. Hearing that Latin classification from her lips is like a melody from childhood, half-remembered and suddenly played in full. Things I did not know had been askew fall back into place inside me.

I miss you, I want to say.

"I think the talc is dry," I say instead.

The talc has turned a faint brown, and it crumbles like plaster when I scrape it off with my fingernail. Max pushes his nose into the discarded chunks until Johanna hisses at him that he is a filthy creature and absolutely should not eat that. He does not seem particularly deterred.

"Did it work?" she asks, hands pressed over her eyes.

I heft the not inconsiderable amount of material into my arms and stretch the offending patch between my hands for an examination. "It's not entirely gone, but if you don't know it's there you can't hardly tell."

"Promise? I'm trusting you because I can't see it."

"You can trust me." I falter. The fabric of her dress suddenly feels slick as buttered glass between my hands. "I didn't know your mother was in Japan."

Johanna tugs on her necklace, pulling the clasp back into place. "She was quite a lot of places. When she died—"

"She died?" I interrupt, the words coming out in a sharp breath. "When?"

"Last year. Near Algiers."

"Johanna, I'm so sorry."

She shrugs. "I never really knew her."

The lie of that hums behind the words like a hive. I did not know much of Johanna's mother—I never met her—except that she had left an abysmal marriage and was away (in Japan, apparently), and when Johanna's father died, her mother would not or could not come home for her daughter. That had been the story that had been passed down the church pews and through tea parties and over card games until it finally reached me, because she was gone from my life by then, sent away to a relation in Bavaria because her mother didn't want her.

"Would you like a hug?" I ask.

She frowns at me. "You hate hugs."

"Right, but I could make an exception. If it would help you."

"How about instead . . ." She offers me a hand and when I take it, squeezes gently, the same way we used to when we helped each other up rocks and fallen trees, so we knew the other had a grip. We knew we had a hold of each other. We could step more boldly than we would without a mooring.

Then Max, ever the jealous lover, sticks his nose between our hands until we use them instead to scratch his head.

Johanna and I leave my room together, Max prancing behind us like a show pony. The bow around his neck seems to make him feel very pretty. At the top of the stairs, we nearly smash into Johanna's uncle, who is making a very dramatic ascent with a lot of huffing and muttered curses. "Johanna," he snaps when he sees us. "Where have you been?"

Johanna halts, reaching out for Max's head. "I was . . ."

"All of these insane festivities are for you"—and here he shakes his hands in the general direction of the still-unseen party—"and you can't even be bothered to show up on time. Do you know how much I wasted on flowers alone? It's the middle of the winter and you insist on lilies—"

"I had a problem with my dress," I interrupt, for Johanna looks like she may start to cry, and I don't want to add ruined cosmetics to the list of this evening's fashion catastrophes. "Miss Hoffman was helping me."

"You have a maid for such things." The uncle takes Johanna's arm with a grip that looks like it pinches and starts to drag her away, but then pivots back to me for a last word. "Miss Montague, is it? While we're on the subject, you'd best keep a closer eye upon that maid. I chased her out of my study this morning."

"What?" The hair on the back of my neck stands up. I didn't see Sim much this morning, but I have also been so preoccupied with reviewing Alexander Platt's treaties so that I could be best prepared for our conversation tonight. "What was she doing there?"

"Lord knows. I gave her a slap and a scold to stay where she was allowed." Sim hadn't mentioned that. She hadn't given any sign of taking a hit. But then I suppose Monty never had either, and he was beaten by our father for years. Or perhaps it's just easy not to see if you aren't looking. Herr Hoffman adjusts his wig, the part down the middle a pale line like a surgical thread pulled taught. "I suggest you not employ negresses, madam. They're slippery and treacherous."

"That's a very grand statement," I reply.

"If you had worked with as many African sailors as I have, you'd be suspicious as well." I start, thinking for a moment he knows Sim is a sailor before I realize he's talking about his shipping company. "Come along, Johanna."

Johanna casts me an apologetic look over her shoulder as her uncle drags her away. "What about Max?"

"I'll put him in your room," I say quickly, for her uncle looks ready to strike her as well were they not about to walk into polite company. I hook two fingers under the bow around Max's neck, then realize that is hardly enough and instead use both my hands to tug him back to my side. He whines, claws pulling up the rug as Johanna and her uncle disappear down the stairs.

"Go with Felicity," Johanna calls. Max only cries louder.

"Come on, you enormous wrinkle." I heave so hard I

hear my shoulder joint pop. Max responds by lying down, a dead weight made possible to drag only by the fact that his fur is very slippery upon the polished wood floor. But I am not dragging this reluctantly dragged behemoth anywhere, particularly because in the process, he is leaving enough hair behind that two other dogs could be fashioned from it.

"Max." I let go of the bow and instead make a fist, which I hold out to him. "What if I told you I had a treat for you in this hand?"

He sits up at once, tail thumping and all abandonment forgotten, then stands and follows me as I back down the hallway. I lead him into Johanna's room, then open my hand and let his nose, the size of my palm, make a thorough exploration to be certain there's nothing there. The thought of food got him salivating, and when he snorts and pulls his snout away, my hands are thick with slimy drool. The whole affair is a bit like being lovingly caressed by a dead fish.

I'm about to go when Max lets out a low woof, more threat to it than I've heard from him before. I turn back from the doorway as Max growls again.

Sim is standing at Johanna's writing desk, the drawers open and their contents strewn over the top. She has a ring of thin files looped around one thumb, the metal picks clinking against each other like coins. Her sleeves are pushed up past her elbows, and I get a flash of that pirate ink in the crook of her elbow, a dagger running parallel to her veins, capped by a crown.

I have interrupted a burglary.

Sim must have frozen when I opened the door, for we stare at each other from across the room. I wonder if she's armed, that marlinespike or worse within her reach. I wonder if I should run. But I've seen her, and she's seen me, and she knows where I sleep. Running won't change any of that.

Max lets out another ominous woof from deep within his chest. If there is to be a fight, at least I have the heaviest thing in the room on my side.

"Sim. What are you doing?" I say, trying to keep my voice as low and even as I can, though I'm reaching for the doorknob behind my back.

She doesn't answer. The hard line of her jaw pops as she grinds her teeth.

"Are you stealing from the Hoffmans? Is that why you came here? You fed me nonsense about that book so that I wouldn't notice you were a thief?"

"Let me explain," she says, but I don't give her a chance. Behind my back, my hand finds the door latch, and I spin around, trying to throw it open and bolt, only to find Max's not insignificant rump is entirely in my way. The door bounces straight off him and slams again.

Sim launches herself across the room and grabs me, trying to pull me back into the room and away from the door. I have no idea what she intends to do once she has me where she wants me, so I take an example from Max and throw my dead weight in opposition. Instead of trying to pull me up, she tackles me, launching me backward so that we both smash into the wardrobe hard enough that it rattles against the wall. Inside, I hear something fall off a shelf and shatter, and the noxious scent of spilled rose water blooms around us, so thick we both cough.

Sim's scrabbling behind me, trying to keep me pinned and reach the desk as well, and I'm almost sure she's groping for some sort of weapon. While I don't know much about fighting, I do know how revolting drool is, so I reach up and clap her face between my hands, still thick with Max's saliva.

She yanks away from me. "God, what is that? That's disgusting."

I take a great lungful of air, ready to shout thief, but Sim leaps again, this time toward the desk. She snatches a single letter off it, the seal cracked in half and its folds fluttering, then bolts for the door.

I seize her by the back of the dress and yank hard. There's a ripping sound as her skirt tears away from her waistband. She seems willing to leave her modesty behind if it means escaping—she's still pulling for the door—so I adjust my grip and instead fasten my arms around her waist and we both crash to the ground again.

There's another ripping sound as we fall, this one from my dress, and I feel my mannish shoulders break through the stitching where the sleeves connect to the bodice.

Max is barking. He's also dancing around us with his haunches in the air and his front paws upon the ground like this is a game, cementing his status as the least effective guard dog of all time.

"We had a deal," I say to Sim, my words coming out in short, sharp gasps. "Nothing . . . stolen."

"Let go of me." Sim is trying to claw her way to the doorway on her stomach, but I'm still attached to her waist and doing my best to snatch that letter from her. I manage to get my hands around one end, and I pull, hoping it might come free, but instead it rips. I'm thrown backward, half the letter—including the seal—crumpled and slobbery in my hand. Sim's chin cracks the ground hard, but she's up so fast it seems like she bounced. I'm still dazed from the fall as she opens the bedroom door and slips out.

I sit up, immediately greeted by a hard butt on the forehead from Max, who still thinks this romp is for his entertainment. I push him off, struggling to my feet, and smooth the scrap of my letter out against my dress. Between my damp hands, violent grip, and the fact that I am in possession of only half of it, the letter is entirely unreadable, but the seal has held well enough that I can make out the words *Kunstkammer Staub, Zurich*.

I don't know what else she would have taken had I not walked in on her. But she was taking things. She is a thief. I let a thief into Johanna's house. Doesn't matter what she's after or what she wants; I brought her here. From the moment she pulled the marlinespike on the sailor in London—perhaps even sooner—a part of me suspected it. But the bigger part of me ignored that entirely. She could have told me from the first word that she was here to slit someone's throat in the dead of night, and I likely would have gone along with it because I would have turned a blind eye to anything for the chance to meet Alexander Platt. *Primum non nocere. First, do no harm*, that's the oath. I can't start down a path with those words in hand knowing that I stepped on Johanna to get there.

I need to warn her. I was a fool to bring Sim here. A fool to think she'd hold up her end of a hollow promise. But ambition can infect your sensibilities and poison them like a well. There's a reason most geniuses have failed marriages and no friends.

I leave Max in the room and dash down the stairs. The Polterabend is spilling outside from the grand parlor in the back of the house. There are tables stacked with china to be ceremonially smashed, guests retrieving their dishes to be broken upon the stones outside. There is an excess of lamps to illuminate the cards and dice being played around the room, though hands are starting to be dropped and parties shuffled outside toward the traditional smashing, now that the bride has arrived. There's a quartet playing in one corner. The violinist has legs too long for the small stool he's been confined to, and they're folded under him at an awkward crimp, one foot twisted almost impossibly around for balance, like an unstrung marionette that has landed in a tangle. I think of Percy and suddenly want to be home so much it hurts. Or not home so much as . . . I don't know what I'm missing. It's a queer thing, to have a vacant space inside you and not know what it is that carved out the absence.

There's the crash of a dish prematurely broken out on the veranda, and a few people begin to howl with laughter. I follow the sound into the night, feeling so hot a cloak would have been redundant until the winter air gets its teeth in me and I shiver. Above me, the sky is murky with clouds, stars scattered between them like seashells on a beach.

On the veranda, everyone is wrapped in furs and velvet, some of them masked with feathers and scales painted or pasted over the frame. Others have the same feathers and scales pressed straight onto their faces like pox patches. Women have whole birds in their hair, wings attached to the sleeves of their dresses or the hems of their cloaks. The servants carrying lanterns are dressed in black feathers so that the lights look like they're floating. The light flashes off the pottery everyone is holding, glazed and shimmering like cupped fireflies between their hands. Everything feels overwrought and over-drawn, too bright and too loud and too disorienting. No one looks like themselves, or even truly human.

I should be looking for Platt. He asked me to be here, told me he wanted to talk about my work and study. I should be thinking of myself and my future and my career.

But all I want to do is find Johanna.

I spot her talking to a man with octopus tentacles woven into his wig and a wineglass in each hand. In the silvery light of the lamps on the snow, she looks like a mermaid, or the figurehead of a ship, the sort of plump, heavenly siren that would have sailors throwing themselves into the sea at just a crook of her finger. The feathers sewn onto her dress move slowly in the breeze, like kelp underwater, and when she turns toward the faint light spilling from the house and tussling with the stars, the powder on her skin makes her cheeks sparkle.

She shrieks with delight when she sees me com-ing, like this is the first time we've seen each other all night—or perhaps simply as an excuse to abandon the man trying to force one of the glasses upon her—and holds out a hand for me to take. "Felicity! I've been look-ing for you! I'm sorry I left you with the dog; he didn't give you any trouble, did he? Oh no, what happened to your dress?"

I pull the wilted sleeve up over my shoulder. It slips down again at once. "I need to talk to you," I say. "Alone."

"All right. I'll be back, my Lord; don't make a move until I return." She taps the geriatric kraken's nose with her fan, then lets me drag her away, up onto the porch and out of the circle of lantern light. "Do you think it looks all right?" she says as we go, trying to turn to get a look at the back of her dress. "I don't think anyone can tell, but I can't stop worrying about it." I halt so abruptly she steps on the heel of my shoe and I almost stumble out of it. "What is it? What's wrong?"

If I tell her, there will likely be no chance of working with Platt. What respectable physician would hire an outsider who had used devious means to gain access to him, lied her way into his home, and left his fiancé vulnerable to robbery?

But it's Johanna beaming down at me, and all I say is "I'm sorry." My voice comes out as thin as smoke.

A small crease appears between her eyebrows, the only blemish upon her face. "What are you sorry for? You did such a good thing for me earlier—"

"No, I have to tell you something."

"Can it wait? I have to—"

"No, stop. Just stop talking, please, and listen to me." I take her hands and she stills, her mouth pulling down into a frown. "The girl with me—Sim—she's not my maid. She's . . . I don't know. A sailor. Maybe associated with bad people. She was looking at a book in your library, and your uncle caught her in his study, and I found her just now in your apartments robbing you, and she tried to make off with this." I press the letter into her palms.

Johanna stares at me, then down at the letter. Her thumb traces the outline of the wax seal. "You're a thief?"

"No, my maid is. She's not my maid, she paid my way here in exchange for getting her into your house. I only came because I wanted to talk to Dr. Platt about a job. I'm not going to school. I'm not in touch with my family. I've been in Edinburgh for a year trying to get a medical education and no one will have me and if I don't find work soon, I don't know what I'll do. I thought Dr. Platt could help me."

"You lied to me."

"Yes. Yes, I did." I'm absolutely clutching at her hands, like that will keep her from leaving me without atonement. The scrap of the stolen letter crumples between us. "But I'm telling you now."

"You think that matters?" she says, her already trilling voice rising to a whistle tone. "You're telling me *after* I've been robbed. *After* you let this person into my home. *After* you let her into my rooms."

"She told me she wasn't here to steal anything."

"And you believed her?" she demands. "Better

question, why did you ally yourself with someone who had to make a clarifying point that she was not a thief? What did you think she was doing here? What did you think she wanted with me?"

I can't even look at her. I comb back through my interactions with Sim, every moment from that first time we sat down in the pub, and I know Johanna's right. I assumed the best, even while I told myself I was being suspicious and careful enough, because more than Johanna's safety, more than any real concern for what Sim was doing, I was thinking of myself. "I had to talk to Dr. Platt," I tell her. "You don't understand what it's like to be so stuck you'll do anything to get out."

She pulls in her lips. Bites her cheeks. Squeezes my hand. "Don't I?"

It's that moment that Dr. Platt himself, as though summoned, appears at her side, one hand fastening around her elbow. "Johanna. Where have you been? Your uncle is looking for you." He spots me attached to her wrists and smiles. "Miss Montague, good evening. I was beginning to think you'd forgotten me." His smile flips as he stares at my shoulder, and I realize one of my sleeves has puddled in the crook of my elbow. "Is your dress torn, or is that the fashion these days?"

I look between Johanna and Platt, mute. I think for certain she'll tell him about what I've done, out me as the ambitious monster that I am. But instead, she presses the scrap of the letter back into my hand and folds my fingers over it before turning to Dr. Platt. "I'm ready if you and Uncle are," she says, and suddenly she's herself again, an actress composing herself before she steps on stage and becomes someone else.

"Let's get on with it, then. May I?" he asks, and I realize I'm still holding Johanna's hands. Or perhaps Johanna is holding mine. When she lets go, she leaves behind small half-moons on my knuckles from where her fingernails bit, and that damp, withered scrap of paper, the waxy seal starting to go soft from so much handling.

Anger rises in me as I watch them walk away, blotting out the guilt and panic like sand over ink. I'm not sure if she doesn't believe me or simply doesn't want to believe me, and why didn't she tell Platt or show him whatever correspondence was snatched or at least tell someone so that everyone in the house is ready to tackle Sim if they see her.

I watch Johanna and Platt descend the stairs, meeting her uncle halfway. He hands them each a plate, then raises his hand to the courtyard and calls for silence. The musicians break off. The crowd hushes.

Hoffman looks to Platt, who clears his throat and steps forward, letting Johanna's arm fall from his. "We're so happy," he says, though his voice sounds flat and rehearsed, "you are all here to celebrate with us. I'm very lucky to have formed a partnership with the Hoffmans."

He nods to the uncle, then seems to remember this is actually meant to be about Johanna and adds, "And lucky as well to have found a woman who will tolerate a mad doctor for a husband." There are a few laughs. I swear Johanna looks back at where I'm standing. And she looks like she wants to run. "If you'll please join me . . ." Platt looks to Johanna's uncle, who has a fixed smile while his face goes slowly red. What was likely supposed to be a grand speech from the groom was a mere two lines, but Platt raises his plate in the air, then reaches behind him and grabs Johanna's hand, pulling her to his side. *"Scherben bringen Glück!"*

Johanna raises her plate, and the guests raise theirs, and they fling them to the ground, where they burst, shards streaking through the air like comets as they catch the lantern light. The air turns dusty with china plaster, a thin haze hovering over the evening and turning the barrels of light foggy with motes. There are screams of delight and laughter, and music begins to play as dishes are thrown, toppled, flung, and stepped upon.

Every one of them smashed.

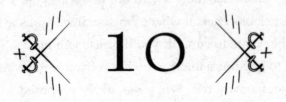

10

Johanna disappears almost as soon as the china is broken, and I don't dare approach Dr. Platt. If she told him about Sim—and who could blame her, to assure there was no chance of me entering their lives after I had gone on and on about how I had put her in danger just to meet Platt?—any hope I had of working with him or any connections he might have provided will be snuffed. He may be a rebel in the operating room, but I imagine offering his new bride up to a robber will put a permanent tarnish on a relationship.

I return to my room to find Sim's knapsack gone. Which is part relief, part dread, because with her goes my way back to England. I wrangle myself out of my dress—more rip myself out, for it's already beyond saving—and change into the weathered tartan skirt and bodice I arrived in. There is no point staying for the wedding now. Johanna will want nothing to do with me. She'll likely turn Platt against me. I'm not certain how I'll travel back to England—perhaps on credit, then show up on Callum's doorstep and accept his proposal so long as he takes on the massive debt I have mustered in returning to him. Perhaps I'll go back to London and try again. Perhaps I should take up factory work and hope that someone's foot gets sucked into a machine occasionally and I have the chance to practice what I've spent so much time studying. Perhaps I should go back to my parents, tail tucked, and give it all up.

But it feels like living without a heart. Until now, I was chasing something, no matter how far in the distance it was. But now my only choice is going back, and going back means resigning myself to a life without work. Without study or purpose. And what kind of life is that?

Perhaps, like walking with a lamp in the dark, I must move forward before I am able to see the next bend in the road, but for now, I pack my things, then sit on the bed and wait for the sun to pearl along the horizon, feeling trapped within a shrinking box in an indifferent universe.

The first noise I hear does not come from the house raising its head in preparation for a wedding, but rather from the grounds outside. Someone is whistling, then a child's voice cries in German, "Come on, doggie! Run!"

I stand and cross to the window. The sky is peach

colored outside my window, the pine trees dark blades in silhouette against it. On the lawn, blanketed in snow still studded with flecks of broken china, a tiny girl with shocking blond hair and enormous ears is running circles around Max, who seems to have deflated, so flat is he lying on the ground. I wonder suddenly if it's my fault he got out—perhaps I didn't shut Johanna's door properly last night and poor Max has been loping around the grounds in the dark.

I let myself out of my room, then dart down the stairs in my slippers and out onto the veranda, stopping upon the last step so I don't wet my toes. "Max!" I call, and his head shoots up, spraying snow off his ears.

The girl stops running and stares at me, then throws her hands at the beastie as though in presentation. "I've brought the dog," she says in German. "Money, please."

"Did he get out?" I ask, making a tentative crossing of the snowy lawn toward her. My slippers, made for ladylike treads across carpet, are soaked by the time I reach her, but there is no chance the dog will be moved by this girl as delicate as a snowflake.

The girl puts her hand atop Max's enormous head, giving him a two-fingered stroke between the eyes. "No, the lady at the carriage stop in Stuttgart gave me a *kreuzer* and said if I brought the dog back to the pink house, someone would give me another. But he looked so sad I thought he might want to play."

I'm not sure how this small creature got Max any-where, particularly when she hooks a hand around his bow and tries to pull him over to me. She seems to be throwing her whole weight into the act, and he barely budges. Stuttgart is at least two miles of playing carrot and stick with this creature away.

I suddenly realize I have entirely missed the key word of her statement. "Sorry, what lady?"

"The lady from the pink house in the country. They wouldn't let her bring the dog on the diligence so she said you'd give me a *kreuzer*—"

"I don't have a coin for you," I interrupt. "You can go ask around the service door if you want your payment."

As the girl prances off through the yard, I bend down and stroke Max on the head. "What were you doing in Stuttgart? You should be upstairs with Johanna getting dressed up for the big day." He snort-whines, expelling a puff of frozen slobber from his jowls, and nudges his face into my skirt. His black lips pool against my knee. "Come on, let's go find her." I drag him up by the loose skin around his neck—I swear I lose sight of my hand in all the fur and folds—and pull him back into the house, then up the stairs toward Johanna's room. He's a reluc-tant companion, whining and dragging his massive paws and offering such passive resistance that I'm winded by the time we reach the door to Johanna's apartments. Max shakes himself off, and I'm drenched in a combination of the snow thrown from his fur and long ribbons of slobber. I swear some fly off and adhere to the ceiling, where they cling like rock formations in a cave.

Hunched over with the dog cuffed under one arm, my hair in my face, and most of me soaked in muddy snow, I'm a proper vagrant when I knock on Johanna's bedroom door. "Johanna?" I can feel the sleeve of my dress slowly soaking as Max leaks saliva into it. "Johanna, I've got Max—I think he got out." No answer. I knock again, harder this time. "Johanna?"

I give a tentative push on the door and it swings open. Max presses his massive forehead into the back of my knees, like he's trying to hide, but instead ends up nudging me into the room. It's empty. Her wedding dress is hanging unworn, her bed made, and the fire cold, unstoked since the night previous.

Max galumphs in ahead of me, makes a slow heft of his girth onto the bed, and turns around three times before flopping down. I take a few more steps inside. "Johanna?" I call, though it's obvious she isn't here. The washroom is dark, the essential items of her toilette gone, and the bedsheets cold but where Max has already begun to sink into them.

Johanna is gone.

Not just gone, but seemingly not here at all last night.

I have to tell someone—it will delay my own departure, but there's a whole wedding party about to assemble in her honor, a garden full of flowers being arranged below stairs, a chapel full of guests who will be left staring at an empty aisle. Not to mention the humiliation for the groom to be standing at the altar, waiting and waiting and waiting, only to find his bride has vanished.

I have to tell Dr. Platt.

I'm fairly certain I know which room is his, though the first door I knock upon is answered by the deaf relative I sat beside at my first dinner. I apologize and move on to the next, rapping upon it so hard my knuckles smart. Dr. Platt answers in a banyan and cap, his eyes bloodshot. "Miss Montague." He scrubs a hand against his face. "It's . . . early."

"Johanna's gone," I blurt out.

He blinks hard several times, like he's trying to translate my words from a language of which he only knows a few words. "What?"

"Her room is empty, and there was a girl in the yard who brought Max and said that she was given a coin by a woman getting on a diligence to bring him back to the house."

"Come inside." He ushers me into his room, closing the door behind us. Cleanliness is clearly not a prominent water feature in the courtyard of his life, as he seems to have nothing in his wardrobe and everything upon the floor. There are sets of dishes with dried crusts of food stacked on a table by the fire, which he pulls a chair from and offers me. He retrieves his snuffbox from the nightstand before pulling up a stool for himself. "Do you need a drink?" he asks, and I shake my head, though even sitting down, I am unable to be still, my knee bouncing up and down. "Tell me slowly now, from the beginning."

When I'm finished explaining, he asks, "Are you certain she's gone? She may be elsewhere in the house. Did you check—"

"She didn't sleep in her bed last night," I interrupt. "It was still made. The fire was cold. Things were missing from her dressing room."

"Did the child say where the diligence was headed?" I shake my head. "Do you know where she would have gone? Or why?"

My mind flits briefly to the night before, the letter clutched between us and Johanna furious and serious and entirely not herself. But there's no proof that was due to anything other than her learning that I had set her up to be robbed. "No, sir."

He nods, tugging the sash on his banyan tighter. "I'll have the staff search the house and grounds, to be certain, and alert her uncle. Let me dress, and then you and I can go to Stuttgart and see if we can find out where she's gone."

Platt sends the butler to the chapel to let the priest know the service may be delayed, while I do my best to shake off the bridal attendants beginning to assemble in the parlor. By the time Platt and I depart for Stuttgart, Johanna's uncle and the groundskeeper have his hunting dogs on leads, ready to launch a search of the woods that frame the house.

Platt and I take a carriage from the house to the diligence stop in the city, where the clerk confirms that a young woman and her giant dog arrived early this morning seeking a departure. However, while the dog was sent back to the house with the girl due to not fitting comfortably inside the carriage, Johanna got herself on the first southbound coach this morning from Frankfurt to Genoa. The clerk counts out the next stops for us on his fingers. "Rottenburg, Albstadt, Memmingen, Ravensberg, Schaffhausen, Zurich . . ."

Zurich. I can see it on the seal of the letter I tore from Sim. Did Johanna tell Platt about Sim? Did it matter at all to her? Did she dismiss it when he interrupted us because it didn't matter, or because she didn't want him to know? Do I have a hand in her sudden departure, or is it just a severe manifestation of nerves before a wedding and my betrayal was just an enormous coincidence?

What were you thinking, Johanna?

Outside the travel office, Platt slaps his gloves against his hands absently, blowing a long, milky breath into the air before he declares, "I'm going to send word to the chapel that we're postponing the ceremony, and then follow the route. See if I can't catch up with the diligence or find her at any of the stops. She can't have gone far; she'll miss all the comforts she's used to within the day."

I'm not certain he's right about that. Johanna Hoffman may seem like a girl who would be out of her depth in a mud puddle, but I don't think she'd run without a plan. Or at the least, a very good reason, though I can't fathom what that might be.

"I think . . ." I start, but falter when he looks at me. His gaze is hawk sharp, and the chance of the letter I intercepted being in any way tied to her flight is so thin it feels likely to snap as soon as it's tested. I take a deep breath. "She may be heading to Zurich."

"What makes you think that?" he asks.

"Last night, I caught my maid robbing her. She tried to take a letter, and the seal was from Zurich."

"A letter? Do you have it with you?" I shake my head. "Do you remember anything about it?"

"Kunstkammer Staub. That was on the seal." I trip so badly over the pronunciation I blush, suddenly feeling foolish not just for my poor German but also for thinking this was worth mentioning. "It may be nothing."

"Or perhaps not." He rubs a hand over his chin. He hasn't shaved, and his cheeks are peppered with coarse stubble. "We should go to Zurich. I've a house rented there for our honeymoon, so at least we'll have somewhere to set up."

"We?" I repeat.

"Ah, yes." He tucks his hands into his coat pockets with a smile. "I was going to speak to you of this last night, but we never found each other. I gave quite a lot of thought to how I might best use you, and I can certainly find space for you on my expedition staff."

It's like the whole world shifts. The light gets brighter. The snow whiter, the sky glacier blue. The bitter wind clattering shop signs against their chains quiets. For one quiet moment, the world is still, and it is mine. My legs feel firmly planted under me for the first time in years. Maybe my whole life. Nothing has been ruined, no rift in the earth opened between me and the greatest living physician. I left out the damning details of how Sim got into their house, but either he didn't notice or didn't care. He still wants me.

Platt pulls his scarf up over his nose, squinting down the street and seemingly oblivious to the fact that in one sentence he has given me a chance I would have cut off my own feet and eaten them raw for. "Though this damn expedition will never get off the ground if we can't find Miss Hoffman."

The wind picks back up, and a spray of muddy snow splatters across the hem of my dress as a passing carriage strikes a rut. "Why not?"

He's pulled out his snuffbox and tipped a thimbleful onto the back of his hand, shielding it from the wind with a cupped palm, but he pauses, eyes flickering to me. Then he says, "What sort of man would leave the country while his fiancée is missing?" He takes a snort and shakes his head a few times. "Please come. You're her friend; she trusts you. Whatever has inspired this hysteria, perhaps you can talk her down from it. Miss Montague, I need your help."

It was not quite the context in which I had imagined Alexander Platt would ask me for my help. In my fantasies, it was from the other side of an operating table, in a time of crisis, with everyone panicking over a tangled intestine no one could unravel until I stepped up. But I'll take whatever scraps I'm thrown. No matter how tired I am of not having a seat at the table.

"Let's find Johanna," I say.

Platt wastes no time on public transport. He hires us a carriage and a driver and foots every bill for accommodations. Which is a vast improvement upon my original plan of limping back to England by way of public coaches and sleeping at the sheltered stops along the way. And though I am not particularly fussy and have done my share of sleeping in open fields with only my own two arms to pillow my head, I prefer beds and roofs and heated foot warmers in an enclosed carriage when they are made available to me.

Platt is a gentleman. He doesn't sit on the same side of the bench as I do and lets me ride forward while he sits with his back to the coachman. He takes quite a lot more snuff than I have ever seen a man ingest, and I lived with Monty—though of all his vices, Monty was never one for snuff. Platt snorts it like clockwork, a deep inhale through the nose every quarter hour, and when we stop for the night, he leaves our inn and ventures out into the frigid winter to purchase more. The next morning over breakfast, he adds laudanum to his coffee and complains of the poor quality of tobacco to be found in this town.

It reminds me of my brother, who, before our Tour, would take brandy in the mornings after a night drinking himself sick at the clubs, smelled of whiskey more often than aftershave, and who, had he ever dueled, he would likely have been saved from a fatal bullet by the flask in his breast pocket. I know now why: after years of abuse at the hands of our father, he had felt himself unable to experience the world sober. It makes me wonder what demons Alexander Platt keeps barricaded away with that small box of shimmering powder.

I am not certain how to speak to him, and so at first we do very little of that. I want to ask him everything— about his work, his research, the wards he's walked and the ships he's sailed on, what he thinks about Robert Hook's presentation of artificial respiration before the Royal Society, whether he agrees with Archibald Pitcairne that fevers are best cured by evacuating medicines, because that had always seemed overly simplistic to me—but none of this seems appropriate to ask a man whose bride has fled the altar. Even if he is one's hero.

But one can only spend so long bookless in the company of another human before one feels compelled to make conversation. Particularly when one of those humans has just offered the other an opportunity that has her stoked as a just-fed fire.

"So about the position."

I say it so fast and with so little grace that he looks up from notations he's been making in a small book with a frown. "Pardon me?"

I swallow. "I was hoping. Maybe. You could tell me more about the sort of work I'll be doing for you."

"Work?" he repeats.

"The position with your expedition."

"Oh, of course." He closes his book around the pencil, marking his place. "While I'm away in the Barbary States, it would helpful to have someone at my office in London to keep track of my correspondence and finances, transcribe notations sent from abroad. I can't pay you much, unfortunately—but you know how these things are, always so short on funds." I don't know, actually. I am not sure what things he's referring to—medicine, or expeditions, or any position that's held by a woman.

"So I'd be your secretary," I say.

"Assistant," he corrects. When I don't reply, he adds, "You look disappointed."

"It's not quite what I had in mind," I say, as tactful a response as I can muster. "I was hoping for something more practical."

He's fishing in his jacket again, and I expect to see the snuffbox, but instead it's a handkerchief. He blows his nose, then, when he finds me still silent, laughs. "What more would you want?"

"I'd like to study," I reply. "And work. Not just take notes for someone who is."

He swipes a thumb over his chin, then folds his handkerchief with such precision it makes me want to scoot away from him, though there's nowhere to go in this carriage. "Miss Montague," he says, "let me be clear about something. You'll not be given many chances for employment in this field because of the inferiority of your sex. I'm kind enough to offer you this when most physicians wouldn't entertain the idea of a woman in their office managing their research. This is not an opportunity you'll be offered again, from anyone."

It is a blunt battering ram of a tone. The sort that makes me suddenly aware that it is just the two of us in this small space on this empty country road. He leans back, kicking one foot up on the opposite knee with such grandness that his toe knocks into my shin. "Might I suggest some gratitude? It's far more becoming."

"I'm sorry," I say, and I hate that I am apologizing to him when it is he who kicked me, he who has made me feel that I'm in the wrong for daring to ask for something. Not even something—for anything. He has me apologizing for asking for the minimum that is granted to most men.

"You needn't apologize for ambition," he says, flipping his book open again and taking up his pencil. "Just know that most men will find it unseemly in a woman."

I turn away from him and stare out the window, watching the white countryside pass us by and trying to resist the urge to open the door, step out onto the road, and make my own way rather than spend a minute longer in this coach.

"Once we get to Zurich," he says, and his voice feels floating and far away, "you'll help me find Johanna. Won't you, Felicity?"

"Yes, sir," I reply, and the conversation between my hero—*your hero, your idol, your favorite doctor*, I remind myself over and over in time with the clattering carriage wheels—whittles into nothing.

Zurich

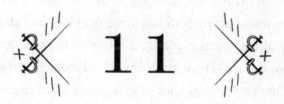

11

The house in Zurich is ready for us when we arrive. Well, not us. Johanna and Platt. It's a modest townhouse near the shore of the lake, not so close that you can hear the port, but not so far away as to be overly fashionable. The staff is just a cook, a housekeeper, and a valet, who all do an admirable job of hiding their surprise when Dr. Platt introduces me as Miss Montague rather than Mrs. Platt.

We arrive late in the evening, the streetlamps already glowing and the lake a glassy reflection of the sky. The housekeeper takes me up to my room, brings me supper on a tray, and heats coals for my bed warmer before leaving me to sleep. I'm flattened from the traveling, but the house keeps me awake—perhaps it is just being unaccustomed to strange sounds of a strange place, and a strange city as well. Perhaps it's the way I can hear Dr.

Platt in the sitting room below me, his footsteps on the floorboards, the clink of a decanter against the rim of a glass more times than seems advisable.

I drift off without realizing it, but I'm woken abruptly by the sound of my bedroom door opening, and the faint beam of a lantern being unsheathed, which disappears almost at once. There are a few rough footsteps, then my bedroom door bangs shut, and an unfamiliar male voice asks in English, "Who is that?"

"Keep your voice down," Platt hisses. "God, you didn't have to barge in."

"I knew you were lying. I knew it."

"I didn't lie—"

"That's not your wife, Alex."

I don't move, debating whether they'll be back, whether it is wiser for me to continue to feign sleep or to bolt suddenly awake. The intensity of their voices—and that they are two men and I a woman alone—sits deep in my bones like a bad fever.

"So where is Mrs. Platt?" the stranger's voice asks, farther away now. The stairs creak beneath their feet.

Their voices peter out as they get farther down the stairs. I sit up, straining to hear. I am no dropper of eaves, but it seems in my best interest, and Johanna's, to know what is being said about us behind closed doors. Or, rather, in the hallways outside them.

I scramble out of bed and to the door, then ease

myself out as quietly as possible and glide sock-footed to the top of the stairs. From that vantage point, I can see across the entryway and into a sliver of the sitting room where they've taken up residence. From where he's seated on the couch, Platt's shoulder and the back of his head are barely visible. ". . . in the city, somewhere," he's saying. "She's also not Mrs. Platt yet."

"Dear God, Alex. I thought you could handle this."

"I can—I am. Handling it."

"What was wrong with taking her to Poland?" the stranger asks. His accent is English, with a crisp precision that reeks of hunting parties and Cambridge classrooms.

"She would have suspected a proposition of elopement—" Platt starts, but the man cuts him off.

"What do you do if she gets there before you?"

"It doesn't matter. They'll never let her near the archive. She needs me—"

The second gentleman cuts Platt off with a growling sigh. He's standing too far away for me to see him, but I get a brief view from the waist down as he crosses in front of the fireplace—a thick wool gray coat and tall boots crusted with salt. Sailor's boots, but far too fine for a seaman. They look like pieces of a uniform.

There's a strangled silence. Platt is staring at the floor, his elbows on his knees. "I will fix this," he says at last.

"You'd best." The decanter clicks again. Platt reaches

out for the glass he's offered. "So," the second man asks, "who is the girl in your bedroom, if it isn't Miss Hoffman?"

My heartbeat jumps, and I lean forward just as Platt settles back into his seat, his elbow perched on the armrest at such a jaunty angle that some of the liquor sloshes out of his glass. "You won't believe me if I tell you. Do you know Lord Henri Montague?"

My fists close on the banister, the hard ridges of the wood jutting into my palm.

"The English earl?" the second man asks.

"The same." Platt tips a finger over his shoulder, toward the stairs above which he thinks I'm sleeping. "That's his child."

"What?"

"His kidnapped girl in the flesh. His Lordship has been telling the whole peerage that his children were taken by slavers in the Mediterranean, but as it happens, they ran away." He takes a loud slurp from his drink, then lets it dangle between his thumb and forefinger. "Can you imagine the scandal if the truth got out?"

My palms start to sweat against the banister. Monty and I both wrote to our parents when we first resolved not to return home after our Tour, me to a stifled existence and a loveless marriage, Monty to likely the same, but with a good deal more damage from our father done to him along the way. And while we didn't exactly send a forwarding address, Father's lack of reply had led Monty and me to optimistically agree that he had decided to quietly blot our names from the family tree, bet his estate upon the new baby son, and let us go our own ways. Apparently, he has taken a far more dramatic route, telling everyone we were taken by corsairs, and now Platt has the evidence to prove otherwise.

In the parlor, I hear the second man say, "You're going to kidnap the daughter of a lord and blackmail him?"

"There is no kidnapping," Platt replies. "She came willingly. Miss Montague will help me find Johanna and see us married. Then we collect Sybille Glass's work and send the ladies back to England, and Montague's help will keep us afloat and see Herr Hoffman paid for his ships. See? All in my control, Fitz."

I should be afraid—I'm certainly trembling. Platt knows who I am and will use me to find Johanna, and then plans to send me back to my father. All the while I'd thought us allies, I'd been no more than a pawn. And that has my vision spotting with anger. Anger for being used. For being thought foolish. For knowing that he'd likely never thought me capable of medical work; he'd just recognized my name.

I need to leave this house at once and find Johanna and warn her that whatever love Platt professed to have for her is false, and the wedding is a sham. If it was Platt she ran from, I've led him straight to her door. She may think she's safe until the moment his jaws snap closed around her, all because of me.

The conversation in the parlor has moved to sailing, and if I do not leave now, I may not get another chance. I slip back into my room and change from my nightdress into my tartan skirt and bodice. They're reeking from the travel, the hem muddied up to the knees and the material crusty with sweat that has dried and then dampened over and over again as we went from stifling carriages to frigid station stops. My cloak is in a closet below stairs, and I do not dare creep down for it, nor do I dare bolt into the cold without it. Instead, I strip the quilt off the bed and wrap that around my shoulders.

Then, the much more complex task at hand: the actual escape. Ice on the window cracks when I shove it open, and a gust of wind pushes back so hard I almost lose my grip. The pelmet curtain is sucked out, and the shutters clap against the side of the house. Below is an unhelpful drop to the street—no footholds, ledges, or loose bricks promised me by every fiction book I have ever read. Not even a convenient hedge to drop into.

I have never been in possession of any particular acrobatic skills and, having the proportions of a corgi dog, do not anticipate a burst of natural athleticism to manifest just in time for me to scale the side of a building.

I drag the windows shut, then take a breath and an inventory. Resources at my disposal: very few. The sparse furnishings of this room, which would only be valuable if they could be subtly pushed out the window to create some sort of precarious tower. My knapsack full of nothing useful—stockings and underthings and a few books. I open the cupboard in the corner and find additional bed dressings and towels.

The only idea seems to be taking up the role of the towered princess who grows weary of waiting for a knight: a rope made of her bedroom's drapery.

The sheets tear quietly and braid easily—years of keeping my hair in a long plait has finally done more than garner ire from fussier peers. I tear, braid, and braid again, then tie a firm knot around the rod hammered into the wall to hold the pelmet over the window. I sling my knapsack over my shoulder, test my weight upon the rope to be certain I won't fall to my death if the plaster is ripped from the wall (well, death is rather grand—perhaps fall to my two broken ankles, more accurately). Then I brace my feet against the casements and rescue myself.

In the shelter of the bowing streets, the city is warmer than the countryside, and in spite of the snowfall, I've sweated through my scarf by the time I arrive at the diligence stop where the carriage from Stuttgart comes in daily. I pay the linkboy lighting lamps for me with coins left over from supper the night before and then stand alone on the side of the street, the sludgy snowflakes trickling through the clouds making lace trimmings on my eyelashes, trying to think where I would go if I were a girl alone in a city, likely coming in in the dark and the cold.

Which I am, I realize. But I try not to linger too long on that lest my fear swallow me whole.

I think of Johanna. Everything I know of her. Where I would go if I were her.

I would go home to Stuttgart and my giant dog and my frilly dresses, is the first thing I think, but the Johanna I knew back in Cheshire had once slept for three nights in her father's stables in winter in hopes of seeing the snowy owl she suspected had made its nest in the rafters. Had fallen through ice on a pond and pulled herself out before anyone could help her. A girl who had survived without a father, and a mother who wouldn't come home when she lost him. Perhaps she is still made of that stone foundation I watched her build as a child. Perhaps it has not eroded with time but grown stronger. And been draped in silk and dog saliva.

If I were Johanna, I think, I would want somewhere Platt wouldn't find me. Not somewhere he'd expect her to stay, a guesthouse along the river with polished floors and silk sheets. I'd want to hide. I'd want somewhere tongues didn't wag and runaway girls weren't noticeable and men were not allowed. Somewhere like the boarding-house I had called home in Edinburgh. And, if I had a trunk in tow, somewhere nearby.

The streets of the old town are steep and winding, a combination of cobbles so slick with snow it's almost necessary to take them upon all fours and rough stair-ways just as treacherous, but with more sharp edges when fallen upon. The diligence stop shares its corner with a trinket shop advertising tarot readings, shut up and looking as though it hasn't been opened in weeks, a cobbler with faded velvet slippers in the window, and a café spilling violin music and the soft clink of a night that's crowded but not busy.

I make my way inside, picking through the tables populated with drunk artists staring into the bottom of gin bottles and painted ladies swooning around them. The man behind the bar is wiry and thin, with a thick mustache and a weathered kerchief tied around his neck. He's missing two teeth on the bottom, and he greets me with a rasping, wet cough before asking in a gritty voice, "You want something to drink?"

"No, sir, actually . . ." I make a big show of swallow-ing, willing myself to get tears in my eyes, just for fullest effect. "It's my sister."

"Your sister?" he repeats.

"She's run away from home because our father is a tyrant who would see her shipped off to an asylum just

223

for being a girl who reads books." I am poaching a bit of everyone's life story for this lie, but I press on. "She's come here to Zurich and I know she's just arrived and I'm trying to find her and I think she came in here a few days ago and please, sir . . ." The damn tears just aren't coming—I've spent so many years training myself to not show any sort of weakness, even under desperate circumstances, that my face seems utterly confused about what it is I'm asking it to do. I'm screwing up my nose and snuffling and I think it looks more like I'm about to sneeze than trying to cry, for the bartender just looks confused. "Please, sir," I squeak, trying to put a teary wobble in my voice and overshooting so it instead sounds like I just inhaled a mouthful of pepper. "If you know anything . . . of where she might be . . . I just want to find her."

He gives me a heavy-lidded look, still wiping endless circles around the glass in his hand. I likely could have told this bartender that I was looking for Johanna so I could murder her in cold blood and he wouldn't have cared—he doesn't seem to give a fig about my tragic, albeit fake, story or my similarly-tragic-though-only-because-of-their-fakeness tears. "Why would I know?"

"Surely you see unfortunates in here begging for your help."

"Unfortunates are the only kind we see here, madam." He coughs again, this time pulling up the kerchief around his neck to cover his mouth. The material is wet and worn, the striped pattern faded into pilled cotton around the edges, like he often pulls it up. There are no blood stains, though, so if he's coughing into it often, it's not a consumptive hack. This close, I can hear his lungs cracking every time he takes a breath, like the spine of a book opened for the first time.

"Do you suffer from asthma, sir?" I ask before I can stop myself.

He pauses in wiping down glasses and, for the first time, seems to pay me attention. "Do I what?"

"Asthma," I repeat, and hope I'm pronouncing it correctly—it's a word I learned from reading Dr. John Floyer's treaties and I've never said it outside my own head. "A respiratory condition that causes labored breathing and chest contractions."

"Don't know," he replies.

"Do you often have trouble breathing deeply?"

"Most days. I take laudanum for it."

"Have you tried tar water and nettle juice instead? They're much better for a constricted throat, and there's less risk of dependency. Less expensive too. Some quacks will tell you that boiled carrots help the lungs, but tar water has proved the most effective treatment. Any pharmacy should carry some, or make it up for you."

He stares at me, trying to decide whether I'm making a joke, then coughs again, this time with his mouth closed so that his cheeks puff out.

"It's remarkable the difference a good deep breath can make," I offer.

He huffs, presses his fist to his chest, then says, "She's really your sister, is she?" When I nod, he says, "We get lots of unsavory types in here looking for girls who don't want to be found."

"Do I look unsavory?"

"You've got no cloak."

"That makes me unfortunate, I should think."

He huffs again, wiping his nose on the back of his hand. "When we get girls wandering in, I send them to Frau Engel's near the chapel. She's a boardinghouse for waywards. The only one you can walk to from here. Your sister may be there."

"Do you remember a girl with—"

"We get a lot of girls," he interrupts. "And I send them all to Frau Engel."

"Thank you, sir."

I start to leave, but he calls to me, "What was it? Tar juice?"

I turn in the doorway. "Tar water and nettle juice. I hope it helps."

He nods. "I hope you find your sister."

Frau Engel is similarly unmoved by my tragic story, though she has no illness I can diagnose to soften her heart. I make no attempt at tears this time. "Could be anyone," she says. She's in her nightdress and cap, but the lit clay pipe between her teeth assures me I didn't wake her. Her large frame occupies most of the door. "I get a dozen girls in and out of here each day. I don't know them all."

She looks as though she's about to close the door in my face, so I throw out a preemptive arm against the frame, in the hope that she will at least have enough pity in her heart not to crunch my fingers, and say, "Please, you must remember."

She shrugs, her clay pipe bouncing between her teeth. "All girls are the same. You want to pay me for a bed, you can wander around and try to find her yourself, but make the decision quick so I can get back to bed."

I give her all the coins I have left without a clue of what she's charging. I'm fairly certain it's too much for a single night, but she doesn't offer me anything back. Just harrumphs, then gives me a tin plate, a cutlery set, and a blanket made of rough ticking that smells as though it were last used to rub down a horse. "Two girls to a bed, three if you can't find a spot. Washroom's on the second floor."

"I'm not actually staying, I just want to find my sister."

"Still two to a bed," she says, drawing back so I can pass, then adds, "And don't run off with my blanket." She says that like the withered carcass of material would have any value. There are so many holes it seems like it would not even serve the most basic purpose of blanketness. "And don't wake me again," she calls as she galumphs back to her room, a thin finger of smoke from her pipe lingering behind.

The boardinghouse is packed above stairs and smells of mold and wax. Large pieces of the wallpaper are peeling away, leaving raw patches of damp wood that splinter when I brush them. I wander the second- and third-floor bedrooms, feeling invasive and downright criminal as I peer at all these sleeping girls, squinting through the darkness to see if any of them is Johanna. I'm not sure what I'll do if I find her—wake her or sit beside her bed and keep vigil until morning or perhaps lie down beside her and sleep myself, though the question is rendered irrelevant as I finish my lap and find her nowhere.

Most beds are full, and most with more than two girls. I see four knotted up together upon one small, stiff mattress, the littlest no more than twelve and all of them curled around each other like kittens. They're all thin and pale. One girl keeps coughing into her fist, trying to stifle the sound. Most are asleep. A few are gathered in one corner, whispering around a lamp and a deck of cards that they're using to tell fortunes. Another is sitting naked and shivering as she stitches up a seam in what must be her only dress. I almost give her my horse blanket to cover herself, though that feels as if it may do less good than my intentions would merit.

On the third floor I find two girls wedged into the windowsill, looking out at the snowfall and giggling as they press their lips together. When they notice me in the doorway, one of them starts hissing in French I can't understand simply for all the extra air in her words. When I don't reply or react, she unpeels herself from her friend and starts coming for me. I bolt, stumbling over the end of a bed and dropping my blanket-cutlery bundle with a clatter that jolts half the room awake, and then there are more than a few girls who seem to want to skin me alive. I dash back into a hallway, down the rickety stairs, and smash headlong into the girl coming out of the washroom so hard that I nearly knock the lamp from her hand.

"Felicity."

It takes me a moment before I recognize her. "Johanna."

Without powder, pomade, or cosmetics, she looks a different person. Her skin is cratered with scars—I had forgotten she had measles when we were ten—and blotched with dry spots from the harsh winter air. Her hair is loose and falls to her waist, kinked from its plaits and lank with the sweat of a long journey.

We stare at each other through the darkness, the thin beam of Johanna's lamp bathing us in a rosy glow.

"What are you doing here?" she hisses.

There are footsteps on the stairs, the two kissing

girls likely leading their floor in revolution against me for waking them. Johanna's eyes flit over my shoulder, and I worry she might try to escape me before I've had a chance to explain, but instead she grabs me around the wrist and drags me into the washroom, bolting the door behind us. The lantern in her hand bobs like a drunkard.

I stumble into the washroom, the backs of my legs connecting painfully with the washbasin. Johanna stands with her back to the door, facing me. The washroom is hardly big enough for the two of us, and my shoes cling to the sticky floor. "How did you find me?" she demands, her voice still absurdly high even when hissed through a clenched jaw.

"Did you think it would be hard?" I retort.

"Yes, I thought it was quite a good flight."

"Oh, please. You tried to take your elephant of a dog on a diligence with you."

Her frown turns inward, disappointment in herself rather than me. "Yes, that wasn't as sneaky as I wanted. But I couldn't leave Max! You didn't bring him, did you?" she adds, her voice brightening for a moment before she remembers she's furious with me. "Wait, no, tell me why you're here."

"I'm here to warn you."

"Warn me? About what?"

I take a deep breath. "I have reason to believe that Dr. Platt's intentions with you are not noble."

I expected her to gasp, step back, and press a hand to her chest in the sort of theatrical shock ladies often indulge in. At the very least, a whispered *"No!"* Instead, she crosses her arms and gives me a withering stare. "Really? That's the revelatory information you came all this way to deliver?"

I nearly execute the step back and hand press I had been so ready to judge her for. "You knew?"

"Knew what? That he's a crook and an addict and a degenerate? Of course I did. He's laid out more often than he's sober, and all his business with my uncle is done on credit because he's spent a fortune on opium."

"I thought you were in love with him."

She laughs, a brittle sound like a step upon thin ice. "You think I'm so stupid that a strange man shows up at my door asking for my hand and I just swoon and say yes?" I don't say anything, which only confirms that I do think her shallow enough to fall so hard and so fast for the first man she met who could fill a pair of breeches.

"So why were you going to marry him?" I ask.

"Because I didn't have a choice," she replies, sinking down so that she's sitting on the edge of the tub, then immediately standing again and wiping something off her nightdress. "My uncle was forcing me, and I didn't know how to escape him. I was scared."

"So you ran away to honeymoon on your own?"

"No, I came to Zurich because that letter your maid

stole—it's from the cabinet of curiosities my mother was working for when she died, and they have all her effects."

"Effects?" I repeat.

"Everything she had with her," Johanna explains. "The idiot curator will only give them to a male member of my family. When you told me your maid or friend or benefactress or whatever she was had tried to snatch the letter, it was enough of a push to finally do the thing I had been afraid to and come here myself, to get them before she could."

"You think Sim's after your mother's effects?" I ask. I had been so focused on Platt, trying to use Johanna's story to fill in the gaps I'd overheard in his, that I'd forgotten Sim.

"Why else would she care about that letter? I think it likely she convinced you to bring her to my home because she assumed we had already collected them and hoped to steal them, but then learned from that letter they're here in Zurich, at the Kunstkammer Staub."

"I think Platt's after them too," I say. "I overheard him talking about his voyage, and he said something about the archive and a cabinet. Did he ever mention that to you?"

She shakes her head, forehead creasing. "No, never. He asked about my mother and father when we first met, but I asked about his. Just getting-to-know-you."

"What work was your mother doing that's so valuable

to both him and Sim?" I can't come up with something that would wed their two worlds.

"I don't entirely know," Johanna replies. "She was working as an artist assistant to a naturalist on an expedition to the Barbary Coast. One of many journeys."

"I didn't know that."

"My father said he'd send me to a plantation in Barbados if I told anyone. He was so embarrassed by her. To have a wife literally run from your home in the middle of the night to sail with unspeakables?" She runs her fingers through the ends of her hair, pulling at the knots. "But she wrote to me on all her voyages. Sent me such strange things."

"All your stories," I say, realization dawning suddenly upon me. She looks up. "When we were children, you always had such great adventures we would pretend to go on. Those were from her letters."

"You remember that?"

"Of course I remember that! Those were . . ." The lamplight jumps against the wall, making skeletons of our shadows. "Those were the best days."

"They were, weren't they?" Her nose wrinkles up into a sly smile. "Dr. Brilliant."

I roll my eyes. "Ha, ha. I was only six. I had not yet peaked creatively."

"No, it's sweet." She laughs. "Everyone should give themselves an aspirational fake name."

"Well, what about you, famous naturalist—" Were my revelation any more sudden, it would have knocked me flat. I actually have to reach back and steady myself against the basin, I go so lightheaded.

Johanna, still oblivious, continues with that goading smile that wrinkles her nose. "Go on, do you remember?"

"Sybille Glass," I say, and I hear it in my head in Platt's voice. "Was that your mother's name?"

She nods with a wistful sigh. "I wanted to be just like—"

"Johanna, I overheard Platt just now," I say, "talking to some English bloke about Sybille Glass and collecting her work."

She almost drops the lamp. "Platt is in Zurich? You brought him here?"

"No, he brought me," I explain. "The cabinet will only surrender her things to a male member of your family, yes? Do you think that's why he wanted to marry you—so he'd have legal claim to whatever it is she was working on?"

Johanna sucks in her cheeks hard, mouth puckering. Then she lets go a breath laced with "Son of a bitch."

It is not a situation for laughing, but I do anyway—in her lilting soprano it's like hearing a curse in a homily. "He can't get them, so long as you aren't wed."

"Doesn't mean he won't try." She presses a fist against

her chin, thumb tapping in rhythm to her thoughts. "I'm going to go to the *Kunstkammer* tomorrow to see if they'll give me my mother's effects."

"No, you have to get out of here before Platt can force a ring upon you," I say. "The effects are legally yours, so long as you don't marry him—he has no claim. Come back to England with me. We can figure things out there—about him and Sim, if you think she's after them too."

"Are you encouraging me to run from a fight?" she says, and it almost sounds like a challenge. It's too dark to properly tell what kind of smile is flirting with her lips. "I thought you were the brave one out of the pair of us."

"What? No—no fighting," I say, then add, "And you were the intrepid explorer in our games, remember? I was the levelheaded tagalong."

"Yes, because make-believe is most fun if you can pretend to be something you're not. It took me until the night before my wedding to leave because I've been so afraid to be alone." She scrapes a hand through her hair, pushing it back from her face. "Maybe I shouldn't have run. Maybe there was another way, or I should have asked for help or not acted so spontaneously. But I'm here, and I am determined, and I am going to the museum tomorrow and—"

"You don't have to defend yourself," I say quickly. "Not to me."

"Oh. Good. Well, I'm possibly still making defenses in my own head." She smooths out her nightdress between her fingers, then looks up at me. "Do you need money?"

"Money?" I repeat.

"To get back to England. I don't have much, and I can't say I feel particularly obligated to give you a comfortable way home if I'm paying."

Home. I have nowhere to go. No Platt, no Sim, no family. No lifelines. I cut my ties and am drifting alone, a lifeboat in a windless surf.

"Could I come with you?" I ask. Johanna looks up sharply, and I add, "I already paid for a night, and I can't go back to Platt, so I might as well stay here. And I'm not . . . I mean there's no hurry . . ." I peter into a shrug and a toe scuffed against the floor. Or, rather, an attempt at a scuffed toe, for the floor is so sticky that it's more of a squelch. I don't dare look at her for fear she'll say no, so before she can, I take my pieces off the board. "Sorry, never mind. You probably don't want a thing to do with me. I mean, if you want me to come, I thought maybe I could. But you probably don't, so I'll leave first thing."

"Are you having a conversation with yourself?"

"No. I'm conversing with you."

"Then give me a chance to answer, will you? You can come. If you'd like. Though I can't imagine Dr. Platt will look favorably upon any of his future protégés conspiring against him."

236

If I join Johanna, I will give up on any chance of working for Dr. Platt. Even after overhearing his conversation back at the house and knowing he'd use me ill, it is such a large thing to let go of. Staying with Johanna means I'm betting on nothing.

Except her. And her mother. And myself.

"Well," I reply, "good thing I'd rather not be any man's protégé."

12

The *Kunstkammer* is located on the Limmatquai, its back sloping into the river. The water froths fast and dark in the miserable weather. The sky is gray, and it snows with intermittent strength as we make the trek across the city, and when Johanna and I arrive at the collection, we are both soaked through our cloaks, mine borrowed from Johanna so I don't damage our already shaky credibility with dodgy outerwear. A layer of snow-flakes dust our shoulders like sugar atop a bun. Johanna made a valiant attempt to arrange her hair before we left that morning, and at her insistence I made a val-iant attempt to help her, though was dismissed from my responsibilities when I stabbed her in the back of the head with a pin so hard it drew blood. In her flight from her father's home, though she couldn't bring her dog, she did bring a trunk's worth of extravagant dresses, and a pink skirt hemmed with mint-colored ruffles peers out from under her cloak. In my plain Brunswick, I'm much more likely of the pair of us to be taken seriously by the men who dart behind the exhibits of bugs and stuffed animals here.

"I wish I had Max," Johanna says as we cross the entryway of the cabinet to the ticket desk, eyeing the stuffed form of some kind of devilish-looking wild cat rearing over us from a pedestal in the center.

"I don't think he'd win against that," I say with a nod up at the cat.

"You've never seen him really go after a slipper," she replies.

We step up behind a woman paying for admission for herself and a tiny boy with beautiful blond curls that have somehow thwarted the snow and remained perfectly ruffled. Johanna takes a long, tight breath, one hand pressed against her stomach. "I just always feel better with my dog."

"Don't be nervous," I say. "You've got right on your side."

"When has that ever mattered?" she murmurs.

The woman and the blond boy move away from the desk, and Johanna and I step up to the attendant. "Good morning," Johanna chirps, and I immediately cringe at how high her voice is, how pitchy and giggly she sounds, and how silly that pink dress looks. "I was hoping I might speak to the curator, Herr Wagner."

The clerk, who had been prepared only to take our money and write the date upon our admission tickets, looks up very slowly, his brow creased. "Were you invited?"

"Herr Wagner and I have been corresponding." Johanna peels a letter out of the carpetbag she brought along—a bit optimistically hoping she'd be leaving the *Kunstkammer* with it full of her mother's final effects. The bag fared no better than we did in the snow, and the letter emerges as damp as the rest of her. The ink has become splotchy and streaked. When she leans forward to hand it to the attendant, a lump of snow slides off her hood and lands with a plop upon his desk.

The clerk frowns as he reads the letter, then holds it up for us to see, as though we hadn't had a chance before. It's pinched like a dead mouse between his thumb and forefinger. "This says the presence of your husband or father is required."

"My father's dead," Johanna replies.

If she hoped to elicit pity, her effort is entirely ineffective. "Where is your husband, then?"

"He has . . ." Johanna and I look at each other, and then she says, "Venereal pox," at the same time I say, "Business."

The clerk's eyebrows slope. "Then Herr Wagner will meet with your husband when he is available."

"But I'm here now," Johanna says, pressing herself against the desk so that her breasts make a seat of its surface. "It will only take a moment, I swear. If you could just tell him Johanna Hoffman—"

"Girls," the clerk says, and the word sets my teeth on edge, "Herr Wagner is a very busy man. He doesn't have time to meet under pretenses."

"It's not a pretense," Johanna says. "I have business with him."

"Then go fetch your husband, and it can be completed."

I step in. "Sir, I'm not sure you understand."

"Young lady," he starts, and that's as far as he gets before I snap back at him, "Really? First *girls*, and then *young lady*? That's how you feel it is appropriate to refer to us? Like children?"

"Your current comportment is excessively so," he replies.

"And your current comportment doesn't give me much reason to believe your brain is your best asset," I reply. "Will you please tell Herr Wagner that he has left the daughter of one of this century's greatest naturalists standing in his lobby dealing with a ticket monkey who doesn't recognize a legend when she drops snow upon his desk?"

I hope I might at least get him quaking with the threat of disrespecting a legacy. No matter how overdrawn that legacy may be. I would have thrown in Johanna's mother's name except that I don't think naming that naturalist to be a woman would help our case against this pile of moldy pudding formed into the shape of a man.

He blinks once, slowly, then says with spiteful deliberateness, "*Ladies*, I must ask you to leave. You are causing a scene."

I'm ready to spin on my heel and stomp out, well and truly making that scene we have been accused of, but Johanna says with shocking cheer, "No, thank you, sir. If we're not to be permitted to see Herr Wagner, we'd like to see the *Kunstkammer*." Then she smacks her coins upon the table and gives him that devastating smile of hers.

He stares very hard at the coins, as though he is hoping they are actually crackers or buttons or something that will give him a legitimate reason to refuse us. Finally, he places his palm overtop and slides them along the desk toward him, their edges making a hair-raising scrape against the wood grain that's far more of a scene than we were causing. Men are so dramatic. He hands us two admission tickets, then Johanna takes me by the arm and we stalk, dripping and indignant, into the gallery.

"Well, that went about as expected," she says at the same time I say, "What a disaster."

We cross into the first room of the exhibition, a collection of items from the South Seas. The walls are lined with glass-fronted cabinets, and there's a massive skeleton of some sort of long-necked bird articulated in the center of the room. We stop side by side in front of the first wall, where polished gemstones in iridescent turquoise and green are laid out upon dark velvet. I can feel Johanna's carpetbag knocking against my knees, heavy as a history book in its emptiness.

"That's what you were expecting to happen?" I ask her.

She shrugs, hefting her bag into the crook of her elbow. "I hoped it would go differently. I thought I might charm him."

"I think I might have ruined that."

"Yes, thoroughly." She glances sideways at me with no attempt to conceal her frustration. "Charm has never been a flower that blooms in your garden, has it?"

Charming is not a word I'd use—or ever want used—to describe me, but the way she says it prickles me. It's the sort of thing I feel entitled to say disparagingly about myself, but from someone else, it feels blunt and unkind. "Well, you're hard to take seriously in that dress," I retort, and then move on to the next case, to examine a set of poison-tipped arrows.

Johanna chases after me, her heels—zounds, she brought *heels* on her escape!—clacking on the tile. "What's wrong with this dress? It makes me feel pretty."

"It's very feminine," I say.

"Is there something ridiculous about being feminine?"

"To men there is."

I keep walking. She keeps following. I don't even stop at the next case, just barrel forward into the second gallery, hoping she'll grow weary of chasing me in those ridiculous shoes and relent. "But you're the one who said it to me, and you're not a man," she says, somehow still at my elbow. "Would you ever wear this dress?"

"That's not the point."

"Answer it anyway."

"Why does it matter?"

She steps in front of me, trapping me with my back against a cabinet of pinned butterflies, which is a rather metaphorical display to be cornered in front of. A few people are already staring. The woman who was in front of us in line has taken that beautiful blond boy by the hand and led him from the room at a quick trot. This is feeling far too close to the argument that cracked us apart back home. Me cornered and her demanding. Both of us lashing.

Johanna puts her hands on her hips and tips her chin at me. "You think this dress is ridiculous, and you are afraid of looking ridiculous."

"I didn't say that."

"Do you think it's ridiculous?"

"You're talking too loud."

"Tell me."

"Yes, fine, all right?" I snap. "I think it's a stupid dress, and I think if you keep dressing like that and speaking in that voice and smiling all the time like a fool, no one will ever take you seriously. You think you could present in front of the Royal Society dressed like that and anyone would listen? Men won't take women seriously unless we give them reason to, and that dress is not a reason to. It makes us all look pathetic. Can we please go now?"

She stares me down for a moment, then says, her voice no longer loud but prickled as a rosebush, "Now I remember."

"Remember what?"

"Ever since you showed up, I've been thinking, Felicity is so funny and kind and clever, why did I ever stop being her friend? But thank you. I just remembered." Her head tips to the side, regarding me. I want to look away. "It's because when I stopped running around with my petticoats hiked up to my waist and started enjoying the social scene and caring about what I wore, you never stopped taking shots at me for it."

"I never took shots," I protest. "It was you who decided you couldn't bear to be seen with me because I was so embarrassingly unfeminine. *You* abandoned me. You tossed me out for prettier friends."

"Felicity, I never abandoned you. I made a choice to remove myself from our relationship because you thought that me liking pearls and pomade meant you were superior to me."

"I did not."

"Yes you did! Every time you rolled your eyes and every little smart remark you made about how silly it was for girls to care about their looks. You refused to let me— or anyone!—like books *and* silks. Outdoors *and* cosmetics. You stopped taking me seriously when I stopped being the kind of woman you thought I had to be to be considered intelligent and strong. All those things you say make men take women less seriously—I don't think it's men; it's you. You're not better than any other woman because you like philosophy better than parties and don't give a fig about the company of gentlemen, or because you wear boots instead of heels and don't set your hair in curls."

I'm not sure what it is that I'm feeling. Something like anger, but with far more shame attached. Anger as a means of defense, anger I know is completely misplaced. But I still snap at her, "Don't tell me how I feel."

"I'm not telling you how you feel, I'm telling you how you make me feel. I felt so silly for so long because of you. But I like dressing this way." She spreads her arms. "I like curling my hair and twirling in skirts with ruffles, and I like how Max looks with that big pink bow on. And that doesn't mean I'm not still smart and capable and strong."

I am combing back through my memories, those last few weeks before Johanna and I ruptured, trying to remember what I had forgotten. But I hadn't forgotten a thing. I had just always cast myself in the role of the misunderstood and sympathetic heroine, Johanna the traitor who had buried a knife in my side and abandoned me for girlier pastures. But Johanna and I had parted ways because of me, and because I thought survival meant stepping on others.

I want to apologize. I want to explain that I had felt then like I was losing the only person who knew me and still liked me, had tried to keep her unchanged because while all the other girls were growing out of their childhood fancies, mine were starting to root in my soul, leaving me strange and unruly, but Johanna made me feel natural. I want to tell her I've spent my whole life learning to be my own everything because I had parents who forgot me, a brother who never lifted his face from his drink, a parade of maids and governesses who never tried to understand me. I have spent so long building up my fortress and learning to tend it alone, because if I didn't feel I needed anyone, then I wouldn't miss them if they weren't there. I couldn't be neglected if I was everything to myself. But now, those fortifications suddenly feel like prison walls, high and barbed and impossible to cross.

Johanna starts to turn away from me, but then lets out a small gasp and instead grabs my hand. I panic, thinking that she has spotted Platt or Sim or some other threat to our well-being that managed to sneak up on us while we were reliving our childhood traumas, but she's staring at the framed pages hanging from the upper gallery. "Those drawings."

"What about them?"

"They're my mother's."

They're so high above us, it's hard to see them, but Johanna rushes up as close as one can get, and when I join her, we stand below, our necks craned. "This must have been the work she was doing for the *Kunstkammer* when she died," Johanna says.

"Come on." I take her hand, drag her over to the tight stairway that leads to the bookshelves in the upper galleries, and step over the rope keeping the public off them, and we squash ourselves upward. These stairs were clearly designed for men, for the tight spiral isn't compatible with so many petticoats. Johanna has to turn sideways so that her wide hips will fit.

We dart along the gallery until we are above the paintings, then together grab the wire and haul the first one up so we can see it better. There's a generous layer of dust along the top, and it sticks like frosting to my fingers. The drawings are of dolphins and sea birds, though they look more like hasty sketches, not finished prints to be delivered to a patron. The artistic style and the handwritten notations remind me of the portfolio I saw Sim examining in the Hoffman library.

"Look here." I direct Johanna's eye to the plaque at the bottom of the frame—

Aquatic Life of the Barbary Coast
Dr. A. Platt
HMS *Fastidious*
17—

"That's a lie!" Johanna cries, her voice so loud and in my ear that I almost lose my grip on the frame. "These are my mother's; I know it! I've looked at her art my whole life. That's her writing, and her sketching style. The Barbary Coast was her last voyage. That's the same ship and the same year she died."

"Here." I hand her the weight of the frame, and while she searches it for any sign of her mother's name, I fish my list of reasons to be admitted to medical school out of my pocket, the one Alexander Platt had scribbled his opinion all over. I hold it up to the sketches for comparison. "It's not his writing."

"Of course it's not, it's my mother's!" she replies. "Why is his name on these? What does he have to do with any of this?"

"Did Dr. Platt know your mother?" I ask.

"It certainly never came up if he did. I know he's been to the Barbaries, but he never mentioned it was on the same expedition as her. Which seems like something you would tell your fiancée." We look back at the drawing together. At the top of the frame, two sea birds chase each other, one with its wings tucked and the other spread, a few delicate bones outlined beneath the feathers. "Aren't they gorgeous?" Johanna says, the blade that had been in her voice a moment ago suddenly blunting.

"The drawings?" I had thought they were rather hasty, like the map of the human body I had done on my boardinghouse floor in Edinburgh. Not something I'd want hung in a gallery and presented as my best work.

"No, the animals. Look, they're sandpipers. *Tringa ochropus*. They nest in marshes and pick food out of the swamp. And each variety has a different bill that allows them to dig in the mud to varying depths, so they don't compete for nutrients. They all live together in harmony." Johanna reaches out and presses a finger to the tip of the bird's wing, leaving a smudge on the glass. "And the dolphins. I thought I saw dolphins when I crossed the Channel after my father died. It was most likely just very pointy seaweed, but I'd just gotten a letter from my mother about dolphins, right before she decided not to come home for me." Her finger wanders down the sketch, stopping just below the bottom corner. "What's that?" She pokes one of the drawings, and I have to tilt the frame so I can see past the glare.

"I don't know." It's a serpentine shape, long and curled, with a barbed tail and frills along its belly. "It looks like a snake."

"Aquatic life." She taps the plate at the bottom of the frame.

"Birds aren't aquatic."

"Yes, but there are most certainly no snakes in the ocean. And look, it has little flippers." She taps a nail against the glass, at the snake's feathered stomach, then leans forward, like pressing her nose to it might give her a better idea. "What *is* this? It doesn't look like a snake; it looks like a dragon."

"That's—" My attention snags on something in the same corner, just as, from below us, someone bellows, "Ladies!"

Johanna and I both jump. Below is the ticket clerk, his hands cupped around his mouth as he shouts, as though we are a great distance away from him. There's a second man standing next to him, an anxious-looking fellow with a very shiny forehead. When he tips his head back to see us, his wig nearly slides straight off.

"You are not permitted to be up there," the clerk calls, his hands still cupped around his mouth.

"Or touching the collection," the man beside him says.

"Or touching the collection!" the clerk hollers, though we both heard the first time. "Come down at once!"

"Credit my mother for her art and I will!" Johanna hollers back.

"That work was commissioned by the collection and is our property," the second fellow shouts, mopping his shining brow with his sleeve. "Come down now or we will call for the police!"

Johanna looks like she's going to rip the painting off the wall and claim it, so I preemptively wrestle it from her, then let it fall back into place, bouncing on its wires. Both the clerk and his sweating companion gasp. As it falls, I get one quick glance of the sketch beneath the finned serpent, no bigger than my thumbnail: a crown hovering above a thin blade.

The crown and cleaver.

"This is your final warning!" the clerk calls.

I drag Johanna down the stairs and together we stalk past the clerk and the curator, who I suspect is the Herr Wagner we were not permitted an audience with. Making our plea for Sybille's things now that we have broken every rule of the *Kunstkammer* seems futile, particularly when Johanna says "Shame!" very loudly in both their faces as we pass. The clerk follows us all the way across the lobby to make certain we leave, while the curator retreats through a door marked *No Admittance* behind the ticket desk. He opens it with such a dramatic flourish that I am offered one brief but impactful glance behind, into a set of rooms lined with glass cabinets. Surely this place must have bowels to hold its treasures not on display to the public, but I'm offered hardly a glimpse of them before the door is shut hard in our faces.

Outside, the snow has swollen into a blizzard. I pull my scarf up over my face—it reeks after days of me pushing my wet breath into it to keep my mouth warm.

Johanna is vibrating with anger. I swear the snow steams and melts when it strikes her skin. "How dare they?"

"Johanna."

"They deny me what's rightfully mine."

"Johanna."

"They refused to acknowledge her work."

"Johanna—"

"They hang her renderings without any credit—"

"Johanna!" I step closer to her—the initial idea was to get her attention, but it's so much warmer huddled together that I press myself into her side. The fur lining the hood of her cloak brushes my cheek. "Your mother and Platt must have been on the same voyage, and he must know about whatever she was working on when she died. If he got his name on those drawings, perhaps he's trying to take credit for whatever it is she was researching. We need to make sure you get what she left behind, not him."

"What's your plan to make that happen, exactly?" She pulls her face down into her cloak, like a tortoise drawing into its shell. "They won't give me her things."

Sybille Glass and Dr. Platt are tied up together in this work somehow, and if we want to unravel it rather than just batting it around like cats with a ball of yarn, we need Sybille's last effects. "If they won't surrender them, then we'll steal them."

Johanna looks up at me. "What?"

"We steal them," I say. "If we don't, Platt will. Or he'll convince Herr Wagner you're married or find some other way to claim them. We've got to get them before he does."

Johanna regards me, and I can't tell if she thinks me reckless or inspired until she says, "Wasn't Dr. Brilliant the one who was always telling Miss Glass to quell her reckless spirit lest she get herself killed?"

"Well, Dr. Brilliant isn't here," I reply, "just you and me. And I say if there were ever a time for recklessness, it's now."

She presses her fingers to her lips, surveying me as a slow smile spreads across her face. "I like Dr. Montague quite a lot better than Dr. Brilliant." When I laugh, she adds, "I mean it. And it was a good list."

"Oh." I touch my pocket, where my medical school admission plea is again tucked. I hadn't realized she had read it while I had been comparing Platt's handwriting. "Thank you. It has been entirely ineffective thus far. Dr. Montague remains in the realm of fantasy with Dr. Brilliant."

"Give it time," she replies. "It won't be a story forever."

13

The cabinet is open to the public two afternoons a week, and while we are prepared for theft, I'm not certain we're equipped for a full-scale dead-of-night bolted-doors-and-barred-windows break-in, so we have a single opportunity to get inside the following day before having to wait another six for the next. We decide that I will do the actually thievery, and Johanna will cause a distracting ruckus, as she has, in her words, a figure that is not made for sneaking. "Were I required to ascend one of those tight stairways again, but this time in a hurry," she said, "I might be wedged." Which we both agreed would not be particularly subtle.

I make my entrance first—thank God it's a different clerk minding the desk than the one Johanna and I made a scene with the day before. I linger near the cloakroom, making a long affair of brushing the snow off my shoulders and also taking an assessment of the lobby. The door at the back of the room didn't seem locked yes-. terday when the curator made his dramatic exit. Or if it was, he had left it unlatched when he had come out to shout at us. Which I'm hoping will happen again.

A few minutes after my arrival, the doors open, and in comes Johanna. If she had her way, she would have roped a feral dog from the streets, shined it up, and brought it with her on a lead to make a real meal of her distraction. Alas, feral dogs are reluctant to be roped anywhere, unless there's some sort of steak involved, and we're trying to save the limited coinage we have left. But even without the dog, her entrance is grand— her confidence blasts through the room like a wildfire, hot and bright and beautiful, but also the sort you want to watch from a distance. She does not look toward me but rather tosses her scarf showily over her shoulder and makes her way to the desk. The ruffles of yet another ridiculous dress whisper against the floor behind her.

Not ridiculous, I correct myself. Softness can be an armor, even if it isn't *my* armor.

Johanna buys her ticket, trading a few sweet remarks with the clerk, who is as red as a beet by the time she floats off into the gallery, looking doe-eyed and help-less, a beautiful girl who knows it but pretends she is unaware. I count at least three men whose heads turn as she passes, and as she disappears from my sight, I feel a surge of confidence in our plan. These boys will be falling over themselves to come to her aid.

She's been out of sight for a few minutes when there's an enormous crash from one of the galleries—much larger than I expected. She must have gone for the articulated bird. Behind the desk, the clerk stands up, craning his neck like he might magically be able to see through the wall to the source of the noise and determine whether he needs to leave his post to attend to it. Then Johanna's histrionics start—crying out and apologizing and shrieking. The clerk bolts from behind his desk and takes off at a run toward the commotion. Several other men follow, and those who don't try to act like they all just happen to be making their way over to the ruckus at that exact moment.

The door at the back of the room bangs open, the same harried-looking curator from the day before poking his head out. Had he not appeared, I was ready to rush up to his door and make a zealous cry about a commotion in the gallery he needed to see to straightaway. He follows the noise, which has turned into wailing, then a gasp from the onlookers, which I imagine means that Johanna has fainted. I make a path across the lobby, like I too am chasing the excitement, then divert at the last second, catch the door the curator came through, and duck inside the offices.

I don't know what trove I was expecting, but the room

is disappointingly bare. The glass cases that reflected the light the day previous are full of books—which would ordinarily thrill me, but now is not the time. There are some skeleton bits sitting upon a table beside a magnifying glass as if they were abandoned midexamination, a filing cabinet, and a desk that looks to be merely somewhere to set paperwork. In one corner of the room a spiral staircase leads up to a second-floor gallery with smoking chairs and large windows overlooking Zurich, but the steps go down as well, under the building. I dart over, heft up a handful of my skirts, and start the descent.

The lower level is unfathomably dark, windowless, and thick with the smell of dust and old paper. Through the pale light leaking down from the stairwell, I can make out the long rows of shelves filled with a seemingly random assortment of skeletons and stuffed animals and feathers and eggshells and beaks and stones and sand samples in glass jars and glistening emerald beetles the size of my hand stuck through with pins and pressed between glass slides. Dried palm leaves fan out from beneath a stack of golden masks. A clock lying upon its side ticks away merrily, though it has no numbers and its hands are moving backward. The shelves seem to stretch infinitely before me and on either side, though I know it's just a trick of the light. Or, rather, lack of.

I start to make my way toward the shelves, though

I barely get far enough to step out from the direct light off the stairs before my body makes it known to me that it is not keen on this venture. My pulse elevates. Chest tightens. The room feels crowded with the darkness and so many strange things, like mourners at a funeral all whispering and morose, strangers to each other but here for a common purpose.

You are Felicity Montague, I tell myself, and the darkness, and my heartbeat, in an attempt to rein it in. *You have climbed through catacombs darker than this, you escaped from a second-story window with only your bedsheets, and you should not be frightened of the darkness, but instead be sure that the most frightening thing in it is you.*

I pick two shelves at random to walk between, making a slow study of some kind of preserved organs in milky liquid, a green snake stuffed and coiled up beneath a glass bell, its fangs in a jar beside it, a skull stuck through with a spearhead the size of my forearm, trying to discern any system for organization. I'm going to live out the rest of my life down here if I search each of these shelves for Sybille Glass's last possessions without direction or truly knowing what it is I'm looking for. Maybe it *is* the snake.

I double back to where I was and examine the shelves again, hoping for some clue as to where I should be looking. There are large wooden letters that I missed the first time, nailed to the end of each aisle. The shelves nearest the stairs are labeled *Aa–Ah*, the second set *Ah–As*.

No woman on earth has been so delighted by alphabetization as I am in this moment.

I look down into the darkness—the G's for Glass feel a long way away, though I remind myself I'm fortunate that Sybille's surname didn't begin with a zed.

It's more and more difficult to read the alphabetical designations the farther I get from the stairs and the light. I have to reach up several times and trace the letters with my fingers to make certain I haven't gone too far. When I find the G's, I turn down the aisle and nearly smack face-first into an enormous ape, stuffed so that its body is reared back, arms stretched above its head, like it's ready to claw at my eyes. I stumble backward out of the aisle, barely managing to choke back a scream. The tag attached to the foot reads *Gibbon (Family Hylobatidae), from the island of Java, 1719, Capt. W. H. Pfeiffer.*

"You furry little bastard," I hiss at the gibbon. "Whoever placed you there is very cruel." The gibbon says nothing in return—thank God, or else I might have sincerely shat myself.

And then, down the aisle, something moves.

Fear, according to Descartes, is one of the passions that originates where the body attaches to the soul. Having almost one hundred years and quite a lot more books at my disposal than Descartes, I'm not certain I believe this, for all my symptoms in that moment are purely physical. I go light-headed. My muscles seize, then begin to tremble. Sweat breaks out beneath my arms. And it's only the clinical analysis of these effects that keeps them from knocking me over entirely.

There's someone here, creeping around in the dark with me. Someone who must have been here all along. I don't know whether to run or press forward, betting on the hope that the movement was a draft or a precarious arrangement collapsing. Perhaps it's Platt, just as stuck as we are in his attempts to claim Sybille Glass's effects and resorting to the same methods. I shrink backward, and my elbow knocks a flower lying upon the shelf, disrupting it. It doesn't fall like a flower. It drops hard and shatters.

There's a very human gasp. Through the darkness, I can make out a silhouette, framed by the motes of dust. The figure raises its head, then begins toward me, stride picking up from a quick walk into a run.

I turn and run too, cursing my short Montague legs that give me no speed or advantage over the panther chasing me. I feel someone snatch at me, and I turn, flailing with my fingers tensed into claws and trying to find eyes or the soft meat at the throat or some part of the body that's mostly thin tissue I can dig my nails into. But before I can, I'm grabbed around the waist and tackled into the gibbon, all three of us—me, my attacker, and the gibbon—crashing to the ground. My neck goes stiff, an instinct to protect my head from striking the floorboards, and I feel the wrench as I land.

My attacker is overtop of me, straddling me, and I can feel the tight material of a skirt pulled around my waist. She grabs my arms before I can move, pinning my hands to the ground at my side, then leans in close enough that I can see her face.

It's Sim.

She looks as startled to see me as I am to see her. Her grip on my arms loosens, and had I not been so dazed by the fall, I might have had the foresight to pull free. But I can hardly breathe, let alone shimmy out. Between gasps, I manage to choke out a single word—her name. "Sim." It does not come out as I intend it to, which is like a squirt of citrus into the eye. Instead, it's a small, wretched mewl.

She's far less winded than I am, which is embarrassing, for it was she who did the actual sprint and tackle—all I had to do was fall. "What are you doing here?" she hisses at me.

It's not a question I feel the need to answer, so I retort with "Let me go!" It comes out a bit stronger than my previous statement. Not so much a kitten as an adolescent cat.

Sim lets my arms go, giving them a bit more of a shove into the ground than is really necessary. "Get out of here, Felicity. This hasn't anything to do with you."

"And those things aren't yours; they're Johanna's."

"What things?"

"Sybille Glass's things!" I say, louder than is advisable, for Sim clamps a hand over my mouth.

"Keep your voice down!"

I bite her thumb, and she lets go with a curse. "That's what you're here for, isn't it?" I demand. "You thought Sybille Glass's work was at the Hoffmans' house. That's what you were hoping to find there."

Her jaw sets. "It belongs to my family. In the wrong hands—"

"Your hands are the wrong hands! Get off of me."

"I don't want to hurt you—"

"Then don't!"

"Then stay out of my way." She pushes herself up and starts back down the aisle, but I grab her around the ankle. She trips, crashing to the ground and taking out a shelf of ceramics with her. I scramble to my feet again, climbing over her with a high step so she can't pull the same trick on me before darting down the aisle. Sim grasps a handful of my skirt, both pulling me backward and dragging herself up with me as counterweight. One hand is clawing at her boot, and I remember the marlinespike. I kick her hard in the shin and she yelps, stumbling sideways into a shelf. A pod of seeds bursts into the air like a disrupted beehive, and we are enveloped in a strange, chalky dust that starts us both coughing. My eyes burn, and I double over, hands pressed to my face and trying not to rub them, though the temptation is strong. Sim grabs my arm as I stumble blindly down the aisle, and I throw an elbow, hoping to hit her in the face, but she ducks, and I slam instead into a case of delicate spiral shells that crumble under me. We are single-handedly wiping out a slew of the world's natural wonders.

Sim twists my arm behind my back, but I step hard on her foot in retaliation. She must barely feel it, for she's got monstrous clomping boots on, but it's enough that when she tries to move it throws her off balance. I snag one of the tags from the shelf before me and take a wild look, trying to gauge where we are. Thank god the case is weighted down with actual rocks, or I would have ripped it straight off the shelf. *Girasol.* We're getting close.

Sim grabs me by the end of my plait and jerks me backward hard enough that I shriek for the first time. "Has anyone told you," she hisses, her breath damp and warm against my neck, "that you are tenacious?"

"Thank you," I reply.

"It wasn't a compliment."

"Anything can be a compliment if you take it as one."

I grope around on the shelf behind me for an adobe pot and aim to crack it over her head, but she flings an arm up and it breaks over her elbow instead. Shining black powder that smells volcanic rains down between us. Sim doubles backward, a stream of dark blood dripping down her arm, and I wrench myself away from her and start fumbling for tags. On the lowest shelf, there's a hard leather case for documents with a shoulder strap, as well as a canvas sack splattered with a crust of chalky mud. The name stitched into the seam is *S. Glass.*

I grab the leather case and throw it over my shoulder, then snatch up the canvas sack. The drawstring isn't pulled as tightly as I thought, and half the contents spill onto the floor. There's the tinkle of delicate glass breaking, and I scramble to scoop it all back into the sack. I'm groping through the darkness, my fingers brushing something damp, just as, from behind, Sim jumps on top of me. I think she'll try to wrestle the bag from me, but instead she clamps a hand over my mouth. "Shut it," she whispers. Her voice has suddenly taken on a different tone than before—more wariness than fight. I try to throw her off, but she snaps, "Felicity, stop, someone's coming!"

I go still. Sim raises her head, peering down the aisle into the darkness we came from. I can't hear anything for what feels like long enough that I'm ready to dismiss her warning as a distraction in hopes I'd lower my guard, but then a light starts to play along the ceiling.

Then a man's voice calls out, "Is someone there?"

Sim starts to scramble down the aisle on her hands

and knees, in the opposite direction from the voice. And the stairs. I scramble after her, praying she has another way out. There are footsteps at the end of the aisle, and the lamp grows closer. "Who's there?"

Sim breaks into a run and I follow suit, thick dust and shards of pottery crunching beneath our boots. The case knocks against my shoulder blades.

I chase Sim down the aisle and to a cellar door in the back corner of the basement. She yanks a large, sturdy-looking vase over so she can stand tall enough to unbolt the doors and fling them open. Sim hoists herself up and onto the snowy lawn, then looks back at me. I think for a moment she's going to slam the doors shut in my face and leave me to the mercy of the curator, but she throws down a hand to help me up after her. It seems a moment of compassion before I realize I have Sybille Glass's things and it's likely that she's saving more than me.

She's bad at the hoisting—her hands are slick, and my knee bangs painfully into the frame when her grip slips. She ends up dragging me through the snow while I kick at the air, struggling for purchase. I get a lump of ice down my dress and leave a sleigh track across the lawn with my face. Sim kicks the cellar door shut as I clamber to my feet, spitting out mouthfuls of mud, and we take off at a run away from the cabinet, our heels kicking up sprays of wet snow.

Johanna is at our appointed meeting spot—a statue two squares over of a man on horseback who no doubt did something heroic. She's sitting on the step up to the plinth, just beneath the horse's rearing hoof, but stands when she sees us sprinting toward her. Her shoes have cut tiny, perfect prints in the snow, like the tracks of a mouse, that Sim and I stamp out as we approach.

Johanna shrieks when she spots my companion and points an accusatory finger. "You!"

Sim doesn't answer—she's doubled over, gasping for air.

"Did you lead her here as well?" Johanna demands of me, then before I can answer says, "All my tormentors in one convenient place!" She pivots back to Sim. "You sneak into my home to steal from me and now dare to follow me here to see your job finished. Well, consider yourself soundly foiled yet again. I will see you arrested; I will see you prosecuted; I will drag you back to Bavaria by the ear and take you to court there if I must." Now back to me. At least her speechifying is giving us a chance to catch our breaths. "Did you find them?"

I hold up the case for Johanna's inspection. I expect she'll be pleased, but instead she yips, "You're bleeding!"

I look down—I thought the dampness was coming from the snow I had been yanked through, but my arms and the front of my cloak are streaked with blood. "Am I?" I ask in alarm. "I don't think so."

"You're not," Sim says, and then she collapses.

Onto me. She staggers sideways and collapses *onto me*, and while I can't truly blame her for her lack of aim, it is not a particularly comfortable thing to be fallen upon. We both tumble back into the street. My cloak is strangling me, and my skirt is rucked up to my knees so I'm sitting in just my stockings in the snow. The scarf around Sim's head is coming undone, wet enough that it's plastered to her forehead.

Instinct takes over, and I start stripping back her clothes, trying to find where the blood is coming from. It doesn't take long—one of her arms is slashed to ribbons from palm to elbow. I cracked a pot over her arm, but the cuts are studded with small shards of amber-tinted glass, the largest the length of my thumb. I remember something glass shattering from Sybille's bag when I pulled it free. Sim must have slid across it, the thick wool of her skirts and petticoats sparing her knees but the thin linen shirt no match.

The glass will need to be removed. The cuts stitched. But not now, and not here, in the middle of a muddy street. Right now, the bleeding must be contained. I wrench off my scarf and wrap it around her arm. As I tug the cloth tight, I notice again the ink upon the inside of her arm; the cuts stopped just short of cleaving the dagger in two.

I look around for Johanna, only to find that she's

bolted from our statue and is waving her arms to catch the attention of a policeman passing by. *"Hallo! Polizist! Hilf mir bitte!* I am a maiden and I am in distress! Pay me attention."

"Stop it," I snap at her.

"Stop it?" She whirls on Sim and me. "That girl has been apprehended as a robber and should be arrested."

"Yes, but I was also robbing," I say, pulling the make-shift bandage tight around Sim's arm. "If Sim's arrested, I should be too."

"But you are reclaiming stolen property that is right-fully mine," Johanna argues. "She's just stealing it."

"She's right here," Sim mumbles, pulling out of my grip. She tucks her injured arm to her stomach, and when she shifts, I can see the blood has already soaked through my scarf and spotted the front of her bodice. She heaves herself to her feet, then immediately tips over again and sits down hard beside me.

"I won't leave her," I tell Johanna. "She's hurt and she needs help, and I can help her." My whole body is aching from our tussle in the archive, so I'm not feeling any particular goodwill toward Sim either, but leaving her bloody and freezing in the snow goes against every-thing I believe. Everything I am and want to be. Johanna must know this, but she still glares at me until a wicked breeze throws handfuls of needled flakes from the snowy lawn in our faces. We both flinch. I pull my collar up over my chin, trying to protect my skin laid bare by the absence of my scarf. "We need to get out of here."

"Back to the boardinghouse," Johanna says.

"I can take care of myself," Sim mumbles to me, trying to pull herself up again.

"I'm not letting you stagger off into the city with a bleeding arm," I tell her. "Where are you staying?"

"Not far from here," she replies. I can see the hard lines of her jaw jutting out as she clenches her teeth against the pain.

"Let us walk you," I say. "I'll see to your arm, and then we can work out what to do next." Johanna starts to make a protest, but I cut her off. "Frau Engel wouldn't allow a girl with a hangnail in, she's so petrified of a sickness spreading. You can leave if you'd like, but I won't."

Johanna lets out a huff, and it frosts white against the frigid air. "Fine," she says, then snatches up the canvas sack from where I abandoned it on the pavement. "But I'm carrying my mother's things."

Sim directs us back into the old town, where the bright colors of the shopfronts are muted by the storm. The snow is beginning to stick, gathering in piles on banisters and windowsills and making the road treacherous and slick. We try our best to walk as close to the shops as possible, so that the oriel windows jutting out over the boulevard shelter us. I keep a hand on Sim—her stride is growing less steady with every step. I consider telling her we need to stop somewhere closer than this mystery location we're delivering her to and let me do something about the blood, but I can't imagine any of the pubs we pass would be keen on me performing surgery on their barroom floor.

The street Sim finally calls for a halt upon is so narrow that the three of us side by side take up the entirety of it. No carriage could have a prayer of squeezing down it unless they were willing to knock their lamps off. The shops look unadorned, their fronts missing the bright hues and alpine imagery of the main roads. Instead, they're simple and sand-colored. The shutters bang against the windows, testing their tethers in the wind.

"Here." Sim tips her head in the direction of a dark shopfront. I'm nearly carrying her at this point, and when Johanna holds the door open for us, a bell jangles. I look up at the hanging sign, swinging wildly in the wind, but I don't speak enough German to understand the words.

As soon as we have crossed the threshold, Johanna screams. I would have screamed too, had she not done it first and made me very much not want to look so silly and afraid. But even as a woman whose stomach rarely turns at a grisly sight, I feel myself go a bit light-headed. For a moment of weightless shock, Sim and I are holding each other up.

The room is full of human remains. Shelves of hands

stripped of their skin so that the braided muscles are visible, legs from the knees jutting out of a bucket, a row of delicate ears and the thin, curled husks of noses. A long curtain of hair hangs upon one wall, a slow variegation from a fine cornsilk to thick black. Several busts stare at us from the counter, eyes sightless and mouths dangling open, each in varying states of decay.

No, not decay, I realize as I force myself to look closer, though my brain is screaming that what I should really be looking out for is the violent ax-wielding man who is no doubt sneaking up to turn us into so much human confetti. The faces do not look decayed as much as unfinished, like this is the workbench of some heavenly being who paused in the midst of the creation of man to get a snack and a tea.

"What are they?" Johanna asks beside me, her fingers strangling my free arm.

"They're wax," Sim says. She staggers to the counter and rings a bell before slumping backward against it. In the gray light leaking in through the grimy windows, her skin looks slick and sweaty.

"Wax?" I take a careful step toward a hollowed-out torso and touch a cautious finger to the rib cage. It's sticky and firm, but I can feel the potential for give. It smells like honey, and when I pull away, I can see the whorls of my fingerprint left there.

A curtain behind the counter parts, and a woman

peers out. Her skin is darker than Sim's, and her long hair is wrapped in coils that are in turn wrapped around the top of her head. She has a leather apron thrown over her clothes, sleeves pushed up to her elbows though the workshop feels nearly as cold as the street to me. "Sim," she hisses in English. "You said you were gone."

"I was," Sim says, her voice drowsy.

"You say gone, and then you return with two more unfortunates in tow. This isn't a hotel!"

Johanna and I exchange a glance, and she mouths *unfortunates?*

"I haven't room for you all here," the woman says, bustling around from behind the counter and flapping a hand at us like we're stray cats wandered in from the street. "Herr Krausse will have words. Are these your father's bastards, too?"

"It's just me," Sim says. "They're going."

The woman turns to Sim, then reaches out and takes her arm. "What's wrong with you?"

"I'm fine," Sim says, but she doesn't pull away. I'm not sure she has the strength.

"You're clearly not," I say. "She's hurt. Here, let me look at it."

"Miss Hoffman has somewhere . . . she wants to be." Sim's breathing is getting labored, her grip on the counter less a steadying one and more a crutch.

The shopkeeper's face puckers. "Sim?"

"Sorry," Sim mumbles. "I . . . I can't feel my arm anymore."

"All right, that's it." I take Sim by the waist, hoisting her good arm around my shoulder, then turn to the shopkeeper. "Do you have somewhere—"

I don't even finish before the woman is pulling back the curtain behind the counter and ushering us forward. Johanna steps up to Sim's other side, hoisting her with me. Sim is small, but she's still dead weight, and neither Johanna nor I have had much occasion in our lives to heft more than an encyclopedia. Johanna has her mother's bag and the leather case slung over her back, and it gives me a good clock in the back of the head when we duck around the counter.

Behind is a workshop, full of more disconcerting wax figures, all in various states of assembly and some with clockwork pieces jutting from the hollow limbs. One corner is littered with broken plaster, another crowded with a bench with a lamp upon it that looks just vacated—the tools are balanced on the corner beside a head, half of the scalp carefully threaded with dark hair. Opposite the bench, there's a stove, with a pallet laid out beside it, and Johanna and I lay Sim upon it.

"Do you know what you're doing?" the woman asks as I unwind the scarf from Sim's arm for a better look.

"Yes," I say, with more confidence than I'm feeling. "Could you fetch me water, and a clean towel?" I fish into my pocket for my spectacles, give the lenses a quick rubdown upon the tail of my skirt, then smash them onto my nose. "And waxed thread and a hefty needle, if you have it."

"There's nothing in this shop that isn't waxed," the woman says, throwing a shawl hanging beside the door over her shoulders. "The pump's half a mile. I'll run."

As the woman leaves, I toss the scarf from Sim's arm aside and bend over for a closer look at the cut. It is not as much blood as I anticipated—though if there's anything I've learned from being a woman, it's how not very much blood can manage to smear itself around and masquerade as a great deal more than it truly is. It's also not an excessively deep cut—no more than one-fourth of an inch, I estimate, with no fat or muscle peeking through. The blood is not spurting. The skin around the wound is not overly warm. The edges not particularly jagged.

But somehow, this minor abrasion upon the forearm seems to be affecting the entirety of Sim's body. She's awake but, in just a few minutes, almost entirely unresponsive. When she blinks, it's slow and lethargic, like her eyelids are sticking, and I notice she hasn't swallowed in far too long. Her breath is coming fast and shallow, like she's struggling for it.

I can feel my forehead creasing, which Monty has always been quick to remind me will cause me to wrinkle even more prematurely than squinting at tiny print in textbooks will, but there are certain levels of bafflement that require a good pinched forehead to truly be considered.

Johanna brings me the lamp from the wax woman's workbench, her petticoats blooming behind her like tail feathers when she crouches beside me. Since there's really no way for me to be close to Sim without being on top of her, I swing a leg over her waist and straddle her, tipping her mouth open to see if there's something blocking her throat and preventing the air from getting in. The bleeding has stopped, but her arm is beginning to swell, skin turning the mottled purple and black of a day-old bruise. The edges of the cuts are pulling inward before my eyes, like leaves curling into a sunbeam. "There must have been something in it," I say, mostly to myself, but Johanna asks, "Something in what?"

"What she cut herself on." I make a careful extraction of the longest piece of glass in Sim's arm and hold it up against the lamp. Beads of blood slide off a dried brown substance coating it. "Venom? Poison?"

"And now it's in her blood?" Johanna is looking at me for an answer, her face pale, and I realize she thinks she's about to watch someone die. Someone who has given her quite a lot of trouble, but still a living, breathing being, slowly fading out before us like a shadow in the twilight.

And all I can say back is "Yes."

Because I don't know what to do. Nothing in any of

the books prepared me for this, not a word of Alexander Platt's doctrines on blood and bone even touched upon what it felt like to sit helplessly watching as death the vulture circles closer and closer. It didn't mention how to think quicker than your panic, look fear in the face and hope it blinks first, steady your hand, and believe in yourself when you think there's nothing you can do. Sim takes another heaving breath. I can still feel her heartbeat, but her lungs seem to be failing her. It wouldn't matter if I knew what it was that had been in the glass; it's moving through her too fast to do anything, and I don't know how to get it out.

Think, think, think! I scold myself. *Keep calm and think!*

"Johanna, what's in your mother's bag?" I don't know if there's anything to be learned from it, but it's something to do that isn't helpless staring.

She wrenches the bag open and starts shoveling the contents out in handfuls. There are artist's tools, a palette knife and turpentine, along with a box of charcoal and watercolors, squares of color gone chalky with age. There's a leather roll, which Johanna unfurls like a carpet. The top flap contains three unmarked vials, each full of shimmering powder in an opalescent blue the same shade as the shallows of the Mediterranean. Below, a whole row of vials, each containing a different substance, with their corks waxed shut. There are several missing, and one just a cracked rim and stopper clinging to its loop. I drag the lamp closer to me and squint at the vials. There is a word inked atop each, though most so small and cramped I can't make them out. Except for one, which in clear block print reads *HEMLOCK*.

It's a pouch of poisons. Or rather, most likely all poisons. The top three vials with the crystal powder are the only thing that appears duplicated, and none of them have writing on their stoppers, though they're marked with the mathematical symbol for infinity followed by a vertical line. I pop the stopper off one and sniff. It has a faint brine smell, like something collected from a beach.

Sim's hardly breathing now, and each gasp shudders through her whole body. I can feel it in the places we touch each other, my legs around her waist and her hand cupped in mine. The edges of her lips and eyelids are beginning to tinge blue.

Infinity what? I think desperately, staring down at the vial. *Why infinity?*

Unless it's not infinity. I turn the vial horizontal to me, and the infinity is replaced by what looks like a number eight crowned with a single stroke. It's an alchemical symbol, shorthand used by pharmacists and apothecaries, which I learned from Dante Robles in Barcelona. It means *to digest*.

So this is not a poison. This may be an antidote.

278

I pour the contents of the vial into my palm and press it to Sim's face. Her breath is slow and infrequent, and I worry her lungs are too withered to take it in. But then a gasp, and when I pull my hand away, the powder is almost half what it was. A long, painful moment before her next breath, which takes in the rest.

There's nothing more I know to do but sit and listen to Sim's gasping, trying to suck down lungfuls of air and hope. I stare down at her, my hips overtop hers and my own breath ragged inside me. I've two fingers pressed to the pulse point on her wrist, braced for the moment it stops. A piece of snow caught in my hair melts and drops down my cheek. Beside me, Johanna has her eyes closed, hands clasped before her. She might be praying.

And then Sim's breath starts to come easier. It still sounds like the gasping of someone who has been running, but it seems like less of a fight. Her pulse starts to slow, no longer working quite so hard to make up for the rest of her body failing. She blinks, once, then her eyes slide closed as she takes a steady breath. A slip from unconsciousness into sleep.

"What did you give her?" Johanna asks, her voice hoarse.

"I don't know," I reply, my fist closing around the tiny vial, now empty in my hand. Maybe it's medicine. Maybe magic. Maybe it's enough for a woman to cross an ocean to find. Enough to give your life to the study of. Enough to kill for.

When I let the vial fall, the sweat from my palm has transferred the inky symbol from the glass to my hand.

14

The waxwork woman, who introduces herself to us as Miss Quick (most certainly not an actual name, but I don't press), returns with a bucket of water and roots around the shop for the rest of my requested items. When she realizes I'm prepared to remove the glass shards with my bare hands, she offers a set of tongs the length of my palm from her kit. "I only use them on the wax," she says, but I still wash them before digging into Sim's arm.

With the shards removed, I clean out the cuts and stitch them shut. Short of shredding Quick's blankets or my own bodice, there's nothing to use for bandages, so I unwrap the scarf from Sim's head and use that for bindings. Beneath it, her hair is coarse and cropped close to her head.

When I'm finished, I push my spectacles up onto my forehead and press the heel of my hands against my eyes.

They're stinging from doing such delicate work in poor light.

"Is she going to be all right?" Quick asks from behind me.

"I hope so," I reply. "She's no longer actively dying, which is a start." I toss the towel Quick offered into the bucket of water, now brown and murky with blood. "Are you two related?" I ask her, then realize what an ignorant question it was, as it's based entirely upon their shared skin color. "Or how do you know each other?"

Quick laughs. "We know each other in the way everyone who sails under the Crown and Cleaver does." She pulls up her sleeve, revealing a landscape of raised brands and scars and thick, ropey veins. At the inside of her elbow, she has the same inked illustration of a crown and a blade, hers much cruder and more faded into her skin than Sim's, like she could have been born with it.

"What's the Crown and Cleaver?" Johanna asks.

"A corsair fleet that makes berth in a fortress out-side Algiers," Quick replies. "And with one of the largest holdings in the Mediterranean."

My throat goes dry. In spite of my early suspicions since I met Sim, *corsair* rings like a rock dropped into a bucket. Next to me, Johanna pales. "You're pirates?" she asks. "Both of you?"

"Only if you ask the Europeans," Quick replies.

"Are you a thief too?" Johanna asks. "Just like her?"

"If all the thieves in Zurich were hung," Quick replies, "there'd be no one left."

"I'd be left," Johanna replies.

Quick picks at something under her nail. "Well, you're English, aren't you? You have the accent."

"How did Sim find you?" I ask.

"Her father has his people in every city, if you know where to look," Quick replies. "We watch out for each other if our paths cross. When she came to me, I put her up."

"So it's true, then?" Johanna asks. "There is some kind of code among the pirates? Honor among thieves and all that?"

I had been preoccupied watching Sim's chest rise and fall with a steadier breath, but I realize suddenly what Quick has said. "Sorry, what? Her father? Who's her father?"

"Didn't she tell you?" Quick picks up a handful of kindling from beside the stove and starts to pack it into the belly before reaching for a flint. "She is the daughter of Murad Aldajah—his only daughter." When Johanna and I are clearly less impressed by this name than expected, she qualifies, "He is the commodore of the Crown and Cleaver fleet. Hundreds of men sail under his command." The kindling catches, and Quick shuts the door of the stove with a clang. "You want something to eat?"

"We're not part of your fleet," Johanna says. "You don't owe us anything."

Quick shrugs. "I like to help the less fortunate than me. And there aren't many."

Even with the stove lit, the workshop is bloody cold. A necessity, Quick tells us, or else the waxworks melt. Johanna helps her assemble turnips and potatoes for a stew as I watch over Sim, though my gaze drifts along the walls to the wax forms lining them. "What do you make them for?" I ask, unable to look away from a set of organs cast in wax—a heart, a set of lungs, and a stomach on stands.

"Some for curios," Quick replies. "They have wax replicas of the royal family in England that move with clockwork, you know."

"Well, that will haunt my dreams," Johanna mutters.

"The Venuses are for medical schools," Quick says, pointing with the tip of her knife to the body I'm staring at. "They commission them in Padua and Bologna and Bern and Paris, so they needn't cut open cadavers to teach their students what the inside of a person looks like."

I press my fingers to Sim's pulse point, an absentminded monitoring, and it is a strange duet to feel that steady thump against my skin while looking at a perfect model of a human heart, veins and arteries and chambers exposed.

"How did you come to make waxworks if you were raised in a pirate fleet?" Johanna asks, only a tiny bit of judgment bleeding into the word *pirate*.

"The same way any African comes to Europe," Quick replies. "The ship I served on was captured. My crew was enslaved. I was purchased by Herr Krause the wax master and brought here to be trained."

"I didn't know slavery was legal in Switzerland," I say.

Quick halves an onion with a single, neat cut. "It's legal everywhere there's money in the slave trade. And the bankers here have deep pockets."

Quick only has a single bowl for the stew, so we pass it among the three of us, handing the spoon back and forth and sometimes fishing out chunks of potatoes and cabbage with our fingers when the others take too long. Outside, the storm batters the shop, the planks moaning and the stove rattling as the wind whips down the chimney. Strong weather can make even the safest place feel haunted.

My clothes are still damp from the snow, and the soup is so hot it scalds my tongue, but I keep shoveling it down until I can't taste a thing; it just feels so good to be warm inside and full of food. I think of the crusty loaves of bread Callum would bake to pair with the winter stews that I learned to make using scraps from his pasty fillings. It was a process, and Callum put up with many nights of overly salted meat and broth so thick we had to chew it. Once, after a particularly miserable showing at venison and tomatoes, he said the bread deserved butter and I said he also deserved butter than the stew I had given him, and though I generally find puns to be the lowest form of humor, I said it because I knew Callum would like it. And he laughed, the sound as warm and round as a fresh loaf.

Maybe that was love? Who knows?

Quick lets us sleep in the workshop that night while she takes the loft above the stairs. Herr Krause, she assures us, left for Padua last week and isn't due to return until the end of the month. There are no windows in this workshop, and as the fire starts to die and the threat of putting out the lamp grows imminent, the pieces of wax assembled around the room seem to grow more ghoulish. Not threatening, but present, like statues of saints in a cathedral keeping a vigil.

I check on Sim again before returning to Johanna, who is sitting with her mother's effects spread on the floor before her, her back to the stove and knees pulled up so that her skirt canyons between them. It's a most unladylike way to sit, and it reminds me of childhood. I crouch down across from her. "Do you want to stay the night here, or go back to the boardinghouse?" When she doesn't answer, I tap a finger against her shin. "Johanna." She looks up. "What did you find?"

She scrapes a hand through her hair, pushing a few errant strands out of her face. "Other than those vials, there isn't much in the bag. Art supplies and toilette and a petrified piece of cheese."

I glance at the leather folio, lying untouched in front of her. "What about the papers?"

"I haven't looked yet."

"Why not?"

"Because what if she was working on something awful?" She presses her hands to her face. "What if she and Platt were conspiring? What if she's not who I thought she was? All my life, I was sure I could be whoever I wanted because my mother was herself in all things. But what if that was just an excuse for ugliness?"

"Then let her be ugly," I reply. "Because you're not her, and you're glorious."

"Even though I like shoes and lace and anything brightly colored?" She looks down at her hands, the fringe of her eyelashes casting smoky shadows down her cheeks. "Even though I'm not who you want me to be anymore?"

Of course she wasn't the same as she had been when we last parted. She was a brighter, polished version, silver purified in the belly of a crucible until it glinted star-bright. Beside her, I feel stale and molding and unchanged, because if I had not believed entirely in who

I was and what I wanted, I'd never survive. Johanna had let the world change her, let the winds polish her edges and the rain wear her smooth. She was the same person I had known. Had always known. Just a version that was more completely her.

"There's no one I'd rather you be," I reply.

She runs her fingers along the edge of the folio, sucking her cheeks in, then carefully unwraps the string binding it closed. The hard leather snaps at the release, and Johanna and I both peer inside.

The folio is stuffed with papers, some bound together with twine, others loose and weathered. Johanna and I both reach in, scooping out a handful of scraps of notes and sketches and mathematical equations with their answers circled. I skim a few, trying to read the splotched, frantic hand and make sense of anything I'm seeing.

"Look here." Johanna pulls a single page from the folio, double the size of any of the others and folded into quarters to fit inside. Johanna unfolds it, then she and I both take an edge and hold it up to the lamplight.

It's a map, though that's all I know to say of it. It's hand drawn like all the other pages but clearly meticulous, careful work. It is done in ink rather than pencil, thick, confident strokes, the sort one sits at a desk in good lighting and steadies their hands before beginning. There's the start of an intricate border around the edges, and a compass in one corner. A few places are splotched with color, as though she hadn't time to finish filling it in.

"Was your mother a cartographer?" I ask.

"I don't know. Though she lived in Amsterdam for a time." When I look back at her blankly, she clarifies, "That's where all the best mapmakers are. What's it a map of, though?"

I fish my spectacles from my pocket and smash them onto my face, nearly poking myself in the eye as one of my hands is occupied keeping the paper in place. "Look here, that's Algiers." I point. "And the Alboran Sea, so that's Spain. There's Gibraltar." I trace my fingers along the fine lines inked over the water, the paper puckered slightly where she had begun to watercolor.

"So what's this here?" Johanna taps an island in the Atlantic, all the tides and current lines seemingly centering around it.

"I don't know. I saw a fair number of maps of this area when I was traveling, but I've never seen that before. It's very small. Maybe too small for most cartographers to mark it."

"Or maybe that's what she's mapping," Johanna says. "Maybe whatever she was looking for or working on— perhaps it's there." She glances up from the map. "Do you think she knows?"

"Who?"

"Your sailor pirate friend Sim."

"I think she knows something about it," I reply. "More than we do."

Johanna presses her teeth into her bottom lip, her fingers tracing the dotted lines of the map. "Maybe we could ask her."

"She may not tell us anything. Even if she does know."

"But this is what she was looking for, isn't it? This map? She's a sailor, and she wasn't after my mother's paintbrushes. It's got to be this map. And if she wants it, she must know where it leads. And why it's so valuable."

"So what are you saying?" I ask.

"I think we should stay here," Johanna says. "Frau Engel is paid for the night—she won't mind if we aren't sleeping in the beds so long as she has her coin. We can go tomorrow and get my things. But I don't . . ." Her eyes dart over to Sim. "We need to talk to her. Zounds, I hope she'll talk to us."

Johanna falls asleep before me, curled around the stove with her mother's folio, carefully restuffed, for a pillow. I stay up for a while, sitting at the workbench, sort of watching Sim and sort of thinking about Sybille Glass's map and that shimmering powder. I'm tempted to make a quiet rummage through the bag for another look, but I resist.

But I want to know more. I want to know what it is and how it works and why it saved Sim. When all my indignance over inequality, the plight of women in the world, and the education denied me is boiled away, what is always left is that wanting, hard and spare and alive, like a heart made of bone. I want to know all of it. I want to look at my own hands and know everything about the way they move beneath the skin, the fine strings that tie them to the rest of me and all the other intricate components that fuse together to make up a complete person. The mysteries of how a system as delicate and precise as the human body not only exists, but exists in infinite variables. I want to know how things go wrong. How we break and the best way to put ourselves back together. I want to know it all so badly it feels like a bird trapped inside my chest, throwing its body against my rib cage in search of the strong wind that will carry it out into the world. I would tear myself open if it meant setting it free.

I want to know everything about my own self and never to have to rely on someone else to tell me the way I work.

I think again of abandoning my hope of working with Platt and where I have left to go from here, which, in short, is nowhere. No time to keep searching for schools, no money for apprenticeships, and not enough strength to hope that if I keep banging down doors, someday it will pay off. Not enough. The idea of working with Dr. Platt felt like my fingers scraping a star, but that flared out and faded into the darkness so fast. Or perhaps it exploded in my face and then laughed at me. That was more what it felt like.

I don't know where to go from here. The panic caves inside me, like a paper curling in the grip of a flame.

I do not know where to go.

Across the room, Sim mumbles, "Something's wrong with my arm."

I look up as she raises her head, blinking hard like she's still trying to rouse herself. I abandon my perch on the bench, already thumbing through possible complications—gangrene, infection, pain, discoloring in the skin that signifies decreased blood flow.

But she lets her head fall backward so she's staring up at the ceiling and says, "I think I cut it."

I stop on my knees next to her, then sit back on my heels. "To put it mildly."

"I can't move my hand."

"I'm not surprised. Are you feeling any pain?"

"My ribs hurt," she says. "It's hard to breathe. Did I fall?"

"No, I think you were poisoned," I reply. "It entered your body through the cuts upon your arm. Based on your symptoms, I'd wager it's a paralytic that attacks the skeletal muscles."

"You're still here," she says, her eyes still fixed upon the ceiling. "Why are you still here?"

"I had nothing better to do."

Her eyes flick over to me, her gaze more focused. "You're being sarcastic."

"No, actually I was being flippant, but I can do sarcastic if you'd rather." I smooth my skirt against my knees with flat hands. "Best keep a close eye on your arm, though. There's still time for gangrene to set in, and I have never amputated a limb, so this would be a new experience for us both, and I can't imagine it would be as neat as the stitches. Embroidering pillows doesn't give you quite as much practice for amputations."

"You didn't have to help me," she says, her voice very soft.

It feels like such an absurd amendment to gratitude that I respond with vinegar before I can stop myself. "You're right; I didn't. Why didn't you tell me this a few hours ago? You would have saved me so much effort and worry."

I expect she'll bristle, my hard edges once again knocking someone away. But instead she grins. "I do like your sarcasm better."

I laugh in surprise. "Well, it is with entirely no sarcasm—which is hard for me, I assure you—that I say I stayed because I wanted to be certain you were all right."

"So why did Miss Hoffman stay?"

"Less noble reasons, though I assure you she was concerned for you as well. Johanna wants to speak with you about her mother's work. I told her you may refuse, as you have a tendency to be stubborn and inscrutable."

"Inscrutable?" She lets out a short breath of laughter. "Coming from the prickliest girl I've ever known."

"Prickly?" I say. "I'm not prickly."

"Felicity Montague, you are a cactus."

"Debatable." My knees are aching against the hard floor, so I stretch out on my stomach parallel to her, propping my chin on my hands. "My botanical equivalent would more likely be . . . what are those plants that shrivel as soon as you touch them? I'd be one of those."

She pulls herself over on her side with a wince, her good arm curling under her head. "Not something medicinal?"

"Perhaps," I say. "Though that's a rather obvious answer, isn't it?" I stack my fists atop each other and rest my chin upon them. "Or maybe I would be a flower. But a really tough flower."

"A wildflower," Sim says. "The kind that are strong enough to stand against wind, rare and difficult to find and impossible to forget. Something men walk continents for a glimpse of."

I wrinkle my nose. "I'd rather not be glimpsed by men. Perhaps we can set up some sort of trap so that they fall off a cliff if they try to pluck me from the ground." I stretch my hands out before me, making a study of my nails, which have grown long and filthy in our travels. Longer than I like to keep them, for practicality, though the thought makes me feel foolish. I'm not running a practice and being called upon daily to perform surgeries. It's a needless routine that suddenly feels silly and aspirational. "But you're right—whatever I am, there would likely be spines. Or thorns. They keep people away."

Sim rolls onto her back again, her neck arching in a stretch. "I didn't think I'd see you again."

"Sorry to disappoint you."

She looks sideways at me. "It wasn't a disappointment."

"Well, you wouldn't have, except that Johanna disappeared the morning of her wedding and Dr. Platt recruited me to help find her in exchange for a job."

"So you got what you wanted, then?" When I don't say anything, she prompts, "You're working for him."

"I'm not. He's . . ." I consider saying *conspiring to kidnap me*, but am too tired to explain, so instead I finish, "not what I expected."

Sim does not seem moved. Her tone is the verbal equivalent of a shrug when she says, "So you'll find someone else to teach you medicine things."

"It is nowhere near that simple."

"Because he's your hero?" she asks.

"Because I've wanted to study with him for so long," I say. "I've wanted to *study*. Full stop."

"Who's keeping you from that?"

"No one's keeping me from it, but I can't just read

books forever. I want to work and learn and be taught by someone smarter than me. I want to help people. Which I am not allowed to do because I am a woman." I sit up and dust off my elbows, cross that I left myself slip into familiar territory with Sim, for if I'm a cactus, she's a very argumentative rosebush, and I've drawn my own blood again by reaching out. "Maybe I was foolish to let you seduce me away to Stuttgart and expect everything would miraculously fall into place for me. And maybe Alexander Platt wasn't what I expected, but it's not as though I have many chances to learn medicine."

"Of course you don't," she says, pushing herself up on her good elbow. "You're trying to play a game designed by men. You'll never win, because the deck is stacked and marked, and also you've been blindfolded and set on fire. You can work hard and believe in yourself and be the smartest person in the room and you'll still get beat by the boys who haven't two cents to rub together."

It's the sort of sentiment that kept me awake in Edinburgh, long nights of sleepless panic that I was wasting my time trying, that someday I would wake up and find I was old and had wasted my life trying to wage war armed with only a great deal of indignation, which is about as useful as a bowl of cold porridge in battle.

But then Sim says, "So if you can't win the game, you have to cheat."

"Cheat?" I repeat.

"You operate outside the walls they've built to fence you in. You rob them in the dark, while they're drunk on spirits you offered them. Poison their waters and drink only wine. That's what Sybille Glass did." The silence hangs between us, underscored by the last embers popping in the stove. From the shelves, wax ears eavesdrop. "I'll talk to you and Johanna tomorrow," Sim says suddenly. "Because you helped me. And because I want to see the map."

"How do you know about the map?"

"It was a hope until you just confirmed it, so thank you."

"Oh. I mean . . . what map?"

She rolls her eyes. "Are you going to keep a vigil over me while I sleep?"

"To make sure you don't steal the map? If there is a map."

"I meant to make certain I don't die, but yes, let's keep trust at an arm's length." She slides over on the pallet. "Come lie down with me. At least you'll be warm."

I hesitate, then lie down beside her and pull the quilt over both of us. She takes another deep breath with a steadying hand to her chest, then looks sideways at me and says, "Did I really seduce you to Germany?"

Now it's my turn to roll my eyes, regretting I ever

used the word. "It was a combination of you and Alexander Platt. And look: now you're both the banes of my existence."

"You need to be more discerning about who gets their talons in that brilliant brain of yours."

I snort, louder than I mean to. "I'm not brilliant."

She purses her lips with a soft humming sound. "You're right, *brilliant* is quite a strong word. But you seem very bright. Or if not bright, you're at least confident. And often people can't tell those two things apart."

I don't feel confident—I feel like an actress, a pretender, someone who wears a brave face because the moment a strong-willed woman shows weakness, men will push their fingers into it and pry her apart like a pomegranate.

But I don't correct her. I'm still afraid that, the first chance she gets, she might crack me open too.

15

Sim, Johanna, and I leave Quick's the next morning for a coffee shop down the road to take breakfast. In the wake of the storm, Zurich is cold and bright. A thin-fingered mist sits above the streets, making the frost sparkle and the stones emanate light. Even my breath, white as it strikes the cold air, seems to shine. Down the road, a pot clangs as it's slung over a cook fire. Chestnuts pop in a frying pan. A blacksmith's apprentice strikes his anvil, a call to his master that the forge is hot. A dog barks somewhere out of sight. I'm surprised Johanna doesn't go chasing after it.

Women are barred from English coffee shops—most institutions pride themselves on being havens for discourse and educated thought, though most of their clientele are men who slept through Cambridge regurgitating multisyllable words and proving they know who

Machiavelli was. Here, the customers remind me more of the crowd that would frequent Callum's bakeshop—working class, quiet and polite. It's mostly men, but the sheet of rules posted beside the door makes no notations about sex. No one gives us a second glance.

We pay our coins for breakfast and take a table farthest from the door beneath a noticeboard and a stuffed crocodile with his jaws wide. I can hardly taste my coffee after I so thoroughly scalded my mouth the night before on Quick's stew, but every swallow makes me feel warm and more awake. Johanna brought her mother's bag and the leather case. She keeps the bag pinned between her feet under the table and the case over her shoulder, even though it requires her to sit on only half the chair, and every time she shifts, it smacks the back of her head with a crack.

Sim watches Johanna struggle, the corners of her mouth turning up. "Don't worry. I've only got one good arm now." She tugs on the sling around her neck. "You could fend me off."

Johanna sighs with frustration, then reluctantly hangs the strap of the case over the back of her chair. "I still don't trust you," she says, but Sim just shrugs in reply, unconcerned.

We sit in silence for a long minute. Sim murmurs a prayer of *"Bismillah"* before she blows on her coffee through pursed lips, making the surface jump. I had expected she would be more reluctant to come with us, but thus far, she's been suspiciously cooperative. I awoke this morning when she left our shared bed, certain she was running, but she was only rising to pray with Quick. She let me check her injured arm and tie the sling, then borrowed a scarf from Quick and wrapped her head again.

"So, who is going to speak first?" Sim says at last. "Or should we keep wasting time waiting on each other?"

Johanna and I look at each other. She doesn't say anything, just tips her head toward Sim, like I am supposed to answer. Sim blows harder on her coffee.

"All right. I'll start." I clear my throat. "Where did you meet Sybille Glass?"

Johanna, who has been shredding a piece of cut meat between her fingers, startles and looks at Sim for the first time since we sat down. "You knew my mother?"

Sim sets down her mug and cracks the knuckles of her good hand against the edge of the table. "She was captured by my father's men when she was mapping in our waters."

"Mapping what?" Johanna says. "She was an artist on a scientific expedition, not a cartographer."

"She was," Sim replies, "and on the side, she was mapping the nesting grounds of dragons."

"Dragons?" Johanna and I ask at the same time.

"Sea dragons," Sim clarifies. "The ones you

Europeans draw upon charts for decoration. All the dragons that are left nest and swim within my father's waters, and we protect them. We keep invaders away from each other."

"My mother was not an invader," Johanna says.

"No," Sim agrees. "She wanted to study the dragons. She was making maps tracking their migration patterns and trying to plot their nesting grounds. Not even my family knows that anymore. But my father was sure that any Europeans in our waters would mean extinction for the beasts and our fleet. She was alone, but she would bring more. He wanted her to destroy her map and agree not to take what she knew back to London. And she wouldn't."

"Did your father kill her?" Johanna asks bluntly. I almost choke on my coffee.

"No," Sim replies. "But she died at his fortress. She was sick when we took her prisoner, but she refused our treatments because she was experimenting."

"What exactly was she experimenting with if she was just making maps?" Johanna asks. "That seems like a very good story to cover up a murder."

"The dragon scales," Sim says. "They have a sort of . . . I'm not sure how to explain it. They elevate you."

"Literally?" I ask.

"No, not literally," she replies. "No one's flying. It's a stimulant." She lets her hand fall into her lap. "Sailors used to carry them on strings around their neck and chew them before a fight for strength. They were taken once a day to ward off illnesses. Your mother"—she looks to Johanna—"was testing their properties on herself."

"Lots of doctors do that," I explain when Johanna still looks unconvinced. "If you can't find a willing subject to try a new medicine or procedure, you use yourself. John Hunter gave himself gonorrhea to test his theory about its transmission."

Johanna wrinkles her nose, then looks back to Sim. "If she was sick and you didn't save her, you murdered her."

"She wouldn't take our help," Sim replies. Her good hand is fisted upon the table. "She said she had to complete an experiment. She would only take the scales as treatment."

"And you had them and wouldn't give them to her?"

"My father has outlawed taking them in our holdings." I can hear Sim grinding her teeth, and I'm tempted to put out a cautionary hand to Johanna. She has as much right as Sim to be angry, but Sim isn't using her emotions like a cudgel the way Johanna is. "He won't let them on his ships, because you don't have to take them many times before it's all you can think about. And when you strip the scales off the backs of the dragons, they don't regrow. We didn't let her die; she let herself die."

Realization dawns suddenly upon me, and so I turn

to Johanna. "Let me see your mother's things."

"What?" She snatches the bag up from under the table and presses it to her chest. "Why?"

"The vials, the ones we used yesterday," I say, flapping my fingers at her. "Let me see them."

Johanna roots around in the sack and comes up with the leather roll and unfurls it upon the tables. I unhook one of the remaining vials filled with the opalescent powder and hand it to Sim. "Is this them? The scales."

She uncorks the vial with her teeth and takes a careful sniff before dipping her pinky in and scrubbing it against her thumb. "I think so. Though she didn't have any of this with her when I met her."

"It would have been on her ship. This is what saved your life yesterday. It worked as an antidote against the poison." I unfold the other half of the leather skin so that the vials of labeled poisons are on display. "If Sybille Glass was trying to create a compound made from the sea dragon scales that worked against poisons, it would explain why she had a bag full of venomous samples. She wasn't sick; she poisoned herself to test her theories. If Platt was on the expedition with her, do you think he knew about the dragons and the scales too? He's going back to the Barbary States—maybe he's hoping to follow her maps and find the sea monsters."

"And then he takes samples back, and all your English sailors come to my family's territory and kill our beasties and us with them," Sim murmurs. She's still pressing those flakes of scale between her fingers, and I half expect her to touch them to her tongue. I wonder just how addictive it is.

"What if there were a way to duplicate the compound found in their scales?" I say. "Something man-made and nonaddictive that could be used medicinally? If it has anything close to the restorative powers we saw yesterday, it could help a lot of people."

"But you'd first need the scales," Sim says, "and my father would never allow it. Once these waters are open to Europeans, our fleet won't survive. Particularly under its impending leadership."

"You mean you?" I ask. When she looks quizzically back at me, I prompt, "I thought you were the legendary daughter of a legendary pirate king."

"No one said legendary," she replies.

"Quick did."

"My father may be a legend, but I won't be." Sim jabs her knife at her egg. The yolk breaks, spilling gold across her plate. "I am my father's oldest child, and I have claim to the Crown and Cleaver fleet when he dies. But he'd rather see his sons take up his title because I'm a woman. He'll leave me *something* because the law forces him to, but it will be half of what my brothers get, if that, and it will not be the fleet. I have spent my whole life fighting for what would be mine without question if

I were a man, and to be better at it than my brothers, because women don't have to be men's equals to be considered contenders; they have to be better." She slumps down in her seat, rubbing her injured arm. "That's the lie of it all. You have to be better to prove yourself worthy of being equal."

"So this is how you cheat?" I ask. "You bring Sybille Glass's lost map to your father, and that wins you his favor?"

"And what do two English princesses want with maps that lead to monster nests?" Sim challenges.

"What my mother wanted," Johanna says, and her eyes are suddenly bright as new-forged bronze, the same way they used to flash when we would collect samplings of plants from the countryside in hopes of discovering an unknown new species. "Can you imagine the scientific advancements this could lead to? What else will we learn about the sea if we know about these creatures and how they live and what they eat and how they hunt and sleep and . . . everything? Why do you say 'English' like we're all wicked? You're pirates! You're not exactly sinless."

"But we don't come into your countries and drive you out," Sim says, worming her knife farther into her egg. "That's what you do to us. You expect me to believe that just because your intentions are noble, all the English are? Or all Europeans? The Imazighen—who you would call the Berbers," she adds, "have already fought wars over these creatures. We don't need to fight you too."

"So what if we don't bring the English into it?" I ask. "Your father has ships and men at his disposal. What if you bring him the charts, and the daughter of Sybille Glass—not as a prisoner," I say quickly, for Johanna looks like she's ready to raise a sound protest to my phrasing, "but as a companion. Someone to work with, who wants to pick up where her mother left off in order to better understand them. Johanna wants an expedition—why not ask Sim's pirate lord father to fund it?"

Sim frowns. "My father doesn't want another Sybille Glass. He doesn't want to make a study of the dragons or their nests or their scales or any of it. He just wants to keep them undisturbed. And he wants the map to make sure others do too. That's what I went to Stuttgart for— to make certain that if it existed, it was returned to us."

"Then we change his mind," I say. "Protecting these creatures isn't the same as simply not destroying them. I know it's a risk, but we can make a case."

"Where do you come in?" Johanna asks. I expect her to be looking at Sim, but instead she has her eyebrows raised at me.

"What about me?"

"*Man-made and nonaddictive that could be used medicinally,*" she parrots. "That sounds right up your street. You want to make a name for yourself in a way Platt never could? Make it yourself."

I purse my lips against my mug, aware they're both watching me. I think of all the doors I've had slammed in my face, the fact that even when Platt had dreamed up a fictitious position to lure me to Zurich with him, the most he could imagine of me doing was paperwork. And even if that had been a real offer, what would I have done after? Who would I have to fight next to be permitted to go broke sitting in on lectures at a university where I would never be allowed to matriculate? And even if I did somehow walk out of the university with a degree in hand, would any English hospital employ me? Any patients seek my advice for anything other than midwifery or herbs? How long before the men came to chase me out of whatever corner I carved for myself?

How much would I rather be in the company of this mad girl who loves creatures like Francis of Assisi, on Sim's boat unfolding layers of scientific discovery? Finding knowledge that is not just new to me, but new to the world? It pimples the flesh along my arms to think of it. Though my heart has always been fixed to medical school like a compass point, that legitimacy necessary to prove my worth, this small shift in course may lead me somewhere entirely new, but perhaps still somewhere I want to go.

When I answer, I worry it will feel like setting a dream on fire. "I would go with you," I say, braced for it to sting, but it doesn't. It feels like the first step on a new continent.

I look to Sim, and she looks to Johanna, and Johanna looks at me, and I realize that, in that single moment, like a flash of heat lightning over a bare moor, all three of us are in control of our own futures. Our own lives. Where we go now. Maybe for the first time. With my side pressed to Johanna's and Sim's dark eyes meeting mine, I feel newer than I've ever been.

Everyone has heard stories of women like us— cautionary tales, morality plays, warnings of what will befall you if you are a girl too wild for the world, a girl who asks too many questions or wants too much. If you set off into the world alone.

Everyone has heard stories of women like us, and now we will make more of them.

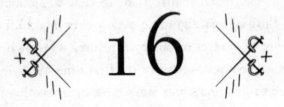

16

The plan is thus: we will travel by all means available to the southern shore of France, from where we can then take a ferry to Algiers. It's a pirate port, Sim tells us, overrun with buccaneers and smugglers and without even a European toe stuck in for a foothold, but with Sim and that crown and cleaver upon her, she's certain no one will dare touch us. We will rally with her father's men in the city, who collect taxes from the European shipping companies, and they can take us to his fortress.

Johanna has some coinage she digs up from her trunk at Frau Engel's before abandoning the rest of its contents and manages to secure some funds from an account of her uncle's. It's enough for the three of us to travel to the coast, though not well—our journey's closest kin is the trek Monty, Percy, and I undertook from Marseilles to Barcelona.

I expect that traveling with Johanna and Sim will be like trying to wrangle kittens into the bath, both of them with minds of their own and distrustful of each other, Johanna homesick and wanting to pet every dog we pass, Sim determined to do the opposite of any instructions given her just to aggravate me. But to my great surprise, I end up being the dead weight of the trio. I'm always the first to call halt for the day or ask to stop for a meal because I'm about to faint with hunger. The one who falls asleep in coaches and diligences and would have missed the stop had Sim or Johanna not woken me. Though even my lowest levels of competence are the equivalent of high-functioning for most, and we are by far the most proficient trio I have traveled with to date. But I'm a bit rudderless without someone to boss around at all times.

They are also both shockingly agreeable. Sim is quiet; Johanna speaks enough for all three of us. She's friendly with everyone we meet and seems to find a way to compliment every sour-faced cook or innkeeper on exactly the thing that softens them, and in such a sincere way that we are slipped steaming pastries and mugs of beer with no charge, and once booked on a diligence we were previously told was full and that we'd have to wait three days for the next. She makes us play word games as we travel, or tells us facts about animals and makes us guess whether they're real or if she's made them up. Sim is better at the guessing, though when I contribute medical facts, they're both hapless. Johanna believes me for several confusing minutes that, after my brother lost his ear, it grew back.

I wrote to Monty before we left Zurich, informing him I was safe and in, if not good, at least neutral company, and that I would not be back in London as soon as I'd planned. I did not mention that there was a good chance I might be running off to join a pirate expedition to protect sea monsters. I have a sense that would get his breeches in a twist.

We leave European soil on a creaking ferry from Nice to Algiers. The boat departs at midnight and is a far cry from even the utilitarian packet that Sim and I took from England to the Continent. It seems to be built neither for cargo nor passengers, but is determined to shove as much of both as possible on board. The three of us end up on the top deck, the benefit of which is fresh air rather than the stale haze that swells on the lower decks, but that fresh air is bitter cold and thick with the misty spray of the sea. We huddle against the rail, with Johanna's cloak over our shoulders and mine wrapped around us from the front, tented in with as much warmth as our bodies can generate. The night is clear for the first time in days. The round belly of a not-quite-full moon sits low and bright over the water, sprinkled on all sides by stars. Every breath blazes warm and white against the night.

As I watch the other passengers, it's hard not to

notice that Johanna and I are some of the only fair-skinned Europeans aboard, and the three of us are some of the only women I can see. I have often been the only girl in the room, but I can't think of a time I was in the minority like this. It must be daunting for Sim to travel Europe knowing that everywhere she goes, she won't be around people like her. Of course, I'd thought of this before—particularly while on the road with Percy—but there's something about being here, curled up on this deck with her and Johanna, that distills the loneliness of it for the first time. In that moment, the sky feels closer than home.

Johanna falls asleep before we've left the port, her arms resting upon her knees and her face burrowed into them, leaving Sim and me alone with enough silence to fill the ocean. I had not realized how much space Johanna's bright, giddy presence took up among the three of us until she was snoring at my shoulder.

Sim and I haven't spoken alone since Zurich, the night we slept side by side in the waxworks. Now, with a moon the color of lamplight above us and her dark skin dewy with the sea spray, she looks softer than I've seen her. Her face seems less guarded, the hard set of her jaw swapped for parted lips. Her injured arm is still bandaged, but unslung, and curled against her stomach.

"Do you think she's sad?" Sim asks suddenly.

"Johanna?" I ask, and Sim nods. "Seeing as she got

her mother's things and escaped Platt, I can't see why she would be. Though I suppose she misses her dog."

"I mean sad that she's not going to be married."

Since so much of our conversation lately has been about natural philosophy and sea monsters, this is not what I was expecting. A small part of me had even forgotten Johanna was engaged to begin with. This girl beside me felt worlds away from the one who had danced in her ridiculous costume the night of the Polterabend. But she's not, I remind myself. If given the chance, Johanna would likely chase sea monsters in that same indigo dress. "I don't think she's bothered by it," I say. "At least, she's not bothered she isn't being married to Platt."

"But if he'd been a good man and not a prick," Sim says. "It must be a shock, to think your whole life is about to change and then . . ." She flicks open her hand in wordless demonstration of the vanishing.

I cup my hands over my mouth and blow on them for warmth. "I think it would be a relief, actually."

"Wouldn't you like to be married?" she asks.

"Would you?" I counter.

"Someday."

"Really?"

"So long as I got along with him. It would be nice to have someone to grow old with. Someone to keep you warm."

I wrinkle my nose. "I'd rather keep myself warm."

"What would you have instead of a husband, then?" The curl of the moon looks back at me from her dark eyes. "A giant dog like Johanna's?"

A cold wind rises off the water and Sim presses closer to me, her cheek against my shoulder so that when I speak, I can feel the material of her headscarf against my skin. "I think I want a house of my own," I start, the words a discovery as they leave my mouth. "Something small, so I don't have much housework, but enough room for a proper library. I want a lot of books. And I wouldn't mind a good old dog to walk with me. And a bakery I go to every morning where they know my name."

"And you don't want anyone with you?" Sim asks, raising her head. "No family?"

"I want friends," I say. "Good friends, that make up a different kind of family."

"That sounds lonely."

"It wouldn't be lonely," I reply. "I'd like to be on my own, but not alone."

"That's not the sort of lonely I meant."

"Oh." I'm not sure why I'm blushing, but I feel it swell in my cheeks. "Well, that sort of aloneness doesn't feel lonely to me."

Sim tips her head backward against the rail, the faint starlight reflected on her skin like seed pearls overturned from dark earth. "You only say that because you've never *been* with anyone before."

"Have you?" I challenge.

"No, but I want to be."

"I don't think I do."

"How can you know that if you've never had anyone?"

"How do you know you want to?" I reply. "I've never drunk octopus ink, but I don't feel the need to. Or like I'm missing anything in not having tasted it."

"But octopus ink might become your new favorite. Do not roll your eyes at me, Miss Montague." She gives me a hard poke in the rib cage. "Have you ever kissed anyone, at least?"

"Yes."

"Anyone you *liked*?"

"Not with that emphasis. I have kissed men whose company I enjoyed."

"And . . . ?"

"And . . ." I make a gesture that looks like I'm juggling invisible balls. "It was not altogether unpleasant."

Sim snorts. "A ringing endorsement of kissing."

"It didn't make me hear violins or go weak in the knees or want to do any more than that, which I think is the evolutionary point of the kiss. It's just a thing people do." I feel strange suddenly, the old itch of fear that I am a feral girl in a domesticated world, watched by everyone with pity and concern. There are men like Monty, with perverse desires, but they find each other and carve out small corners of the world, and likely women too who find themselves only drawn to the fairer sex. And then there's me, an island all my own. An island that sometimes feels like a whole continent to rule, and sometimes a cramped spit of land that sailors are marooned upon and left to die.

Sim is staring at me—no pity or concern, but those enormous eyes reduce me to hand flapping and a half-apologetic, half-frantic "I don't know. Perhaps my mouth doesn't work."

"Of course your mouth works."

It's dark enough, in only the light of the talon moon, that I almost don't realize she's moved until I feel her hand upon my cheek, and when I turn to meet her, she presses her lips against mine.

It is entirely different from kissing Callum. It is, for a start, significantly less wet. Less impulsive and frantic and out of control. It feels bold and shy both at once, like giving and taking. Her lips are chapped but her mouth is soft as milkweed silk and rimmed with salt water from the cold spray kicked up against the side of the boat. When they part against mine, I open my mouth in return. Her thumb skims my jawline, feather-light.

But beyond the physical observations, it's nothing. Not wholly unpleasant, but neither something I'm anxious to repeat.

Just a thing people do.

She pulls back, her hand still upon my cheek, and looks at me. "Did that work any sort of magic?"

"Not really."

"That's a shame." She settles back into our little nest of cloaks, pulling the collar higher around her face. "It worked for me."

Algiers

17

Algiers sits upon the crook of an iridescent bay. Even in the weak sunlight as our ferry makes its slow progress against the dawn, the buildings sparkle like they're inlaid with precious stones, the white sand beach a jewelry box to house them. The city makes a slow climb up the hillside, flat roofed and whitewashed, with the bony fingers of minarets poking out. Clouds stretch across the horizon in wispy streaks.

Johanna and I, pasty English girls in very European clothes who speak no useful languages here, stick out sorely. I've heard a great deal of renegades have come from Europe to seek asylum in Algiers from whatever trouble drove them off the Continent, but we look far from criminals. It is positively unfair how unrumpled Johanna manages to look after weeks upon the road. Somehow she's kept her skirt pressed—likely something to do with the loving layout she gives it each night, no matter where we are staying, while I am more inclined to step out of mine and then let it lie in a puddle upon the floor so that I can sooner fall into bed.

The plan is to hire camels, then ride to a garrison of Sim's father's men several towns from Algiers. From there, we'll go to the Crown and Cleaver fortress. Sim leads the way through the city with a confident stride. I expected that here, we might see a different version of her, relaxed and at ease so near to her home. But instead, she seems tense. She keeps pulling on her headscarf, fiddling absently with the knot holding it in place. My own hair feels exposed in contrast to the veiled women in the city. Johanna and I aren't the only bare-headed women, or the only ones with fair skin, but something about the concentration of both, so much lower than I'm used to, makes me feel very obvious. As well traveled and hard to shock as I pride myself on being, I realize when I meet the eyes of a woman across the road and she stares at me that I know nothing about this world.

We stop for breakfast in the medina, a market made up of tapered streets rendered smaller by vendors' wares jutting into the footpaths. Men lead donkeys by the nose, their backs laden with woven baskets and their hooves clapping against the stones. The air is hazy with the smoke from cook fires where women roast rabbits spattered in vivid sprays of saffron. The street tips upward into long, cracked steps. Tiled mosaics and alcoves inter-rupt the shopfronts, studded with sea glass and scripture painted on ceramic.

Johanna is rapturous, wandering through the haze like she has been transported into a fantastical dream. If she shares any of my discomfort of being a stranger in a strange land, she doesn't show it. The sun streams through the awnings and splinters over her face, thread-ing her hair with gold as she lets her fingers press into the inlaid tesseracts along the walls. She stops at a stand with emerald birds lined up like soldiers, their feet knot-ted to their perch, and has to stroke the domed feathers of each of their heads. Sim whistles at her to get her walking again, and all the birds whistle in reply.

"Are you all right?" I ask Sim as I struggle to keep up with her quick stride, Johanna traipsing happily behind us.

"Fine," she replies, though that strong jawline is jut-ting out.

"Are you certain? You seem tense."

"Of course I'm tense. I've got you and Miss Hoffman—keep up!" she calls over her shoulder at Johanna, who has stopped to feed the rest of her breakfast to a stray dog lounging on the stoop outside a mosque. "The two of you don't blend in well."

"That's not our fault."

"Doesn't change the fact that we're easy to spot."

"And you think someone's trying to spot us?"

She glances over at me, so quick it's almost lost in the folds of her scarf.

A parrot squawks right in my ear, and I swat without thinking. It nips at me, and I yelp, turning to glare at whatever negligent shopkeeper is failing to monitor their fowl. The woman is sitting on the ground, in front of a blanket spread with varying bottles and amulets and medicinal-looking charms. Amid the jumble laid out upon her cloth, a flash of blue catches my eye.

I pull up short. Johanna crashes into me, and a woman behind us carrying two wicker baskets almost smashes into both of us. Sim stops when the woman curses loudly—in spite of the unfamiliar language, it's very easy to distinguish a curse—and turns back to us. "What is—"

"Sim, look!" I point down to the blanket, where six blue scales the size of my palm wink back at us.

Sim comes to my side, Johanna on my other. The shopkeeper's face is completely covered by her veil, but through the slit in the material, her eyes dart between us. "She shouldn't have those," Sim says. "It's illegal in my father's territories to own or sell the dragon scales. Or use them. Or hunt the sea monsters to get them." She steps forward, crouches down on the balls of her feet so she can address the shopkeeper in Darija. Johanna and I stand behind her, helpless and dumb. As she speaks,

Sim jerks up her sleeve to show the woman her ink, and the woman shies.

"Don't frighten her," I say to Sim.

"I'm not," she replies in English without looking at me. "She's frightened because she's done wrong and she knows it." She picks up in her native language again, and the woman squeaks back a few words in reply.

"What is it?" Johanna asks as Sim stands and faces us again. The woman has her hands clasped before her in penance, her shoulders shaking.

Sim knots her fingers behind her neck, starring down at the scales on the woman's blanket, then up at the sky. I can hear her grinding her teeth. "We need to delay finding my father's men."

"What?" I say. "Why? What did that woman tell you?"

"She told me where the scales came from. Just outside the city." Sim holds up a hand to shield her eyes from the sun as she turns to us. "There's a dragon washed up on the beach."

Beyond Algiers, we follow a rough road that snakes through the countryside for almost an hour. Every step drops handfuls of sand down the backs of my boots. The houses turn to farms, then the flat terrain to a rough hike up a hillside of loose soil and scrub. All three of us lose our footing more than once when the soft earth gives out from under us. As we climb, the air grows thick with the smell of a beach and something decomposing upon it. Johanna and I both pull the collars of our dresses up over our mouths. Sim covers hers with her headscarf.

When we crest the hill, Johanna gasps. I have to hold my hand up to shield my eyes from the sun before I see it too. Below us is a horseshoe inlet, hidden from the open water by cliffs. The sickle of white sand is framed by that radiant blue water and thick patches of greenery. And washed up on the beach, still half in the waves so that the surf froths with blood, is a dragon.

By my best estimation, it's likely over one hundred feet long, though I can't be sure from its haphazard sprawl and its tail disappearing into the water. It resembles most closely the serpents from Sybille Glass's drawings in the cabinet. It has a long body, the same sparkling blue of the sea, though the scales have been diluted by sand and blood. The armored forehead narrows into a pointed snout, with what looks like antennae sprouting from it like kelp snagged upon its eyebrows.

There is a scattering of people on the beach, most clustered around the creature and picking at it with axes or knives, prying scales away and carving handfuls of the doughy flesh beneath. Some have even brought ladders and wagons along to aid with their take. A boy who can't be more than ten is sitting upon the head, trying to hack off the tips of the antennae.

"Bloody scavengers," Sim hisses. "They cut up the

corpses and sell the scales as a drug and everything else as sham remedies. The fat for clear skin and silky hair. Spine bones as lucky charms."

"Vertebrae," I say.

"What?"

"The spine bones," I reply, my eyes still on the creature. "They're called vertebrae."

"Thank you, but that's not what I'm concerned about right now."

"If you're going to say something, at least say it right."

Her hands flex into fists at her side. "These rats are going to strip this corpse, flood the markets in Algiers, and then sell the runoff in Nice and Marseilles. Your Dr. Platt won't be the only one looking for dragons."

"What do we do?" I ask.

"I have to fetch my father's men," Sim replies. "We drive the scavengers away when this happens, and keep watch over the corpse until the tide takes it back. I'm going to run to the garrison and bring them back."

"I want to stay here," Johanna says.

"Why do you want to stay with a rotting monster?" Sim asks.

"Because I've never seen one before," Johanna says. "And I'd like to have a proper look."

"That seems ill-advised. You can wait for me in Algiers." She looks to me for reinforcement.

"I'd rather stay here too," I say. Even dirtied by the

sand, those scales in the light are like liquid sapphires.

"Please. You don't need us," Johanna says to Sim, like we are children begging our mother for one more slice of cake. "We'll probably just raise more questions with your father's men. And you'll travel faster alone."

Sim curses under her breath. "Fine. But stay up here. Don't go down to the beach. I say that knowing neither of you will heed me, but these people are leeches." She jerks her chin down at the beach. "Don't try to take anything. If anyone starts to scold you or shout at you or pulls a knife, just run. They want to scare you away from their salvage. It's not a joke," she says when Johanna giggles, though I imagine it's more from the delight at seeing the monster than at Sim's words. "This isn't a romp with your dog in the garden."

"Max and I don't romp in the garden," Johanna replies. "It dirties his paws."

"People have died for much less than one dragon scale." Sim presses her hands flat against her lips, then says, "I'll be back by nightfall. If I'm not, sleep here tonight and then go back to the city in the daylight— the boars and foxes hunt along the road after dark. And they won't want a cuddle," she says, for Johanna looks absolutely swoony with delight at the prospect of animal friends.

"Anything else, Mother?" I say.

Sim purses her lips, so hard her skin mottles. "Here."

She reaches down into her boot, pulls out her marline-spike, and hands it to me. "Don't do anything stupid," she says, then takes off at a run back down the hillside.

As soon as Sim is out of sight, Johanna turns to me, her hands clasped before her. "We are not staying up here."

"Obviously."

She squeaks in delight, bouncing toward me on the balls of her feet. "And here I thought I might have to fight you for agreement. You're such a rascal, Felicity, and I do love it. Come on!"

We stagger down the cliffside path and emerge on the beach, our feet leaving pulsing halos in the damp sand as we approach the dragon corpse. One half-open eye stares sightless at us, the glassy pupil slit. A thin forked tongue spills from between its teeth.

"It's like a snake," Johanna says, hiking her skirts up as she bounds down the sand toward it. "An enormous snake that lives in the ocean. How does it breathe under-water?"

"*Does* it breathe underwater?" I ask. There's a wound in its side, between the soft flaps around its neck. Not gills, but vulnerable enough that something was able to dig its way in and tear up the flesh like the ground after a tree is uprooted. Maybe it's the wound that killed it. "There are no gills."

"Maybe they're hidden," she says. "Or maybe they

breathe like frogs through their skin."

"Is that true, or is this revenge for telling you ears regrow?"

"It's the truth! Don't you remember the toads that swam in the pond on the Peeles' grounds?"

"I don't remember them breathing through their skin."

"And if they really are like snakes, they must have a more effective means of regulating the salt concentration of their blood. Or"—she steps up close to the mouth, the jaws as wide as she is tall, and peers fearlessly into it, steadying herself against one of the teeth as long as her hand—"filters around the tongue?"

I walk along the side of the serpent, watching the way the scales reflect the light like water. Birds are perched upon the spine, picking at the scales to get to the soft meat below. I test one of the scales in my hand—even with decay, they don't split easily. In spite of Sim's warning, I tug at it. It resists, so I use the marlinespike. Even with the metal as a lever, it takes a lot of prying before it cracks off in my hand. I fish my spectacles from my pocket and press them to my nose. Up close and whole, the scale is the shape of a corn kernel, round and tapered where it connects to the body. The color looks more pearly and reflective than it does when ground down into that sapphire powder.

I don't know how powerful the scales truly are, so I press it against my tongue with a light hand. It tastes of brine, though perhaps that's just the residue of the sea, along with something like bone—is it bone? Are they bones and not scales? What creature wears its bones outside its body? I break off a piece of the scale the size of my thumbnail, press it to my tongue, and let it dissolve. When I swallow, it prickles the back of my throat, a bubbly, bright feeling that turns my senses to champagne.

I know it is fast-acting, so I wait, wondering if I've even taken enough to feel any sort of kick or lift or difference at all.

And then I stop wondering.

It's like the world sharpens. The colors become brighter. The sound louder—I can hear two men down the beach arguing in Darija, every word clear though I don't understand them. I feel like I could learn it.

I look down at the scale in my hand, and my vision blurs. It takes me a moment to realize it's my spectacles. When I push them up on my forehead, the eyesight I lost long ago from squinting at tiny print in poor light has returned. I take a breath, and it's like chambers inside my lungs that I never knew existed open, letting so much air flood me I fear I will float away. I'm not sure if it's real, or simply my perception, but I swear my heart has never beat with strength like this. It's not fast with fear, or ragged like after running. It's strong. It makes me feel strong.

I wish I had a book. I could read it at twice my usual

speed. I wish I had a problem to solve, something mathematical and complicated, with a right answer. I flex my fingers in and out of fists, trying to decide if I want to run or swim or start listing every word I know.

My heart begins to feel like it's beating too fast. My whole body feels too fast, and at this speed, even a prickle of fear feels like panic.

When it leaves me, it's abrupt, like picking up a box you expect to be heavy and finding it weightless. The first thing I think—it comes to me without my consent—is that I will never truly breathe deeply again. I'll spend the rest of my life feeling like my heart is not beating fast enough, my lungs not opening enough.

"Felicity."

I look up. Johanna is standing in front of me, her hem splattered with dark sand and her eyes upon the scale in my hand. "You tried it."

"Just a bit."

"How did you feel?"

"Powerful." She holds out her hand, and I pass her the scale for examination. "This is dangerous."

She runs her thumb along the smooth edge, then back against the grain. "We need to take samples."

"Sim won't like that," I say.

"Well, Sim doesn't have to know." She swings her mother's bag off her back and tucks the scale into one of the pockets. "Do you think they're different, depending on what part of the body they're taken from? Or are they all the same? How did you get it free? Did you use your hands?" I hold up the marlinespike. "Good, use that. I'm going to see if there's a way to collect some of the blood."

She darts back down the beach, her bag bouncing on her hip, and I set back to the task of wiggling more scales free. I've hardly got the marlinespike wedged under one when someone shouts. I look up and there's a man running at me, thin and hunched but moving alarmingly fast. He's shouting in Darija, and I don't understand a word of it, but he's waving his arms like he's trying to shoo me away. I step back, raising my hands, but he keeps coming, now flinging his hand toward the glint of the marlinespike I'm holding.

Sim had said run, so I turn and I run.

He doesn't follow me far, but I keep going after he's stopped and returned to his salvage. There's a stone outcropping on the edge of the inlet, its fanged tops domed with emerald moss. Craggy rocks are scattered at its base, water collecting between them in pools, their sides thick with fluttering sea flora and a few dotted with bright-orange fish.

I lose my footing and step up to my knees in the ocean. Something slick and wet brushes my leg, and I shy. To my surprise, whatever brushes me shies too, and lets out a strange cry. It's like a shriek but registers deeper in my ears than most sounds. My whole body jerks with it. The surface of the water, already puckered from my splash, ripples.

I look behind me, but no one on the beach seems to have heard it. It comes again, and I clap my hands over my ears, peering down into the water to see what it is that is screaming at me.

I heave myself out of the pool, my petticoats gasping, then crouch down. I touch my hand to the surface, and something presses back from beneath the waves. I fall backward in surprise, sitting straight into one of the thankfully less-deep pools and soaking my skirt. There's the sound again, but softer this time and with more of a purr. Enough to be sure it's coming from this pool.

There's a jet of mist, then two nostrils poke above the surface, the slits of skin that keep out water opening as they surface. I scramble back to the edge of the pool, and looking back at me is one of the sea dragons in miniature, its scales short nubs and thin fins poking from its belly, translucent and twirling like ribbon beneath the water.

"Johanna!" I shout over my shoulder, so loud that several of the people on the beach turn. Johanna, absorbed in an examination of the dragon teeth, is not one of them. "Johanna!" I shout again, and this time she looks. I make a frantic wave, and she reluctantly detaches herself and trots to my side.

The baby dragon pushes its nose against the edges

of the pool, trying to hook its head on the rock and hurl itself out. I can see a spot along its neck that's been rubbed raw and bloody from trying. "Oh, oh, oh! Don't do that!" I scuttle along the rocks, trying to block the creature from harming itself again. When I touch it, it howls again, and I pull away. Beneath the water, its scales feel like velvet.

Johanna, now close enough to hear it too, lets out a shriek of her own as she covers her ears. "What was that?" she calls to me.

"Come here!" I reply. "There's a little one!"

"A what?" Johanna scrambles to my side, tearing the edge of her skirt on the stones in her haste. She lets out a small gasp when she sees the tiny dragon, its tail thrashing against the confines of the pool, and seizes my arm. "Felicity."

"Yes."

"Felicity." Her voice is a feather. "It's . . ."

"I know."

"A baby!"

"Or it could be a pocket variety."

"Felicity." Both her hands are on my arm now, strangling the fabric of my dress. "Felicity."

"That's me."

"We have discovered a new species."

Her face is like sunlight on a river, an already resplendent beam made brighter. I don't want to be the cloud and remind her we haven't, though. Sim and her family have sheltered these animals for decades. The scavengers on the beach, the people in Algiers—these dragons are not new to the world, only to our very small part of it.

Johanna puts a tentative finger into the water, and the tiny dragon wraps its lips very gently around it, suckling. "It doesn't have teeth," she says, her voice squeaking. "The big one does but—oh no, little one, is that your mother?"

"How do you know it's a female?" I ask.

"Parental unit of indeterminate gender, then. Oh, I hope not, you poor thing. We can be orphans together."

It is radical, I think as I watch Johanna, both of her arms submerged to the elbows as she strokes the dragon's head, the compassion she has for this thing. Most natural philosophers don't carry this sort of tenderness for the things they study. Most doctors don't. The hospitals in London are proof of that. The beetles and lizards and bats hunted for collections and then stuck with pins to a wall behind glass are proof of that. Men want to collect. To compete. To own.

Johanna runs a finger along the bridge of the dragon's nose, and a jet of mist shoots from its nostrils as they break the surface. It smells like seaweed and sugar. "Did you ever think," she says as the dragon purrs at her fingertips, "all those years ago, when we played at exploring, that we'd ever actually be here? Or find something like this? This feels like a dream." She pulls her hand from the water, shaking the water off, then turns to me. "Do you really think we can keep this to ourselves?"

"It's not ours to share."

"We could take this to the Royal Society. They'd have to take us seriously with a discovery like this. We could be the first women ever."

"First women to do what?"

"Any of it. All of it. We could lead expeditions. Publish books and papers and give lectures. Teach at universities. Can't you imagine it—you and me and the sea?" She spreads her arms and throws back her head, neck dipped like a dancer's. "Maybe it's worth sacrificing a few creatures so that we can better understand them all."

"What about sacrificing a few African cities?" I reply.

She sighs, letting her arms fall to her sides. The dragon raises its head from the water and nuzzles upward into her palm. "It's all very complicated, isn't it?" she says. "Or is it simply that I am not a good person because I even think that?"

"I'm not sure anyone is all good when you break us down to raw materials," I say.

"Max is all good."

"Max is a dog."

"I don't see how that changes anything. He's a good dog." The sea monster flips in the water, its tail cresting

337

the surface to reveal a small barb like a prickly burr. Johanna flinches with a laugh at the splash. "Maybe this little thing is all good."

"Or maybe she'll sink ships one day."

"Oh, shush." She dips her hand again into the water, and the sunlight strikes the waves like the ocean is made of precious stones. "Let me dream that there is something unquestionably pure in this world."

Johanna and I manage to free the little dragon from its prison in the tide pool, but it seems reluctant to swim out into the open ocean. Instead, it keeps darting back to where Johanna and I stand, up to our knees in the ocean, and winding itself between us. Johanna wades out with it under the pretense of luring it to deeper waters, but it's clear they're both playing. Her skirt bubbles around her like a jellyfish, pulsing with the waves. She chases the tiny dragon through the water, and it lets out another screeching purr, which makes Johanna shriek, though it seems to be a noise of pleasure from deep within them both. She dips a hand into the water, and it comes to her touch, its tail wrapped around her round calf like a living ribbon beneath the sea.

I return to the shore where Johanna left her mother's bag and folio, and draw a handful of the loose papers from inside. Pages and pages and pages of notes, most that it would take time and a magnifier and less potent sunlight that doesn't butter the lenses of my spectacles to decipher. There are several sheets with drawings of the dragons, each one a little different as she formed a more complete picture of what they look like. There is a long list of chemical compounds with two columns beside them, one with the word *obtained* dotting it and the second marked with either a P or a G.

It reminds me of something, and I dip into my pocket and pull out the list I have been carrying since the hospital in London, now ripped and spotted and practically molded to the shape of my thigh after so long pressed against it. The only line still completely legible is at the top: *I deserve to be here.*

I'm not sure I believed it when I wrote it. As much as I boasted a stiff upper lip in the face of rejection, every man who turned me away raised in me a fear that maybe they were right. Maybe I did not deserve a space among them. Maybe there is a reason women are kept in houses, minding children and making supper. Perhaps I never can be half as good a doctor as any of those men, simply because of a natural inferiority, and I am just too stubborn to see that.

But if I cannot always believe in myself, I can believe in Johanna. And Sim. And Sybille Glass and Artemisia Gentileschi and Sophia Brahe and Marie Fouquet and Margaret Cavendish and every other woman who came before us. I have never doubted the women who came before me or whether they deserved a seat at the table.

I crush the paper in my fist and let the ocean carry it from my fingers and out to sea.

I do not need reasons to exist. I do not need to justify the space I take up in this world. Not to myself, or Platt, or some hospital governors, or a pirate ship full of men with cutlasses. I have as much claim to this world as anyone else. No one will offer Johanna and me permission to make this work ours, to take up her mother's maps and follow their headings to the horizon's edge, where the sea and the sky smoke together. First of our name, first of our kind.

There's a bellow from the cove, and I glance over my shoulder. We're mostly sheltered by the rocks, but a sliver of the beach is still visible to me. The scavengers are leaving. They're leaving fast. They're running up the hillside, their faces turned to the sea so that they lose their footing on the sand. Some of them left their tools and bounty behind in shimmering heaps along the beach.

My skin prickles. Something is wrong.

I shove Sybille's papers back into the folio, then hike up a handful of my skirt and trek back to the beach, away from the shelter of our cove so that I have a full view of the empty sea beyond the bay. The sun has traveled farther than I expected. It sits just above the horizon, the yolk of a broken egg tipped out along the edge of the sky. The water is beginning to bronze beneath the spill.

And silhouetted against that syrupy sky is a massive warship, sails pulled in, anchor dropped and longboats lowering into the water.

I spring back down the beach and stagger into the cove. "Johanna! There's a ship!"

She looks up from the water. "What? Is it Sim's?"

"I don't think so."

"More scavengers?"

"No, it's a big ship. A warship. If it's European men, they won't let us walk away quietly. At best we'll be questioned and taken back to the Continent." I don't have to say aloud what the worst case is. "We have to hide."

"Where?"

"Stay here. Lie low."

"We're hardly out of sight here. As soon as they make landfall they'll spot us. And we'll lead them straight to her." She glances down at the water, where the dragon pup is twirling between her legs, oblivious to any danger.

"Then what do we do?"

"We run. It's the only thing we can do. Get over the dunes and hide there and wait for Sim like she said. We have to go now."

Johanna starts to hike toward me, her steps high in the water, but then stops. "No, stay here!"

It takes me a moment to realize she's talking to the sea monster, still curling around her ankles with every step. She tries to shoo it back into the cove, but it's not as well trained as Max. "Stay! Stay here! Don't follow me."

I run through the water—as much as one can run when the waves are pressing you the opposite way and the sea floor keeps abandoning your step—to where Johanna is begging a creature that does not understand her. I splash as loudly as I can, batting the water right in its face. It shimmies away from Johanna with another one of those ear-splitting whines. It is a horrible thing, to cause so much fear in something. If it were older and had a few more teeth, it would turn predatory. I know—I've felt that sort of fear too. I've felt cornered and turned on, and I've bitten back.

Instead, the little dragon looks cowed, floating a few feet away from us, its big wet eyes fixed on Johanna but too scared to return.

I'm sorry, I think. *I wish you understood.*

But it doesn't, and Johanna and I leave it behind in the cove, frightened and alone with its mother rotting upon the beach.

We pull up short at the edge of the rocks, crouching behind them and out of sight of the ship. The longboats have almost reached the shore. The sailors in them are distinctly European—all of them fair skinned and light haired and speaking English to one another. They're none of them in any sort of uniform, but they are out-fitted with hatchets, and several are hauling cases for collection between them. They drop them on the beach and unfold them into sample boxes, glass jars, vials. Rifles are fired into the air to scare off the few remaining scavengers upon the beach. They all go scrambling for the dunes.

The English know about the dragons already. They came here knowing about the beached monster, to harvest it. We're too late.

"Do we run for it?" I whisper to Johanna as we peer out from our hiding spot. "Or do we sneak for it?"

"I don't think they'll follow us if we run," she says. "They just want the area clear. We get up over the hillside and wait for Sim."

There's really no way to sneak. It's scrub and sand and the crumbling cliffs. But if we can get up among the trees, I think we can hide. "Come on."

Johanna and I start to scramble over the rocks. On the beach, the men are so absorbed in their work that it seems a good chance they won't notice us. Then, in the cove behind us, the tiny monster lets out its most earsplitting scream yet. It stops the world, but only for a moment. The sailors all look straight at us, and Johanna and I both start running.

Though running in sand is perhaps the most futile task one can undertake. Johanna is bigger than I am, and with no shoes and her sopping dress weighing her down, she's slower. I almost stop, but there's nothing I can do to help her other than offer words of encouragement, and words never won a race.

I had expected the sailors would leave us alone once they saw we were leaving—at most, they'd fire a gunshot in the air—but instead, they're advancing. I was prepared to be chased off but not to be pursued. "Johanna, hurry!"

But we're pressed against the rocks, the sailors closing in and cutting us off from the path. I try to dodge around one and he grabs the back of my skirt, yanking me off my feet. I sprawl backward in the sand, and the sailor flips me over, then pins me to the ground with my hands twisted behind me and his knee pressed into my back. I'm spitting out mouthfuls of sand. It's in my eyes and my ears. I kick backward at him, hoping it will land hard enough to weaken his grip, but instead, the marlinespike wedged in my boot flies free and lands in the sand, out of my reach. Another man snatches it up. Johanna screams, and I raise my head as high as I can, just enough to see her hit the ground beside me, then a heavy boot, black and shiny as a beetle, presses into her back.

It is perhaps a very conventionally feminine thing to say I recognize those shoes. But when the only bit of a man you get a good look at is his footwear, and when that footwear appears again, this time pressing your friend into the dirt, shoes tend to make an impression. I crane my neck to look up at him, though I wouldn't have recognized him, for I never actually got a good look at the man in Platt's living room in Zurich. But I'm certain it's him. He's tall and fair skinned, his cheeks red with the sun and hair beneath his cornered hat cut short, like it's usually tucked under a wig.

"Alex!" he shouts down the beach, and my heart sinks. "Are these your lost girls?"

A shadow stretches up the beach toward us. Beside me, Johanna lets out a whimper. I half expect the little dragon to answer again, their fear matching in pitch.

His shadow strikes my face and I flinch like it burns. Dr. Platt looms over us, a curved cutlass in one hand and his shirtsleeves already stained with the dragon's blood. He looks ill; his hair is greasy and his skin like it's one of Quick's waxworks. Perhaps it's the time on the ocean, but the sun tends to lend color to a man's cheeks, not turn them pallid and bruised.

"They are indeed." He pushes a toe under Johanna's chin and tips her face up to his. "I had a sense we might cross paths here."

"How did you find us?" I ask, and it comes out with a mouthful of sand.

Platt spins to face me, his feet tipping as the sand caves under them. "We followed the monster."

I remember the wound on its side, the ripped-up flesh around its neck. Like something from a harpoon. "You killed it."

345

Platt doesn't answer. Instead, he turns to the man with the boots and says, "Do we tie them up?"

"Probably best while we harvest."

"Harvest?" Johanna cries, and while we had just considered taking samples ourselves, these men look ready to extract far more.

Platt doesn't acknowledge her. Instead he says to his sailors, "Bind them together. We'll take them back to the ship when we're done here."

I want to scream. I want to spit and writhe and kick my feet like a child. This pathetic, deceptive man I wasted years of my life idolizing, followed across a continent on a chance, who had his knife so deep in my side I didn't feel it until he twisted. I've never wanted so badly to punch someone in the face as I do him in this moment.

Where are Sim and all those threatening pirates when we need them? As much as I believe in the power and strength of a woman, what I wouldn't give for a flock of barrel-chested men with cutlasses for limbs to emerge from the hilltops and leap to our defense. But instead, Johanna and I are bound back to back, our wrists knotted to each other and legs tied at the ankles and knees, with a length of coarse cloth looped around each of our mouths. We are then made to sit and watch as the sea dragon is stripped of its scales in chunks that scatter along the beach like shells. Even after they've been collected, they leave dark circles of blood in the sand.

The sailors work long into the night. They light fires, burn the fat from the leviathan body for fuel. The men take turns standing watch over us. Johanna is facing the ocean; I have my back to the sailors, looking up at the tops of the cliffs. So it's me who sees the pirates when they appear at the top of the hillside, dark silhouettes that feather from the shrubbery and spread. The moonlight makes their weapons look like they're made of smoke. Me who sees Sim creep to the edge, the same spot we three stood this morning, and hold up a hand, watching Johanna and me, and the English sailors and the ship. Calling a halt.

And then a retreat.

I'm the one who watches them disappear into the darkness, leaving us tied on the beach as Platt's men strip the dragon to its bones.

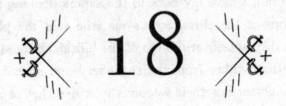

18

We are kept upon the beach until the sun rises and the men begin to load their spoils into the longboats to be ferried back to the ship. The carcass of the monster is rotten flesh and raw bones now, the remaining skin pinked and bloody and bare. It looks like a vein burst open upon the shore. Johanna and I are unbound from each other and hauled into the last longboat, then forced to sit wedged on the floor between cutlasses and hatchets, their blades clinking together like coins in a purse. We've hardly cast off before my socks and skirt are soaked through with the blood and bile collecting in the bottom of the boat.

The sailors stink of the rotten entrails they've been picking apart, all of them punchy from whatever they've been chewing to keep themselves awake and popping blisters upon their palms from where their work has rubbed them raw. I could tell them that will lead to nothing but infection, but at this moment, I'd prefer if all their hands fester and rot off. Any man who takes a lady against her will deserves a far more sensitive body part than the hands to drop off slowly. As our boat is hauled up to the deck, I catch a glimpse of the name painted upon the side: *Kattenkwaad*. Dutch or Germanic, and though I couldn't say which, I'm certain it's a ship from Johanna's uncle's fleet.

We are marched to the captain's cabin at the back of the ship, where we are at last untied and ungagged. My tongue feels hairy and dry after so long pressed against the thick material. Beside me, Johanna sucks in her cheeks, trying to generate moisture in her mouth.

Platt is waiting for us in the cabin, leaning against the captain's desk like it's holding him up. His eyes are bloodshot, his skin even yellower than it looked on the beach. Before him is Johanna's trunk, left behind at Frau Engel's in Zurich—he must have tracked her there, same as I had, and I say a quick prayer of thanks that we didn't spend another night there before we left. A prayer rendered pointless by the fact that he's caught us now. He also has Sybille Glass's bag and the leather portfolio collected from the beach. The bag has been ripped apart, emptied, and then turned inside out so that its contents are strewn across the floor. The papers have been far more civilly looted, leafed through, and left lying in stacks upon the desktop.

Johanna and I both stop as the cabin door slams at our backs, the trunk in between us and Platt. "Where's the map, Johanna?" he demands with no prelude.

"What map?" she says, really leaning into that girlish trill of her voice. The pitch could shatter glass.

"Your goddamn mother's goddamn map. Where is it?" Platt pushes himself up and staggers around the trunk. I'm not entirely sure what the answer is—I didn't see the map when I flipped through the folio earlier, but I had assumed it was there. Either Johanna had taken precautions or it had been lost somewhere along the way, though that seems impossible. I think briefly of Sim, seeing her lurking upon the top of the hill watching the English ravage the dragons they'd sworn to protect. Perhaps she had taken the map without us noticing, and all these noble intentions had been a lie. Or rather, more of a lie than previously thought, for no matter her motives, she had still abandoned us.

Platt kicks the trunk out of his way, and Johanna takes a step back, straight onto my foot. I grab her by the elbow and push her behind me, putting myself between her and Platt. "We don't know what you're talking about," I say. My voice is hoarse after a night with my mouth full of wool, but at least that disguises the fear that would have dried it out anyway.

"I know you have it," Platt says. His legs tremble

under him, the ship's bobbing in the water seeming to unsettle him more than it should. "You've every other damn thing she left behind on that ship. You wouldn't have left Zurich without it. You wouldn't be *here* if you didn't have it." He picks up the portfolio case and shakes it at us. He's already emptied it, so it is a gesture made primarily for symbolism. "Where is the map?"

"We left it behind," Johanna says. She has her elbows pulled into her, hands balled over her stomach. "It's back in Algiers."

Platt's eyes flash with panic, but then he swallows hard. "You're lying. You wouldn't go all the way to Africa to leave it behind. Did you meet with someone? Did you sell it? Did those pirates make a deal with you?"

"How do you know about the pirates?" I ask.

He laughs, a savage, raw sound. "Because the Crown and Cleaver owns every inch of water we sailed in. We were paying them taxes just to be allowed into their territory. And her mother"—and here he thrusts a shaking finger at Johanna—"used the voyage for her own gain. She was mapping her way to these monsters' nests and then she was going to take that information to return to England and make a name for herself. If she hadn't been certain this discovery would make her impossible to ignore, she wouldn't have cared about these beasties. Miss Sybille Glass would have done anything for attention."

"So how are you any different?" I shoot back. "You can't claim noble intentions either, after you just stripped a corpse."

"For resources," he replies, his jaw clenched around the final word. "Resources that the corsairs who own that land would have let wash back out to sea and waste. They rob the world of valuable substances by keeping them hidden." He's groping around in his coat. He looks manic and wild, his hands shaking as he paws for his snuff box in his inside pocket, but when he flicks it open, it's empty. He lets out a low growl and instead takes up the rolled leather case fallen from Sybille's bag and unfurls it, fumbling for one of the vials of powdered scale.

The back of my mouth burns at the sight of that glistening powder, my lungs suddenly very aware of how light my breath is, how much stronger than me Platt is. I want to reach out and snatch it from him but instead I say, "Don't take that. It's addictive."

"You think I don't know that?" he snaps. "Not all of us are born as privileged as you, Miss Montague. We don't learn about addicts in our medical treaties, we are born to them and raised by them and we're hooked from the moment we first breathe."

"That's what you've been taking all this time," I say. "It's not snuff or *madak* or opium. It's those scales."

His hand fists around the vial, so tight his knuckles

turn white. I'm shocked it doesn't break. "Your mother," he says, jerking his head toward Johanna, "roped me into her experiments. Poison and antidote and poison and antidote, all treated with the powdered scales she found in black markets and bought off pirates. She told me it was a drug that could end sickness. Asked me to take it regularly and promised it would get me off opium. Said I could go back to England a sober man and get my medical license back and she'd credit me for my help. It was a wreck of a ship, a damned voyage paid for as cheaply as possible by that man who wanted a collection but had no idea the lengths it took to get one. We were all sick from the rot and the rats and the food. We thought we'd sink before we got to the Barbary States. Every man on board that boat was only there because he had no other options. Your mother was no different."

"No one wanted to work with her because she was a woman," Johanna argues.

"No one wanted to work with her because she was a bitch," Platt says, and Johanna cringes. "She used anyone who could give her a step up. Used them and then discarded them."

"She had to fight for recognition," Johanna says. "You're the one who took credit for her work in the cabinet."

"It was my work too—it ruined my whole damn life, and if she hadn't gotten herself killed, she wouldn't have given me an inch," he replies. "Your mother was ruthless. Just as much of a degenerate addict as I am. She was a slave of her ambition, and that made her a slave of her drug."

He can't get the seal broken on the vial, and with a growl of frustration, he cracks the top off against the edge of the desk and empties it into his hand. "Don't!" I grab his hand and the powder spills, blossoming in a cloud between us before settling upon the desk, the floor, down the front of both our clothes, no speck salvageable.

I look up at Platt just as his hand connects with the side of my face.

It's a stunning pain, unlike anything I've ever experienced. The bright sting reverberates through me. My vision goes blurry and I stumble backward, sitting down so hard that I feel the shudder through every inch of my spine and popping in my neck.

Johanna shrieks. I blink hard, trying to clear my vision and the ringing in my ears.

"I'm sorry. I'm so sorry," Platt is saying, his voice ragged and breaking. He's bent over the desk, his shoulders shaking. "I didn't mean to—"

"You've lost your mind!" Johanna shouts at him.

There's a knock on the cabin door, then the man who visited Platt in Zurich enters. "What the hell is going on here?" he snaps, pushing the door shut behind him with one of those expensive boots, their toes speckled with sand from the beach. "We're loaded, and we need a heading. Good God, Alex?"

Platt motions wordlessly to the gent, and the two of them stagger out onto the deck, the door clapping shut behind them.

As soon as Platt is gone, Johanna is beside me. "Are you all right?" she asks, brushing away the tears the slap pried from my eyes with a gentle touch that still stings. "Zounds, I can see his whole handprint on your face."

"It's fine." I spit out a mouthful of blood from biting my tongue, but all my teeth are still in my head and a quick exploration of my face with my fingers confirms no bones broken. Outside the door, I can hear Platt and the other man arguing. Forcing myself to ignore the pain, I motion to the door, and Johanna and I both crawl forward and press our ears to it.

". . . losing your head," the man is saying. "Where's the map?"

"She has it, Fitz," Platt replies, his voice cracking. "I know she does."

"But you haven't seen it?"

"I . . . no."

"Is it stashed somewhere on the beach? Or back in the city?"

"We have to take her back to England and then to court. They'll force her surrender."

"We don't have time to return to England and get a

court to pry documents out of her hands," Fitz snaps. "Without a marriage certificate, your legal claim is tenuous at best. And by the time a judge has heard your case, you'll not have any investors left."

"But—"

Fitz presses on overtop of him. "The moment this case shows up in court, we lose our only asset in this expedition. Our first claim. By the time we have the map, someone else will have discovered your nesting grounds."

Silence, but for the sound of Platt taking several deep, strained breaths. The door creaks as he leans against it. "What about the Montague girl?" he asks at last.

"If you think you can extort money out of her family, we're going to need that. Send her back to England with a letter to her father."

"We don't have another ship."

"I'll find someone for you."

Every word tightens like a fist around my chest, making it harder and harder to breathe. I should have stayed in Edinburgh with Callum. I should have settled for life with a baker who would have tolerated me. I should have known I wasn't a forest fire, but a small flame that could be snuffed out easily by the first man who turned my way with a heavy breath. There is no winning for women in this world. I was foolish to think there ever could be for me, and now it's like pouring salt in a wound to know that

I spent so long sustaining myself on such misplaced hope.

You are Felicity Montague, I think, trying to force some courage into my heart, but all I can think is, *You are Felicity Montague, and you should have settled for a simple life.*

"Right now," Fitz continues, "we have samples, but they can be easily dismissed. That won't secure a charter, but it will get every other naturalist in London to put their nose to the ground and sniff out these creatures before you can. You need the map, you need the island, and you need to return to England with eggs. So tell me: What's our heading?"

A pause. Both Johanna and I hold our breath. "Gibraltar," Platt says at last.

Beside me, Johanna lets out a small squeak, one hand flying to her mouth. *Gibraltar?* I mouth at her.

"English soil," she replies. "He's going to marry me."

It will be at least a week at sea before we reach the lone spit of British soil at the tip of Spain. The blessing of a small ship ill-equipped to hold ladies who are not quite brig-worthy prisoners but who are also most certainly not to be left to their own devices is that Johanna and I are locked together in the cabin, with big glass windows that look out across the ocean billowing behind us. It seems at first foolish for them to leave us with such an easy escape until I, in truly thinking out the logistics an attempt through the windows would take, realize that it's no exit at all. The windows do not open, and even if we smashed through enough panes that we could climb out without lacerating our flesh on the shards or drawing attention to the noise, there is nowhere to go. Above is a ship full of men. Below the vast, unforgiving sea. Aside from a plan of leaping overboard with a pocket full of hardtack and the hope of being scooped up by someone with more noble intentions than our current captors, we've no relief.

Once we're certain Platt has left us alone, I ask Johanna, "Do you have the map?"

"Of course I do." She pats her stomach.

I may have been hit harder than I thought, for I stare blankly back at her. "You ate it?"

"No, it's laced under my corset. I was worried someone might snatch the bags while we traveled, or we'd lose it or something terrible would happen. Something like this." She gestures around at our cell. "And I assumed that if we did find ourselves trapped by men who would want it, none of them could get a corset unlaced if they tried. Or even think to look there." She tugs at the bodice of her dress, trying to shake off the sand that has dried along it in clumps. "Though it won't do any good. If he marries me, he could rip all my clothes off and steal it and force himself upon me and still be protected by the law."

I shudder. As soon as the vows are exchanged, anything Platt wants to do to her would be within his rights. And while I don't think that's where his head is at, I've learned from years of stories passed in whispers that men have needed much less of a reason to do much worse to a girl.

"We could destroy the map," I say weakly. Johanna closes her eyes, a crease appearing between her eyebrows, and I feel the same twist inside me, like a cloth wrung dry. Destroying that map would mean giving up on my last chance of escaping a life with Callum. A life on my own terms, with Johanna and a ship and something to study. Work I could own, that would make me impossible to ignore.

"You saved Sim because of the dragon scales," Johanna says. "We can do good things with this."

"Can we? Or are we just going to use them the same as Platt?"

"You mean Platt *and* my mother?" Johanna flops down upon the cabin bed, her loose hair tumbling in snarled ribbons over her shoulder. "We should have let Sim take the map. At least then Platt couldn't have it."

"Yes, but if that had been suggested to you before we knew he'd found us, you would have led a mutiny. And I'm not certain Sim has as much goodwill toward us as we do her."

"I thought you didn't have any, what with all your

goading each other."

"Yes, well, turns out arguing a lot with someone can make you rather fond of them." I cross to her trunk and begin to rifle through it, hoping there will be something there that will give us some comfort or hope of escape or maybe even a box of those macarons from Stuttgart so we can do a proper sorrow-drowning in some excessive decadence. It's mostly a tangle of dresses and overskirts and bodices. Muffs and black stockings. A bottle of melon water and a case of tooth powder. A tiny miniature with a sketch of a woman who must be Sybille Glass in one frame and a lock of hair pressed into the other side. A sewing kit.

"You were very prepared," I say as I sift through.

"I wasn't intending to go back," she says. "At least, not for a long while. That's far less than I wanted to take. I planned to bring Max, remember?"

I toss a drawstring bag of hard biscuits onto the desk. "I can see that."

"Do you think Platt was right?" she asks.

"About what?" I say without looking up.

"That she wasn't . . ." She scrapes her heels against the floorboards, prying sand off the soles. "That my mother wasn't what I thought her to be. I've spent my whole life looking up to her, this brave woman who left an unhappy marriage to work in the field she loved. She left me, but that could be forgiven because she did it for the work. But maybe she did it for herself. And she used Platt. Probably others too. And maybe she didn't care for these creatures at all. She would have done anything to be noticed."

I glance up. She's unraveling the embroidery along her bodice, a flower coming unstitched petal by petal between her fingertips. "You can't believe what Platt told you."

"It's the only thing anyone has ever told me of her," she replies, her voice breaking. "Except for the letters she wrote me herself. And she'd never cast herself a villain."

"I don't think she was."

"She wasn't a hero, either."

"So she can be both." My fingers scratch the bottom of the trunk, pulling up the brocaded paper lining it. I stare down at it, absolutely throttling my brain to come up with something—anything—that would get us out of this without having to destroy the map entirely. That would be the right thing to do, and we both know it. But it's also a surrender. A surrender as self-serving as anything Platt or Glass ever did.

"We could make a copy of the maps," I offer, though it's hardly a suggestion. In anticipation of our imprisonment, the room has been stripped. Every desk drawer is empty or locked. All they've left us are bedclothes, towels, and a washbasin. Nothing that we could make any use of in map duplication. The most promising method would be carving it with our teeth into the single bar of soap.

"We're not going to be able to make a copy," Johanna says. She jerks the undone thread on her stomacher and it unfurls in her hand.

Which is when an idea occurs to me. "What if we stitch it?"

"Stitch what? A copy of the map?" When I nod, she looks down at the thread tangled around her fingers. "You mean embroidery?"

"Why not? I had scads of lessons, didn't you? We could embroider a copy, then destroy the actual paper version. Throw it in a fire and let it burn beyond anything Platt could fish out. If you don't have the map, he has no reason to want to marry you. You can refuse to give it to him, and he can search forever and never find it because it's gone. Then we walk away with a copy he doesn't even know exists."

"What do we stitch it on?" she asks, her eyes darting around the room. "We can't very well go carrying the bedsheets away with us without raising some sort of suspicion."

"You've got petticoats, don't you?" I say. "No one will see those."

She chews on her bottom lip for a moment, then says, "No, not my petticoats. Yours." She bounces off the bed,

362

tossing her hair over her shoulder. "He'll be less likely to suspect it from you."

Johanna does not have an overabundance of thread in her sewing kit, which was meant only for tasks like sewing a button back on, and as my fingers are smaller and more suited to tiny stitches than hers, she assigns herself the task of carefully unpicking thread from all of her dresses from the trunk, as well as the bedclothes, while I begin our meticulous copy of the map on the inside of my petticoats, stitch by single stitch.

It's no small project. Even with my spectacles, my eyes are stinging by the end of the first morning and my fingers are sore by night, knuckles cramping and pinched. Johanna and I swap positions, though the muscles in my hand are so prone to random contractions that I'm a liability to our limited supply of thread. I'm more vigilant after those initial days of arthritic pain to stretch my muscles, pulling my fingers back until I feel the strain to keep them limber.

We can't afford to waste precious time—the distance between Algiers and Gibraltar suddenly seems to be nothing more than a few quick strides—so though I'm likely going to end up with stiff joints before I've even reached the appropriate age to call myself a spinster, there's not time to wait for the pain to subside. Johanna knows how to read a map better than I do, so she tells me what pieces can be left out, what numbers and angles are most critical to get right. We use the ribbons from her dresses to measure the distances between points on her mother's chart and mark them with pins upon our fabric.

By the time we reach Gibraltar, we've made an almost complete copy of the chart upon the underside of my petticoat.

Gibraltar

19

Boarding a ship in Africa, the farthest from home I'd ever felt, and then stepping off in Gibraltar to find a tiny slice of Britain is nearly as disorienting as trying to get my land legs after our time at sea. Though we see even less of Gibraltar than we did of Algiers—we hardly get a view of the Rock before we're taken straight from the ship to a second cell, this one a captain's house along the waterfront, manned by a staff so aggressively English that, although we were clearly brought here against our will, tea is delivered to us in our rooms as we are locked inside them. The staff addresses Fitz as Commander Stafford, and he seems master of the house, though I'm not sure whether he owns it or it's a navy holding.

Johanna and I are kept here, confined in separate apartments for several days. The map is again tucked inside her stomacher and laced tight against her stays.

We are very nearly finished with our copy, but not quite enough to destroy the original with confidence. Johanna wanted to see it through before we made landfall, cut our losses and set it aflame from the lamp in our cabin, but I had insisted not. Any hasty decisions could compromise this plan entirely. Our embroidered map is impressive, but nowhere near as detailed as Sybille's.

The next time I see Johanna, a maid escorts us downstairs together. On the stairs, Johanna catches my eye and touches two fingers over her stomach, a silent indicator that the map is still there.

We're shown together to the parlor, where both Stafford and Platt are waiting for us, Platt jittery and pacing, smacking a folded sheet of parchment against his palm.

Johanna does not wait for him to settle or seat us or offer biscuits like this is anything resembling a civilized meeting. "I don't know why you thought bringing me here would change anything," she says, crossing her arms and giving the two gentlemen a stare that would have cracked granite. "I will not marry you, and I will not give you the map. I shall scream all the way down the street and refuse to sign the papers and tell every man, woman, and child in this city that I am a prisoner of you and my hand is being forced. I will never call myself your wife, nor Mrs. Platt, and anyone who addresses me as such shall hear the full story of how you deceived and abused me. So I say to you, sir, that this is your last chance to avoid a kidnapping charge, for do not think for a second I won't take you to court."

I nearly applaud. It's a speech I heard her practice a few times while we were picking at our embroidered map, but she delivers it with poise and ferocity that I had not seen in full before. It's like staring into the sun, so strong and bright she stands, and my heart swells with a sudden adoration for her, my proud and lovely friend.

Stafford looks at Platt, who tugs at the collar of his shirt like it's choking him. His fingernails are yellow around the edges. He takes a short breath that sounds as though it sticks like toffee in his chest, then crosses to Johanna and holds out the paper in his hand without a word.

She doesn't take it. "What's this?"

"Some information that may change your mind," Platt replies.

"Nothing will change my mind."

"Read it, Miss Hoffman," Stafford says over Platt's shoulder. "You will not be asked again."

Johanna glances at me, though I have no advice to offer her, then takes the paper. The tips of her fingers are bruised and swollen from our needlework, but either Platt does not notice, or doesn't understand what it may mean. I watch as her eyes skim the page, trying to decipher what it says from the set of her brows. Then all the color leaves her face, and she sways like a boxer on her last legs. I worry for a moment she may swoon. "Johanna?" I say, reaching out, but she crumples the letter and throws it back at Platt. He lets it strike his chest and bounce off without flinching.

"I do not believe you," she says, her voice wobbling.

Platt spreads his hands wordlessly.

Johanna's bottom lip is trembling, eyes welling. All that fierce confidence suddenly wilted like a paper caught flame. As she sinks, my panic rises. I want to dash across the room, snatch up the letter, and see for myself whatever Platt has found to hold over Johanna, but before I can, Stafford has taken up the sheet and tucked it inside his coat.

"I'll give you the map," Johanna says breathlessly.

"What?" I say.

Platt glances at Stafford then shakes his head. "Not good enough."

Someone tell me what is going on! I want to scream. Tell me what rut our plot has struck. The only thing worse than knowing is not, for my mind is unfurling every possible horrific message that could be contained within that letter. He's threatened her. Her uncle. Me. Our families. Our friends. Every person we've ever known. The whole of England. He'll poison them all if she doesn't comply.

Johanna swipes a hand over her cheek, but another tear replaces the one she pushed away. "All right," she says, her voice breaking. "I'll marry you."

"No!" It escapes me before I can stop it. Stafford is already heading for the parlor door, and Platt has snatched up his coat and is tugging it on. Johanna is statued at my side, still and weeping silently. I take her by the hand. "What did it say? What's he done to you?"

She shakes her head. "I can't tell you."

"Johanna, whatever it is—"

"Miss Montague," Stafford barks. "With me, please."

I don't let her go. "Whatever threat he has made against you—"

"Montague!"

"Don't marry him," I say, my voice a cracked whisper. "You'll never be free."

Before she can respond, Stafford has me by the shoulders and drags me toward the front hallway. I look back as Platt extends a hand to Johanna and she takes it, civilized and silent.

The marriage is to be performed at King's Chapel, a small and brown and very Anglican church on the fringe of the sea. The other places of worship in the city are all mosques stripped and rechristened as Christian halls, but there's something about this tiny chapel built by Franciscans with its thin interior aisle and brick front that makes me feel like I'm back in Cheshire. Particularly with the prayer books written in English, the priest a pasty man with a greasy wig and thick blue veins standing out under his skin. The money that trades hands in exchange for a hasty ceremony is English. The priest asks no questions about why it is that Platt is determined to be wed to this girl half his age with no notice, or why the bride looks as though she's about to vomit and one of her witnesses is pinning the other to him, his arm a vise clamping her to his side.

Platt and Johanna could have said their spousals on a hill without anyone knowing and so long as they were on English soil it would have been legal, but I suspect Platt wants any case he may someday need to make for the legitimacy of this union to be as strong as possible, so they have the Bible read, rings provided by the chapel exchanged. They sign the registry book, then Stafford does, before holding out the pen to me. With every step I take toward the podium, I can feel the silky embroidery inside my petticoat brushing my thighs.

Platt presses a chaste kiss to Johanna's mouth and all I can think of is what could have been in that letter that has kept Johanna silent all this while. She raised no protest. She did not scream. The only words she's uttered since we left the house were the *I do*. What was written on that page that has so stopped her mouth? I'm sick with imagining.

After the ceremony, we're marched back to the house, where Johanna and I are left alone in the parlor, sitting side by side upon the couch for a few precious moments while the gentlemen convene in the hallway. Johanna is crying again, her cheeks swollen and cherry red and her tears absolutely silent. I take her hand on the couch between us.

I don't press her. I don't ask what the letter said. But after several minutes of silence she chokes out, unprompted, "You're going to think me the silliest girl who ever lived."

I glance sideways at her. "Why would I think that?"

"Because of what I've done . . . for . . . You'll never forgive me." She pulls her hand from mine and covers her face. "You thought me silly and vain before, but this will truly seal it."

"Johanna, please, tell me. I swear, whatever it is, I trust you. I trust your heart. I won't think—"

"It's Max."

"What?"

She lets out the first audible sob I've heard from her, unexpected and brutal as a hunger pang. "He would have sent the letter back to Stuttgart, instructing them to shoot my dog, unless I married him." Her hands are shaking against her face. Her whole body is shaking. "I know it's foolish. If I had told you I was going to sacrifice my independence and my life and our work for some dog, you wouldn't have let me. You would have told me I was silly."

"You're not."

She peeks at me overtop of her hands. "What?"

"You're not silly. Or foolish." I don't know how to say it and make her believe me. Sincerity suddenly feels like a pantomime, particularly after all the time I spent slyly and savagely telling her just how silly I found everything she loved. But I have no ounce of ill will toward her for it, and nothing seems to matter in that moment more than that she believes me when I say it. "You are protecting what you love."

She shakes her head, then slides a hand down the front of her dress, fishing around in her stomacher before she emerges with the tattered map, now stuck through with pinholes and smudged with a few drops of blood drawn from needles. Her eyes flick to the fire snapping in the grate, merry and oblivious.

I press my hands over hers, the map in between them like a shared prayer. "Don't."

"I'm so pathetic," she says, and I can't tell if she's laughing or crying. "I'm soft and selfish and sentimental."

"You're nothing of the sort, Johanna Hoffman," I reply. "You are a shield and spear to all the things you love. I'm glad to be among them."

She lets her head fall over onto my shoulder, and I press my cheek against it. Her face is damp against my neck. We're both quiet for a moment, then she sniffs and says, "Sorry."

"Don't apologize for—"

"No, I'm a messy crier, and I've gone and slobbered on your shoulder."

"What? Oh." She sits up and I laugh at the damp, slimy spot she leaves behind. She laughs too, a little wetter than a laugh ought to be, but at least recognizable. "Max would be very proud."

The parlor door swings open and Platt strides in. I look behind him for Stafford, but he's absent. Platt stops before us and folds his hands behind his back. "Do you want to make a theater of this?"

"No." Johanna stands up and squares her shoulders. Faces her executioner on her feet and extends the map.

Platt snatches it from her and unfolds it, a small cry that may be delight or pain or some compound of both flying from his lips when he sees it. "Did you alter it? Remove information?"

"No."

"If you have—"

"I know," she interrupts. "Please don't say it."

He folds the map with surgical precision and tucks it into his coat pocket, then keeps his hand pressed over-top of it like he's afraid we may make a snatch for it or a heavy wind will whip through the parlor and pull it from him.

"You have what you want," I say, rising to my feet to stand beside Johanna. "The map and the folio and all her work. You don't need us any longer."

"A good attempt at negotiation, Miss Montague," he says, his fingers tripping into his pocket again and tracing the shape of the map. "But with your wit and your mouth, I would not trust you to leave this home unchecked."

"I won't say anything," I say. "So long as you uphold your end and Johanna and her . . ." I'm not sure what word best describes Max, so I just say, "family remain safe."

But Platt is shaking his head. "Commander Stafford has hired a captain with an English Letter of marque to take you both to England. Miss Montague, you'll be returned to your father, and Mrs. Platt to my home in London. Any whiff of trouble, and I'll send word to your uncle in Stuttgart at once."

"There won't be," Johanna says softly.

But Platt doesn't have a cuddly puddle of a dog to hold over me, and I had certainly not expected to be sent anywhere so soon. I thought we had more time here, or at least more time to reorient ourselves now that our plan has changed. "That wasn't part of the arrangement."

"Then would you rather I have Mrs. Platt committed to an institution for her hysteria and you tossed back into the Barbary States without a penny? How far will that mind of yours get you then? You'll truly learn what a woman must do to survive alone in this world." He takes a step toward me, and I fight the urge to retreat. I can still feel the sting of his hand against my cheek, but I will not back down before this man. It may be a small, hollow gesture, but the refusal to surrender is all I have. He stops, fists clenching at his sides. "I am doing you a kindness, Miss Montague. You should be returned to your family."

"A kindness?" I repeat with a wild laugh. "You think yourself kind to me? Is that what you tell yourself so that you can sleep at night?"

"Your ambition will eat you alive," he replies. "Same as it did Miss Glass. I cannot let that happen to you."

Zounds, does this fool actually think he's saving me? Another storybook hero to swoop in and rescue a girl from a dragon or a monster or herself—they're all the same. A woman must be protected, must be sheltered, must be kept from the winds that would batter her into the earth.

But I am a wildflower and will stand against the gales. Rare and uncultivated, difficult to find, impossible to forget.

The bell echoes through the house, then footsteps and the front door opening. Stafford's voice raised in greeting to the captain who has arrived to return us to England.

"You have not saved anyone," I say to Platt, as low and dangerous as I can muster. "Not me, not Johanna, not yourself."

"You don't understand."

"Neither do you," I snap. "At least I know enough not to delude myself into thinking imprisonment is a kindness."

"Imprisonment?" Someone says from the doorway. "That's very dramatic. Will she make this much of a theater about everything?"

For a moment, that voice in this house with my stomach calcifying in slow despair is so out of place I'm certain I am imagining it. Or if not imagining it, I am at the very least mistaken. I almost don't dare look for fear of breaking the spell and resigning myself well and truly to my fate. Hope in any form feels fragile as spun sugar.

But there he is, swaggering into the room in a way that would have been ridiculous had he not been so good-looking, all scruffed up and mussed like he's been weeks on the unforgiving sea. Had he not lost that ear, he'd be far too pretty to pass as a convincing sailor.

It's Monty.

Thank God the commander is occupied making introductions under some assumed name I don't catch and Platt is just as occupied making a handshake with the young man he must think is a very legitimate British shipping agent, so neither of them sees me trying to scrape my jaw off the floor. Monty raises a fuss about his payment, and how he can be assured it will be received, and how half up front doesn't seem like enough, perhaps they can negotiate something higher. They trade all relevant information of the accounts to be collected and deposited into, and exactly what doorstep I'm to be dropped on, and it's hard not to go from gaping at my brother to grinning when he meets my eyes for the first time. I expect that, in his rascally heart, he won't be able to resist a wink, but instead he sizes me up with a peery eye that nearly has me fooled. Were he ever inclined to take to the stage, he'd make a very good actor. "How much trouble can I expect?" he asks Platt. "They look contrary."

"No trouble," Platt assures him with a hard look at Johanna and me.

Monty points to me. "That one's got a squint like she reads too many books."

I shall break into a thousand pieces with the effort it requires not to roll my eyes at him. He's taking such great pleasure in his clandestine crowing that he's going to give us both away.

"Feel free to use any restraint you see fit," Stafford replies. "And upon the delivery of this letter"—and here he hands Monty a sealed sheet of parchment that I imagine my brother will take great delight in ripping up once we're gone—"you can expect sufficient compensation from her father."

Stafford walks with us to the docks, holding on to Johanna while Monty keeps his arm on me. "Dear sister," he murmurs, so low only I can hear, "look what you get yourself into when I'm not around."

"Dear brother," I reply, "I have never been gladder to see you."

I am near ready to faint with relief when I see the *Eleftheria* among the British ships in port. Monty trades a last handshake with Stafford, then escorts Johanna and me up the gangplank. There are a few men on board, most of whom I don't recognize, but at the helm, Ebrahim straightens from the knot he's clearly pretending to tie, first to trace our progress, then, after a brief moment of eye contact with Monty, falls into step behind us as Monty leads Johanna and me down below the deck.

Monty offers me a hand on the stairs, so steep they're practically a ladder, and I take it, careful not to catch a toe in my skirt and unravel all our hard work on my petticoat. When he extends the same hand to Johanna, not only does she not take it, but she leaps unaided the rest of the way down to the lower deck, then deals Monty a sharp kick between the legs. He buckles like a hinge.

"You should be ashamed of yourself!" Johanna cries, smacking him across the back of the head with her muff. "You are a terrible man for accepting money to deliver human cargo who are obviously taken against their will. You're no better than a slaver and a pirate!"

"Johanna—" I reach out for her, but she bats me away with the muff.

"I don't care what he does to me! I don't care what any of these bastards do! There's nothing left to take from me, and I just want to hit something!" She swings her muff at Monty again, nearly clipping Ebrahim as well, who stops just in time on the stairs.

"Johanna, stop!" I seize her by the arm and pin it to her side. "Stop it, he's not going to hurt you."

She squirms, trying to pull free of me. "Well, I want to hurt him!"

"Stop it, Johanna. He's not a sailor. This is my brother."

"What?" She stares at me, then pivots sharply to Monty, still doubled over. "Henry Montague?"

Monty groans in affirmation, straightening slow as if he were thawing out. He places his hands carefully over his most vulnerable areas, then says, "Miss Hoffman." Her voice is nearly as high as hers. "My compliments to your cobbler. What are those shoes made of and from where exactly was it mined?"

"You're . . . weren't you . . ." Johanna looks wildly between Monty and me, like she's studying our faces for a resemblance. Then she blurts, "I remember him taller."

"You and him both," I reply.

"Oh. Well then." She straightens her dress and holds a hand out to him. "I'm sorry I didn't recognize you."

"Not sorry for the kick?" Monty asks.

"No, not particularly," she replies.

There's a heavy step from the fo'c'sle behind us, and before I can turn I'm nearly knocked flat as Percy wraps the entirety of his long limbs around me. "Dear Lord, Felicity Montague," he says, and somehow he holds me even tighter. "I've been sick over you."

I don't say anything, just press my face into his chest and let myself at last be held. Behind me, I feel Monty's arms wrap around the pair of us, the long-ago threatened Monty-Percy sandwich manifested, and I don't mind it. It feels safe, and good to have been missed after so long thinking I had no one to return to.

But all that sentiment can be enjoyed just as easily without my face squashed into Percy's scratchy coat and Monty breathing down my neck—literally. "All right, that's enough, I think." I extricate myself from the two of them as best I can, feeling a bit like I'm wiggling out from a tight canyon.

Monty lets his arms fall away, but Percy keeps a hold on my shoulders and peers very seriously into my face. "Are you all right?"

"Yes."

"You haven't been taken advantage of in any way?"

"No."

"And you know that you have driven us absolutely mad since you left. I swear to God, Felicity, I'm never letting you out of my sight again."

"That I have some objections to," Monty says from behind me.

"You came for me," I say, looking between them.

"Yes, we have quite literally followed you to the end of the earth," Monty replies. "And there was only mild complaining."

"Incorrect use of literally," I tell him, then remember Johanna hanging slightly behind, watching this maudlin display with a timid slant to her shoulders. "Oh, this is Johanna Hoffman." I lead her over to Percy for an introduction. "I don't know if you two ever knew each other."

Percy takes her hand, and Johanna looks suddenly less misplaced and more shy and girlish. Her cheeks are a pleasant pink. "Mr. Newton."

"We met a few times," Percy says, pressing Johanna's hand in between his. "We're just as glad you're safe."

"Would you like a hug as well?" Monty asks, then quickly steps back, hands shielding himself again. "Though perhaps not from me."

"How did you find us?" I ask, looking between him and Percy.

"When it became apparent you had absconded with a member of Scipio's crew, I consulted him for information about your partner in crime," Monty says. "At which point he informed me that the woman you had chosen to hang your hopes upon is a member of the Crown and

383

Cleaver fleet and that any dealings you might have with her were likely to be criminal at best."

"Why did he take Sim on if he knew she was dangerous?" I ask.

"I was raised under the Crown and Cleaver," Ebrahim says from the stairs, and I jump. I had forgotten he was there. "I vouched for her."

"Which of course led to him feeling responsible," Monty says, "and Scipio feeling responsible, and also Percy and I felt responsible and we were all determined to get you out of whatever trouble you had so determinedly gotten yourself in. Don't look so surprised. We'd move heaven and earth for you. Unless of course there is any actual heavy lifting involved, in which case, I'll abstain, but don't believe that in any way tarnishes the sentiment."

"Did you sail to the Crown and Cleaver outpost?" Johanna asks. Her cheeks are still very pink.

"We did indeed," Monty replies. "Ebrahim still has the ink on him, which, as it turns out, literally opens doors."

"Again, incorrect use of literally," I mumble.

He swats that away. "Stop. I'm telling the story of our heroic rescue. So we were intending to hold an audience with the pirate lord himself and beg for your freedom, but your lady love beat us there."

"My . . . who?"

"Your pirate paramour," he says. "The one you made that bargain with. She showed up with a group of very brawny gentlemen who had no qualms about leaving their shirt sleeves unfastened—"

"Careful," Percy says, but Monty butts his forehead against Percy's shoulder.

"Please. You were looking too."

"I wasn't."

"How could you not? It was like some very lascivious god sculpted them all with a very generous hand—"

"Monty, focus," I snap.

"Ah, right, yes, your pirate girl. Turns out she's the firstborn of the commodore, and she informed us that his very valuable map had fallen into the hands of an English rascal called Platt who would use both it and you two ill."

"Is she here?" I ask.

"She is indeed," Monty replies, "and she's desperate to see you."

Ebrahim returns to the helm to keep a watch as Monty leads the way down to the second deck where the cargo is stored, Percy at his heels. Before following, I take Johanna by the arm. She's still very flushed. "Are you all right?" I ask. "You needn't worry about kicking my brother. I know he's dramatic, but he's fine."

"No, it's just . . ." She covers her cheeks with her hands. "I never told you this because it was right when we were being terrible to each other, but I used to be very, very smitten with Percy Newton. And apparently still am. How is it that we've just been kidnapped and extorted and practically sold, and yet I still can't look him in the eye because I was so infatuated with him when I was thirteen?"

I want to laugh. More than that, I want to hug her, an impulse that so rarely strikes it startles me. But there is something about that single moment, treacle in a swig of vinegar, that swells my heart. Those small, precious things do not cease to exist in the shadow of something large and ominous, and hearing her say it makes me feel human again, a person beyond these last few weeks of my life.

"Johanna Hoffman," I say, and it takes everything in me to keep my face straight. "You are a married woman."

On the lower deck, a makeshift seating area has been arranged out of crates and barrels pulled into a formation of chairs around a table. It's like a child's attempt to build a fortress from his bedclothes and chair backs.

Scipio, Sim, and a man I don't recognize are seated around the table, with several more corsairs standing behind the stranger. Sim is back in the wide-legged-style trousers she was wearing when we first met, and her bare feet are pulled up in a knot under her. Scipio and the second man both stand when we arrive. Scipio gives me a quick kiss on the back of the hand—I have a sense he'd like to lecture me about my recent irresponsibility, but bites his tongue—and gives Johanna a hand as well, before turning to Sim and the man beside her. His skin is a few shades darker than hers, and he's got the Crown and Cleaver inked on the side of his neck, thick and ornate and showier than hers. The men behind him have it too—one on his wrist and the other peeking out from the collar of his shirt.

"This is Murad Aldajah, the commodore of the Crown and Cleaver fleet out of Algiers," Scipio introduces him. "And you know his daughter, Simmaa."

I'm not sure if I should shake hands with Aldajah or bow or even look him in the eye. His gaze is the sort of steely that passes judgment and falls for nothing. He's bald-headed, with a thick beard and gold hoops in each ear.

Johanna, seemingly of a similar confusion on this subject, bobs a quick curtsy and says, "Your grace," like he's the king of England.

He doesn't laugh, but his nostrils flare. "Sit down," he says, motioning all around.

Johanna and I share a seat on the crate across from Sim, and together, we explain to our crew what has happened since we parted ways with her.

"So Sybille Glass's map to the nesting island is in the hands of the Europeans," Aldajah says when I'm finished, one hand running over his beard.

I look over at Sim, her shoulders braced against her seat. She looks different in her father's shadow, somehow more like a soldier and a child at the same time. She sits straight as a lectern, her gaze sharp and mouth set, like she doesn't know which way an independent thought given voice will tip the scales. Like some days he's her father and others, her king.

"Platt has the map, yes," I say. "But we have a copy, too."

"Was there a duplicate?" Aldajah asks.

"There is now," I reply. "We made one. And Platt and Stafford don't know it exists. Platt and his men are leaving soon to find the island and take specimens back to England to secure full funding for their voyage."

"Then give us your map," Aldajah says. "And we will make certain they're stopped. We have another ship waiting for us off the coast."

"It's my mother's map," Johanna interrupts. "It's her work."

"It's our land," Aldajah counters. "Our home."

"Well, we won't tell you where it is," Johanna says, and crosses her arms over her chest.

Aldajah folds his arms as well, mirror to hers. "This is not a negotiation, ladies."

"You're right, because you have nothing to negotiate with," I say.

"You're aboard my ship."

"*My* ship," Scipio interrupts. "They're under my protection."

"And you sailed colorless into our waters," Aldajah counters. "Your ship and your men have been seized."

"We are not your property," Scipio says. "We are in your employ."

Aldajah spreads his hands. "More men on this ship are loyal to me than to you."

"Stop it," I snap. "If you're so determined to make this a pissing contest, Platt will be back in England with his boat full of eggs before we've weighed anchor. This is not about you or your ships or your manly pride. Now, shut up and listen to what Johanna has to say." My ferocity silences both Scipio and Aldajah. Behind their backs, Monty gives me a silent round of applause, which Percy grabs his hands to stop.

"Are there any terms under which you would agree to surrender your duplicate?" Aldajah asks Johanna.

She clears her throat. "Yes. First, you will take Felicity and me to the island with you to stop Dr. Platt and his crew. Once he's thwarted, my mother's original map will be restored to me, but you may have the duplicate. You will have claim to their crew—any men willing to join your ranks will be yours, and you can have their ship as well."

"And it's quite a fancy one," I add.

"But we will take one copy of the map," Johanna says. "You the other. Then you let us return to England safely, with the *Eleftheria* and their crew."

"Then we trade one kind of European invader for another," Aldajah says. "You're no different from your mother."

"Maybe not," Johanna says, "but those are our terms. You can accept them, or we part ways here."

Aldajah runs a hand over his beard, curling the tip around his finger. Beside him, Sim looks like she'd very much like to say something but grinds her teeth instead.

"Your English ship will not give up without a fight," he says at last.

"So?" Johanna crosses her arms. "You're pirates, aren't you? You know how to brawl."

"Pirates avoid a fight," Aldajah replies. "Don't want to waste men or damage your prize. But this expedition will not be so easily intimidated by a shot across the bow, I think."

"This ship," Scipio adds, spreading a hand to indicate the whole of the *Eleftheria*, "and *Makasib* are not made for a battle. That English ship will rip us apart."

"But there are two of us and one of them," Johanna replies. "Surely that counts for something strategically."

"And their crew is likely mutinous," I add. "Or they will be by the time they reach the island. Platt's losing all his investors, so they can't be paying their men well. They're more likely mercenaries than navy men. They may be better equipped than us, but their crew will likely be greener and sicker."

"And Platt and Stafford are at each other's throats already," Johanna adds.

I nod. "Platt's a mess of a man, and Stafford seems rather tired of playing nanny to him."

"Father?" Sim says, her voice softer than I'm accustomed to. An ask rather than an answer. Her father flicks his gaze toward her but doesn't turn. "It may be time for a change."

"And what change is that, Simmaa?" Perhaps he senses there's an undercurrent to her words—a change in leadership, a change in his fleet, a change that starts with his daughter inheriting his world instead of his sons.

But if Sim means any of that, she doesn't betray it. She keeps her gaze low and says, "We have kept these creatures secret for so long, but we've also hidden the resources they could provide."

"Provide at a cost," Aldajah says, but Sim presses on.

"But we can control the cost if we accept that change is coming. We cannot fight the turning of the world, but we can prepare for it. And we can prepare our world for it."

Aldajah clenches his jaw—the same nervous tick I've seen in Sim, though he doesn't grind his molars together like she does. The same vein on his temple presses against his skin. His eyes slant in the same way when he looks at me, then Johanna.

"Fine," Aldajah says, then to Johanna, "I accept your terms. Now show us your map."

Johanna looks over at me and nods. A small smile tugs at the corner of her mouth, victorious and conspiratorial. I reach down and start to pull up the hem of my skirt, and all the men in the room make a protestation as one—Monty does an exasperatingly dramatic throwing of his hands over his eyes and exclaims, "Dear God, Felicity Montague, keep your clothes on."

"Like you've never seen the outline of the female form before." I pull up my skirt to my knees, careful to keep myself as covered as possible lest one of these brawny gentlemen need a couch to faint upon, and manage to untie the petticoat from my waist.

"How is taking off your underthings any better?" Monty says, watching through his fingers as the petticoat falls to my ankles and step out of it. I flip the petticoat inside out, letting it blossom and float before I spread it across the table so they can all see the replicated map Johanna and I stitched there.

There is not, as I expected, an astonished and impressed gasp. None of the men seem to catch on to what it is. Most of them are too busy avoiding looking at my underthings to make any deductions. It's only Sim who, with a slow, slick smile sliding over her face, says to Johanna and me, "You're quite the rascals."

"Thank you," I say. "We had some time on our hands."

"It's not as complete as we hoped it would be," Johanna says. "The map Platt has is far more detailed and legible. But is this something you can make a heading from?"

"I think so." Scipio looks like he wants to take up the petticoat, but then stops, unsure what the most gentlemanly response is to being handed a lady's drawers for navigational purposes.

"The *Eleftheria* will keep the map," I say to Aldajah. "And Johanna and I will stay aboard here. You can follow us in your second ship."

"Then Simmaa stays here as well," Aldajah says. "To keep you honest."

It isn't a question, but Sim still nods. Johanna nods too. "Acceptable."

I want to leap to my feet and thrust my arms aloft in victory. We're back. We're at our own helm again. My life as an adventurer, a researcher, an independent woman with a world to discover has unfurled its sails yet again after a near miss with captivity. Johanna darts a glance sideways at me, like she senses how badly I want to execute some sort of ridiculous dance in celebration, and presses her shoulder against mine.

"Miss Hoffman," Scipio says at last, "will you join me at the helm and help me decipher this . . . unorthodox guide?"

Johanna takes up the petticoat, letting it wave behind her like a flag as she follows Scipio up the narrow stairs. A hand up from Percy leaves her flustered more than helps.

Aldajah and his men follow, and I start to go as well, but Sim steps in front of me, blocking my path. She doesn't say anything for a moment, just stares at my shoulder and toes the planking. I wait.

"I'm glad you're all right," she says at last, her words stepping on each other's heels in their haste.

"I'm glad you didn't abandon us," I reply.

"Did you think that I had?"

I offer a noncommittal shrug. "You must admit it looked very incriminating."

"A guns-blazing charge down the hill would have done you no good."

"It would have given me quite a bit more confidence in your noble intentions. Though I suppose you wouldn't abandon us, so long as we had the map."

"There are other reasons I wouldn't abandon you," she says, and her eyes disappear behind the thick fringe of her lashes as she looks down again.

"You didn't tell me your name was Simmaa," I say.

Her nose wrinkles. "I hate it. My father picked it up

394

sailing when he was young and vowed he'd call his first daughter Simmaa."

"Why do you hate it?"

"Because it means bravery." Her mouth twitches. "I think he meant for it to be ironic."

"But you're brave."

"But not brave enough to lead his fleet. I don't think he ever intended for that daughter to have an opportunity to be brave."

I purse my lips. "Should I call you Simmaa now, or would you prefer captain? This ship is under your command now."

She lets out a laugh. "Have you ever seen a command post so begrudgingly awarded?"

"But at least it was awarded." She's staring at the ground. I push my toe against hers. "I'm sorry your father doesn't see it."

"See what?" She raises her eyes to mine, and we trade a look that feels like a dare.

"How bloody brilliant you are," I say.

"Am I?" She tugs on her headscarf, pressing a crease behind her ear. "You must be rubbing off on me."

Then she hauls herself up the stairs and disappears onto the upper deck.

Monty manifests suddenly at my shoulder like an obnoxious ghost, grinning at me in a way that makes me realize how close to my ear Sim was speaking.

"I think she likes you," he says.

I roll my eyes. "Just because you and Percy live in unholy matrimony doesn't mean every same-gendered pair also wants to. And we only kissed once, and that was more an experimentation to see if kissing can be an enjoyable experience for me. And the answer is no, though I'd say she's the best I've had. But the point is moot as I don't think it's ever really going to be good because I just don't seem to desire that sort of relationship with anyone the way everyone else does. But just because she kissed me doesn't mean she likes me. I once saw you necking a hedgerow."

Monty blinks. "I meant *likes* as in begrudgingly respects, but my word, how long have you been bottling that up, darling?"

"Dear God, you really are the worst." I stalk past him toward the upper deck, trying my best to ignore his hooked talon of a smile. "Is it too late to be unrescued?"

20

Even if we had a map in a medium other than needle-point, the journey to the island would not be a brief one. First we have to rally with Aldajah's ship, the *Makasib*, off the coast. It's a skinny skeleton of a rig, smaller even than the *Eleftheria*, but it cuts through the water like a hot knife through butter. Were we not in possession of the map, and therefore taking the lead, we'd be limping behind it, the Crown and Cleaver flag snapping from its mast calling for us to keep up.

We are upon the sea for a fortnight. A tense, monotonous fortnight of following an embroidered map and losing our heading where my stitches got knotted and running afoul of some winds I did not have time to embroider as thoroughly as I wanted to.

The distance is great, and nothing is so hard to find as something that no one has yet found. There still seems a chance we will sail straight through the spot Sybille Glass marked to find it's nothing but another stretch of empty sea, or that we will discover the true reason maps were not made out of thread and fabric, which is that they are impossible to follow. We could be wasting weeks chasing our own tail while Platt happily collects sea monster eggs undeterred.

The further the *Eleftheria* plows into the Atlantic, the more it begins to feel like winter again. The open water turns the weather so damp and cold that I am soon certain my hair will never again lie straight, nor will complete feeling be restored to my fingers. The air is thick, a combination of the sea spray and low, coffee-dark clouds that spit rain intermittently. It only takes a day before I abandon my spectacles—they grow too misty to be seen out of as soon as they're placed upon my nose. Monty catches some sort of head cold three days into the voyage and collapses into histrionics, which Percy only encourages with doting concern. Since he's given up spirits, Monty has leaned in even harder to his addiction to attention. His good ear is blocked up by the chill, rendering him almost entirely deaf, though I think not as deaf as he pretends to be when I mention a remedy I read in *An Easy and Natural Method of Curing Most Diseases*, in which a head cold can be doused by rolling up an orange's peel and shoving it up both nostrils. When he refuses to listen but continues to moan, there's somewhere else that I consider threatening to shove it.

As the days creep on, we all grow more restless, and though none say it aloud, I'm certain I'm not the only one sinking into the dread that Platt and his men will not just arrive before us, but depart as well. We may already be too late.

So it is a great shock when the first call that comes down from King George in the crow's nest is not of another ship sighting, but of land.

Sim and I, playing cards under the overhang of the top deck, both spring to our feet and run to the rail. The thick mist rising off the ocean is almost opaque. I don't know how he saw anything through it. Sim calls for a flag to be run up, signaling for the *Makasib* behind us to halt its progress too, and it glides to our starboard side, both ships bobbing in the rough swell. On the opposite deck, I can see Aldajah crossing toward the bowsprit, a spyglass unfolding in his hands.

I squint forward into the mist, my hair plastered to my face by the sea spray. If I work at it, I can make out a dark shape through the fog, an illegible inkblot looming over the ocean. Then the pale outline of a craggy cliff breaks through the clouds, and suddenly it's in silhouette before us, a small, rugged fist of land thrust up from the waves. The sort of place mutineers would maroon their captains. Somewhere you leave a man to die.

Scipio comes up behind me, his own spyglass pressed

to his eye before he passes it to Sim. I hold out a hand for my turn, but clearly am not in charge enough, for after a scan of the horizon, she returns it to Scipio. "Do you think that's it?"

"It must be."

"Then where are they?"

"Who?" I ask.

"The English," Sim replies. "I can't see another ship."

"Perhaps they're on the other side of the island," I offer.

"Doubtful," Scipio says. The spyglass is pressed to his eye again. "They would have approached from the same direction as we did. They'd have no reason to navigate around—there's too great a chance of running aground when you're this near land in unfamiliar waters. It would be easier to go by foot overland if needed."

"Maybe the eggs are on the other side of the island," I offer. "That would be enough reason to risk it. Or perhaps they got lost and had to retrace their steps."

"Maybe they've come and gone already," Scipio says.

"Or perhaps they haven't come yet," Sim adds.

Scipio lowers the spyglass, folding it in and out in nervous thought. I squint forward again into the fog, trying to make sense of any details of the island beyond a shadowed mass. I can see the outline of trees crowding the cliffsides, their trunks bare and their tops bushy. The cliffs themselves drop straight into the ocean, sides polished from the constant battering waves that break white and frothy against them before settling back into a green that courtly ladies would have cut off their thumbs to have their dresses dyed. The whole landscape looks rough and inhospitable, not a place made for human life. No wonder it hasn't been found—even if stumbled upon, no ship would stop for such a wasteland.

The shallows around the island seem to wink when the waves retreat, an opalescent flush like the seafloor is made of pearls. "Let me have a look," I say, and Scipio passes me the spyglass. Magnified, it looks like huge bubbles are collecting beneath the waves, visible only when the water stills between beats.

Then I realize. They're eggs.

There are dozens of them, cocooned along the shallows with a shiny, translucent netting connecting them to each other and tethering them to the seafloor. Their insides glow green, the source of the water's color, their outer shells so translucent and soft that they pulse when the water hits them.

"The eggs are in the water!" I'm so excited, I forget I have the spyglass and nearly knock Sim in the face when I spin to face her. "In the shallows, you can see them netted together. They tie their eggs to the island but keep them in the water. Look!"

"What's going on?" I hear Johanna ask behind us, and a moment later she's at my side at the rail, leaning so far over I nearly grab the back of her dress so she doesn't tip overboard.

"We found it. And there are eggs, look! You can see them in the water."

"That's it?" Johanna asks.

"It's got to be," Sim replies. "But the English aren't here."

"Then who's that?" Johanna asks, pointing.

Sim drops the spyglass, and she, Scipio, and I squint forward, following Johanna's finger but seeing nothing.

"There's smoke," she explains. "Someone's lit a fire on the shore."

Sim curses under her breath, tearing away from my side just as I see it too. A small, thin finger through the mist, black and rising in a column from the beach.

"They're here!" Sim has her hands cupped around her mouth and is shouting across the water. I don't know if her father can hear her, but he turns, one hand held up to shield his face from the spray. "The English are here already!"

I look to Scipio. "What does that mean?"

"They're waiting for us," he says. "This is an ambush."

My stomach drops. When I look to the water again, the *Kattenkwaad* has torn itself from the fog and is gliding toward us, a silent predator with toothy guns already rolled out from its lower decks.

"How did they know we were coming?" I ask. I can

hardly catch my breath.

"They must have spotted us on their tail, or had men watching us in Gibraltar." Scipio is already rooting around in his belt, coming up with a powder canister and a handful of grapeshot. "Get down to the d—" he starts, but he's interrupted by the first shot from the *Kattenkwaad*, a warning shot that sails over our bow. Several long, still seconds pass as they give us a chance to run up a flag of surrender. Then their front-facing gun belches a set of twin cannonballs connected by chain that hurtle through the air and wrap themselves around the foreyard of the *Makasib* with speed enough to knock the foreyard to the deck with a crash that sends the men scattering.

"All hands!" Sim is shouting. "All hands to stations! Load the guns and give no quarter!"

"Bring her around to starboard," Scipio calls. I can hear similar shouts from the *Makasib*, and I realize that not only is the *Kattenkwaad* much larger and better gunned than us, but they're in motion, barreling toward us with swivel guns and cannons already loaded, and will easily pivot so we'll be facing down an entire hull of artillery before we can even bring ourselves around.

"Felicity! Johanna!" Sim shouts. "Get down to the gun deck! Out of the open!" I grab Johanna by the hand and we sprint together to the stairs, tripping over each other and the steep incline as we tumble onto the gun deck.

I nearly smash into Percy, standing barefooted at the bottom of the stairs and frantically trying to wrap his hair back into a knot. "What's going on?"

"The English," I gasp. "They caught us by surprise."

The deck is flooding with men, everyone scrambling to their positions around the cannons and trying to hastily load the least hasty weapon in human history. "What do we do?" I shout to Ebrahim, who is worming debris from the barrel of the biggest gun with a spiraled rod.

"Get the swivel guns on the deck," he shouts to Percy. "You remember how to load it?" When Percy nods, he says, "Take Monty and arm yourselves." Percy bolts for the arsenal, and Ebrahim calls, "Johanna, open the gun ports. Felicity, to me!"

Johanna and I both stagger as another shot rocks the ship. A hammock flies from its hangings and whips like a serpent's tail through the air, nearly slapping me in the face. We have drilled for this, and know our stations, but it feels unreal as Ebrahim tosses me a set of heavy leather gloves, their insides crusty with sweat. "Cover the vent," he calls, and I press my thumb over the small hole at the base of the cannon while he loads the first charge.

"Hold for fire!" Sim shouts down the stairs. "We're coming around!"

Our pivot is painfully slow. The three small swivel guns on our deck are all we have to fight back with while the *Eleftheria* heaves itself around so that the hull is parallel to the *Kattenkwaad*. Ebrahim and I wait, my hand clamped over the vent and both of us peering out the small square that the nose of the cannon juts through. It's a narrow window that gives us a view of nothing but the gray sea and the grayer sky inching past. I'm trembling with the wait, the helplessness, the stillness, my thumb pressed so hard to the vent it goes numb. Beside me, Ebrahim has the linstock clamped between his knees, striking flint and a rod in his hand, ready for the call. There's another shot from the *Kattenkwaad*, accompanied by a crack.

Ebrahim grits his teeth. "They're bringing down our yards."

I can hardly breathe around my heartbeat. It's digging itself into my lungs and throat and making me feel controlled by fear. *You are Felicity Montague*, I tell myself. *You are a brilliant cactus and a rare wildflower who survived capture and imprisonment and extortion, and you shall survive this.*

And then, Sim's voice down the stairs. "Open fire!"

"Fire in the hole!" Ebrahim shouts, and I let my finger off the vent and throw my hands over my ears, my body curled away from the cannon.

We never actually fired during our drills, and the blast rattles my teeth. The cannon kicks back, narrowly missing my toes. I don't look where the shot lands, but the gray sky through the gunport has been replaced by a square of the *Kattenkwaad*'s hull. It's somehow less terrifying than the empty sky and waiting, and also more, because now we're in the fight. Through the mist, I can see the faces of their sailors at their own gunports, loading weapons larger than ours. Along the hull of the ship, beneath the waves, nets are strung, pinned like barnacles to the side and dragging in the water. I can't fathom what they are until I catch the same pearly wink I saw through the spyglass. They've already collected the eggs, and have them dragging along the ship in rope nets.

A man slings himself out from the gunport across from us to swab the barrel before his partner has a chance to pull the gun back into the deck. Ebrahim whips a pistol from his belt and takes a shot through the gunport and straight into the swabber. He pitches forward in a tumbling pinwheel into the ocean. My stomach heaves, and I look away. Blood has never bothered me. Not sickness or injury or dying, but battle is entirely different. Ebrahim, whom I've played checkers with and who taught Percy how to dive and wound Georgie's hair into tight braids along his scalp, just shot a man dead. But maybe that man would have shot us first. Perhaps it can be considered self-defense. In advance.

Can't think of any of that.

I grab a rope on the cannon, and together, Ebrahim and I drag the gun backward again. There's another pepper of fire, this time smaller pops of rifles from the *Kattenkwaad*, followed by a scream from our upper deck.

My shoulders and hands are aching after only a few shots. Down the deck from me, Johanna is passing cannonballs to one of Aldajah's men, her face black with soot and one hand bloody from a splintered shot that burst our hull. Ebrahim scorches his hand on loose embers as he swabs the barrel—they slip down his sleeve and he has to pat them out against his skin before they spark his shirt. I lose count of how many rounds we fire, not because of how great the number is, but more because of how time seems to play by different rules in a skirmish. The time between shots pass like hours. The moments it takes for a cannonball to travel down the length of the barrel, for the linstock to catch, is half a lifetime. But the shots from the *Kattenkwaad* come thick and relentless, an impossible pace we can't match. The only thing to be done is to keep yanking the gun back into place, keep covering the vent, keep throwing my hands over my ears and letting the recoil jostle my bones.

I'm only pulled out of the fight by the sound of my name from behind me. "Felicity!"

I turn. Sim is hanging down from the stairway leading to the upper deck. Her headscarf is speckled with blood, though there's no indicator it's hers. She jerks a frantic hand at me, and, at a nod from Ebrahim, I stumble across the deck toward her.

"You're needed—" I can't hear her over another of our cannons fired. The whole ship pitches, and she grabs me around the elbow, hauling me up and pressing her mouth against my ear. "—shot" is all I hear before she's dragging me up and I'm scrambling up the steep stairs on all fours.

The deck is chaos. Yards have fallen and are tangled in the rigging, dangling like tree limbs in a jungle canopy and pulling the masts off balance so that they sway dangerously, their bases cracking. The bowsprit and figurehead have been blown off. One of the sails is on fire, two men perched upon the mast trying to beat it out. Smoke chokes the air.

Scipio's leg is slashed open and dripping a puddle of blood around where he's crouched on the deck, a rifle jammed into his shoulder. Sim pushes me down so that my head is below the rail—I had started forward to help him without a thought to the gunfire—but she shakes her head and redirects me, shoving me toward the stern. She's already tipping black powder down the barrel of her gun again, and I want to ask where she wants for me to go and what I'm meant to do, but as soon as I look in the direction she pushed me, I know.

Monty is crouched below the rail, one hand steadying the swivel gun he's been charged with and the other pressed to Percy, who's slumped against the deck, unmoving. I scramble forward on my hands and knees, my palm sliding in a puddle of blood. Flaming shreds of the sail waft from above.

A gunshot buries itself in the deck just ahead of me, and I flatten myself against the ground. Monty grits his teeth, then swings himself to his feet behind the gun. Percy doesn't move. I can't even tell if he's breathing. Monty is pale as milk, blood all over his shirtsleeves and his hands shaking as he rips the top off a powder cartridge with his teeth. One palm bears a bright red burn, likely from grabbing the hot barrel too many times, but he doesn't flinch.

I scramble forward to Percy and rip back his coat and shirt, searching for the source of the blood. It's not hard to find. He's been shot in the center of his torso, too low for the heart and too high for the stomach. It's a small bullet, though that's little comfort.

"Percy," I say, giving his shoulder a small shake. He doesn't respond, but his lips part. His breath is coming in long, labored gasps that rattle on the end. Each one seems to be too much work and have no effect. "Percy, can you hear me? Can you speak?"

Monty drops down beside me, dragging the back of his hand over his face and smearing it with blood. "They had a sharpshooter up in their nest," he says, his voice gravelly. "Sim took him out, but we didn't see until—"

Percy takes another breath that rattles his whole

body, wheezing like a punctured bellows. Monty's words trickle into a whimper, like the pain is shared. Percy is making a valiant fight to keep his eyes open, but he's losing. His eyelids flicker.

"Why is he breathing like that?" Monty asks, swiping at his face again. "He was awake and speaking right after it happened, and he wasn't breathing like that."

And maybe it's the fear in his voice. Maybe it's that I notice Monty has tried to stop the blood by pressing that ridiculous hat Percy knit for him against the bullet hole, but it's slipped down and nestled against his side. Maybe it's that Percy isn't just precious to me, but he's half my brother's heart. I've never seen fear like this in Monty. I've never seen fear like this in another human, as Monty presses his hands to Percy's face and his forehead to his and begs him to open his eyes, to breathe, to survive.

I'm struggling to focus. Struggling to think. My mind has fallen into the trenches of habit and coursed straight to Alexander Platt's *Treaties*, every paper of his I read about the chest cavity, the lungs, the heart, the circulation, the rib cage. And it's nothing. Not a note, not a blot, not a single comment about a clean gunshot caving in a chest. Platt never wrote a word on what to do when every breath seems to be killing a man slowly.

So I don't think of Platt. I don't worry what Platt or Cheselden or Hippocrates or Galen or any of those men may have written on the subject or how they would have directed my hand. I can do more than memorize maps of vessels and arteries and bones; I can solve the puzzle of what to do when those pieces come apart. I can write my own treaties. I am a girl of steady hands, stout heart, and every book I have ever read.

You are Felicity Montague. You are a doctor.

Percy takes another sickening breath, and it's like a diagram unfolds overtop of him, showing me where the bullet would have lodged, what it struck, and how it's disrupting everything else. An open chest wound like this, with only a knit cap and a hand pressed intermittently to it, is an airway in both directions. Blood is escaping, but air is entering, filling up everywhere it shouldn't be, collapsing the lung and separating his chest cavity from the tracheobronchial tree. It's like a map in my mind, a muscle memory, a poem I can recite by heart. I know what to do.

"I need something sharp," I say.

Monty gropes behind him on the deck and comes back with the cannon worm, passing it to me by the corkscrew tip that goes down the barrel of the cannon before each shot to probe out debris. The handle is slick when he presses it into my palm.

With a chest wound collapsing the lungs, suction should be applied through a blunt-tipped flexible tube, and anticoagulant fluids injected posthaste. Being short on either option, I make do with what I have, and start in on a counterincision between the two lowest true ribs, four fingerbreadths from the vertebrae and the inferior scapular angle.

I press my fingers to the base of Percy's chest, counting his ribs, then hold the tip of the cannon worm to the same spot. I don't doubt myself for a second.

I jam the corkscrew tip in with the heel of my hand until it breaks through the skin and I feel it test his bones. Percy's body jerks, and when I withdraw the screw, he takes a gasping breath, like surfacing from water. I gasp too. The cannon worm clatters from my hand and skids across the deck.

"Keep pressure on it!" I shout to Monty. The gunfire is making my ears pop—I can hardly hear my own words over it. I turn down the deck, ready to run back to the cannons or anyone else who may need me, but Sim pushes me back, shaking her head until I stop. "Dry!" I finally hear her shout, and I realize suddenly how quiet our gundeck has gone—we're nearly out of firepower. What we have left will be single cannonballs or musketballs that expose us to the enemy. Across the water, the bowsprit of the *Makasib* is on fire, flames climbing up the masts and licking the sails, but they're still putting up a valiant fight. One of their cannons bellows and the *Kattenkwaad* answers with a shot through our rail. Splinters burst and skitter across the deck, and I throw my arms over my face. Dust fills my lungs, dust and smoke and the thick metallic smell of blood.

Through the fog, I can still see the island waiting for us, and all I can think is, *This can't be how this ends.*

It is not what I had expected to think as I stared death in his hungry eyes. It's not hopelessness, it's just pure stubbornness. Not even so much a will to live as a refusal to die. Not yet, not now, not here, not when we have so much left to do. There isn't a goddamned chance I'm dying on this rig.

A scream rips the air suddenly, so harsh and otherworldly and at such an impossible pitch it is more a vibration than a sound. I clap my hands against my ears, doubled over with the pain of that sound bellowing up from the ocean and coursing through me. I can feel it in my feet, in my lungs, in the way my teeth knock together. All over the deck, pistols fall and rifle barrels drop. Men grab their ears, screaming alongside it, and the humanness of that sound is almost comforting. The fighting stops, just for a moment on both sides, as everyone reels.

Beside me, Monty shakes his head, like he's trying to clear the ringing. "What was that?"

The ship shudders. Not with a cannon hit, but like something has passed beneath us. A wave crashes over the deck, soaking my knees. "We've run aground!" Sim shouts, but we're still so far from the shore, and the ship settles again almost at once. We're not stuck on any-thing, nor have we caught our keel on a reef or bar.

But something has passed under us.

I fly to my feet and splash to the rail, just as Johanna claws her way up from the lower deck. Her hair is a wilted heap around her shoulders, face speckled with burns from the gunpowder, but she reaches out for my hand to steady herself, undeterred by the blood. We both peer over the rail, as far as we dare look lest we expose ourselves to British guns. "Felicity!" I hear Sim shout. "Johanna! Get down!"

Neither of us moves. We both recognize the sound, from the miniature version we heard in the bay in Algiers. Beneath the bow of our ship, the water shimmers sapphire, something iridescent and gleaming passing under the waves.

Johanna grabs my arm. "It's a dragon. It's under us."

As though in answer, the ship lurches again like we've crested a wave.

"It's not a reef!" I shout back to where Sim is crouched against the helm. "It's one of the beasties! She's under us."

There's that unholy scream again. A ripple goes through the water, knocking the waves flat. The ship heaves. "We have to stop firing!" Johanna shouts. "She's doesn't want to fight; she wants her eggs!"

"She?" Sim shouts back.

"The dragon!" Johanna does a frantic pantomime of pointing down, then miming a snaking motion with her hand. "The warship has her eggs! There's a sea monster under our boat, but if we're still and don't disturb her, she'll leave us be. That's why they leave your father's ships alone! You don't fight them! We have to stop shooting. No cannons, no guns, no anything. We can't move."

"Are you insane?" Sim returns.

"Signal your father. They have to stop!"

Scipio is staring at Sim, looking for an order, though from his face it's apparent what he wants that order to be. His bloody leg is trembling under him. Sim's jaw tightens, the hard set of her mouth betraying her. She doesn't want to surrender. She's a girl raised to claw her way through a fight by her fingernails, to never give up. Always be faster, be smarter, be the last to call halt. Show no weakness. Show no mercy. Sink before surrender.

But across the deck, she looks at Johanna, and then to me. When our eyes meet, I see her chest rise in a single, deep breath.

"Cease fire!" she shouts. "Don't make a movement."

"Belay that!" Scipio cries, snatching at her arm. "We'll be sunk."

Sim jerks from his grip. "No guns, no cannons. Send up flags to my father."

"We won't survive," Scipio cries, but Sim is already

scrambling across the deck and slinging herself down to the stairs. Scipio mumbles something under his breath, then shouts up to his men on the upper deck, "Cease fire and take cover!"

"We aren't yet dry!" one of them shouts, but Scipio returns with a sharp "Do as I say!"

It takes a moment for the message to go through the ship, but when it does, an eerie stillness falls over us. The sound of the battle is replaced by the shush of the water breathing against the side of our boat, the creak of the ship bowing under the damage.

Sim staggers up from the deck, back to where Johanna and I are crouched at the rail. We watch the signal travel in flags between our ship and her father's—since there isn't a signal for *don't upset the dragons*, it's just a call for surrender.

"Please," I hear Sim whisper beside me, her eyes on her father's ship. "Please trust me."

She reaches out and takes my hand, her palm damp and shaking. I take Johanna's in my other. She's so fixated upon the sea, watching for that flash of emerald, that I don't think she notices, until she squeezes my fingers in return. A reminder that she's here. That she's got me. We're holding each other up.

The next round of artillery rips into the ship, a barrage of gunfire and cannon blasts. The top is blown off one of our masts, spraying the deck with shards of wood.

The three of us collapse into one another. Sim's hand is pressed against the back of my neck, sheltering my face with her own.

And then there's that scream again, so high that there is no sound to it, just a vibration that makes me feel as though every blood vessel in my body is straining to burst. I swear my teeth come loose. And then there's a different sound, a cracking, crumbling, like something scrunched up in a giant's fist. I raise my head just as a massive coil of blue scales with a barbed back rips itself from the water, looming high above the English masts and whipping into the air like a snake striking. Another tidal wave hits our boat, this one spilling off the dragon's back, and we tip precariously. I seize one of the rails, both my arms wrapped around it, fighting to keep my head up against the spray. Sim makes a snatch, misses, and instead catches me around the waist, clinging to me. The dragon flails, the middle of her body collapsing overtop of the English ship and splitting it in half with a crack like a tree falling. The masts collapse. Sails shred against her back. She loops her tail once more around the hull, the long barb on the end wicking at the air like a punctuation mark before she dives, pulling the English ship down with her so that it disappears entirely, even the colors swallowed by the water. The eggs float to the surface, still webbed together and glowing.

A moment later, the water ripples again and the dragon's nostrils break the surface, just to the side of our boat. I hold my breath.

The dragon lets out a great puff of misty air, then hooks her nose around the net of eggs. She shakes her head, ripping the sailing ropes apart with the sharp hooks above her nostrils. The eggs bob to the surface, still webbed together by the thin membranes that knotted them to the shallows around the island. The antennae at her eyebrows hook around them, pulling the eggs onto her back, where they nestle like barnacles clinging to her scales.

The dragon raises her eyes. Sees our ship. Snorts another puff of damp air that catches the breeze and blows hot and salty into our faces.

Then she takes a breath—gasping and fathomless, like it made the wind—and dives, the barb of her tail flicking up through the waves before she disappears into the dark water.

And at last, the sea is still.

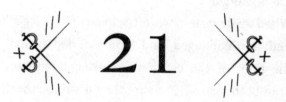

21

It would have been a dramatic sight indeed for Johanna and me to step off the longboat and march to Platt's camp on the island, alone and powerful, two ladies with cutlasses and no fear.

But that's simply not practical, so instead we are two ladies sans cutlasses, still shaking from battle, doused in blood, and accompanied by a flock of pirates—the ones with the grisliest scars and the most threatening stature. It took several hours after the water settled for us to actually make the expedition to the island. At our backs, the *Makasib* has put out its fire, but the front half of the ship is a charred, smoking shell. The *Eleftheria* is attempting to salvage the fallen yards and repair the broken masts. It's no small task. My fingers are stiff from bone setting and the delicate work of extracting bullets from injured sailors. We didn't lose many men, but almost no one escaped without a mark on them. Johanna trailed me around the deck, helping where she could, holding skin and bones in place, unaffected by the sight of exposed muscle and organs.

When we departed, we left Scipio with his leg stitched, cleaned, and bandaged, and Monty curled against Percy on the floor of the captain's quarters, neither resting easy but both resting. I'm sure they'll still be there when we return, likely with Monty stroking Percy's hair as he sleeps, his breathing even and his chest bandaged. Survival not a guarantee—infection and gangrene and all those other sneaky sons of bitches still have time to get their hooks in—but a likely prospect. I've read accounts of duelists shot through the chest who, when treated via intubation, were seen on their feet the next day. The danger now is the sort that comes with any wound. When he returns to his senses, the pain will be brutal, and I wish ferociously that I could give him something to ease it or speed the healing. Some version of opium or the dragon scales that doesn't get its paws around your throat before it's done you any good. There's got to be a way.

We row for the shore when the tide goes out, and drag the longboat onto the only beach that isn't a sheer cliff. The black sand squelches under our feet as we hike, then turns to flaky slate slick with algae and kelp. Milky strands of the sea monster eggshells dot the shore, though whether they were hacked apart by English blades or long ago hatched and washed up with the tide is hard to say. The mist is low, the ocean so still it's almost standing water. It collects in the hollows of the rocks, making pools where sea stars and tentacled sponges wave at us in a paintbox of colors. They seem too bright for nature, these small rose windows beneath the sea.

We find first the camp of sailors Platt brought with him to the island to collect his specimens, all of them fickle-hearted and more than willing to surrender before our pirates have even had a chance to properly threaten them. "Where's Dr. Platt?" I ask one of them, and he jerks his head up the hillside, where smoke is still trickling into the sky.

Johanna and I hike along the hillside, trailed by a few of the men. We have to scramble on all fours in places where the shelf steepens. The trees are bare up to their necks, and the green, shrubby tops sit in the fog, flat and symmetrical. A few patches of yellow flowers dot the hillside, unbent by the winds and waves that batter the island. Rare and wild and impossible to forget.

Platt is sitting alone upon the hill, a burned-out shell of a man. He must have seen the fight, seen the monster sink his ship. His skin looks thin as smoke, and so pale I can count the blue veins in his neck. His hands are raw and blistered as he feeds Sybille Glass's notations one by one into the fire, but he's either so doused or so resigned that he doesn't seem to feel the burn. The flame jumps each time a new page falls upon it.

He raises his head as we approach. His eyes are bloodshot, cheeks sunken and taut so that he looks like a wallpapered skeleton more than an actual man. He does not leap or run or fly into a rage when he sees us coming, nor when we stop on the other side of his fire. Instead, he stands, calmly, though his legs shake beneath him, and takes up Sybille Glass's map of the island from where it sat beside him. He extends it toward us, and I think for a moment he's handing it over, all the fight puddled in his boots, but he stops as the map rests over the fire. The smoke stains the backside black.

Johanna freezes, her boots slipping on the rock. I think it might be a panicked pull-up-short, but instead, she's calm as a summer sky. She crosses her arms. Surveys Platt. Gives him no power. "You can burn it," she says. "If that's what you want."

His hand is shaking. The paper quivers. If he had expected hysteria, her calm must be unsettling.

"It was your work too," she goes on. "Whatever happened between the two of you, my mother wasn't blameless. And if you want to destroy it, so be it."

"It wouldn't have stopped her," he says.

"It won't stop us, either," Johanna replies.

Platt lets go the map, but instead of dropping into the fire, it floats upon the smoke, defying all known laws of gravity for a moment as it hangs on a gust of hot air.

Then Johanna reaches out and plucks it from the trench of smoke, her hands returning sooty and leaving a trail of black fingerprints down the edges of her mother's map.

Platt lets the pirates take him. He doesn't struggle against them or resist in any way, and I wonder what it's like to be too beaten down to fight anymore. I hope I never learn.

Johanna and I meet Sim upon the black sand beach. She comes in a longboat from the *Makasib*, the two men with her swapping her space in the boat for Platt and taking him back to the ship.

"Where's your father?" I call as she hikes toward us.

"With Scipio on the *Eleftheria*, making a plan for their repairs." The wind picks up suddenly, and she presses a hand to her head, holding her headscarf in place. "Did Platt give you the map?"

Johanna holds it up for her to see with a grin. "Should we draw straws for which of us gets which map? We needn't pretend the petticoat is the most desirable version. Or should we each take half of each and then pin them together? Just to be fair. Or perhaps—"

Johanna keeps going, but Sim isn't looking at us. She's staring at the ground as she turns the sand over with her toe, then glances over her shoulder at the longboat rowing back to her father's ship. "Sim," I say, and when she looks back at us, Johanna falls silent.

"You can't have the map," Sim says.

Johanna pulls back, pressing the leather portfolio of her mother's drawings rescued from Platt against her chest. "We had an agreement."

"I know. But my father . . ." Sim looks down again, her eyes shining. "I wish it could be different."

"It can be," I say. "We can talk to him. Make an arrangement."

But Sim is shaking her head. "He won't change his mind. He doesn't want this secret to get back to London. He has men on both ships, more than Scipio does. He'll rally them if you resist."

Johanna stares at her, cheeks sucked in hard for such a long moment I begin to worry for her respiration. Then she lets out all the air in a sharp puff and says, "Well then, I'm not leaving!"

"Johanna—" Sim says, but Johanna pushes on over-top of her.

"I'm not. I'll maroon myself on this island and make the English camp my home and learn to eat that orange moss on the trees and drink sea water and I shall find someone to bring me Max and then I will make this island my continent and my classroom and I will learn everything your father is too cowardly to, and the map won't matter." She crosses her arms, legs spread, a defi-ant general. "You can't stop me. If you will not let me take the map back to England, then I'll stay here."

"I will too," I say.

Johanna jumps, like a fly landed suddenly upon her, and pivots to me. "You will?"

I lost myself in the wanting to do everything right, to get the certificate, the membership, the license, and the diploma. I thought I needed it to all be the same as what men were given, or else it did not count. I have been tripping my way down the same path as Platt and Glass, less of a care for the work than the fact that I wanted to be noticed for that work, and that I was doing it in a way the boards back home would recognize as legitimate.

I had lost sight of the fact that I want to do work that matters. I want to understand the world, and how it moves and how the intricate strings of existence weave together into a tapestry, and I want to weave those tapestries with my own two hands. I am filled suddenly by that wanting, to know things, to understand the world, to feel myself in it. It floods me with a ferocious strength. This world is mine. This work is mine. If it is selfish to want, then selfishness shall be my weapon. I will fight for everything that cannot fight for itself. Block the wind and keep away the wolves and put supper on the table. I am suddenly swollen with more than wanting to be known—I want to know.

The dragons are not ours to expose. The Crown and Cleaver is not ours to throw open the gates to. But this world is still ours. We deserve our space inside of it.

Whether that space earns me a spot on the walls of the surgeon's hall in London or not.

Sim looks between us, and while she must have known neither of us was the sort to go gently, she must be wishing she had picked less willful companions. "Please," she says at last, and holds out a weak hand. "Don't make this harder."

"We're not," Johanna replies. "Your father is, by going back on his word. If you want someone to pat you on the head and tell you you're pretty and absolved, go run back to him, for you won't find it here."

Johanna begins to stalk off, then seems to realize halfway up the beach that she has nowhere to go, as this island is deserted and inhospitable, but after only a short stuttered step goes on with her charge up the mountain anyway, as though to prove just how ready she is to tame this wilderness. Even when that wilderness snags her skirt and she has to rip it free, leaving behind a small flag of pink silk waving from a thin-fingered tree.

Sim looks like she wants to run too, though not in anger. She looks hollowed out and halved, two allegiances doing battle but the one that has been sewn into her blood since birth winning out, no matter how much she may be doubting it. Part of me wants to tell her that I understand, that it's all right, that I don't blame her. The other part wants to say she's a traitor and a coward and should grow a spine and stand up to her father. But that's a very simple thing for me to say.

"What happens to Platt?" I ask at last.

Sim drags a hand over her eyes. "My father and I will take him back to our garrison. See if there's any of him left and make certain he doesn't return to London." A flock of black birds nesting upon the cliff behind us takes flight. She looks at me, strangely expectant, and when I raise my eyebrows, she says, "You didn't ask me if we're going to kill him."

"Oh. I assumed you wouldn't, because that's what I'd very much like to do, and you're far more decent than I am."

Her lips part, the ghost of a smile. "When we first met, you would have assumed the worst of me."

"I would have, and that was terribly unfair," I reply. "Though in my defense, one of our preliminary interactions involved you pulling a knife on an innocent man."

"Because you needed him to punch your brother in the face."

"Not punch him! We decided no punching." She laughs, and I lean my shoulder into hers. She lets my weight sway her sideways like dune grass in the breeze. "How long have you known your father wouldn't give us the map?"

"He never told me outright."

"But you knew."

She shrugs. "Pirates."

"He should have been a man and told us himself instead of sending you."

"He'd rather follow in the great tradition of women cleaning up the messes made by men."

"Ah, the history of the world." I push a handful of my hair out of my face. It's gone greasy as bacon over the last few weeks, and I almost wipe my hand upon my skirt as soon as I've touched it. "I suppose he wouldn't believe you if you said it was lost and let us keep the petticoat."

"He wouldn't."

"And I suppose you agree with him, that the dragons should be left alone and undisturbed."

"If we leave them undisturbed, we also leave them unknown," she says, and it sounds so much like something Johanna would say that it catches me under the chin. Sim cants her head to the side, one finger tracing the shape of her bottom lip. "It may be his choice, and he may be the commodore, but I don't think it's the right one."

"That's very bold of you to say."

"It would be bolder if I were saying it to him. I've thought for so long that the only way he'd ever consider me a contender was if I made myself into the best version of him in miniature that I could, so that he'd know his legacy wouldn't be disrupted if he gave his landholdings to me. But I don't want to be my father. I don't want things to stay the same. And if that costs me my birthright . . ." She falters, resolve weakening when faced with voicing it.

"What will it mean for the dragons?" I ask.

"I don't know," she replies. "But there are always consequences. Even in standing still. And I'm tired of stillness."

We stand side by side, staring out at the ocean, watching the waves fan across the shore, leaving constellations of white shells behind. A beached starscape at our feet. "Do you ever wish time could be lived backward?" I ask. "So you could know if the decisions you were making were the right ones?"

Sim snorts. "Are there right ones?"

"Righter ones, then. Ones that won't end in wasting your life and getting nowhere chasing something that might never be anything more than a mythology."

"Mythology is all shite anyway," she says. "It never has stories about people like us. I'd rather write my own legends. Or be the story someone else looks to someday. Build a strong foundation for those who follow us."

I wrinkle my nose. "That's not very glamorous. Foundations are buried in dirt, you know."

"Since when have you cared for glamour?"

"I don't. It's you I'm worried for." I pluck at the loose

fabric around her thigh. "Wouldn't want anything to happen to those fashionable trousers."

She tips her head at me, eyes narrowing. "You're mocking me."

"I am," I reply, as solemnly as I can muster.

That oil slick of a smile spreads over her lips, and I want to touch a candle to it and watch her smolder, this dangerous, gorgeous, wildfire of a woman. "Just because you've never seen me cleaned up doesn't mean I can't lean deeply into the princess part of my piracy."

"Oh, can you now?"

"Felicity Montague, if you saw me dressed for Eid in my blue-and-gold kaftan, you'd faint dead away. You'd propose marriage to me on the spot. And maybe my kisses aren't magic for you, but of course I'd say yes, and I'd treat you right and we'd be very happy together. You could have your house and your books and your old dog, and I would have a ship and sail for years at a time and only stop by to see you on occasion, so you'd never grow tired of me."

"And would we be happy?" I ask.

"Ecstatic," she replies.

Her tongue darts out between her teeth and her eyes flicker to my mouth. I think for a moment she might kiss me again. Every amatory novel would say this is the moment for a back-bending, knee-weakening embrace, lips on burning lips, though I can't imagine there's any book in existence in which two people like us kiss. If we are not the stuff of myths, we are certainly not the coupled lovers of any modern fiction either.

"We'd grow weary of each other eventually," I say. "We're cactus girls. We'd prick each other with a glance."

"I withdraw my cactus comparison," she says. "Or, if you're to be a cactus, you're one of the furry ones. The ones that look like they have spines but if you're brave enough to press your hand against it, you realize it's soft."

I roll my eyes. "That sounds fake."

"Then you'll be the first of your kind. Wild and rare and impossible to forget." She opens and closes her fist, flexing the striped scars along her arm from the broken glass. A reminder of the strange things the ocean grows. All the mysteries of the world we still don't know. Questions we haven't even thought to ask.

"I can't give you the map," she says. "But if you'll let me . . . and if Johanna will let me . . . there may be another way."

We find Johanna at the skeletal remains of the English camp, releasing her rage by methodically destroying anything Platt's men left behind that will not prove necessary to her survival should she have to make good on her promise of installing herself as queen of this island. She stops when she sees us coming, a pan in her hand already dented from several times struck against a tree trunk. "What?" she calls flatly as Sim and I pull ourselves up the hillside toward her.

Sim halts at the camp's edge, takes a moment to catch her breath, then says, "Would you hear a proposition?"

"I'll hear it," Johanna says, "but I may not entertain it."

"What if," Sim starts, "you return to London—"

"With the map?"

Sim hesitates. "No."

"Then the answer is no." Johanna flings the frying pan into the shrubs, startling a pair of birds into flight. She squeaks, looks like she might apologize to the birds, then realizes that would undermine the fury she's trying so valiantly to put on. "I told you, I shan't leave without it."

"Well, hold those convictions for a moment and let her finish," I say.

Sim takes another deep breath, looks as though she'd like to move the rest of the cookware out of Johanna's reach just in case, but then says, "Go back to London. Mapless. Make certain everyone knows that Platt's ship sank and his expedition failed and everything he was studying was nonsense. He was a crazed addict. He was out of his mind."

"So far none of this is proposition-worthy," Johanna says.

"Then, as his wife, take whatever finances of his remain for yourself."

"He won't have much," she says. "Opium is expensive, and he's been without a post for a long while."

"But you have a dowry," I say, "which will have reached his bank accounts by now."

She pauses. Considers this. Then scowls again. "All right, so I have some money. What do you propose I do with it?"

"Purchase whatever equipment you'd need to do this work right," Sim says. "Get your house in order, fetch your giant dog, pay these corsairs to fix up their ship and bring you to the Crown and Cleaver garrison when the time is right. And then I'll bring you back here, and we do this work together."

Johanna was so ready to flatly refuse any offer from Sim that she looks put out by how reasonable this solution is. "And what then?" she demands. "What happens when we find a way to entirely end death by using the dragon scales?"

"I don't know," Sim says. "We'll have to work that out together when the time comes."

"Though if we've ended death, we'll have a good long while to figure it out," I add.

"What about you?" Johanna asks me.

I look to Sim. "You could go with Johanna," she says. "Or, if you wanted . . . come back to Algiers with me.

Our medical institutions are different from yours, but we have surgeons and physicians in our fort. You could learn from us. With us. And make certain I uphold my end of this bargain."

"Yes, I'd feel much more comfortable with that," Johanna says. "Felicity will keep you pirates honest."

"I know it's not what you wanted," Sim says, and I can feel her eyes on me.

It isn't. It's leagues away from what I pictured years ago, reading medical books in secret and romping through the grounds with Johanna and harboring an illicit vision of a future away from my father's estate. It isn't what I wanted. But I don't care. It is not a failure to readjust my sails to fit the waters I find myself in. It's a new heading. A fresh start.

"We can't disappear from London forever," Johanna says. "We'd have to keep some sort of contact back home if we want to go back. If Platt has accounts, or a home, or any assets, someone will have to manage that so I can keep a claim to it and we have something to go back to when the time comes."

"My brothers," I say, and the word feels warm and round against my tongue. "Monty's rubbish at figures, and his penmanship is a disaster, but he and Percy could handle it. Monty can charm investors and Percy can make certain all the sums even out. And they can live in the house while you're away. I'm sure Monty would be thrilled to impersonate your husband if need be. He's gotten very enthusiastic about playacting."

"The three of us could rally at my father's garrison in a year and return here together," Sim says. "I know it's not what we promised, but it's a start. It's the best I can do."

"You're right," Johanna says. "It's not what you promised." Her voice is so sharp my heart sinks, but then she goes on, "But it's the start of something. And I'll take a start." She holds out a hand to Sim, like she wants to make a formal stamp upon this accord. When Sim doesn't take it, Johanna says, "Is there a different way you corsairs seal your bargains?"

"We can shake, if you want." Sim stares at her open palm, then adds, "But I have a better idea."

"Am I going to catch some ghastly disease of the blood from this?" Johanna asks as she watches Sim mash lampblack and laundry bluing in with the white of an egg. The mixture shifts from milky to the bluish obsidian of the underside of a raven's wing. Sim spits into the bowl, then tests it with her thumb.

"Almost definitely," I reply. We three are sitting on the deck of the *Eleftheria*, our skirts spread like puddles collected from a rainstorm as, all around us, the men make ready to cast off. They've done enough repairs to limp back to the mainland, with Johanna aboard, while

435

Sim and I will go with her father's men, back to Algiers. Scipio, who only stays off his bad leg when I'm looking, is shouting orders from a perch near the helm. Percy and Monty are nearby as well, Percy stretched out on his back with his head in Monty's lap. They're both soaking in the sun, which has appeared for the first time since the battle. Percy doesn't color in the sun like Monty does, but it makes him look glowing and healthy and—thank God—*alive*. Monty says something I can't hear, and Percy laughs, then puts a hand to his chest with a wince. Monty flips at once, from goading to doting, pressing his hand overtop Percy's as he whispers admonitions I can't hear but are almost certainly something like *steady on*. Or perhaps they're far more explicit descriptions of what he plans to do to Percy once he's healed. When it comes to my brother, both are equally likely.

"And you do know how to draw, don't you?" Johanna asks Sim, scraping her nails against her palm as she bounces up and down like a tea kettle trying to let the steam out. "I'm not going to end up with a permanent mark upon my skin that looks like a penis with a party hat on, am I?"

"No, that's a different piratical fleet entirely," I reply dryly.

Sim flicks her eyes at me with a glancing smile, then turns back to Johanna. "I'll draw it out in charcoal for your approval before I do the ink." Johanna lets out a wild giggle. "Why are you laughing?"

"Because it's going to hurt! And this is how I cope!" She throws her arms around my neck, nearly pulling me over into her lap. "Comfort me, Felicity. I haven't Max to hold so you'll have to do. This is going to hurt terribly, isn't it?"

"Yes, it will," Sim says, but I shake my head when she turns away. Johanna looks between us, not sure whose credentials to believe.

"Where do you want the mark?" Sim asks us. "Before you answer, consider that, in order for it to be most effective in a time of need, you'll have to show it off."

"Consider also," I add to Johanna as I lean backward into her embrace, "your fondness for low-cut party dresses."

"Oh, I don't know!" Johanna flaps her hands. "It's too much pressure to choose!

"Do you want me to go first?" I ask. "That way if I don't survive, you can change your mind."

"Yes, please."

Johanna releases me from her strangulating snuggle, and I turn to Sim. "Where am I marking you, Miss Montague?" she asks.

"Right in my elbow, I think," I say, fiddling with the button on my sleeve.

"Same as mine?" she asks, and I hesitate.

"Yes. Is that strange?"

"No," she replies. "It's symmetrical."

As promised, she draws the sketch upon my skin in charcoal first—no partying phalluses, just the faint outline of the Crown and Cleaver on my forearm—then picks up her instrument. She's wrapped needles from the ship's surgical kit together with string to create a tiny, many-toothed nib. It's certainly not the dodgiest tool that has been used to put a permanent mark on a person's skin, but still far from the sort of instrument that would have been approved for use by the governors of Saint Bart's.

But I'm rather finished with wondering what those men would think.

Sim dips it into the black ink, then takes my forearm in her hand. A flock of terns launches from the sea and into flight, a wild burst for the sky that speckles shadows across our faces.

"Am I shaking?" I ask.

"Not a bit."

"I don't want to look!" Johanna cries, though she makes no move to cover her eyes or even close them. Sim's thumb floats over the soft skin of my forearm, stretching it tight, then she leans down and deals a quick kiss to the spot. "For luck," she says.

As she raises the needle, I look between her and Johanna. In the company of women like this—sharp-edged as raw diamonds but with soft hands and hearts, not strong in spite of anything but powerful because of everything—I feel invincible. Every chink and rut and battering wind has made us tough and brave and impossible to strike down. We are mountains—or perhaps temples, with foundations that could outlast time itself.

When the needle breaks my skin, the pain is as cold and bright as the horizon of a cloudless winter sky. In this moment, this place, this perch upon the edge of the world, it feels like the view goes on forever.

Dear Callum,

I've been staring at this page for an hour at least and that's all I've written. Dear Callum.

Dear Callum,

I'm not sure how I have so much to say and no words to be found. Also pardon the blood—it's only a small drop, and it's mine, and it's only from having a pirate symbol carved upon my arm.

Drat. All that contemplation for such a poor beginning.

How I should have started was with I'm sorry, for I intend for this to be an apology letter to the both of us.

First to you, for taking advantage of your kindness and your fondness. I hope you aren't sorry for that kindness, and I hope you do not falter the next time you feel the urge to give a cream puff to someone in need, simply because I burned you.

Second, an apology to me, for trying to force my heart somewhere it didn't belong, and for thinking myself odd because it didn't fit there. And then again to you for also thinking myself odd in the way of a wildflower, brilliant and rare and better for that rarity, and you too common a blossom for my garden. I'm sorry I looked down upon your life.

I'm sorry that you thought you had to save me from myself. Sorry more that we live in a world that raised you to think that way. I used to wish terribly that I wanted a bakery and a baker and a brood. I used to wish that was all I needed to feel complete. How much simpler life would be. But nothing is simple, not a life in a bakeshop in Scotland nor one exploring the world's untouched trenches. And thank God, because I do not want simple. I do not want easy or small or uncomplicated. I want my life to be messy and ugly and wicked and wild, and I want to feel it all. All those things that women are made to believe they are strange for harboring in their hearts. And I want to surround myself with those same strange, wicked women who throw themselves open to all the wondrous things this world has to offer.

Perhaps I'm spiraling into sentimental prose, but at this moment, I feel that I could swallow the world whole.

I hope you live a life you're proud of. I really do. I hope someday we can sit down again over cider and pastries, and you can tell me your story and I can tell you mine and we will both burst like overripe fruit with pride in ourselves, and each other. I couldn't be a baker's wife, but someone will, and you'll be good to her, and happy together, and as much as this new life is mine, that will be hers. I'm learning there is no one way for life to be lived, no one way to be strong or brave or kind or good. Rather there are many people doing the best they can with the heart they are given and the hand they are dealt. Our best is all we can do, and all we can hold on to is each other.

And, zounds, that is more than enough.

Yours,
Felicity Montague

Author's Note

Women in historical fiction are often criticized for being girls of today dropped into historical set pieces, inaccurate to their time because of their feminist ideas and independent natures. It's a criticism that has always frustrated me, for it proposes the idea that women throughout time would not see, speak out, or take action against the inequality and injustices they faced simply because they'd never known anything else. Gender equality and the treatment of women is not a linear progression; it has varied throughout time and is dependent upon a slew of factors, like class, race, sexuality, location, religion, etc., etc., etc. We tend to think of history as less individual than we do our modern experiences, but most general statements about *all women* in any historical context can be proven false. By exceptions, not rules, of course. But still disproved. Just as there is no single story for women today, there is not one for historical women either.

Here, I will address the three women in the novel and their respective aspirations, as well as the research and real-life women of history that inspired each of them.

Medicine

It is indisputable that medicine in eighteenth-century England was dominated by men. They were not all educated—medical care ranged from barbers who would shave your face, pull your teeth, and perform surgery all with the same tools to professional, educated surgeons whose services were usually only available to the wealthy (and whose ranks were generally made up of those already born into wealth). At the time, there were only a handful of universities offering medical degrees, so a surgical education was often gained from lectures, courses, and dissections sponsored by hospitals or private physicians. A prospective doctor would have to sit an exam before receiving his license, though many unlicensed doctors still operated around the country.

Women were restricted to certain corners of the medical field, like herbal remedies and midwifery, though the growing trend of male midwives, as well as the development of and subsequent monopoly on forceps by male surgeons, was boxing women out of that. However, the idea that women were excluded from all medicine—or, really, all "men's work"—is false. In many professions we now think of as traditionally male—including medicine—wives often worked alongside their husbands and, if the husband died or was unable to work, served as a "deputy husband," meaning they took up their husband's profession. Lady doctors were more accepted the farther you got from big cities and big hospitals and their regulating boards.

Felicity, a woman who wants to be educated and taken seriously in the sciences, would by no means have been ahead of her time. At the same time the novel is set, Laura Bassi received a doctoral degree in physics from the University of Bologna after defending her thesis at age twenty, and went on to a professorship—the first woman to earn a university chair in a scientific field. In Germany, Dorothea Erxleben, inspired by Bassi, was the first woman to receive a Ph.D. in medicine and, in 1742, published a tract arguing that women should be allowed at universities.

Things moved slower in the United Kingdom—it would be one hundred years after Felicity before medical schools welcomed women into their student bodies. (And welcomed is far too generous a word.) The gender barrier was finally broken in 1869, thanks to the consistent efforts of countless women who fought without ever seeing the product of their struggle, but who paved the way for the Edinburgh Seven, the first group of matriculated undergraduate female students at a British university: Sophia Jex-Blake, Isabel Thorne, Edith Pechey, Matilda Chaplin, Helen Evans, Mary Anderson, and Emily Bovell.

But even after they were granted admission, they were educated separately from their male counterparts. Their tuition was higher. Male students harassed them physically and verbally. When the Seven arrived to sit an anatomy exam, they were met with a mob who threw mud and rocks at them. And even after they'd completed their coursework and exams, the university refused to grant them degrees.

But as more women joined their ranks, they formed a General Committee for Securing a Complete Medical Education for Women, which helped pass the Medical Act of 1876, which allowed licenses to be granted to both men and women. Jex-Blake, the leader of the Seven, helped establish the London School of Medicine for Women and eventually returned to Edinburgh as the city's first woman doctor. The epigraph of this book is a quote from her biography. Go ahead and flip back to it. I'll wait.

The medical texts, practitioners, and treatments that Felicity references throughout this book are all real and all products of the eighteenth century, but I played fast and loose with their timeline. Some of the writings she mentions would not have been published at the same time the book is set, and several doctors mentioned would have technically come after her, but I chose to include them to create a more rounded picture of the weirdness that was medicine in the 1700s.

Naturalism

The eighteenth century was the age of enlightenment. Most of the world's major landmasses had been discovered, but thanks to technological advancements, many locations were being mapped for the first time. Scientific missions, commissioned and funded by kings, governments, and private collectors, were focused on creating these maps, as well as bringing new flora and fauna back to Europe. Fields like natural history, botany, zoology, geography, and oceanography expanded. These voyages of discovery almost always included artists, who were used to record the landscapes and natural wonders. Before photography, artists were critical to capturing precise details of nature so that they could be compared and analyzed.

Johanna Hoffman and Sybille Glass were inspired by Maria Sibylla Merian, a German naturalist and scientific illustrator whose work spanned the end of the seventeenth and beginning of the eighteenth century. Like Sybille Glass, Maria Merian separated from her husband and was hired as an artist on a scientific expedition to Suriname. She spent two years in South America, accompanied by her daughter Dorothea. Later, the two women ran a business together selling prints of Maria's scientific illustrations. Today, Maria's work is considered to be among the most important contributions to modern entomology.

Naturalism and medicine were closely related fields to eighteenth-century scholars. Physicians joined expeditions, not only to administer first aid to the crew as needed but to conduct their own research and collect samples of natural medicines for further study. Experiments, procedures, and dissections were often performed on animals (both dead and alive, because history is the worst). Many physicians believed that facts learned from these animal experiments could also be applied to the understanding of the human body—false, but good hustle, eighteenth century.

Piracy

The pirates of the eighteenth-century Mediterranean were not the white, roguish swashbucklers that populate most of our best-known modern buccaneer narratives. They were mostly African men and women from the Barbary States who worked to expand and protect their own territories and fleets. They defended themselves from and fought against both other pirates and Europeans. The slave trade was alive and well in the 1700s—Europeans enslaved Africans, and Africans enslaved other Africans. However, of all the liberties taken for the sake of an adventure-novel plot, I have to cough up to one in particular: pirates were no great fans of tattoos, as it was a far too obvious and permanent way to declare your allegiances.

Within every pirate fleet, there was often a complex internal organization that included electing officers and leaders, dividing plunder, and maintaining social order. Much of this order was kept in balance by pirates marrying each other. Not all marriages had romantic components—some were only to determine who would inherit what if someone died in battle—but many marriage contracts that have survived do include clauses about intimacy. Sailors have long been practitioners of "situational homosexuality" as a result of long months at sea without sexual release, but for pirates, these relationships could be open and legitimate. The term for these unions was *matelotage*, which was eventually shorted to mate, and then matey. Sim, as a Muslim girl, likely would not have been kissing anyone, but views of homosexuality, particularly relationships between women, were as complex and variable as they are today.

Sim was initially inspired by Sayyida al-Hurra, the sixteenth-century Muslim woman who used her position as governor of Tétouan to command a fleet of pirates that conducted raids on Spanish ships as revenge for the genocide and exile of Muslims, though her character and story line evolved considerably over the course of writing this novel. And while women at sea were outnumbered by men in the Barbary States, Sim is part of a long, rich heritage of women at the head of pirate fleets, including Ching Shih, Jeanne de Clisson, Grace O'Malley, Jacquotte Delahaye, Anne Dieu-le-Veut, Charlotte de Berry—they could fill an entire book (and have! Have you read *Pirate Women: The Princesses, Prostitutes, and Privateers Who*

Ruled the Seven Seas by Laura Sook Duncombe? It's rad).

There are many things that make this book fiction, but the roles women play within it are not. The women of the eighteenth century were met with opposition. They had to fight endlessly. Their work was silenced, their contributions ignored, and many of their stories are forgotten today.

Nevertheless, they persisted.

Seven Real Women Who Would Have Been BFFs with Felicity, Johanna, and Sim

History is lousy with stories of women from every time and place who demonstrated the same tenacity, courage, and general badassery that Felicity, Johanna, and Sim all demonstrate in their chosen fields. Here are seven painfully brief biographies of some of the real women from history whose stories inspired those of our leading ladies.

Keumalahayati came from a noble Indonesian family, back in the 1500s, when Indonesia was controlled by the power coupe of European colonization: Portugal and the Spanish Netherlands. When Keumalahayati's husband was killed in a naval battle against Portugal, Keumalahayati immediately offered to take over his spot as admiral at the head of his fleet fighting for independence. With the permission of the sultan, Keumalahayati mustered an army of the most powerful soldiers she could find: war widows. Her army gained a reputation as one of the most feared fighting forces in Asia, driving out European colonial forces throughout the pacific. Not only was she the first female admiral in the history of the modern world, she also became Commander of the Uleebalang (the Royal Palace Guard) and a negotiator in foreign affairs.

Hortense Mancini was born in 1646, one of five fabulously beautiful sisters raised in the court of King Louis XIV at Versailles. The downside of being one of these fabulously beautiful sisters was that she was forced to marry Armand-Charles de La Porte, Duc de La Meilleraye, a religious fanatic/general dick twice her age. He kept Hortense isolated from the world and controlled her every move. And Hortense was not into it. She may have been one of the richest women in Europe because of the marriage, but money can't buy a non-abusive relationship. After seven years of unsuccessfully trying to get a divorce granted, Hortense took matters into her own hands and simply left Armand. She fled France where King Louis declared her under his protection. Armand pursued her for the rest of her life, attempting to extend his control over her by freezing her assets and taking legal action. But even when she was ordered by a judge to return to her dipshit husband, Hortense refused. For ten years, she lived as a runaway bride evading the law and her abuser. She never returned to him.

Anna Maria van Schurman entered Utrecht University in 1636, making her the first female university student in Europe. After graduating, she formed the hub of a European network of other highly educated women and wrote important texts that, among other things, advocated the importance of getting girls into classrooms. In spite of being one of the seventeenth century's leading academics, Anna Maria van Schurman often had to sit behind a screen when she attended lectures—even after she graduated—because of her sex. She attended them anyway.

Laura Bassi was a child prodigy who, at age thirteen, began studying medicine and philosophy with a professor from the University of Bologna. In 1732, she was admitted to the Bologna Academy of Sciences, its first female member. She received her degree as a doctor of philosophy after defending her theses, and one month later, after defending a second set of theses about the properties of water, she was awarded an honorary post at the university as a professor in physics. However, because she was a woman, she was not allowed to actually teach at the university, so instead she gave lectures at her home. In 1776, she was appointed to the chair of experimental physics at the University of Bologna, making her the first woman to hold a department chair position at a European university.

Jeanne de Clisson was born around 1300 in Brittany, France. When Jeanne was forty-three, the French king executed her husband, on the off chance he was an English spy. Jeanne's response was to sell everything she owned, buy three warships, paint them black, and out-fit them with blood-red sails. Then she recruited a crew of bloodthirsty buccaneers, named her flagship *My Vengeance*, and made it her mission to destroy as many French ships as possible as payback for her husband's execution. She became known as the Lioness of Brittany and was so successful at this that she was officially recruited by the English to pillage French ships, now on their payroll—she received land, titles, and money for her work. Unlike most pirates, Jeanne wasn't killed in battle or executed—she retired. She married an English lord, settled down, and outlived her great enemy, the French king.

Elizabeth Blackwell was a British physician and the first woman to receive a medical degree in the United States. Her interest in medicine was sparked after a friend fell ill and remarked that, had a female doctor cared for her, she would have been more comfortable and less stressed. Elizabeth began applying to medical schools, and was universally rejected, except by the Geneva Medical College. There, male students voted to admit her, only because they thought her application was a joke. It wasn't. In 1847, she became the first woman to attend medical school in the United States. She went on to found the New York Infirmary for Women and Children with her sister Emily, and gave lectures around the country to women on the importance of educating girls. She also played a significant role during the American Civil War in organizing nurses.

Mary Anning was an English paleontologist who became known around the world for the fossils she discovered in Lyme Regis in southwest England. Her findings, which began at age twelve when she discovered the first ichthyosaur skeleton, contributed to important changes in scientific thinking about prehistoric life and the history of the earth. Mary was not able to fully participate in the scientific community of nineteenth-century Britain, as it was comprised exclusively of men who continued to make rules about how only men could be scientists. However, she became well known in geological circles throughout Europe and America, and was consulted frequently on questions of paleontology. Because of her gender, she was not eligible to join the Geological Society of London and she did not always receive credit for her scientific contributions. The only scientific writing of hers published in her lifetime appeared in the *Magazine of Natural History* in 1839, an extract from a letter to the editor she wrote correcting their claims.

The Gentleman's Guide to Love and Letters

"They are truly impossible to describe."

I'm not entirely certain Percy is listening to me. He's making a careful study of the scuffed billiard balls scattered across the tabletop as he rubs chalk onto the end of his cue. But then he says, "And yet somehow, you've found a way to describe them for the last quarter of an hour."

"They're just . . . very, very blue. Sinjon Westfall has the goddamn bluest eyes I've ever seen." I lean backward against the bar, which is farther away than I thought and what I had meant to be an elegant swoon is more of a lovesick stumble. "Blue as the sky. But different, because they're darker blue. So the sky . . . but different. That's what I'll say when I write him. Or blue as . . ." I grab at the air like I'm trying to catch a scent. "That color women use on their breasts to trace the veins."

Percy snorts. "Do not write that in your love letter."

"But you do know the color, don't you?"

"I don't have many occasions to look at women's breasts."

"We need to get you out more." I reach for my glass of gin, which I swear is both emptier and in an entirely different location than it was when I last set it down, as I hoist myself onto one of the stools. "They're very blue eyes, all right? They're blue beyond words."

"Write that, then. Make it a short letter." Percy leans over the table and hooks a finger around the end of his cue, his other arm drawing back like a bow. The muscles in his shoulder turn tense and round.

"And he rows," I say before I can stop myself. "So he's got these arms like someone carved him out of stone. Stone I really want to sleep with." Percy scrapes his teeth over his bottom lip, his customary gesture before he takes his shot. The single stroke sends one of the balls sailing into a pocket with a hollow rattle. "What's the word for it?" I ask as he straightens.

"Wanting to sleep with a stone?"

"When you're muscled but not in the way that makes you look like you're about to rip the seams out of your trousers."

Percy wanders around the table, one hand tugging up the waistband of his breeches. "Trim?"

"No." I take a sip of my gin. "I mean, he is. But not

what I'm thinking of."

Percy slings himself along the bar beside me, taking up his mug of beer and skimming his lips over the foam as he thinks. "Slender? Lean?"

"That's it, lean." I knock my glass against his. "Sinjon is very lean."

"Like a chicken cutlet," he mutters, neither loud enough for me to hear nor soft enough to be certain I won't.

I frown. "Don't be sour."

"Lean as chicken and dense as stone, isn't that what you said?" He takes up his mace again—our attempts to convince the owner of the hall to let us play with cues instead of maces had been for naught, as he remembered me from the last time we came to play, and I had accidentally punctured a hole in the felt with an over enthusiastic swipe that had missed the ball entirely. "Can we talk about something that isn't Sinjon Westfall, please?"

I kick my foot after him, nudging his thigh lightly. "Help me think of something better to write to him, then. Something about his eyes."

"Oh, you mean 'the sky but different' isn't romantic enough for your confession of adoration?" he asks.

I flick a piece of chalk off the edge of the table at him. "Help me, then. Tell me something blue."

"Your eyes are blue."

3

I scoff. "I can't put that in a love letter. Dear Sinjon, your eyes are as blue as my eyes, which is why I love them. Come now, Perce. I know I'm vain but that's a bit much." He's back to staring at the table again, working out the geometry of his next shot. He always pretends to put some sort of maths into his billiards game, but in the end we're both so rubbish that I know he's guessing almost as wildly as I am; he just looks more thoughtful about it.

When it seems unlikely he's planning to respond, I let out a moan and flop face-first onto the table. My elbow knocks one of the balls, and I abandon my dramatic gesture to put it back before Percy can scold me. "Help me," I plead. "I want to write him while we're apart for the holiday, so that way if it's horrible and he doesn't feel the same, we can ignore each other for the rest of the term, or I can say I got a little foxed at a Christmas ball and wrote it as a jest. Please, I won't be able to think of anything else until this line is settled. Then we can talk about something else, I promise."

Percy narrows his eyes at me, like he's judging how much of a man of my word I am feeling tonight. "Fine," he says at last. "Get off the table; you've already mucked up my shot." I take my hands off the felt and tuck them obediently behind my back, waiting. Percy knits his fingers over the top of his mace and leans upon it, chin resting on his hands as he surveys me for a ponderous moment. Then, at last he says, "A classic: the ocean."

"Not majestic enough," I reply.

"Plenty of poets have found it sufficiently majestic."

"Clearly, none of them ever saw an ocean from England because dear God are they bleak and gray here."

"Blueberries," he offers.

"Your eyes are as blue as blueberries. That's not poetic, that's just repetitive." I press my fist against my chin. "What about crabs?"

I say it just as he takes a drink, which ends up spat back into his mug as he laughs. "Crabs?" He repeats, swiping a hand over his mouth. "You rejected comparing his eyes to the ocean in favor of your eyes are as blue as crabs?"

"You know, the blue crabs!" He's still laughing, so I go on, "The ones we caught that summer in Penzance."

"I have no memory of this."

"Yes you do! It was the summer we found the shipwreck—"

"I remember the summer," he interrupts. "Just not crabs in a shade of blue worthy of a love letter."

"They were about this big," I hold my thumb and forefinger close together for a measurement, "and they were fast and mean and all over that bloody ship, so we tried to herd them into a bucket, and I got my foot stuck in that rotted board and you told me it would have to be cut off."

"Oh yes." His mouth quirks into a half moon. "I do remember telling you that you were going to have to cut your foot off."

"God, did you tell me I was going to have to do it myself? You're cruel."

"Don't blame me," he says, holding up his hands. "Blame the crabs."

I hoist myself onto one of the barstools again as Percy realigns his mace. "I'm going to write Sinjon tonight," I say, "and I'm going to tell him his eyes are blue as crabs and I think his ass looks fantastic in those god-awful trousers they make us wear and also I'm very smitten with him and hoping he feels the same."

"That line about the crabs absolutely will not work," Percy says without looking up.

"It will, and it's going to be grand. We'll be married by the spring." I drain my gin, set the glass on the bar with a flourish, and say "Just you wait."

Percy doesn't answer. When he takes his shot, he misses entirely and sinks the shooter into the pocket with a deadened thunk.

"Blue as crabs is the worst line in the history of the written word."

We are holding up the wall at the back of the chapel, in the corner where the floor is textured with memorial stones to men who paid god knows how much to be certain that, even in death, it was clear just how much money they had. Christmas services have finished and while everyone wanders around showing off their fancy duds and wishing each other a good holiday, Percy and I are tossing coins into a chalice built into a stone monument upon the wall, while also avoiding my father. He's only been back from London for a day and already I have been told I am scruffier than I was when he last saw me, my complexion is worse, as well as interrogated as to why my marks remained so aggressively mediocre, and why, when he met my Latin professor in Cambridge, he had been informed I have twice fallen asleep in his lectures.

"Right," I had said. "Only twice."

He'd slapped me across the face, though I wasn't sure if it was for the sleeping through lectures or the lip.

Percy rolls a shilling between his hands, makes a show of kissing it for luck, then flicks it off his thumbnail toward the chalice. The coin misses by a not inconsiderable distance, then bounces twice against the stones before rolling on its side under one of the pews. "I told you."

"I know, but I didn't believe you because I'm almost always right," I reply, digging my shoe into the groove of one of the monuments beneath my feet. "Particularly about love letters."

"You didn't send it yet, did you?"

7

"No, thank god. I wrote it in a burst of passion and then let it sit on my desk for a week and I swear someone must have swapped it out while I slept. How drunk was I that I thought blue as crabs was a romantic way to describe someone's eyes?"

"You were . . ." He presses a finger to his lips in consideration. "Not entirely sober."

There's a clap as someone drops a hymnal nearby, and I flinch, fumbling the coin I had been tossing between my palms. Percy's head snaps up, glancing first at me, then around the pews for the source of the sound. I swipe a hand over my face, then shake my head a few times, trying to clear it. The two shots of whiskey I downed covertly before we left are starting to lose their bite. On the other side of the aisle, Richard Peele is making a valiant attempt to pretend he's interested in whatever story Johanna Hoffman is imparting to him about some unfortunate creature she and my sister recently rescued from the countryside. His shock of fine blond hair is set in a jaunty curl, shining with pomade even in the dim light of the chapel. Richard's gaze drifts over Johanna's shoulder, and our eyes meet. His nose wrinkles in that uniquely Richard way, where I can't tell if he's smirking at me in confidence or condescension.

I slump behind the pillar sheltering us. "If only I were writing about Richard Peele's eyes, this would be so much easier."

Percy retrieves the ha'penny I dropped and tosses it to me. I catch it between flat palms. "Because you could write Dear Richard, your eyes are the color of dirt."

"Dirt seems too generous. Mud, maybe."

"Or perhaps Dear Richard, your eyes are the color of sh—"

"Percy Newton!" I clap a hand over his mouth. It's a maddening distance to have to reach—when had he gotten taller than me? "How dare you say 'shit' in the house of the lord!"

He shoves me off him with a laugh. "I hate Richard Peele."

"We hate Richard Peele!" I reply, not loud enough for Richard to actually hear but enough to make Percy laugh and shush me at the same time. God, I missed that bright, merry sputter of his laugh while I was away at Eaton. I know it like I know my own shadow, the way it always starts with a burst of surprise, as though delight has snuck up on him. It makes me feel bright and fizzy as champagne, and I wonder if every jape I've ever made is done in hopes Percy will offer up that laugh in return.

I don't want to knock that smile from his lips, so I don't tell him—though I suspect he worked it out—that when Richard and I left the bar within a quarter of an hour of each other two nights previous, it had been for a snog in the alley that had spiraled into trousers around ankles. I'd come back inside with soaked, muddy knees,

9

and my hair standing up in the back from where he'd seized handfuls and tugged hard, too rough for my taste, but one can't really hope for a sweet touch when giving a bar-alley blow job.

I'm sure Percy knows. Even more sure when he glances at Richard again and sucks in his cheeks. I could tell him it hadn't meant a damn thing—it never did with Richard. I could tell him I'd only gone along with it because of how terribly panicked I was about that goddamn letter to Sinjon, and maybe all those eyes he'd been making at me across the library meant nothing, but I'd hung my heart upon them anyway. I could tell him I was so certain I was about to be let down again that I'd gone running to Richard, the only well I knew to drink from when I was this disgusted with myself. I don't know why I care what Percy thinks. He's seen me wander out of bars with plenty of people. Maybe because it's Richard. Maybe because of the letter.

I toss my ha'penny, which skitters off a ridge in the stone chalice and goes wild.

"What if . . ." Percy says suddenly, and I look over at him. He swipes his thumb over his bottom lip. "What if you wrote to Sinjon that his eyes are blue as a flame? You know, when you look into the very center of a candle flame, where it touches a wick. Sometimes that burns blue. His eyes are as blue as the center of a candle flame."

"Really?" It comes out with a peak that would have

embarrassed me had it been anyone but Percy. "Would that work on you if someone said that in a love letter?"

"It would . . ." He runs his tongue over his teeth. A long dribble of wax from the chandelier over our heads splatters on the tiles between us. "Say that his eyes are blue as the center of a flame, and a love unrequited is like holding your finger to that fire, knowing you'll be burned, but it's worth the pain." His gaze flits to mine, then down just as fast, mouth quirking to one side. The apples of his cheeks are rosy in the piebald light. "That would work on me."

"Percy Newton," I say, letting myself tip sideways so my shoulder is pressed into his. "You are a goddamn poet."

"I should have written that his eyes are as blue as crabs."

Percy and I are lying side by side on my father's lawn, three months after that letter found its way into Sinjon's pocket. Two since our first reckless kiss behind the dormitories in the honey light of a new spring moon. Only a week since the seizure of my rooms at Eton, where his reply was discovered and turned over to the headmaster as cause for my expulsion. Two days since my father came to fetch me.

The pain in my ribs isn't as bad lying still on my back, but the bruises are starting to throb, starting to sink so deep I swear I feel them in my bones. I feel like I'm decaying. Like if I pressed two fingers against my check, where the skin around my swollen eye has turned blue and mottled, my skin would give like I was rotten fruit. It makes me want to press, if there's a chance I could make myself into something that might sink into the earth and be consumed.

The grass rustles as Percy looks sideways at me. "What blue crabs?"

"Don't you remember?" I ask. "That first letter I wrote Sinjon. I wanted to tell him that his eyes are as blue as crabs."

"Like the crabs we caught on that shipwreck in Penzance."

"Yes, those bastards." I sniff. The back of my throat feels thick and acidic. "Maybe if I'd written him that he has crab eyes, he would have found that terribly unromantic and never would have written back or kissed me or . . . other things." I blush when I say it, though I can't say why. "Maybe none of this would have happened if I'd committed to the terrible comparison."

"What did you write instead?" he asks.

"Some bit you came up with, about fire. And how the very center of a flame is blue. And loving someone without knowing if they feel the same is like holding your finger closer and closer to the flame, knowing you're going to be burned, but the pain feels too good to pull away."

"I told you to write that, did I?" He turns his face back up to the sky, silent for a moment before he says, "That's quite good." I laugh, a raspy hiss that turns into a whimper when a bright whip of pain cracks across my rib cage. Percy rolls over onto his stomach, his brow puckered. "Please let me walk into town and fetch the doctor."

"Oh god, Father would love a bill from a surgeon, wouldn't he?" I press a hand to my side, feeling like I'm trying to hold myself together, and close my eyes. When I open them again, Percy's face is above mine, one long curl tumbling from behind his ear and brushing my cheek. My heart flutters like a skipping stone kissing the surface of the water. I feel the ripples to my toes, somehow both new and familiar at once, like perhaps this is the way my heart has always beat around him. It felt ordinary until this moment.

"Monty." He's looking so seriously at me that my heartbeat picks up. "Can I tell you something?"

"Course," I say, suddenly aware of every spot on my body where I'm bruised. Like I can map myself with pain. "Always."

"I . . . I want you to know that I think . . ." My skin is standing on end. He swallows hard. Licks his lips. Then says, with grave sincerity, "Your eyes are as blue as crabs."

"You son of a bitch." I'm laughing again, but this

time I don't fight it. Percy lies down beside me again, nose pressed gently against my neck, and I let the pain crackle through me, bright and sharp and so, so alive.

Better to be burned.